Acclaim for **WILLIAM BOYD**'s

An Ice-Cream War

WILLIAM BOYD

An Ice-Cream War

William Boyd's first novel, *A Good Man in Africa*, won a Whitbread Prize and a Somerset Maugham Award; his second, *An Ice-Cream War*, was awarded the John Llewellyn Rhys Prize and was short-listed for the Booker; *Brazzaville Beach* won the James Tait Memorial Prize; and *The Blue Afternoon* won the Los Angeles Times Prize for Fiction. Boyd lives in London.

INTERNATIONAL

An Ice-Cream War

WILLIAM BOYD

An Ice-Cream War

VINTAGE INTERNATIONAL

Vintage Books

A Division of Random House, Inc.

New York

FIRST VINTAGE INTERNATIONAL EDITION,
OCTOBER 1999

Copyright © 1983 by William Boyd

All rights reserved under International and
Pan-American Copyright Conventions. Published in
the United States by Vintage Books, a division of
Random House, Inc., New York. Originally published
in hardcover in the United States by William Morrow
and Company, Inc., New York, in 1983.

Vintage Books, Vintage International, and colophon
are trademarks of Random House, Inc.

Library of Congress Cataloging-in-Publication Data
Boyd, William, 1952–
An ice-cream war / by William Boyd.
p. cm.
ISBN 0-375-70502-3
1. World War, 1914–1918—Africa, East—Fiction.
I. Title.
[PR6052.09192I2   1999]
823'.914—dc21   99-18313
CIP

Author photograph © by Jerry Bauer

www.vintagebooks.com

Printed in the United States of America
10 9 8 7 6 5

For Susan

ACKNOWLEDGMENTS

I would like to thank the following who have helped me in various ways during the research for this novel: Sir Rex and Lady Roy Surridge, Mrs. Valentine Sillery, Mr. Robin Whitworth and the staffs of Rhodes House Library, Oxford, and the Imperial War Museum, London.

Oxford, 1982   *W.B.*

. . . He hurried desperately, and the islands slipped and slid under his feet, the straits yawned and widened, till he found himself utterly lost in the world's fourth dimension with no hope of return. Yet only a little distance away he could see the old world with the rivers and mountain chains marked according to the Sandhurst rules of map-making.

—RUDYARD KIPLING, *The Brushwood Boy*

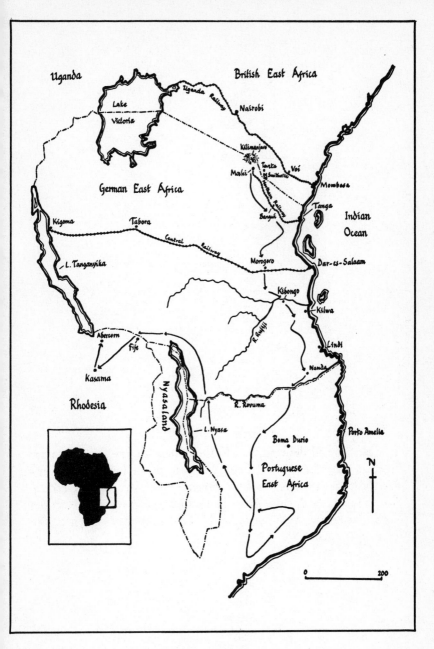

German East Africa,
showing route taken by German forces

PART ONE

Before the War

CHAPTER ONE

6 JUNE 1914

Dar-es-Salaam • German East Africa

"What do you think would happen," Colonel Theodore Roosevelt asked his son Kermit, "if I shot an elephant in the balls?"

"Father," Kermit said, keeping a straight face, "I think it would hurt a great deal."

The colonel roared with laughter.

Walter Smith smiled at this exchange as he supervised the unloading of the horses and equipment. The colonel and his son were sitting on the bench above the cowcatcher at the very front of the train. Walter couldn't see them, yet he heard their conversation as clearly as if they were standing alongside. It must be, he reflected, some trick of the atmosphere, the stillness and dryness of the air.

The train had stopped in the middle of an enormous African plain. A tall sky, a few dawdling clouds. High blond grass, badged with occasional thorn trees and outcrops of rock, stretched away to a horizon of purple-blue hills. Mr. Loring, the naturalist, thought he had seen a male oryx of a species which the hunting party had not yet bagged, and so a halt had been ordered.

Walter told the Somali grooms to lead out four Arab ponies and saddle them up. The Roosevelts, Mr. Tarlton the white hunter, and Mr. Loring the naturalist would ride out in search of the oryx. The side of the long horse-box was lowered to the ground and the first of the small ponies was led down. It paced delicately about, as if testing the earth, and flicked its head and ears in irritation at the corona of buzzing flies that constantly attended it.

Walter took off his thick solar helmet and wiped his forehead on his sleeve. The heat was slamming down on the exposed train and not the slightest breeze stirred the tremendous grass prairie.

He heard, again with astonishing clarity, Colonel Roosevelt grunting as he eased himself down from the cowcatcher and stretched and stumped on the railway ties. He seemed to see him in his mind's eye, almost as in a vision. The plump and rumpled figure wore a baggy army shirt, ill-fitting khaki jodhpurs buttoned tightly from knee to ankle and sagging around his bottom, and heavy boots. He saw the avuncular bespectacled face, with its drooping walrus moustaches, squint into the baleful sun. The colonel windmilled his arms and cracked his knuckles. "Good day for hunting," he said, and paced stiffly up the track a few yards.

But then Walter's view changed—miraculously—to Kermit. He saw Kermit's small handsome features set in a thin smile. Saw him reach for his double-barrelled Rigby shotgun. Heard the oiled mechanical click as the twin hammers were cocked. Saw the barrels slowly rise to point at the colonel's broad back.

"No!" Walter said to himself in horror, dropping the pony's reins he was holding. He spun round and looked up the train towards the locomotive. Sure enough, the colonel stood some fifteen yards up the track, his back to the engine, staring out at the landscape. But Walter could not see Kermit. Astonished at this clairvoyant vision, he sensed that in some way it had been granted to him precisely so he could prevent the assassination of this esteemed military hero and ex-President of the United States of America.

"No!" Walter shouted again, drawing startled looks from Mr. Loring and the black handlers. "No, Mr. Roosevelt, sir, for God's sake don't do it!"

He began to run towards the head of the train, his feet slipping on the earth and stones of the embankment. Again, in a flash of prescient vision he saw Kermit's aim settle between his father's shoulder blades. Saw the knuckle of Kermit's forefinger whiten as the first slack was taken up on the trigger.

"No!" Walter screamed. "Stop! He's your father, for Christ's sake!"

Boom! went the twin barrels. The colonel's shirt erupted in a splash of blood and tattered khaki as the two-foot spread of cartridge pellets pitched him onto his face.

Walter flicked up the mosquito net and sat on the edge of the bed. He stood up and stretched. He was naked. He rubbed his shoulders and chest, slapped his buttocks and touched his cock.

Walter was a small, stocky man in his early forties, about five foot six, with a barrel chest and thick muscular legs. His once-compact frame was still just visible even under the amount of excess fat it was nowadays obliged to carry. He had a sizeable belly and there were two diagonal folds of flesh on his back, running from the nape of his neck to his kidneys. His chest and broad shoulders were covered in thick, greying, springy hair. His jawline had long ago disappeared into one of his chins. His pepper-and-salt hair was cut short and parted in the middle and he had a dark, bushy, drooping moustache that grew well over his top lip. This moustache was such a prominent feature that it was often the only personal detail that could be recalled of him. His nose was small, almost snub, and his eyes were pale and innocuous.

He walked over to the window and opened the shutters an inch or two. From his room on the top floor of the Kaiserhof Hotel he had a good view of Dar-es-Salaam's capacious natural harbour. There, anchored a quarter of a mile offshore, lay the cruiser *Königsberg*. Her 4.1-inch guns sounded the last of her salute. The quayside was crowded with spectators, and bunting was strung from every available telegraph pole, window-ledge and balcony. With a clash of cymbals the band of the *Schutztruppe,* the colony's army, started up *Deutschland über alles* and the guard of honour was inspected by its commander, Colonel Paul von Lettow-Vorbeck.

Walter turned away smiling, thinking about his dream. He hadn't dreamt about Roosevelt for years. He yawned. He supposed he should be grateful to the old swine, really. After all, without Roosevelt he would never have come to Africa. In 1909, as the manager of a small iron foundry in Sturgis, New Jersey, Walter had reached a stage in his life where the only prospects were increasing boredom and frustration. Then he had seen the Smithsonian Institution's advertisement for a manager to run and organise a hunting and specimen collecting trip in Africa. He had applied, got the job and had embarked with the Roosevelts and their tons of luggage two months later. It hadn't lasted long. The Roosevelts shot anything that moved. Worried about the large numbers of wounded animals they left in their wake, Walter had voiced a mild protest. At which Kermit had promptly "sacked" him, as the English said.

Walter screwed up his face. The old man was all right. It was Kermit whom he'd never gotten on with. Yet when the colonel's book—*African Game Trails*—had appeared in 1910 there hadn't been a single reference to Walter. Punishment, he assumed. He asked himself if any reader had wondered how the hunting party, with its immense paraphernalia, had moved from A to B, how trains had been loaded and unloaded? He told himself not to fret; in the long run the Roosevelts had done him a favour, and it was the long run that was important as far as he was concerned.

Walter allowed himself the luxury of a bath and then dressed in his freshly laundered clothes. The Kaiserhof was the best hotel in East Africa, in his opinion. Better than the Norfolk in Nairobi and the Grand in Mombasa. Hot and cold running water, servants drilled with Teutonic thoroughness, and within five minutes' rickshaw ride of an excellent brewery.

After breakfast, Walter stepped out of the hotel onto Arabstrasse. The Kaiserhof was in reality the railway hotel, built some six years before at the commencement of the Dar–Lake Tanganyika central railway project. It was a stone building of some size topped with fake crenellation and it stood at the corner of Arabstrasse and Bahnhofstrasse. Behind Walter lay the harbour lagoon with its newly erected pier, Port Offices and customs sheds. Before him was the festering Indian town, made up of crumbling mud houses packed together in a maze of narrow fetid lanes. If he had walked to the east, continuing up Arabstrasse, he would have come to Unter den Akazien, the main commerical thoroughfare, where evidence of German neatness and efficiency was more apparent. Unter den Akazien's narrow, flamboyant-lined avenue led to the residential areas of Dar. Wooded, spacious roads, solid two- and three-storey stone colonial houses with red tiled roofs, and a large and beautifully laid out botanical garden.

It was this last feature of the town that had brought Walter to Dar, to buy coffee seedlings. His dealings with the colony's director of agriculture, or the *Chef der Abteilung für Landeskultur und Landesvermessung* to give his official title, had been brisk and satisfactory. For a reasonable price, crates of coffee seedlings were being prepared and would be ready for him to transport back to his own farm the next day.

It was a long journey back to Walter's farm, which lay near the foot of Kilimanjaro in British East Africa. First there was the coastal steamer from Dar to Tanga, and then a day's journey from Tanga to Moshi on the Northern Railway, followed by a further day's wagon ride across the border to B.E.A. and his own farm near the small town and former mission station of Taveta.

His business had been successfully completed the day before; he had some money left, so he decided to savour the carnival atmosphere that currently pervaded the town. The German colony was flourishing. The Central Railway had just been completed. It was to be officially opened in August and a huge Dar-es-Salaam Exhibition had been planned to coincide with it. Hence, Walter assumed, the arrival of the German flotilla—the *Königsberg* and several destroyers, survey ships and a fleet tender.

Walter turned and walked down Bahnhofstrasse, past the splendid new station and on to the dockside. A large crowd of several hundred people had turned out to welcome and admire the *Kö-*

nigsberg. In the morning sun its slim lines and three tall funnels stood out with emphatic sharpness. Strings of flags had been run up its masts and its crew lined the decks at attention.

The crowd was carefully segregated. On either side of the Port Offices were the Indians, Arabs and natives. In front of the offices, beneath the brightly striped awnings, the German colonials gathered. A sizeable guard of immaculate askaris was lined up on the quayside. A young European officer put them through some elementary drill routines. They seemed as capable and organised as any European troops Walter had seen. On a temporary dais the *Schutztruppe* brass band blared forth martial music.

Walter looked about him. All the spectators were got up in their finery. The women all wore white dresses with lacy trims and carried parasols. The men wore formal suits with hats, collars and ties. Walter joined the crowd and watched the captain of the *Königsberg* arriving ashore. He was greeted by Von Lettow-Vorbeck, a dapper small man with a completely shaven head, and the Governor of German East Africa, Herr Schnee. They then proceeded to a bedecked and sheltered row of armchairs and there followed a succession of speeches. Walter's German was rudimentary and he understood virtually nothing of what was said. He wandered away.

Moored some distance from the *Königsberg* was the Deutsche-Ost-Afrika liner, the *Tabora*, which the cruiser had escorted for the last half of its journey from Bremerhaven. Passengers from the *Tabora* were disembarking at a jetty. Nearby, gangs of natives unloaded supplies and large numbers of cabin trunks and suitcases from a lighter.

"Hello Smith," came a voice—strangely high-pitched—in English.

Walter turned. He was surprised to hear impeccable English accents among so much German. He was even more surprised to see that it came from an officer in the *Schutztruppe*.

"Good God," Walter said, his American accent contrasting strongly with his interlocutor's. "Erich von Bishop. What are you doing in that outfit? I thought you'd left the army."

Von Bishop was Walter's neighbour. Their farms both lay in the Kilimanjaro region, separated by a few miles and the border between German and British East Africa. Von Bishop was a tall, lean man with a melancholy, clean-shaven face. He had a large sharp nose and an unusually long upper lip which, Walter supposed, was responsible for his looking literally so down in the mouth. He was one of those men who narrowly miss being freakishly ugly; the odd features were just under control. The most surprising thing about him was his voice. It was boyishly high and reedy, full of air and sounding as if it would give out any second. Like Von Lettow-Vorbeck, his commander, his head was shaven to a prickly grey stubble. He wore the brilliant, starched white uniform of a *Schutztruppe* captain and carried a sabre by his side.

"I'm in the reserve," he reminded Walter. "Everyone's been summoned for the celebration; there's a big parade later today. And besides, I'm meeting my wife. She's arriving from Germany"—he gestured at the harbour—"on the *Tabora*."

"Well, I won't detain you any further," Walter said. He had never met Von Bishop's wife, but knew she had been away for over a year.

"No, please," Von Bishop said. "I insist on you meeting her. After all, we are neighbours of a sort."

"Delighted," Walter said. He was, he had to admit, curious. He didn't know Von Bishop well. They had met perhaps four times in the three years since Walter had settled at his farm, but he had formed sufficient opinions about the man—he thought he was extremely odd—to wonder what his wife looked like.

Von Bishop was in his early fifties and, as Walter knew, half-German and half-English. For some reason, in his youth he had gone to the German military academy at Kessel and had come out to East Africa in the nineties. He had distinguished himself in the putting down of the brutal Maji-Maji rebellion in 1907 and had been awarded the honorary title of *von* in recognition of his services. He had a large and thriving farm growing maize and bananas.

The two men moved towards the crowd that was greeting the arriving passengers. Walter saw Von Bishop stiffen with recognition as a woman walked up the steps from the lighter to the jetty. She was wearing a simple air-blue ankle-length dress with small ruffs at the end of the long sleeves. Her face was shadowed by a wide straw hat. Walter waited for Von Bishop to go forward to greet her but he didn't move.

"Ah-ha," he said cautiously. "There she is."

"Who?" Walter asked. "Is that your wife?"

"My dear wife," he said feelingly. He clasped his hands in front of him and stood his ground. Walter wondered why he didn't step forward and welcome her.

"Oh dear," Von Bishop said, making his face sadder.

"What's wrong?"

"She looks . . . she looks different. What shall I say? Very healthy. Yes, healthy."

The woman seemed in no particular hurry either. She stepped off the jetty and looked idly around. Every now and then she reached into her bag and put something into her mouth.

"Erich!" She had seen him and came over. Only then did Von Bishop go to meet her. He politely kissed her on the cheek and spoke some words in German. He offered his wife his arm and led her over to Walter.

"This is Mr. Smith, our neighbour in British East Africa. Mr. Smith, my wife Liesl."

"How do you do," Walter said. "I hope your trip was enjoyable."

"Yes." She spoke slowly in English, with a strong German accent. "It was quite tolerable, thank you. I'm happy to meet you." They shook hands. A strong gust of peppermint came from her mouth when she spoke.

She was a well-built woman, Walter noticed, who looked to be considerably younger than Von Bishop, perhaps in her mid-thirties. She was tall, like her husband, and had broad shoulders and a heavy bosom and hips. Her skin was very pale and creamy and her face was covered in large freckles. Her nose was slightly hooked and her eyes were green. Her mouth was wide and her upper lip was the same size as her lower—if not slightly larger—which gave her a look of constantly biting back her words. From beneath her hat some strands of crinkled bright ginger hair had escaped.

Von Bishop left to supervise the loading of her luggage into a rickshaw.

"And what are you doing in Dar?" Frau von Bishop asked abruptly.

"I've come down to buy coffee seedlings," Walter explained. "We have nothing like your botanical garden in British East. But, I must confess I wanted to see Dar and, um, your splendid new railway." He wondered why he was talking in this ridiculous manner. It was something to do with the almost permanent mood of censure that seemed to emanate from the woman.

"You are not English, I think?" she said, cocking her head to one side, as if she had caught him out in some way.

"No," Walter confessed. "I'm American. From the United States of America. I came over in oh-nine with President Roosevelt on his hunting trip. And I, ah, decided to stay on."

"I see," she said. There was an awkward pause. "What *is* Erich doing? Would you like a peppermint?" She offered Walter a paper bag.

"Why, thank you." He put the sweet in his mouth. He didn't like peppermint that much.

"For . . . *mal de mer*. How do you say it?"

"I'm sorry? What's maldermare?" To Walter's surprise Frau von Bishop energetically mimed a vomiting motion, complete with noises.

"Sick," she said. "At sea."

"Oh. Sea-sick. Yes, mmm."

"Sea-sick?" She seemed irritated at the simple logic of the word. "It's for sea-sick. Peppermint."

Walter nodded his comprehension vigorously. There was another pause. "Well," Walter began uneasily, "it must be nice to be back."

She seemed about to make an answer but was interrupted by the return of her husband.

"They have it all," Von Bishop announced cheerily, referring to the luggage. "Shall we go?"

He and his wife climbed into a rickshaw.

"We are guests of the Governor," Von Bishop said. "Can we take you anywhere?"

"No, thank you," Walter said thankfully. "I think I'll observe the pomp and circumstance a little longer. Then I intend to sample some of your German beer."

"Of course. Goodbye then."

"Goodbye, Mr. Smith," Frau von Bishop said with impressive finality. "A pleasure to meet you."

"Goodbye," said Walter, raising his hat.

"Wait!" squeaked Von Bishop. "When are you going back to Taveta?"

"Well . . . tomorrow."

"Excellent, excellent. We can travel together. Till tomorrow, Smith."

As they drove off, Walter saw Frau von Bishop snapping harshly at her husband. What strange people, Walter thought. He watched the small caravan of rickshaws—the Von Bishops leading three others carrying luggage—move along the gentle arc of the harbour front, past the Catholic church, the post office and the European club towards the Governor's palace nestling in its grove of palm and mango trees at the mouth of the lagoon. He let his gaze swing round to the crowded flotilla on the sparkling water; then he turned away. He moved through the crowd and walked to the back of the Port Offices. He called a rickshaw over and climbed in. The half-naked African pulling it looked round for instructions.

"Die Brauerei," Walter said. If he was going to be travelling back with the Von Bishops he'd better make the most of his last day.

Later that same evening Walter slipped out of the Kaiserhof. It was half past ten and the moonless sky was filled with stars. Unthinkingly his eye picked out the constellations and stars as it always did: Orion's Belt, the rest of Orion scattered vaguely about, the Big Dipper, Cassiopeia, Venus. The streets around him were empty and dark. Electric light shone from the windows of the Kaiserhof, and from the lounge came the tinkling of a pianola. The night was very warm. From the warren of the Indian town sweet smells wafted and there were shouts and drum beats, as if someone were having a party. Walter walked a few yards up Unter den Akazien. He didn't want to go into the Indian town on foot on his own. He saw a rickshaw and called it over. He gave the name of a hotel on Marktstrasse. The rickshaw boy pulled him swiftly through the dark lanes. Walter sat back on the hard wooden seat and enjoyed the slight breeze.

"Here, bwana," said the rickshaw boy. Walter got down and paid him. KITUMOINEE HOTEL, it said, in faded painted letters above the door. Walter walked in. Oil lamps set up a soft, inviting glow. There was a babble of muted conversation. About a dozen sailors from the *Königsberg* sat around tables in the large ground-floor room. Some civilian engineers from the railway played cards. In one corner was a small wooden bar in front of some shelves with bottles of alcohol on them. Behind the bar stood a swarthy Goanese.

"*Bitte, mein Herr?*" he said as Walter approached. Walter walked over and placed his hands carefully on the bar surface. He swallowed.

"*Guten Abend*," he said. "Do you speak English?" Some of the sailors looked round at the unfamiliar accent. Walter felt the close heat in the room cause his clothes to stick to his body. He wondered why he was bothering to go to all this trouble.

"*Englisch?*" said the Goanese. "*Nein.*"

Shit, Walter swore to himself. "Upstairs?" he said, pointing at the ceiling.

The Goanese smiled his comprehension. "Oh, *ja*," he said. Then indicated the sailors. "*Ein Moment, ja?*"

Walter sat down and drank two glasses of beer. Three sailors clattered down the wooden stairs from the first floor, smiling and grinning, and immediately went into a huddle with their friends.

Walter smoked a cigarette. He tried to keep his mind empty of thoughts. He concentrated on the taste of the beer. It was good beer, he said to himself, brewed right here in the city, as good beer as he'd tasted in Africa. . . . He looked round the bar. For a bar it was decidedly quiet, he observed. A muttering of conversation from the sailors, a flip of cards from the engineers, the occasional scrape of a chair on the paved floor. It was as if everyone were afraid of drawing attention to himself, wanted to be as unobtrusive as possible.

Two more sailors descended the stairs. The Goanese proprietor came over and took away his beer glass. He smiled and nodded at

Walter, shooting his eyes in the direction of the floor above. Walter stood up. He was about to walk over to the stairs when the proprietor touched his elbow.

"*Vier Rupien, bitte,*" he said. Walter paid him the money.

He climbed the stairs, acutely aware of the clump of his boots on the wood. On the first-floor landing were three doors. Gently he tested the first, but it seemed locked. He was about to open the second when a German sailor came out. Walter stood to one side and the sailor moved past. He said something to Walter in German that Walter didn't understand, but he smiled wryly, shrugged his shoulders and gave a chuckle. He sensed it had been that sort of remark. Walter moved to the third door, pushed it open and went inside. The room was small and bare except for an iron bed. In one wall was a small window which overlooked Marktstrasse. The shutters of this window were open a few inches and a native woman stood in front of them looking down on the street. On a ledge above the bed was a crude lamp, a burning wick in a bowl of oil.

The woman by the window was chewing something vigorously. She was wearing a rough cotton shift and had a bright fringed shawl loosely about her shoulders. With the toes of her right foot she scratched the back of her left calf.

Walter cleared his throat and shut the door behind him. The woman looked round.

"*Abend,*" she said dully and went over to the bed. She looked a strange mixture of Arab, Indian and Negro, Walter thought. Her hair was long and wiry and tied up in a complicated knot. Around her neck she had ropes of beads and metallic necklaces. On her thin arms she had a large collection of bracelets. The bed was covered in a grey blanket. Walter moved closer. He saw that her hair was thickly oiled, and indeed that her entire body was covered in a thin layer of shiny grease. Dark-blue tattoo marks stood out against the dark-brown skin of her forearms. Set in her nose was a brass stud of a simple flower shape. Her middle parting had been smeared with a rusty, ochreous unguent. A cloying, oddly farinaceous smell came from her body. Walter wondered how many races, cults, theologies and customs were meeting in this small room tonight, and what little portion he would add to the mix.

He looked around him and became suddenly aware of the accumulated filth of the place. He saw the rickety bedstead strengthened with wire, saw the flies and insects buzzing and crawling round the flame of the lamp. He could sense the blanket alive and twitching with bedbugs.

He scratched his head. He'd been in some fairly primitive whorehouses in his time, but this won first prize. Still, he thought, he'd come all this way; it seemed pointless not to see the thing through.

The woman folded her shawl carefully over the end of the bed. With a single movement and a clank of bangles she removed her shift. She was now wearing only her jewellery collection. More strings of beads were wrapped round her waist, Walter noticed. It would be like going to bed with the bric-a-brac counter at a dime store. He wondered vaguely if the beads were talismans of some kind.

The woman sat down and with an innocently lewd gesture parted her legs in order to examine more closely the irritation on the back of her left calf. To his annoyance, Walter realised he was smoothing down his hair. The woman's breasts were low-slung and oddly pointed. The tattoos he'd seen on her forearm were extended over portions of her torso.

Unhappily he unbuckled his belt and undid the buttons on his trousers. He was wearing no drawers but the woman didn't spare him a glance. She only looked up when he stumbled as he tried to step out of his trousers. He'd forgotten, in his absorption with the exotic, to remove his boots.

"Moment," the woman said, and strolled languidly to the window, her low breasts swaying and juddering. She chewed fiercely for a second or two, then spat something out into the night. There was a dull clang as whatever it was hit a tin roof below.

That does it, Walter thought. My God, this is depressing. Tonight was his last night; he was meant to be having fun.

He pulled up his trousers.

"I'm sorry," he said. "Nothing personal, lady. But goodnight."

As he left he heard her bangles rattle—it sounded like a kind of laughter, he thought—as she pulled her shift back on.

CHAPTER TWO

8 JUNE 1914

The Northern Railway · German East Africa

Liesl von Bishop stared out at the towering green humps of the Usambara hills as the train slowly chugged alongside them on its way north to the terminus at Moshi. Her eyes barely registered the movement of game, deer and antelopes, bounding away from the track. She felt an intense boredom settle on her. The air in the compartment was hot and muggy despite every available window being opened wide. She pressed her forehead against the warm glass and shifted her position on the shiny leather seat. She felt her buttocks begin to itch. A fly buzzed somewhere above her head. She rubbed her stinging eyes. Erich and the fat American had smoked continuously, it seemed, ever since they had left Tanga. Why, oh why had she come back to Africa? she wondered for the hundredth time since her arrival three days ago. A night in Dar, suffering the condescension of Governor Schnee and his opinionated milkmaid of a New Zealander wife. Then a heaving, wallowing sea journey in a filthy tramp steamer from Dar to Tanga, the luggage reloaded and unloaded yet again. A troubled stay at the Deutscher Kaiser Hotel in Tanga; Erich and the fat American up all night joking and drinking with red-faced farmers and *Schutztruppe* officers. Erich drunkenly whispering to her as he climbed unsteadily into the creaking bed, then falling into a crapulous sleep almost immediately.

It started again in the morning: three hours in the dust and stink of Tanga station, hot, thirsty, surrounded by piles of luggage. The fat American running about worriedly, looking for water to moisten his wretched coffee seedlings. Erich was sullen and sore-headed. She walked about Tanga's station buildings searching for cool shade, fanning herself with a silk fan her mother had given her as a leaving present. She noticed that each of the three clocks on Tanga station told a different time.

Finally the ancient train backed arthritically into the station. The luggage and crates were loaded on board and they secured their seats in a first-class compartment. There was another unaccountable wait of forty minutes before the train pulled out of Tanga on its daily run to Bangui, midway between Tanga and Moshi. At Bangui they would have to spend another night, as trains between Bangui and Moshi only travelled twice a week. Liesl sighed, thinking of the speed and efficiency of travelling in Germany. From her family home in Koblenz to her sister in München in under one day!

She turned her head and flipped open her fan. For some reason the American was standing up, swaying dangerously to the motion of the train. A small black buckled cheroot poked from between the bristles of his moustache and he was rubbing his buttocks vigorously, pummelling them with his fists as if he were plumping cushions.

He smiled, but his moustache still obscured his mouth; only the changing contours of his cheeks and the disappearance of his eyes in deltas of wrinkles indicated this new facial expression.

He spoke, without removing his foul-smelling cigar from his mouth—a very common man, she thought, having noticed earlier his appalling table manners at the hotel. A common man indeed.

"All this sitting down," he said. "Kinda makes a man stiffen up."

What was he talking about? Liesl asked herself. She could hardly understand a word he said—his whining, droning accent—and she prided herself on her English. She smiled tightly back and resumed her hill-watching out of the window.

"Tell me, Erich," she heard the American say, softening the *ch* to a *sh*. "What's all this talk about war between England and Germany?"

She closed her ears. War war war. She was tired of hearing men talk about war. They were like children. Her father. Her brother-in-law, her nephews. War, politics, war, politics. She sighed again, quietly so Erich wouldn't hear, and she thought about her sister's home in München. Electric lights, water closets, beautiful furniture, the richness and variety of the food. She'd forgotten what it was like; all those years with Erich on the farm, she'd forgotten about the choice and the succulence. She'd eaten so much on this last trip home, as if she were storing it up, like some animal about to go into hibernation. She could feel her hips and belly bulging beneath her corset, loosened to the full extent of its ties. None of her African clothes fitted her any more. She could feel her blouse cutting into her armpits, sense its material stretched—tight as a gooseberry—across her broad shoulders.

Itches ran down the back of her thighs. The heat rash was starting, after only three days! She needed to bathe every day, and she hadn't had a proper opportunity since she'd left the *Tabora*. She cursed her fair complexion, her soft moist skin, suddenly envying the American his freedom to stand up and scratch.

To take her mind off her discomfort she opened her travelling bag and took out the thin wooden box. Turkish Delight, bought in Port Said, her last box. She had bought five, meaning to hoard them, but she had eaten her way greedily through the lot on the voyage out as if it were the last time she'd ever taste it.

She took off the lid. There were three pieces left, like large chunks of uncut precious stone, pale pink, seeming to glow beneath their dusting of powdered sugar. She picked up the little wooden prongs and stabbed them into the largest piece and popped it into her mouth. Saliva flowed. She chewed slowly and carelessly, allowing bits of the sweet to become lodged in her teeth. Two pieces left. She shut her eyes, relishing the pleasure, forgetting her itches for a moment.

"Must be good stuff," she heard the American say. And then Erich's false machine laugh.

"Ah, you see Liesl has developed a sweet tooth."

She opened her eyes and saw them grinning at her like two idiots. She offered Erich the box. He waved it away, accompanying the gesture with a little snort of air through his nostrils. She held it out to the American. He peered in, almost timidly.

"I don't think I've ever come across this before. What's it called?"

"Turkish Delight," she said flatly.

"Hey. All the way from Turkey." Two blunt and calloused fingers plucked a piece out. Only one left.

"An exotic experience," the American said. "Light shines through it too. That's nice."

She watched him as he bit the delicacy in half, raised his eyebrows in approval, then finished it off, licking his fingers. Icing sugar whitened the ends of his moustache.

"Now that's what I call candy," he said, relighting his cheroot. "Very nice indeed."

Liesl knew she had been sulking and in a bad mood all day, but she didn't care. And once they arrived at Bangui there was little chance of an improvement. The guest house was small and dirty and kept by a taciturn railway engineer's wife. Liesl slept fitfully for two hours in the afternoon, saying she had a headache. As dusk gathered outside she got up, washed her face and went downstairs to the bar-cum-dining room that occupied most of the ground floor. She strolled outside to the verandah. Erich and the American sat on cane chairs looking out over the dusty main street. She joined them, assuring her husband she was feeling much better. She asked a native servant to bring her a cup of coffee.

"Here they come again," Walter Smith said, looking up the street.

A squad of about sixty askaris was being drilled by a German NCO. They marched briskly down the street, halted, ordered arms and stood at ease. Then they shouldered arms and marched off followed by a crowd of small boys.

"Now why," Walter said, wagging a forefinger at Von Bishop, "why are your askaris being drilled like this? It looks like you're expecting trouble."

"I'll be honest with you," Von Bishop said. "I don't know what's going on. They say it's for the exhibition in August, but since Von Lettow came, everything has changed. They even called me up." He spread his arms and shrugged his shoulders.

Walter turned politely to Liesl. "Do you think there will be war in Europe, Mrs. von Bishop? Was this the talk when you were there?"

Liesl wrenched her attention away from a lizard which was stalking an ant.

"There was some talk. But with Russia, I think. Not England. I don't know." She smiled apologetically. "I didn't listen very hard. I'm not very interested." Her English sounded thick and clumsy on her tongue. She hadn't had to speak it for so long. She resented having to speak it now, for this American's sake.

Walter frowned and turned back to Von Bishop. "I can't see there being any fighting out here, can you?"

"I doubt it," Von Bishop said. "It seems most unlikely. Von Lettow is just a very cautious man."

Liesl let them talk on. It was marginally cooler now the sun was setting, turning the Usambara hills behind them a golden bracken colour. Crickets began to cheep and chirrup and she smelt the odour of charcoal fires. The boy brought her coffee, and she sipped it slowly. An oil lamp was lit on the verandah and some moths immediately began to circle round it casting their flickering shadows over the few Europeans who sat on chatting. For the first time since setting foot on shore at Dar, Liesl felt she was truly back in Africa; the memories of Europe which she had protectively gathered round her slipped away, or retired to a safer distance.

She looked at her husband. He caught her eye for a moment

and then his glance jumped guiltily away. She wondered if he would try tonight. They hadn't been together for over a year, the time she'd spent away. On the voyage back her mind had turned regularly to their reunion, and she had been vaguely surprised at the vigour of her desire. But that had been on the ship. Now she was quite indifferent.

She looked covertly at his thin bony body, his taut, lined face, his big nose, his soft, thick old-man's ears. She wished he hadn't shaved his head like a soldier. It accentuated the angularity of his jawbone, seemed to deepen the hollow of his temples, made his nose look longer. . . . He was nervous tonight, she could see.

She sighed. She had been away once before to Europe on her own, in 1907 during the Maji-Maji rebellion. Since then it had been six years without a break. During that period the Northern Railway had been completed, Erich had resigned his commission and bought the farm on the northern slopes of the Pare hills facing Kilimanjaro. The farm prospered; the ground was rich and fertile. They built a large stone bungalow. They lived well, and money steadily accumulated in the bank as the crops were transported down the Northern Railway to the port at Tanga.

Oh, but the life! The beauty of their surroundings, the success of their enterprise couldn't make up for the tedium of the diurnal round. Erich was away all day in the plantations, returning exhausted at night. She had many servants to do her work for her, but she was always uncomfortable in the heat; her fair skin wasn't suited to the sun. Every biting insect saw her as a delectable target. She seemed to sweat unceasingly, her clothes rough and chafing against her moist skin. She got fevers regularly. Her neighbours were remote and uncongenial, there were few diversions in Moshi, and Erich was not a man for dances or social gatherings.

Then, last year, she spent an entire month locked in a severe fever, her body trembling with rigors, her teeth chattering for hours. She announced she was going home to convalesce as soon as she began to recover. Erich couldn't refuse. They had a bank account full of money. She could return to her family with pride, armed with purchasing power. She smiled at her spendthriftness.

She'd spent everything she had, bought presents and luxuries, spoilt her little nephews and nieces. How they had loved Aunt Liesl from Africa! It had been a marvellous year.

She smiled again. Perhaps that was why Erich was so nervous. When she left a year ago she had been thin and miserable, still wasted from the fever. Perhaps Erich didn't recognise her now. She touched her neck reflexively, feeling its creamy softness. Maybe Erich thought he was seeing a ghost.

The next morning Liesl, Von Bishop and Walter Smith stood on Buiko station watching two companies of *Schutztruppe* askaris climb onto half a dozen flatcars attached to the rear of the Moshi train.

Liesl fanned her face with her straw hat. Again Erich had sat up drinking with the American. He had eased himself silently into bed, careful not to touch her, thinking she was asleep. Liesl felt irritation mount in her again. Flies buzzed furiously round her face, settling for split seconds on her eyelids and lips. Waking this morning she had counted two jigger fleas beneath the big toe-nail on her left foot. Small red spots, slightly painful to the touch. How could she have jiggers already? Thank God she would be home soon. Her houseboy Mohammed was expert at removing the sac of maggoty eggs the fleas laid beneath the skin. He used a pin: like extracting a tiny winkle from its tight little shell. She never felt any pain when Mohammed did it.

Eventually they boarded the train and it pulled out of Buiko on the final leg to Moshi. The Usambara hills gave way to the gentler Pare range as they rattled steadily northwards through lush green parklands, the hills on their right, the Pangani river on their left.

"There is talk," she heard her husband say, "of banning native shambas and villages from a five-mile-wide strip the entire length of the line. It's such good farmland and so close to the railway."

"Sounds reasonable to me," Walter observed, looking out of the window. "They do it in British East. I only wish my farm was as good as this." He looked to his left at the line of trees that marked the Pangani.

"Ha!" he exclaimed, making Liesl jump. "There she is!"

The train was rounding a gentle curve to the right. They all crowded to the window. There, dominating the view ahead, was Kilimanjaro, bluey-purple in the distance, its snowy peaks unobscured by clouds.

"Magnificent," Erich said. "Now I know I'm home."

The sun flashed on the window of the compartment, blinding Liesl momentarily. She reached into her bag and rummaged around inside it for a pair of coloured spectacles. Kilimanjaro dimmed slightly, subdued by the thick dark-green lenses, but lost none of its grim majesty. Contrary to the elation the others felt, Liesl's heart felt weighted with the recognition. She had lived so long with the splendid mountain facing her house that she did not see it as a glorious monument, but rather as a hostile and permanent jailer, or some strict guardian.

She leant back in her seat, glad she had put her glasses on because she felt her eyes full of tears. How long would it be before she left again? she wondered despairingly.

"Liesl!" came a high-pitched cry.

In considerable surprise and alarm she was jerked out of her morose reverie and saw her husband's quivering forefinger pointing at her, his mouth hanging open in a crude imitation of disbelief.

"What on earth have you got on your face?" he cried. "Those . . . *things!*"

"What *things?*" she demanded furiously.

"Those glasses, spectacles."

"They are coloured glasses," she said, speaking very slowly, trying to conceal her annoyance. "I bought them in Marseilles on the voyage out. To help my eyes against the sun."

"But I don't know if they're . . . correct to be worn," Erich rebuked her, giving her a shrill, nervous laugh for the American's benefit. "I mean, you look like you're blind. Don't you think so, Smith? Like a blind woman who should be selling matches."

Liesl felt angry at this display of pettiness, especially when she heard a loud laugh from the American at Erich's observation. She dropped into German.

"Don't be ridiculous, Erich," she said through gritted teeth. "Everyone wears them in Europe."

Although Smith couldn't have understood it, it was clear he

hadn't mistaken her tone, as he spoke up in her defence.

"I do believe coloured glasses are almost dee-rigger these days," he said. "I see many people in Nairobi wearing them. Why, the Uganda Railway has coloured glass in the windows of their passenger carriages."

"There you are, Erich," she said, her eyes narrowed. "You have been on your farm too long."

Von Bishop grunted sceptically. The atmosphere in the compartment was heavy with tension. The American was smiling broadly at them both, as if his smiles could magically disperse the mood.

He took out his fob watch and opened it. "Ah," he said. "Well, only two more hours to go."

Liesl and Von Bishop were met at Moshi station by two of their farm boys. Liesl's luggage was loaded onto an American buggy drawn by two mules. The Von Bishop farm was not more than an hour's ride from Moshi, due south into the lush foothills of the Pare mountains.

Walter's farm foreman, Saleh, was a Swahili from the coast, a small wizened alert man upon whom Walter relied more than he liked, but there was no sign of him, any farm boys, or the ox-cart with its team of six oxen that was intended to haul the crates of coffee seedlings the ten miles from Moshi to Taveta, the first settlement across the border in British East Africa.

Liesl watched Walter supervise the unloading of the crates onto the low platform. When their own luggage was secured on the buggy she called out to him.

"Mr. Smith. We are ready to go."

He came over and shook her hand.

"A real pleasure to make your acquaintance, Mrs. von Bishop." She found his accent easier to understand. "I must say," he went on, "this, ah, agricultural endeavour of mine has been greatly, um . . . Your company has . . . and I only hope our conversation wasn't too boring."

Von Bishop joined them. "Well, Smith, we must be going. No sign of your boys?"

"No, damn them—excuse me, Mrs. von Bishop. I think I've hired the laziest bunch of niggers in British East Africa."

"Niggers?"

"Natives, my dear," Von Bishop explained.

"Don't let me keep you," Walter said. "I know you must be keen to get home." He shook Von Bishop's hand. "Good to see you again, Erich. Why don't you ride over and visit my sisal factory one day."

"I might just do that, Smith. I might just do that."

They left Walter pacing up and down outside Moshi station. Von Bishop helped Liesl into the buggy and climbed up to join her. He shook the reins, the mules reluctantly started and the buggy trundled off down the dusty street. Liesl looked back and saw Walter take off his terai hat and mop his brow with a handkerchief. He saw her turn and he waved his hat at her. Then his squat figure disappeared from view as they rounded a bend to pass beneath the huge embankments of the new fort the *Schutztruppe* had built at Moshi. Liesl looked up at the stone walls and crude square buildings of the *boma* and saw the black, white and red flag of the Imperial Army hanging limply against its flagpole.

"He's a curious man, the American," she remarked to her husband, to break through the silence that sat between them.

"And a foolish man as well," Von Bishop said with a laugh. "If he thinks he can grow coffee at Taveta he must have more money than sense."

CHAPTER THREE

10 JUNE 1914

Taveta · British East Africa

"Bwana Smith is a great merchant," Saleh extemporised, singing in Swahili and cracking his whip idly in time at the lead bull ox in the lumbering team. They had just crossed the Anglo-American boundary and were making their way along a rough track that wandered between the many small hillocks that were a feature of the landscape at this spot.

Walter saw Saleh glance back over his shoulder to make sure he was listening to the song.

"Bwana Smith has bought coffee of exquisite beauty," he droned. "He will grow many coffee plants, he will become a rich man, his farm boys will praise the day he gave them work."

"Oh-ya-yi!" chorused the two farm boys who plodded behind Saleh. Saleh looked back at Walter again, and rubbed his buttocks through his grimy white tunic. Walter laughed to himself. He had landed three powerful kicks on Saleh's behind when the men had turned up two hours after the train's arrival. He was also forcing them all to walk beside the ox-team as further punishment—normally they would have sat on the back of the wagon, each one taking turns to lead the team. Saleh had sworn that a miserable, monkey-brained swine of a station sweeper had assured him the train was due later in the day, but the reek of corn beer on his breath tended to devalue his protestations of innocence.

Walter's body jolted and swayed as the heavy waggon negotiated the ruts and stones of the track. The country around them was of thick scrubby thorn with the occasional small volcanic-shaped hill. Behind them lay the fertile Pare hills and the purple slopes of the great mountain, its flattish white top obscured by a cloudy afternoon haze. Walter's mind turned to the Von Bishops. What a train journey! Von Bishop seemed nice enough, but *was* he boring. . . . And his voice: three days of that reedy falsetto had almost proved too much.

She was a fine woman, though. Big-breasted and broad-shouldered, with that creamy, freckly skin of one just fresh from Europe. It was hard to keep that look. It wasn't so much the sun and the heat but the constant nagging ailments: the fevers, the attacks of diarrhoea, insect bites and sores that never seemed to heal. . . . They made a very strange couple, he thought. He wondered what it would be like living with Von Bishop: that voice, day in, day out.

Walter winced, and looked at the swarming clouds of flies that buzzed around the rolling backs of the ox-team. Sometimes he wondered if he had been right to bring his wife and young family to Taveta, away from the comparative health and easeful climate of Nairobi. It hadn't been very fair on Matilda or the children, he admitted. But he could never have afforded so much land in the highlands, could never have set himself up as he had down here. He gave a grim smile. Also, he doubted if he could have stood the society much longer: the mad aristocrats with their obsessive horse racing and hunting; the way the tiny society had evolved—almost overnight it seemed—its own rigid hierarchy, its preposterous code of values and bizarre snobbery. A club for senior officials and a club for junior ones. The endless bickering between the settlers and the government. The awesome privilege of riding after hyenas with the Maseru hunt, all hunting horns, tally-ho and view-halloo. God, Walter swore, the English! He was glad to have escaped. Now he had his own farm, a sisal factory and linseed plant that provided him with a steady turnover. He could stay at the Norfolk Hotel when he went to Nairobi now, take his entire family to the Bioscope—every night of the week if he felt like it. He squared his shoulders self-consciously and smoothed his moustache. It seemed better in German East. Less fun, perhaps, but life was organised, and they appeared happy to accept everyone. Look at Von Bishop, he thought, half-English, but a local hero.

"Taveta!" Saleh shouted.

Walter looked up. They had come over a small rise and the township of Taveta lay ahead. Among the dark-green mango trees the sun flashed off tin roofs. Houses and buildings were scattered around haphazardly. The dirt road from Voi, to the east on the Mombasa–Nairobi railway, arrived and became Taveta's main street There was a post office, and a few bungalows belonging to the Assistant District Commissioner, the police inspector and a jailer. Some tin shacks did duty as the ADC's offices and courthouse. Forming three sides of a square were the whitewashed stone buildings of the police askari barracks, the jail and a stable block. An untidy heap of wooden huts and stalls at one end of the street marked the festering purlieus of the Indian bazaar. Sited as far away as possible, at the opposite end of town, was a new wooden store, run by a European. There were a few settler-farmers in the district, like Walter, but not many, as the Taveta–Voi district was not generally regarded as fertile farming land. Most of the farmers were Boers who, again like Walter, were not too enamoured of the British.

Walter's ox-cart creaked slowly into Taveta. It was late afternoon and there was little activity. The place reminded Walter strongly of small western townships he had seen in Wyoming, which he had visited once as a young man in the 1890's. He wondered briefly if he should stop in at the store, run by an Irishman named O'Shaugnessy, and have a drink, but as he still had an hour's journey to go before he reached his farm he decided to press on.

He wheeled the ox-team off the Taveta–Voi road and followed the meandering track that led to his farm, south towards Lake Jipe.

He was only about ten minutes out of Taveta when his attention was caught by the sight of a saddled, riderless mule trotting round a bend in the road, followed, some seconds later, by a tall lanky figure in a white drill suit and solar topee, brandishing a riding crop and screaming foul insults at the animal. As soon as the figure saw Walter and the ox-cart he stopped at once, straightened his suit and dusted it down. Saleh grabbed the halter of the mule as it trotted past.

"I say, thanks a lot," the white-suited figure shouted. Walter hauled on the reins and the oxen stopped at once. The man sauntered over, for all the world as if he were enjoying a Sunday afternoon stroll.

"Ah, Smith," he said, raising the brim of his topee in greeting. "Pleasant day."

It was Wheech-Browning, the ADC from Taveta. He was very young, about twenty-five years old, and very tall, about six foot three or four, Walter calculated.

"Hello," said Walter; he found it difficult to address Wheech-Browning by his preposterous name. "Having trouble?"

"Yes," Wheech-Browning confessed. "I bought this bloody mule from a Syrian in Nairobi, for three hundred rupees, and he assured me the beast was broken in. He trotted out well enough, but then suddenly seemed to go raving mad." He turned to look at the animal, standing motionless now it was attended by Saleh.

"Oh," Wheech-Browning said. "Seems quiet enough now, but I can assure you the little beast bucked me clear off his back." He paused. His face above his collar and tie was bright red and sweat trickled from beneath the brim of his topee. Walter found it extraordinary that this awkward, innocent youth sat in judgement over murderers, thieves and drunks every day in his sweltering tin courtroom, but he seemed to accept his duties unreflectingly. Walter had been in court once as prosecution witness against one of his own farm boys who'd stolen cattle from a neighbouring farm. He had seen Wheech-Browning sentence the quaking man to six months' hard labour. A murder case had to be referred to the

Provincial Commissioner's court at Voi but it was obvious to Walter that Wheech-Browning could happily have condemned the accused to death and then gone out for a game of lawn tennis with the police inspector without a qualm.

Wheech-Browning patted the pockets of his jacket and loosened his tie.

"Would you mind awfully if I cadged a ciggie off you, Smith? I must have lost mine when I was thrown."

Walter took out a packet of cigarettes and offered him one.

"Dumb animals, eh?" Wheech-Browning said, exhaling smoke and looking at his mule. "Thought I'd got a real bargain. And talking of bargains," he said, noticing the crates in Walter's wagon, "what've you got there?"

"Coffee seedlings," Walter said.

"Coffee? Here? Think they'll grow, old chap?"

"Well, we won't know till we try."

"Got a point there, I suppose. Where did you get them? Nairobi? Nakuru?"

"No. I got them in Dar."

"German East? Good Lord, how fascinating. Tell me, what's it like? I'm hoping to get down to Dar for the exhibition thing in August. Our consul there was at Cambridge with a cousin of mine. How did you find the wa-Germani?"

"It's a nice place," Walter said. "Clean and neat. Efficient, too—in Dar, certainly. But it was like an armed camp. Soldiers everywhere."

"What you'd expect, really. Typical Hun mentality, always marching about." He paused. "Well, look, Smith, mustn't keep you. Thanks for catching my mule. Let's hope the beastly thing's more tranquil on the ride home. Don't want to land on my arse again."

He walked over and mounted the mule, an operation that was, for him, as easy as getting on a bicycle. When his feet were in the stirrups they were only six inches from the ground.

"Gee up," Wheech-Browning ordered, and the mule obediently started walking in the direction of Taveta. Walter tried to stop himself from smiling at the ridiculous sight.

"Seems fine," Wheech-Browning shouted over his shoulder.

Then, "Oh, by the way, can you drop in and see me some time next week?"

Walter frowned. "Why?" he called.

"Those coffee seedlings from German East," Wheech-Browning yelled. "You've got to pay me the customs duty on them."

Walter was still cursing Wheech-Browning when he came in sight of his farm some thirty minutes later. "Smithville," as he grandiosely referred to it, did not present an attractive aspect to the eye. His house was built on a small hill—or rather, it was being built. The two-storey wooden frame house had been incomplete now for over two years. The ground floor, consisting of a dining room, sitting room and kitchen, was in working order, but only two of the three bedrooms on the floor above were habitable. The third bedroom, above the kitchen, had walls, a floor, but no roof. It had been left incomplete not so much through want of funds or building expertise but through lack of energy, all of that commodity having been claimed by and directed towards the construction of the sisal factory, which, unfortunately for the house, still remained the centre of Walter's world.

From the house the land sloped gently away towards the small patch of water—some two miles distant—that was Lake Jipe. Across the border in German East (which ran beyond the lake) rose the Pare hills, along whose other side Walter had travelled that morning in the train from Bangui to Moshi.

At the moment Walter's farm was divided into plots of sisal, with their great spiky leaves like hugely enlarged pineapple crowns, and fields of linseed plants. At the foot of the hill on which the house stood was the "factory." This was a large corrugated-iron shed which contained Walter's pride and joy: the Finnegan and Zabriskie Sisal "Decorticator," a towering, massive threshing machine that pulverised the stiff sisal leaves into limp bundles of fibrous hemp. A smaller shed beside it contained smaller, more domestic-sized crushers for processing the linseed berries. Grouped around this central nub of the factory were other shaky lean-tos, relics of failed enterprises of the past.

A large number of fenced-off wooden pens had served first as a pig farm, which had flourished for nine months before swine-fever had decimated the entire herd in a fortnight. Undeterred, Walter had immediately adapted the enclosures for ostrich farming, raising the fencing until it stood six feet high, and taking out some of the intervening walls. He had bought thirty ostriches at considerable expense and had been looking forward to his first harvest of feathers and the outcome of his breeding efforts—eight huge eggs had been laid by the hens—when disaster struck for the second time. One night a pride of lions had broken in and killed every bird. The ostriches trapped in their corral had been absurdly easy prey, their long necks an inviting target, broken with one swipe of a paw or crunch of teeth. Walter could still recall the shock of witnessing the result of the massacre, standing knee-deep in feathers, surrounded by his ravaged, mangled flock. Ostrich farming had proved a costly failure. All the recompense he had received was a week of superb omelettes—for breakfast, lunch and supper—as he and his family had sadly eaten their way through the clutch of eggs.

All the same, Smithville had survived, sustained by the reliable but boring sisal and linseed. Walter had invested in the Decorticator as much in an attempt to liven up the business of farming as to save him the processing fees he had to pay if the hemp was made at Voi. Theoretically, his forty acres of sisal did not warrant the erection of the factory, but it had swiftly become one of the most exciting and joyous moments of his life to set the great Decorticator in motion, its engine belching smoke, the webbing drive-belts flapping and cracking, the tin shed echoing to the crunch and clang of the flails as the bundles of sisal leaves were fed into the jaws of the machine by his terrified farm boys.

It was now almost dark and the sun was dropping behind the Pare hills, sending their blue shadows advancing across the orange lake. Walter had travelled faster than he expected. He got Saleh to unharness the oxen, supervised the careful unloading and storing of the coffee seedlings and looked in briefly on the dark gleaming mass of the Decorticator before he trudged up the hill to the house.

Matilda, his wife, was sitting on the verandah reading, a book propped on her pregnant belly. She had a neat, bright face with round, very dark brown eyes. After Kermit Roosevelt had dismissed him, Walter had found temporary work with the American Industrial Mission near Nairobi, where his expertise had come in useful in the teaching of rudimentary engineering skills to the orphans the mission housed and cared for. Matilda's father, the Reverend Norman Espie, ran a mission a few miles away. Walter was lent to supervise the erection of a water tower and met Matilda. There was something about her enormous calm that attracted him and encouraged him to think of staying to make his future in the new and growing colony. The day he received notification that his savings had been transferred from Sturgis to the Bank of India, Nairobi, he proposed and was, with only a night intervening to allow further reflection, accepted.

Matilda looked up at the sound of his footsteps.

"Hello, dear," she said, returning to her book. "Have a nice trip?"

"I did," Walter said. His wife never ceased to astonish him; he might have popped out for ten minutes. "Very interesting. And successful." He chose his words carefully, conscious of the creeping onset of guilt as he bent to kiss the top of her head. He had a sudden image of the oiled, compliant whore in the Kitumoinee Hotel. Now, in his home, with his wife, family and farm around him, he wondered what had possessed him to visit the place.

"How are you?" he said, a flood of tenderness making his voice tremble. He cleared his throat. "Everything go fine? No problems?"

"What?" Matilda said, looking up and squinting at him. "Oh, yes. All well."

"Good," Walter said. "Good, good, good." He sat down. There was a tray with a teapot and milk jug on it. He cupped his hands round the pot.

"Coldish now, I should think," Matilda said. "Why not have a peg?"

Walter squeezed her hand. "I think I will. Join me?" But she hadn't heard; she was reading again.

Walter went into the house. The dining room table was covered with the residue of some disgusting meal. Enamel plates, glasses and cutlery were assembled haphazardly on its surface among damp spills and pieces of food. His children had been fed—that at least was something. He went through into the kitchen. This room was practically bare. In the centre of the floor stood a table. In a corner was a stoneware water filter and a large meat-safe, a fly-proofed cupboard whose four legs stood in small tins of water to protect it against invasion by the ants that swarmed everywhere on floor and walls. Along one of these walls was a three-foot-high concrete trough, filled with charcoal and covered in thick iron grilles. It was on this crude instrument that all their cooking was done. Walter walked to the back door. In the gathering dusk he could just make out, beyond the privy and a huge pile of firewood, his cook and houseboy's shamba, an untidy collection of woven and thatched straw and grass huts and ill-tended vegetable plots. He saw the plump figure of the ayah waddling up the hill, his baby daughter, Emily, balanced on her hip.

"Ayah," he shouted. She was Indian, inherited from Matilda's family, and spoke English. "Call Joseph," he instructed. His voice carried to the shamba, because shouts and screams of excitement promptly rose up from it, and the small pale bodies of his two boys, Glenway and Walker, hurtled from behind one of the huts and ran breathlessly towards him screaming "Papa, Papa!" in their shrill young voices.

He felt a twinge of irritation at Matilda's complacency. The boys were not meant to play in the cook's shamba. It was annoying to come back from a long and arduous journey to find the house in a mess and his instructions so heedlessly flouted. His two boys— Glenway nearly four and Walker nearly three—reached him and jumped up and down, tugging at his trousers and jacket. He picked them both up. Joseph, the houseboy, loped grinning behind them.

"Joseph," Walter ordered, "one whisky and water, on the verandah, quickly." Joseph ran off to get the whisky while Walter set his two boys back on the ground and then walked round towards the front, holding their hands.

He paused at the side for a moment, looking over his farm: the drying racks, the trolley lines, the factory, the neat rows of sisal and linseed stretching out to the shores of Lake Jipe, now dark and opaque. All around the crickets were trilling; somewhere a hyena barked. He saw Saleh and the farm boys walking back down the road to the village where the farm workers lived, a mile or so away on the banks of the thickly wooded river—the Lumi—that flowed into Lake Jipe. Over to his left, some distance off and invisible in the dark, was a small grove of wild fig trees which contained the grave of his third child, an unnamed baby girl who had lived for barely a day.

Glenway pulled at his arm. "Come on, Papa," he said. "Let's go in." Walter looked down at his children. He found it strange that they spoke with English accents—said *P'pah* instead of *Poppa*. It was an indication, he ruefully admitted, of the amount of time he spent with them. They walked round to the front of the house. Matilda still sat on the verandah, an oil lamp on the table illuminating her book. In the dining room he could see Joseph clearing away the remains of the children's meal. He felt the comforting presence of his family form around him, the reassuring familiarity of the things he owned and the things he had grown or made occupying their appointed places in the gathering dark—from the two hundred fragile green shoots of the coffee seedlings to the imposing bulk of the Decorticator; from the thousands of sisal and linseed plants to the fences he'd erected at his land's perimeter just a few yards from the border with German East. They were like pinions that fixed him to the soil, clamps that fastened and bound him to this new life he'd chosen. He ruffled his son's hair, enjoying the pleasant sensations, his heart big with self-satisfaction and pride.

"Where did you go?" Walker asked him as they climbed the steps to the verandah.

"To another country," Walter said.

"What did you do there?"

"I bought some coffee plants and . . ." He paused, sensing the beginnings of a blush spread across his cheeks. "And, guess what, I saw a big battleship and lots of soldiers."

"Soldiers," Glenway said, his eyes gleaming. "Are they going to fight a war?"

Walter laughed. "Did you hear that, Matilda? A war? Don't be silly, Glenway. There isn't going to be a war. Well, at least not here in Africa anyways."

CHAPTER FOUR

24 JULY 1914

Ashurst · Kent · England

Felix Cobb stepped out of the train at Ashurst Station. He put his bags down on the platform, took off his glasses and folded them away in their case. The wrought-iron railings behind the station building had been recently repainted and bright tubs of geraniums stood evenly spaced out along the length of the platform.

The train puffed off and Felix realised he had been the only passenger to get out. For a second he thought he'd left his hat on the train, before he remembered that he and Holland had decided to go about bareheaded. He waited a little longer. It was clear no one had come to meet him. He felt the irrational hatred of his family, which he'd vowed to keep banked down this weekend, flare up inside him. Typical, he thought: a family of soldiers and they can't even organise someone to meet me off the train. He picked up his suitcases and walked out of the station, handing his ticket to the sleepy collector on the way.

It was eleven o'clock in the morning and the sun blazed down from a washed-out blue sky. Felix felt his clothes heavy on his body. He wore an old tweed jacket and navy-blue serge trousers, a new soft-collared bright-emerald-green flannel shirt and a red tie. Both these last items had been purchased the day before on Holland's instructions.

Felix ran his fingers between the prickly collar and his moist, chafing neck. The station yard was also empty, except for two horse-drawn drays from which churns of milk were being unloaded. The boys hefting the churns looked not much younger than he, sixteen or seventeen. They wore large flat caps, collarless shirts with the sleeves rolled up, coarse woollen trousers that stopped at the ankles, and heavy, clumsy-looking boots. Felix sensed he was being scrutinised. He tried to look at ease and approachable, hoping his coloured shirt would proclaim him an ally. He wished he were still carrying the book he had been reading on the train—it was Kropotkin's *Social Anarchy* after all—but realised that, even if the two boys could have read the name of the author, it would be unlikely to have much significance for them. Instead he kicked casually at a pebble and whistled a couple of bars of "All Night Long He Calls Her," a tune he'd come to like recently. He tapped his pockets, wondering if he had time for a cigarette. Perhaps he should set off and walk the mile into Ashurst village; he could get someone to take him out to the house from there.

"Bloody family," he said out loud. "Damn bloody damn bloody family."

Felix was of average height—five foot nine—and slimly built. His lips were full and a dark pink, almost as if he had rouged them. This vaguely effeminate feature was counterbalanced by his bluish beard, unusually heavy for an eighteen-year-old, spreading on his upper lip from the corners of his mouth and on to his chin, as if it had been blacked in for theatricals. The skin around his eyes had a brown foxed look (which might have indicated a tendency to insomnia), but the most arresting features of his face were his eyebrows, prematurely thick and wiry, barely thinning where they met above his unexceptionable nose.

Felix took a cigarette from his cigarette case, and was about to light it when a car—a Humberette—pulled into the station yard, the klaxon giving a strangled hoot of welcome. When Felix saw who was driving, all the accumulating tensions and irritations of the day cleared themselves. It was Gabriel, his brother. Gabriel stepped out of the car and gave a salute, clicking his heels together ostentatiously. He was wearing a Norfolk jacket, a shirt with a cravat and grey flannel trousers.

"Your excellency," Gabriel said. "Your car is waiting."

"Gabe," Felix said. "You're here."

"Looks like it, old fellow. Can't miss your own wedding, you know." He strode forward, his hand out, smiling. He was tall and broad-shouldered. His pale-brown hair was cut short and parted neatly in the middle. His face was square, as if his jaw muscles were permanently clenched, and his features were even and pleasant. He looked strong and a bit simple. Gabriel was the only member of his family to whom Felix gave his love uncritically and unreservedly. He was twenty-seven and a captain in his father's old regiment, the Duke of Connaught's Own West Kents, currently stationed in India, from where he'd just returned. Felix shook his hand, squeezing hard.

They got into the Humberette, Gabriel driving.

"Ready?" he said. "Off we go."

They turned right out of the station yard and drove off up the main road from Ashurst to Sevenoaks.

"How's the army?" Felix asked, raising his voice above the noise of the puttering engine. "Boring?"

"How's school?" Gabriel riposted, not rising to the bait.

"Over, thank God. And now"—Felix paused, stretching luxuriously—"Oxford."

Gabriel glanced at him. "When did you clear that with Father?"

"Oh, he doesn't bother about me, Gabe. He gave me up as a bad job years ago. Mother told me he didn't mind."

"Lucky old you. But that shirt won't be popular, I can promise you."

Felix took out his cigarette case. "Want one?" he offered.

"No thanks, old chap, not while I'm driving."

Felix lit his and blew smoke at the passing countryside. The bulging hedgerows were bright with flowers, but the leaves on the trees and bushes looked tired and dull. So far, the summer of 1914 had been a good one. The cornfields were bleached and ready for harvest; some fields already contained their line of reapers, scythes swishing rhythmically as they made their slow but steady advance into the ranks of corn.

They turned off the main road and the hedges rose to overshadow the lane. Driving through shade after the sun made Felix shiver.

"It's all so predictable, isn't it?" he said.

"What?"

"Summer. You know: hot sun, corn, birds singing. All that rot."

Gabriel looked at him, smiling. "Honestly, Felix, sometimes I just can't make you out at all."

Felix shrugged. "Never mind." He paused. "Looking forward to tomorrow?"

Gabriel stiffened slightly, then relaxed. "Of course, you idiot. After all, it was *me* who asked her to get married, not anyone else. She—that is, Charis—is looking forward to meeting you." He smiled again. "Can't think why. I've told her all about you. Right clever Dick, my little brother is, I said. *Hey!*"

Felix punched Gabriel lightly in the shoulder, causing the car to swerve.

"Watch out, Gabe," Felix said mock-seriously. "'Bridegroom and best man in automobile accident.'"

"Talking about best man," Gabriel said, "remind me to have a word later on today."

"Words of advice from big brother?"

"Something like that."

They drove on another mile before they reached a gate set in a long stone wall. They drove through it and up an avenue of elms towards the medium-sized country house which was Stackpole Manor.

"Home sweet home," Felix said.

The elms gave way to high rhododendrons. In front of the house was a gravelled square and a lawn on which two little girls in pale-pink lacy dresses scampered, being chased by a small yapping terrier. Three cars were parked in front of the main door.

"Good Lord!" said Felix. "Don't tell me Mother's started a taxi service."

"Just the family," Gabriel said. "Gathering of the clans. Nearly everyone's here."

"Oh, no," Felix groaned. Then, as the two little girls ran up: "Let me guess. These are Albertine's. What are their names, Gabriel? I can't remember."

"My God, Felix, you can certainly spout rubbish."

"Hello, Felix," said one of the little girls shyly.

"*Uncle* Felix, please, Dora. But hello anyway, Dora. And hello to you, Harriet," he said in deep, suitably avuncular tones. "If that's your beastly dog, will you please stop it barking like that."

Felix stood on the gravel and looked up at the manor house. It was a strange building. The front of the house, which faced to the north, was a classical three-storey Georgian brick façade with a neat pillared portico around the front door and regular rows of sash windows precisely descending in size as they moved higher. However, Felix's uncle Gerald, the previous occupant, had added what was in effect an entirely new and larger building to the back, obliterating the austere southern façade with an edifice of modern design. This forced Siamese pairing was, to Felix's eyes, an act of desecration. Now the landscaped south lawns were confronted by a cluttered and inelegant jumble of styles. On the ground floor were three reception rooms sharing a long stone terrace. The ground-floor walls were of red brick but the two above them were faced with hanging tiles, reminiscent of grossly enlarged fish scales. The large bay window of the downstairs drawing room was carried up through the next two floors to form a squat turret. Other bay windows rising from the new dining room and library were half-timbered, the windows filled with leaded lights. Felix's father, Major Cobb, had made his mark on the unhappy building by enlarging the servants' wing to the east—new kitchen, scullery and pantry, wash house and coal cellar. And at the western extremity Mrs. Cobb, not to be outdone, had appended a neo-Gothic conservatory and loggia.

Gabriel stood at the door with Felix's bags watching him with amused tolerance.

"Come on, Felix," he said. "You've only been up to London for ten days. It's scarcely the return of the prodigal."

"Well, that's what it feels like," Felix said. "Even when I've only been away for a night. What possesses them to live in the place?"

He didn't need an answer; he knew why. Stackpole Manor had been bought by his late uncle, Gerald Cobb, who had astutely invested the meagre Cobb inheritance in the electroplating industry. With the money he'd made he had bought Stackpole Manor, built on his new half, and had settled down with his wife, Mary, to raise a family. No offspring had been forthcoming, however, and the deficiency or whoever was responsible for it had never come to light. In 1896 Gerald Cobb drowned in a sailing accident. His widow left the Manor and took her childless grief and increasingly unbalanced mental state to another house the family owned some ten miles away. The Manor, the home farm and the electroplating works in Wolverhampton passed to Gerald's younger brother, Hamish, a major in the Duke of Connaught's Own West Kent regiment. Major Cobb resigned his commission and established himself in the Manor forthwith. And as if to taunt brother Gerald's shade, the major and his wife promptly conceived and produced a child, Felix, some ten years after they had assumed their large family to be complete. Felix had been born and brought up in Stackpole Manor, yet he, of all the Cobb children (there were four others, girls, apart from Gabriel and himself) was the least attracted to the place, the most reluctant to call it home.

They went into the hall. It was unnaturally dark after the glare outside, and deliciously cool. The hall was tiled in black and white marble. A wooden staircase swept up from the middle and divided itself in two against the wall, beneath what had once been a large window. This, however, had been bricked in as a result of Uncle Gerald's extensions, and now the only light came from two small casement windows on either side of the front door. Double doors led off to reception rooms to the right and left and other doors had been knocked through the back wall to gain access to the new apartments. From one of these issued Felix's mother with plaintive cries of, "Felix, darling, darling, you're home."

Felix allowed himself to be enveloped in his mother's plump, odorous arms. She was a large, soft, pink woman, dressed, as ever, in the latest fashions. Today she wore a heliotrope satin tea-gown, fastened at the side with a large hook.

As he had grown older Felix had come to realise that his mother was a redoubtably silly and sentimental woman. But equally, as this awareness had established itself, so had a steadily growing respect for the certain innate qualities of shrewdness and intractability she exhibited. He saw that she treated her marriage to his father as a relentless challenge, an unending struggle under appallingly adverse conditions to get her own way. At first this manifested itself only in the naming of her children, but lately, as she had come to know her enemy, or as he had grown more senile and eccentric, evidence of her own personality long-suppressed came increasingly to the fore. She dressed in the most unsuitable clothes, followed interests that in the earlier years of her marriage would have been banned forthwith, and, for this was her greatest weakness, surreptitiously indulged in her taste for the modern. She had installed refrigeration in the kitchen, electrified the house, bought motor cars and, her current campaign, was trying to move from coal fires to hot-water heating.

Felix was, he now accepted, a living proof of this silent lifelong insurrection. As her younger son, and through lack of interest on his aging father's part, he had been indulged and brought up in a way quite different from that of his brother and sisters. Felix also realised that this triumph of his mother had prompted the animosity that existed between him and his sisters and the mutual near-contempt that he and his father held for each other. From his mother's point of view, the kind of person he now was—independent, self-assured, above all *different,* stood as a monument, living testimony to her own spirit and pluck. But it brought with it its own share of problems.

However, Felix thought, as he allowed his mother's love to wash unobstructed over him, he was glad she had persevered. And besides, he reflected, there was no telling that he might have turned out as he had anyway. Gabriel had been the focus of his father's ambitions and attention all his life and yet he had barely been corrupted by militarism. The two were as close as brothers could be. Parents, he decided, had only a superficial impact on their offspring. As Holland said: you either had the right soul or you hadn't.

He turned his attention back to his mother, who was pushing the lock of hair off his forehead and being sceptical about his health.

"Are you well, Felix? Darling, I *do* like your shirt and tie. Don't you think he looks tired, Gabriel? Do you want to lie down, my dear?"

"No, thank you, Mother. I'm fine."

"Did you have a pleasant time with the Hollands? You didn't do too much I hope."

"Rest assured on that point, Mother. Holland and I do as little as possible. Am I in my own room?"

"Of course. Nearly everyone's here. Yseult and Henry, and little Charles. Oh, he's in your dressing room. I hope you don't mind. We're so crowded. And Albertine and Greville. Did you see the girls outside? We're just waiting for Eustacia and Nigel. . . ." She paused. "Do you want to see your father, dear? He's upstairs, in his study."

"Not really," Felix said breezily. "I'll see him at dinner, shan't I?

After lunch—a veal mould, cold meat and pickles—Felix and Gabriel went for a walk in the garden. From the back of the house a long lawn sloped gently down about fifty yards to three large ornamental fish-ponds, planted round with bushes and stocked with fat, slow carp. On the right was an ornamental rose garden separated from the lawn by a neat briar hedge. Carefully aligned screens carried a riotous freight of ramblers. A path avenued with pleached lime trees led through the screen and flower-beds to a dark yew bower, decorated with spanking-new classical busts. Neglected for a few years, everything now evidenced the most careful cultivation. Ornamental gardens, Mrs. Cobb intuited, would be back in favour soon. On the left of the lawn was an orchard with wooden beehives scattered about it. Beyond the orchard a beech and oak wood grew.

"Heavens," Felix said, "what a heat!" He took off his jacket and slung it over his shoulder. It was one of those flabby, corpulent midsummer days.

"Fancy a swim?" Gabriel suggested.

"Good idea, that, man," Felix said. "Just let me change. I'll get some towels."

Ten minutes later Gabriel and Felix—now dressed in white flannels, open-necked shirt and rope-soled tennis shoes—climbed over the eve-gate at the foot of the orchard, walked across the small bridge that spanned the stream feeding the fish-ponds and set out along a mud path that led through the wood. About a quarter of a mile from the Manor they stopped at the garden gate of a small stone cottage. The lawn had been freshly mown and the flower-beds newly hoed and replanted. Even what Felix could see of the driveway on the other side looked regravelled.

"What do you think?" Gabriel asked.

"What do you mean?"

"Like it? It's where Charis and I are going to live. Father and Mother's wedding present."

"Oh. Very nice. But didn't Cyril live here?" Felix referred to the Manor's young gardener and odd-job man.

"Yes. He's been moved to the village. We had to do a lot of work on the place. Cyril and co. lived in a fair old squalor." Gabriel paused, looking over his new home with pride. "Charis hasn't seen it yet."

"Where is she, by the way?" Felix asked. "She is around somewhere, I take it."

"Yes, you great oaf. She's staying over at Melton with Aunt Mary."

"Aunt Mary? God help the poor girl. Whose idea was that?"

"Not much alternative, I'm afraid. Bride and groom have got to be kept apart. Her papa can't come over from India. . . . Aunt Mary's not that bad."

"She has her days."

"Anyway, I saw Charis yesterday. She's fine."

Felix tested the garden gate, noting the new latch. "I bet Cyril wasn't too pleased about being turfed out."

"Who?"

"Cyril." Sometimes Gabriel was so slow. "Whose house this was." Felix laughed. "Lord, the air must have been blue." But Gabriel had already walked ahead.

"Come on," Gabriel shouted. "Cut along, Cobb, cut along."

Felix caught up with him as they tramped over the dry, crumbling furrows at the edge of a silently restless cornfield.

"Haven't had a dip in the pond for years, have we, Felix?" Gabriel said. "D'you remember that day we pushed Eustacia in?"

"Useless Eustace," Felix said. "Father leathered us, though." He picked up a stick and swished it at clumps of dusty nettles and delicate cow-parsley heads.

"Is this how you decapitate Pathans or fuzzy-wuzzies or whatever you call them, Gabriel?" He brutally hacked down a stand of ragwort in illustration.

"I wish it were," Gabriel said. "I'm afraid I've wielded nothing more lethal against my fellow man than a polo mallet."

"That's good," Felix cried. He always liked to celebrate Gabriel's rare sallies of wit.

"I've stuck a few wild pigs, though," Gabriel said.

"Disgusting habit. Did they squeal terribly? Do stuck pigs squeal?"

"I should say they do. I would squeal if somebody stuck me." Gabriel looked serious for a moment. "I may soon be doing worse than that. We all may."

"What? Worse than sticking pigs?"

"No. Raising arms against our fellow man."

"What *are* you talking about, Gabriel?"

"The Anglo-German war. It's coming, Felix. I'm sure of it."

"Do they only take the *Daily Mail* in your mess?" Felix scoffed. "I've never heard such rot. There's not going to be any war." He ran ahead, leaping and bounding in a theatrical imitation of euphoria. "Holland says everyone is having far too good a time to go to war. Don't you think this is the most wonderful time to be alive, Gabriel?"

Gabriel smiled. "Well, I suppose I do. But then I've got my own special reasons."

"So have I," Felix said. "I think I'd rather be living now than at

any other time. Don't you think so? There's so much in the air."
They climbed over a gate.

"Besides," Felix went on, "they can't have a war. I'm going to
Oxford."

"Oh, well then, of course not. I'm sure the Kaiser will wait
until you've got your B.A."

They had reached the river. It ran turbidly between wheat
fields, before some subterranean impediment caused it to take an
unusually sharp bend. At this point five mature weeping willows
grew over the large pool formed by the swerve in the river's progress. The gentle current eddied and swirled, slowly cutting into the
facing bank. On one side of the pool was a mud and pebble beach.
On the other the overhanging bank shadowed a wide channel some
six to eight feet deep. It was possible to climb the willow trees and
drop into the cool green waters from a considerable height.

"Looks inviting," Gabriel said, unbuttoning his shirt. "It seems
to get bigger every year." He slipped off his clothes until he stood
naked.

"I hope there's no country maiden passing by," he said, and
climbed easily up the accommodating boughs of the willow tree
before launching himself with a whoop into the pool. He swam
splashily across to the far side and sloshed out of the water onto the
beach.

"Superb," he called. "Come on, slowcoach. It's not a bit cold."

Felix stared for a moment at his brother's powerful naked body,
dappled with the knife-like shadows of the willow leaves. He had a
broad slab of a chest covered in a sprinkling of fine blond hairs. His
abdomen was flat and muscled and the line of his pelvis was clearly
marked. His ruddy pink cock and balls, tensed from the cold water,
were compact in their nest of gingery brown hairs that spread
across his groin over his heavy thighs. Water runnelled off his chest
and stomach and dripped in a stream from his stubby cock. His
scrotum, big as a fist, was wrinkled and firm.

Felix felt himself blushing. He folded his trousers and shirt with
undue care and laid them at the foot of the willow. He was conscious of his white half-formed body, his thin chest, his little tuft of
pubic hair. Gabriel seemed so solid in comparison, his body tapering

from broad shoulders. Felix felt feeble and soft. He undid the cord on his drawers and let them fall to his ankles. He climbed the tree and almost immediately felt dizzy and insecure. He looked down at the swirling, shifting mass of the water, the frolicking prisms of light some twelve feet below. It seemed like a hundred and twenty. He hung on to a branch, gathering his courage. Gabriel stood waiting on the mud beach, arms akimbo.

"Jump, Felix. Leap in. It won't hurt."

Felix let go of his reassuring bough and fell.

Felix dried his hair with the towel and ran it one last time over his naked body. A beam of afternoon sun broke through the willow leaves and warmed his left hip and thigh. Holding the towel in front of him, he covertly ran his hand over his cock and balls, feeling the sensations swarm and jostle. If Gabriel hadn't been present, he thought, he would have frigged there and then, in the open air.

Gabriel pulled on his shirt and tucked it into his flannels. He held out his arms and breathed deeply.

"Ah, splendid," he said. "I used to dream about this sort of afternoon when I was in India." He ran both his hands through his damp hair. "Got a comb?" he asked, smiling.

Felix was silenced for an instant with a sudden tingling surge of inarticulate love for his brother. He felt numb and weightless with its power. He swallowed. "No," he said. "Silly. I should have brought one."

"Never mind, never mind." Gabriel clawed his hair into shape with stiff fingers. He looked at Felix.

"Felix, you know I wanted to talk to you about this best-man business?"

"Don't worry, Gabriel. I've been working on my speech for days. Very funny, have everyone in stitches. Nothing improper, mind you."

"Oh." Gabriel looked pained.

"Why? What's wrong?"

"Well, you know I asked you to be best man because I thought that Sammy—Sammy Hinshelwood, in my battalion—wouldn't be on leave. . . ."

"Yes. I don't quite see."

"Well, he is. On leave. He told me last week. He telegraphed."

Felix felt his face tighten.

"Well, old chap, I've known Sammy for ages, and that was the original plan and—"

"You've known me for ages too." Felix somehow managed a laugh.

"I would have told you earlier but it's all been so hectic. Sammy's down here now staying at the pub in the village. Charis knows him too. She'd like Sammy to . . . We had the rehearsal last night and everything. I said you wouldn't mind. But look, old fellow, I'd like you to be chief usher, if you would. Be an awfully big help."

Felix pulled on his drawers and tugged his shirt over his head. He relaxed his facial muscles for the instant his face was covered, then clenched his teeth and shut his eyes. Stupid rotting wedding, he thought, as his head pushed through the collar. I don't care.

"Don't worry, Gabe," he said with a bright, hard smile. "I can see your problem. No, fine. Glad to do your ushering for you. It was a pretty dreadful speech anyway, I'm sure."

Felix gazed out of his bedroom window at the south lawn and the fish-ponds. He saw Cyril, the gardener, trudge across from the orchard, a heavy bucket in his hand, on the way to feed the carp. As if to complement Felix's mood, the brilliant day had suddenly clouded over, as it can in an English summer, and had become cool. The fish-ponds, a deep and placid blue before, were now mouse-grey and crinkled by a breeze.

"Charis knows him too. She'd like Sammy to . . ." The words hummed in his head. He knew who to blame for his bitter disappointment. Damn Charis, he thought. Damn bloody Charis. During the walk back from the willow pool he had been brittle and gay, expressing all sorts of outlandish opinions on white slavery, the Cailloux case in Paris, the assembly of the fleet at Spithead, and had loudly announced his plans to take dance lessons in order to master the tango and maxixe. This was a Felix that Gabriel knew well, and he had laughed and humoured him, apparently glad to see him back on iconoclastic form.

Once back in his room Felix had punched his pillow, sworn and impulsively ripped his best-man's speech into pieces. He was annoyed to find his eyes smarting with tears of frustration and hurt. He resolved to be steely and cynical at all costs. No one should guess how he felt let down and betrayed. Sammy Hinshelwood. Another wretched soldier, boisterous and hearty. How he detested the army!

He lay on his bed and smoked a cigarette, watching the blue braided fumes curl and disintegrate above his head. His trunks from school had arrived while he was away at Holland's, and as he had requested, they had not been unpacked.

Unlocking one, he took out some books and a cardboard cylinder. From this he removed a coloured poster. It was an offer from De Reske cigarettes, one of the brands he smoked. On receipt of six empty packets the poster was sent free of charge. It portrayed a young couple sitting at a table. A slim young man in evening dress leant forward, cupping his chin in one hand, his other resting languidly behind him on the seat back, a smoking cigarette held between two fingers. He gazed dreamily into the eyes of an equally slim woman, who leant forward also, thereby causing her considerable bosom to press against the low-cut bodice of her silk gown.

What fascinated and stimulated Felix about this picture was the marked disproportion of the woman's breasts to her elegant frail form, and the way she leant forward, provocatively offering them in their décolleté, as some kind of reward for her companion's sophisticated taste in choosing to smoke De Reske.

Felix spread the picture on the hearthrug. He weighted one side with an ashtray and rubbed his groin area experimentally through his cotton trousers. Normally the visual and physical stimulus produced instantaneous results, but on this occasion it seemed merely a bored mechanical exercise. He picked up his ashtray, repackaged his advertisement and resumed his seat by the window, staring emptily at the lawn, the ponds and the fields beyond, now shadowed by the passage of evening breezes.

Later, Hester, the upstairs housemaid, drew him a bath. He bathed and changed for dinner. The family, he knew, would be gathering in the inner hall in preparation for the evening meal, but he felt not the slightest inclination to join them. He sat down at his desk and took out some writing paper from a drawer. He scored out "Stackpole Manor" on the letter-head and wrote "Bleak House" in its place. He would write to Holland, his friend and inspiration from school, the only person who could understand him, who could appreciate and share his mood.

"My dear Holland," he wrote,

"My head aches and a drowsy numbness pains my neck. I am home again. This despicable house is like some vast malodorous carcase dropped in Kent, silvery with putrefaction and occupied by sleek pale complacent maggots, most of whom are wearing military uniforms. My family, God save me from my family. There is not one 'soul' among them. (I except, as always, brother and groom Gabriel—though he is not himself. On perusing a copy of my wedding speech he told me it was far too inflammatory and provocative for the intolerant and sensitive ears of my assembled relations. Platitudes, he said, all that we require are platitudes and homilies and perhaps one or two well-known jokes. I of course refused to alter a single word and have, as a result, been demoted from best man to chief usher. I am unrepentant.)

"Shall you know the others? Cressida, my eldest sister, unmarried and rapidly stoutening, humourless and intolerably bossy, who now runs the household leaving my dear mother free to pursue her 'enthusiasms.' As I write, the driveway is filled with motors of every type and description. Then Yseult, pale and simple-minded. Shamelessly compliant and cowed by her grotesque husband, the booming Falstaffian Lt.-Col. Henry Hyams. They are accompanied by their egregious child, Charles, my nephew, currently depriving me of the use of my elegant dressing room. Next we have the twins: Albertine (quite nice, I admit, and cheerful) and Eustacia (horrible, embittered) and their respective spouses. Albertine trapped the hon. Greville Verschoyle—another soldier, captain or major, or something. Eustacia contrived to snare, only last year, Lieutenant Nigel Bathe—

with an 'e,' mark you. The Nigel Bathes must be the most unpleasant couple I know. Soldiers, soldiers everywhere. One of the advantages, for daughters, of having a father who's a major and spending their lives in garrison towns. Even dear Gabriel is a soldier. Revolting Charles will become one, I'm sure. Leaving only me and my two delightful but very noisy nieces (Hattie and Dora: why do they name them after scullery maids?) uncalled to the colours. I have saved the best 'til last. I have talked of my father before, have I not? I have still to see him, though I have been here all day—"

He was interrupted by the brassy crescendo of the first dinner gong. He put down his pen. He had described his family to Holland many times before, but the letter had been therapeutic. He felt quite restored.

He checked his reflection in the cheval-glass that stood in the corner of his room. His hair . . . Holland had abandoned hair cream and macassar, so Felix had followed suit. They were growing their hair longer too. Prudence, however, dictated that tonight would not be a good time to draw his father's attention to its length. He took a bottle from his trunk and poured some oil into his right palm, rubbed his hands together and smoothed them over his head. He combed his hair again, slicking it down close to his head. With his little finger he dislodged a congealed strand so that it fell across his forehead. He made a silent wager that his father would tell him to get his hair cut. He straightened his bow tie. The second gong sounded in the hall.

At the door of his bedroom he bumped into Charles, similarly attired in a dinner suit. Charles was a thin child with sad eyes and a weak chin. He had inherited none of his father's potent geniality.

"Where on earth do you think you're going?" Felix demanded, impeding Charles's progress down the corridor.

"To dinner, Uncle Felix."

"Dinner? Children don't eat dinner now."

"Oh, but Grandmama said tonight we could. All of us together. Seeing as it's the wedding tomorrow."

Felix raised his eyebrows. "Hattie and Dora too?"

"Yes."

This was intolerable. "Good God! All right, you go on down."

Charles left in a rush. Felix lit a cigarette, allowing Charles time to get downstairs well before it was time to make his entrance.

The inner hall was the most comfortable room in the house. It was large and high-ceilinged and more frequently used than any other. The walls were panelled in light oak and cretonne-covered arm-chairs and sofas were grouped in front of a sizeable fireplace with inglenooks. The floor was parquetine and scattered with Indian rugs. It was set to one side of the house, wedged in, as it were, between the original building and the new additions. A leaded window looked out onto the drive and the kitchen extensions.

Most of the Cobb family were present when Felix entered, one hand in a pocket, the other holding his cigarette nonchalantly at waist height. Dora and Hattie sat in one corner wearing frilly lace dresses and accompanied by their governess. They were very quiet and well-behaved. In a large group by the fireplace sat his mother, Yseult and Albertine. Ranged before the chimney-piece were the men: Gabriel, Sammy Hinshelwood, Greville Verschoyle and Lieu-tenant-Colonel Hyams, the last of whom was laughing very loudly, one hand clamped on the shoulder of his miserable son, who stood at his side, head bowed as if expecting a blow. Scanning the room Felix noted the absence of Cressida—who was presumably super-vising the serving of dinner—the Nigel Bathes and his father.

His mother was the first to notice his arrival.

"Felix, darling," she said, rising to her feet. "Come and sit down. You must be tired after your swim." She advanced to take his arm, as if he were some kind of invalid or partially blind. "Should you be smoking?" she added as an afterthought.

"Felix," Albertine cried. "Smoking. Do you mind?"

"It's all right, Mother," he said, gently releasing his elbow from her grip. "I'll stand with the men." He hoped the irony in his tone was evident; he was going to assert his personality tonight come what may. He greeted those members of his family whom he had not yet seen and politely answered a few questions about leaving school and going to Oxford.

"Felix," Henry Hyams called. "Sherry? Can he have a sherry, Mrs. Cobb, now he's old enough to smoke? Ha-wha-wha!"

Felix helped himself to a sherry from one of the crystal decanters that stood on a table near the window, trying to ignore his brother-in-law's imbecile hilarity. There was gin, brandy, whisky and a soda siphon, but he thought he'd better not go too far too quickly. He rejoined the group by the fire.

"Sorry to have deposed you as best man, Felix," Sammy Hinshelwood said. He was a fair-looking young man with a small moustache and a receding hairline. He held one hand behind his back as if standing at ease on a parade ground.

Felix sipped his sherry. "Don't worry about it," he said, darting a glance at Gabriel, who was talking to Henry Hyams. "I was only first reserve anyway. Good that you could get on leave."

"Yes," Hinshelwood said. "It was short notice, but I'm glad I'm around to see Gabbers getting spliced at last."

"Sorry. Gabbers?" Felix said disingenuously.

"Gabbers. Old Gabbers over there. Your bro. Cap'n Cobb, no less."

"Oh, *Gabbers.* Yes." Felix turned to his mother. "Any sign of the Nigel Bathes, Mother?"

"Yes, darling. They arrived half an hour ago. They're getting changed."

"Pity," Felix said under his breath. He could happily have done without the Bathes. Eustacia, though Albertine's twin, did not possess even her modicum of prettiness and was a surly, moody person at the best of times. Nigel Bathe, her husband, complemented her sourness with an endless stream of grievances and alleged injustices which he claimed the world at large was always visiting on him. Wrongly totalled mess bills, unfair allocations of duty, uncongenial postings and the like. The list was endless. It took very little time for the Bathes to depress the tone and atmosphere of any gathering.

Felix drained his sherry and was about to get a refill when Henry Hyams attracted his attention by loudly calling his name and raising his hand as if he were trying to halt a stream of traffic. Henry Hyams was a large, portly man who filled his dinner suit to capacity. The fat on his neck bulged over his stiff collar and he looked hot and trussed up. He had very small pale-blue eyes, a waxed moustache, and his thinning hair was brushed forward over his forehead and stuck there in a curl with hair oil.

"Yes, Henry?" Felix said patiently, modulating his voice in respectful falling tones.

"Oxford, Felix, Oxford."

"Yes, Henry?" Felix repeated, this time on a rising note.

"What's it all about, man? What's it all about? Not entering the church are you? Mmphwaw!" He gave a snorting bark of laughter.

"Certainly not," Felix answered promptly.

"Felix is going up to read, um, *modern* history," his mother interrupted. "That is right, dear, isn't it? I was so pleased to hear it was modern."

"Modern history!" came an outraged bellow from the doorway. "I'll give you modern history!"

Everyone whirled round in alarm. It was Major Cobb.

Felix was always surprised that his family were by and large reasonably tall when he saw his father. Major Cobb was a small man who had once been powerfully built. Some evidence of those early endowments was still visible, but since leaving the army he had grown dangerously fat. Tonight, Felix thought, he looked like a tiny, black and white, angry box. He was wearing—inexplicably—black knickerbockers and white silk stockings, buckled shoes, a tail coat, dickie and stiff wing collar with white bow tie. Across his left breast jingled a row of medals. He looked like a diminutive ambassador about to present his credentials at the court of Saint James's. He was almost completely bald, but, against the fashion of the time, retained luxuriant side-whiskers. His face was puffy and sallow, the colour of old piano keys, as if he were just recovering from an illness or about to be seriously afflicted by one. He had heavy bags below his eyes and his upper lids were plump wattles. The swagged folds of flesh left only thin slits for him to peer through. A thoroughly unpleasant-looking man, all in all, Felix thought. He prayed earnestly that his own old age wouldn't leave him similarly disadvantaged.

He stamped into the centre of the room flourishing a rolled-up newspaper and hurled it into the fire. This gesture would have had more symbolic force if the fire had been lit. As it was, it just rebounded from the fireback and struck the gaping Charles just below the knee.

"That damned villain Carson!" the major said. "He ought to be boiled in oil!"

"Hamish!" Mrs. Cobb shrieked. "Calm yourself! The children are here."

"Modern . . . *wretched* history. I don't know. Where will it end?" He glanced wildly round the room as if noting its occupants for the first time. "Home Rule, syndicalism, militants, suffragettes. *I spit on them all!*" he seethed.

Felix turned away. He'd seen these displays too often to be fearful or even impressed. Little Charles, to whom the last remarks had been addressed, looked as if he had just been sentenced to Sir Edward Carson's fate.

"No point in getting steamed up, Hamish," Henry Hyams said jovially. "Seven-day wonder stuff, don't you know."

The major was led to a chair and seated, a whisky and soda placed in his trembling hand. Felix sidled up to Gabriel as the major began to heap more iniquities on the Home Rule question.

"Why is he dressed like that?" Felix whispered. "Is he going mad or what?"

"I don't know," Gabriel said. "I think it's something to do with the wedding."

"But he wasn't like this at Eustacia's. Mind you, that's understandable. Oh. Talk of the devil."

Eustacia and Nigel Bathe had come in, unnoticed in the wake of the major's tirade, and were still standing in the doorway being offended. Eustacia was very dark, with Felix's colouring, even down to the hint of a moustache, but her face lacked all animation, as if permanently slumped in disgruntlement. Two deep lines were scored from the edge of her nostrils to the corners of her mouth.

"Why, Mother," she plaintively rebuked. "We've been standing here five minutes while you all row and fling newspapers."

Mrs. Cobb rose to her feet for a third time. "How pretty you look, Eustacia," she said serenely, in a dreamy, far-away voice.

"Isn't that lovely. Crêpe de chine?" She fingered the sleeve of Eustacia's blouse.

"Nigel!" shouted Henry Hyams diplomatically. "Sirrah. Come ye hither and meet Sammy Hinshelwood."

Nigel Bathe, a pale blond soft-edged man, joined the group by the fire. Felix peered at him. Yes, he had thought so, Nigel Bathe *had* grown a moustache, a thin, almost white thing that in a certain light was invisible.

"Everybody here at last," sighed Mrs. Cobb as if transported with joy.

"Except Charis," Gabriel added.

"Ah, yes. Except Charis."

"Poor Charis," Greville Verschoyle laughed. "I wonder what Aunt Mary's having for dinner?" Then, remembering that Aunt Mary wasn't his aunt and catching Albertine's reproving look, said, "Sorry . . . erm, I mean, shame she couldn't be with us, what? Eh, Gabriel? Charis, that is . . ."

"Good evening, Father," Felix said to the major, who was staring at the soda bubbles rising in his whisky glass. He looked round as if he were being addressed by a total stranger.

"Wha . . . ? Eh? You're meant to be in London."

"Dinner is served," Cressida called from the door. "Goodness, so many people."

The major leapt to his feet. "Dinner at last," he cried and marched off through his family at full speed into the dining room. Felix watched him go. What a horrible little man, he thought. He hadn't seen his father for three months. He shook his head and put his sherry glass down on the chimney-piece, watching his family organise themselves into the dining room. Cressida, Miss Stroud, the governess, the two little girls, Albertine and Greville, the Nigel Bathes, small Charles advancing before Henry Hyams and Yseult, Mrs. Cobb and Gabriel, and finally Sammy Hinshelwood, who stood at the door and said, "After you, Felix."

Felix walked down the passageway towards the dining room. He went through the door and to his astonishment found his right arm firmly gripped at the elbow. It was his father.

"Got you, young fella-me-lad! Not so fast!" The major wheeled him round to one side to join a sheepish group made up of Charles and a nervous and fearful Hattie and Dora.

"What's going on, Father?" Felix demanded, with an uneasy chuckle. He looked back over his shoulder and saw his mother nervously wringing her hands as the rest of the family milled round the table finding their places to Cressida's instructions.

"Now," the major said, in a hectoring schoolteacher's voice. "Children don't sit down to a meal without their hands being clean, do they? Let's see 'em!"

Charles and the little girls obediently displayed their spotless palms. Felix couldn't quite believe what was happening.

"Just one moment, Father," he said, putting his hands in his pockets and feeling his cheeks begin to burn as he grew aware of the rest of the family silently watching.

"Come on," the major snapped. "One and all."

"Father," Felix persisted with forced patience, conscious of rage setting up a tremor in his voice. "I am *not* one of the children. I am not prepared to go through with this."

"Hands, hands," crowed the major. "I know you schoolboys. Dirty little beggars."

Suddenly he snatched at Felix's wrists, dragging his hands from his pockets.

"Hah!" he yelped. "See! *Ink!* Ink! Dirty little inky hands! I knew it."

"Hamish," Mrs. Cobb trilled. "May we have grace, please."

Felix looked into his father's eyes. Watery slits in a moist sallow face. They appeared perfectly sane to him. The major spun round and clapped his hands.

"Right. Places, everyone. Are we all ready?"

Felix sat between Miss Stroud and Eustacia. The gleaming walnut dining table was fully extended to accommodate the family. The hatred and anger were just beginning to subside. He put down his soup spoon, leaving half his consommé; the scene with his father had ruined his appetite. He glanced up and down the table. Sixteen of us, he thought. How ghastly. The noise was deafening: seven or eight different conversations seemed to be going on at once to the clatter of silver on china as the last dregs of soup were cleared up.

Felix looked at Gabriel, who was sitting beside his mother. It wasn't the same any more, now that he was getting married to this Charis, he thought bitterly. He wondered what she was like. He turned to Eustacia, who was dabbing at her downy upper lip with a napkin.

"Have you met Charis, Eustacia?"

"Me?" Eustacia loaded the small word with as much irony as it could take. "Goodness me, no. Oh, no no no no. We weren't invited. Just the Hyams and the Verschoyles. Leeds, it appears, is too far away to come for a house party. We did ask Gabriel to come up and stay, but it seems it wasn't convenient at the time." Eustacia prattled on, listing further slights, real or imaginary. Felix experienced a sense of boredom so intense it could have been a Pentecostal visitation. Serving maids cleared away the soup plates, and the fish course was brought in. He declined. Snatches of conversation rose out of the hubbub.

"But don't you see," Henry Hyams said patiently. "We'd hardly send our fleet to the opening of the Kiel Canal if we thought the thing was a danger to European peace. If you ask me it makes sense."

"We're just as bad in their eyes," Sammy Hinshelwood butted in. "Just as bad. I know this German chappie who's convinced our King wants war because once, in his youth, in Paris—for various, um, undisclosed purposes—the King wanted to borrow some money off the Kaiser, and the Kaiser refused. Quite right, too, if I may say so."

"Sammy, *really*," Albertine said.

"And they think the King's had it in for the Kaiser ever since," Sammy Hinshelwood concluded triumphantly.

Felix rolled his eyes in dismay, then looked down the table to his mother, who sat between Gabriel and Nigel Bathe.

"What assassination is this you're talking about, dear?" his mother said. "Everyone seems to be getting assassinated these days. I can never remember who's who."

"The Archduke Ferdinand," Nigel Bathe explained. "Heir to the

Austro-Hungarian empire. In Sarajevo." He was losing patience; Mrs. Cobb's face was still blank. "A month ago, Serbia."

"Oh, yes," Mrs. Cobb said uncertainly. "Did I read about that somewhere, Gabriel?"

"Last week's *Illustrated London,* Mother. There were pictures. Sarajevo, Mother. Everyone's been talking about it."

"These names, these places! Where on earth can they be?"

"And his wife too," Nigel Bathe added grimly. "Revolvers." He levelled two fingers at Mrs. Cobb. "Bang! Shot dead by socialists. Just like that. Bang! Bang!"

Mrs. Cobb flinched as the shots were fired. "Oh dear." She seemed suddenly quite distraught.

Felix sat back and rubbed his eyes. Disembodied sentences filled his ears. He felt something like panic course suddenly through his body.

". . . Did you go to Henley this year, Albertine? . . ."

". . . You can't trust Johnny Sepoy any more. Not since the mutiny . . ."

". . . I hope you don't mind me asking, but what age were you when you got your captaincy? . . ."

". . . We want reasonable progress, but not unreasonable change. . . ."

". . . It cost me seventeen guineas . . ."

". . . Henry, would you be a dear and carve? Hamish seems busy. . . ."

Felix opened his eyes and stared at the light fixture that hung above the dining table, an ugly wooden chandelier with six light bulbs, suspended on a kind of weighted pulley so that it could be raised and lowered. Empty candelabra stood in the middle of the table. He heard a thud, which gave him a start. All the silver rattled and one of the candelabra swayed and toppled over.

"Intolerable!" exclaimed the major, silencing all conversations. "Quite disgraceful!"

Felix looked distastefully at his father's sagging face. "What is it, Hamish?" Mrs. Cobb asked with concern.

"Albertine tells me that now they're allowing women to boxing matches. Can you credit it?"

Conversation resumed at once when it was realised nothing significant was happening. Albertine looked a little chastened at the venom her innocent observation had unleashed, as the major detailed the punishments he'd impose on any daughter of his who ever so much as tried to purchase a ticket.

Felix couldn't stand it any longer.

"Aren't you making a terrible fuss about nothing, Father?" he said in his most languid voice. "You'll let a woman nurse soldiers on a battlefield. Why not watch a boxing match, for heaven's sake?"

"That," said the major, sitting bolt upright in his chair, "has got absolutely nothing to do with it. Nursing is a duty, a vocation. This is mere titillation. Pleasure seeking."

"Surely you are not going to deny the fair sex some innocent pleasure?" Felix said.

"Innocent?" the major gasped. He seemed genuinely shocked. "How dare you!"

He banged the table again with his fist and this time all the lights went out. Eustacia gave a little scream at the sudden gloom the room was plunged into. A greyish evening light filtered in through the south windows; everyone looked sick or old. Hattie— or was it Dora?—started to cry.

"For God's sake, Agatha," the major bellowed down the table at his wife. "This is all your fault. What was wrong with the gas? That's what I want to know."

"Don't panic," called Henry Hyams, still clutching the carving knife and fork. "Women and children first!" He started roaring with laughter, which only incensed the major further.

"Ring the damned bell," shouted the major. "The bell. Get a servant in here, for God's sake." He jumped to his feet and followed his own advice, striding to the bell-push set in the wall and, jamming his finger down on the button as if it were a detonator, held it there.

"Father," Felix said, getting up. "I'll go. The generator will have broken down, that's all. By the way," he said casually as he left the room, "you're wasting your time. It's an electric bell." He quickly pulled the door shut behind him as he heard his father's wrath erupt again.

He looked about him. The entire house was in darkness. He could hear a babble of voices from the kitchen. He walked down the passageway and through the swing doors.

"Hello, May," he said to the cook. "Generator gone, I suppose. Cyril about?"

May was a thin elderly woman with a sourer expression than Eustacia's, which effectively contradicted any vernal notions summoned up by her name. She jerked her thumb at the back door, beyond which lay the coal store and wash-house.

"He'm out back, Mister Felix. Shouldn't take him a minute. 'S always stopping these days."

Felix stepped outside. The cool gloom of a cloudy summer night caused him to shiver. He walked quietly down to the wash-house, part of which had been given over to the new electric light plant. Cyril, the gardener and handyman, was bent over the machine, peering at it with the aid of a torch. Felix paused at the door and listened to him muttering.

"Fuckin buggerin no good bit a bloody lump a scrap metal. Most shittin buggerin useless fuckin heap of shite I've—"

"Evening, Cyril."

"*Chroist!* Ooh, God. It's you, Felix. Whew, gave me a bloody fright though. Jesus. How are you?"

Holland had told Felix it was a worthwhile exercise to get on friendly terms with someone from the working classes. Felix had chosen Cyril.

"Very well," he said. "Machine packed in?"

"Forgot to put the bloody Benzol in, din't I?" Cyril rubbed his hands on his waistcoat. He was a big, lumpy young man. Clean shaven with an unlined, almost Chinese look to his face. His hair black and wiry and combed straight back, which gave an odd, streamlined bullet shape to his head.

"Like trying to fill a bucket with a hole in it, pouring Benzol in that machine," Cyril averred. "Here, I'd better get it going. Won't be a tick."

He unscrewed the top from a can of Benzol, placed a funnel in the generator's fuel tank and poured the fuel in with a tinny gurgling sound. The smell of Benzol filled the cool room. Felix smiled to himself. Although it had started as an exercise to improve his conception of true socialist thinking, he found he liked Cyril a lot and enjoyed his candid, foul-mouthed company. Cyril told him anything he wanted to know.

Felix wandered over to the line of huge basins and picked up an oily pamphlet that lay on the draining board. It was an instruction manual for the small motor that charged the battery the lights were run from. Holding it to the faint light coming in a window, he flicked through the pages.

"Cyril," he said, chuckling to himself. "It says here that 'an unskilled servant can do the work without any knowledge of electricity.' What's going wrong?"

Cyril swore again. "I knows all about beggin' electrics. I just don't know how many people are going to be puttin' up at the house, do I? I sees it all lit up like some kind of . . . of a palace down the drive. Christ, I says, Cyril boy, if you don't get some soddin' Benzol in that motor, them batteries're going to be flatter than a stepmother's kiss. And look what bloody happens just as I'm topping her up." He jerked the lanyard on the motor and with a clatter the engine started up again.

"Bastard," Cyril addressed the shuddering unit. The lights flickered and went on. He turned to Felix.

"How are you then, Felix? Looking forward to this wedding, then, are you?"

"Well, I suppose so. I haven't met my future sister-in-law yet. She's not long back from India. Cigarette?"

"Thanks. Don't mind if I do." Cyril wiped his hands on his trouser seat before accepting one. He looked at it. "Turkish?"

"Egyptian." Felix lit both their cigarettes.

"Not bad." Cyril exhaled. "Think I'll stick to Woodbine all the same. . . . Nah, I met her." He adjusted his stance, widening his feet and easing his shoulders. "Day they came to chuck us out of the cottage. Mr. Gabriel, Mrs. Cobb and Miss . . . Whatsername."

"Miss Lavery," Felix over-articulated. "Miss. Charis. Lavery."

"Charis, eh? Funny name. No, but, she seemed nice enough, though. Very pleasant. Sort of apologising. I suppose she were a bit embarrassed, seein' as it were our house, like. Nice little cottage, that was. Mind you, there are good things about living in the village. The pub, for starters."

"Yes."

Cyril ground his cigarette out with a toe of his heavy hobnailed boots, then picked the butt up and flicked it out of the door.

"I better get back home," he said. "Or the wife'll be thinking I'm stopping off for ale." He put on his jacket, which had been draped over one of the basins. He wore a badly cut suit of thick coarse wool, almost like a blanket or felt. He took a wide flat cap out of his pocket and put it on.

"See you in church then, Felix," he said, winking. "Cheer-ho."

"What's she like?" Felix said. "I mean, what does she look like?"

"Who? Miss Lavery?"

"Yes. I was just wondering."

"Ooh. Small. Dark hair. Looks like a little girl beside Mister Gabriel. Spoke very kindly."

"Well. I shall see for myself tomorrow."

"Yep. That's right." Cyril removed a speck of tobacco from his tongue. He smacked his lips. "Don't half leave a rum taste, those ciggies of yours, Felix. Where did you say they come from? Africa, was it?"

"Sort of," Felix said, lost in thought. "Yes. Africa."

CHAPTER FIVE

25 JULY 1914

Stackpole · Kent · England

Felix took his place in the pew and rested his top hat on his knees. The last of the guests were seated and the assembled congregation in Stackpole church awaited the arrival of the bride.

Felix had performed his duties as usher—assisted by Charles—with a fixed polite smile on his face. The congregation was small, composed largely of family, local acquaintances and dignitaries and, on the bride's side, a solitary aunt from Bristol, a small, plump, cheerful-looking person. Charis was being given away by an old friend of the Cobb family, Dr. Venables.

Ever since breakfast Felix had felt he was going to be sick. And once again saliva flowed into his mouth and he had to make a severe effort to prevent his stomach from heaving. He looked down towards the altar and saw Gabriel's broad back, resplendent in his red and blue dress uniform. He watched him lean sideways and whisper to Sammy Hinshelwood. Felix felt bitter pangs of resentment. *He* should be standing there beside Gabriel, on this day of all days, not showing people to their seats like some major-domo. He turned round and looked back towards the church door. Charles had been deputed to stay there and keep watch for the arrival of the bride. Felix saw the two rows of servants from the Manor crammed into the pews at the back of the church. They had been occupying their seats now for almost an hour, having been obliged to arrive well before the guests turned up. Cyril caught his eye and allowed a look of malicious piety to cross his features as he sat beside his thin, hard-faced wife.

Charles scurried self-consciously down the aisle and whispered that the carriage had just rounded the corner up the road. Felix could hear the faint clop of horses' hooves outside. He nodded to the organist, who immediately struck up "Here Comes the Bride," and the congregation rose to its feet. Two minutes later she entered, on the arm of Dr. Venables.

Felix peered closely at his future sister-in-law, but her face was shrouded in a veil. She was wearing a simple dress with a short train, clutched tenaciously by Hattie and Dora. Dr. Venables, tall, pale, his oiled hair gleaming, towered above the bride, who beside him appeared diminutive and girlish. As she passed Felix, he smelt a faint odour of rose-water and saw her hands distinctly trembling as she gripped a bunch of lily of the valley. He heard, he thought, the rattle of the stamens in the tiny waxy bells.

Gabriel stood at the head of the aisle, badly suppressing a broad grin of welcome and relief, splendid in his short red jacket and navy-blue trousers.

Felix felt his nausea return. The church seemed suddenly filled with the ancient smells of dust and stone, mingled with the scent of flowers and rose-water. He clutched the back of the pew in front of him and stared at his whitening knuckles. He did not raise his eyes again until the vicar invited them all to be seated.

In front of the church door the photographers busily packed away their bulky equipment. Felix stood and watched them. The bride and groom had been carried off in the landaulet to the Manor, where a reception was taking place. Most of the other motor cars, traps, carriages and pony carts had left also.

"Are you walking back, Felix?" came a voice.

Felix looked round. It was Dr. Venables.

"Yes," Felix said.

The doctor joined him. "Fascinating contraptions," he said, indicating the heavy cameras being placed in their velvet-lined boxes. "To think that this day has been captured forever. Preserved on light-sensitive paper through the action of silver oxide. Is that right? I don't pretend to know how it functions."

"I think you're right," Felix said glumly, vaguely remembering the dreadful embarrassments of the group photograph. His mother almost swooning from tension; the major refusing to smile; Gabriel and Charis's happiness almost palpable, like being in a warm, fuggy room. He realised now that they had been sharing a joy in each other's company which he found almost intolerable to witness. He had been close to Gabriel—closer than to any other person—but what he saw happening between Gabriel and Charis was an intimacy of a higher order, and one, he was convinced in his tight frozen heart, that he was unlikely ever to experience.

He had glimpsed them squeezing hands, Gabriel's knuckles white with effort, almost as his own had been on the pew-back some half an hour earlier. He felt overwhelmed by the passion of his jealousy and resentment. And the virulence of his own emotional upheavals had made him take less notice than normal of the finer details of the scene which usually he would have savoured with cynical relish. The covert jostling for prominence amongst sisters and in-laws, the Nigel Bathes freely using their elbows to secure their ground and having almost to be physically dislodged from it to allow Dr. Venables and Charis's aunt their rightful positions at the front of the group. Even the features of Charis's face were still indistinct: dark hair brushed forward and secured in a wavy fringe by a satin band, a round face, wide eyes, a firm determined chin, small sharp teeth disclosed by a mouth continually parted in a smile. He shut his eyes and swallowed as he suffered another attack of nausea.

". . . charming girl, I think." Dr. Venables was speaking.

"Sorry, Dr. Venables? . . . Oh, the bride. I haven't met her yet."

"Yes, that's right, you've been away. Lively, intelligent girl . . . I say, are you all right, Felix? You look a bit washed out."

"I'm fine. The walk back'll do me good. I think it's something to do with the atmosphere in churches."

Dr. Venables smiled. "I'll join you, if I may. There was some talk of sending a trap back to fetch me, but I dare say I've been forgotten in all the confusion."

They walked out of the churchyard and turned up the lane that led from the village to the Manor. It was a bright day with a cool breeze and compact scudding clouds in the sky. Felix exaggeratedly inhaled and exhaled as they strode along.

Dr. Venables lived and practised in Sevenoaks, though he had acted as the Cobb family doctor for as long as Felix could remember. He was a large, tall man in his fifties with a curiously smooth and fleshy complexion. He had a good head of hair and it showed no traces of grey. Felix suspected regular dyeing. His clothes were always elegant and well-fitting. His face would have been conventionally handsome had it not been for his corpulence and a certain slackness about his mouth, caused by a full, heavy bottom lip that seemed always to be hanging down from the upper, and which was only held in place by a conscious setting of the chin. Felix liked him and was always pleased to see him, though for no particular reason other than that he seemed a sensible man who was prepared and happy to talk to him as an equal.

"So you weren't too enamoured of the service," Dr. Venables observed.

Felix scoffed. "I think it's ghastly. Not that I blame Gabriel and Charis," he added quickly. "It's just that occasions such as these bring out the worst in my family. I'd vowed that after Eustacia had married Nigel Bathe I'd never go to another wedding." He paused. "Of course I wasn't to know Gabriel would be the next," he added thoughtfully.

"But *they're* happy," Dr. Venables said. "You wouldn't deny them their happiness."

"No," Felix said. "Of course not. It's just that I don't believe in it, somehow. The ritual, the pretence, the . . . the false piety."

Dr. Venables smiled. Felix sensed he was being humoured.

"What *do* you believe in then, Felix?" he asked.

Felix stopped walking and looked about him. He went to the side of the lane and plucked two dogroses, a clump of elderberry and a stem of cow-parsley. He held them out to Dr. Venables.

"I believe in these," he said with grim sincerity.

Dr. Venables gave a great shout of laughter. "Why, Felix," he said. "You . . . you sensualist, you. You're nothing but—what do they call it?—a neo-pagan. That's what you are: a neo-pagan."

Felix dropped the icons of his religion. He had been following Holland's instructions to the letter. He didn't believe in dogroses any more than he did the Church of England, but at least it was different.

"Well," he said, conscious of the ground he had lost and trying to regain it. "At least it's *there*. Visible. I can see them and feel them. . . ." He remembered a line from Holland's favourite, Ibsen. "One must go one's own way," he announced strongly, "and make one's own mistakes."

"Come on," Dr. Venables said, putting a hand on his shoulder. "I think I know what you're driving at. We'd better get a move on, though, or the party'll be over." They set off up the road.

"Now tell me," Dr. Venables said, "how are you looking forward to Oxford?"

Felix toyed with his pudding, pushing the meringue and cream around with his spoon for a while before deciding to abandon it. He sipped at the champagne he had left in his glass. He felt mildly calmer, restored in part by a speech of utter fatuity made by Sammy Hinshelwood, without even one good joke in it, and which had lasted ten minutes too long.

Nigel Bathe, sitting opposite him, had been advising him for the last five minutes not to waste his time by going to Oxford, and informing him how he, Nigel Bathe, had never for one instant—not for a split second—regretted never attending that seat of learning.

"But, Nigel," Felix interrupted reasonably, "you are a soldier. Oxford would have been wasted on you. I have no intention of becoming a soldier, I assure you. Never. Not ever."

"Hoo! I wouldn't let your father hear that," Nigel Bathe said smugly.

"What's this, Felix?" Henry Hyams boomed, leaning across Albertine to thrust his whiskered face in Felix's direction. "What are you going to be then? A slacker? Wah-hah!" He seemed to find this, as he found most things he said, extremely funny.

Felix wondered what profession would most annoy them. "Actually," he said, "I was thinking of becoming a journalist."

"Felix!" Albertine said, in tones of genuine horror. While the three of them ran down the profession of journalism, Felix looked up to the head of the table to where Gabriel and his new wife sat. Felix had been introduced to her before the reception. She had a slim, underdeveloped figure, Felix had noted. Her hair was set in the latest fashion and he'd heard Eustacia pass the opinion that, for a bride, she was wearing too much powder and rouge. Now she was speaking rapidly and energetically to his mother, who was nodding her head slowly in reply. To Felix she didn't seem particularly beautiful or pretty, and he wondered what it was that had attracted Gabriel to her, why he should have settled for less.

Five minutes later, Henry Hyams leant confidentially across the table and said in a low voice, "Shall we repair to that inner sanctum where menfolk may indulge in their favourite weed?"

"And where none may say them nay, more to the point," added Nigel Bathe, glancing up the table at Eustacia.

The luncheon party was breaking up. Gabriel and Charis were being introduced to family friends by Mrs. Cobb; the children were scampering around on the terrace; the major seemed to be asleep. Felix got to his feet and went to join his two brothers-in-law in the inner hall. Cigars were produced and lit, Henry Hyams dispensed brandy. Greville Verschoyle slipped into the room two minutes later.

"Brandy, Greville?" Henry Hyams offered.

"Rather. Some beano, eh? The major's trying to collar a partner for billiards. Made my escape just in time."

"Where's Hinshelwood?" Nigel Bathe asked.

"Caught up in the bridal party, worse luck for him."

"I thought you were meant to be best man anyway, Felix," Henry Hyams said.

"That was the idea. But it was just a contingency plan. In case Sammy couldn't get leave."

"Bloody awful speech, I thought," Greville said, as Henry Hyams lit his cigar.

Felix wandered to the window and looked out over the drive. He felt a sense of bleak sadness spread slowly through him like a stain. Now Gabriel had gone, nothing could ever be the same here again, he thought. Ever. He heard a burst of raucous laughter from his brothers-in-law and turned back to look at the group. He felt like an anthropologist or explorer contemplating some foreign tribe. Henry Hyams was pouring more brandy. Felix went over to get his glass refilled.

"I should think old Gabriel's looking forward to tonight," Greville said with a smirk. "What's the plan exactly? Are they stopping for the night in town? Or going straight to Deauville?"

"Deauville?" exclaimed Nigel Bathe in outrage. "Why on earth are they going to Deauville?"

"It's called a honeymoon, Nigel," Greville said. "They're having a honeymoon in Deauville. It is Deauville, isn't it?"

"Good *God*," Nigel Bathe uttered, appalled, his sense of injustice causing his nostrils to twitch in disgust.

Henry Hyams ignored him. "It's Trouville, actually. Just next door. No, they're going straight over. Being driven to Folkestone. Steamer, then a train to Paris. Then on to Trouville."

"Be a bit awkward on the train, won't it?" Greville said.

Henry Hyams went purple in the face as he tried to prevent the mouthful of brandy he'd just taken snorting out of his nose.

"Are the Cobbs paying for this?" an aggrieved Nigel Bathe demanded. "That's what I want to know. We only went to Brighton."

Henry Hyams was swaying around as if in a railway carriage travelling at speed, lunging repeatedly at an imaginary bride. Greville Verschoyle was stooped over, pigeon-toed, pounding his knee with a fist, his face screwed up around his fat cigar in a rictus of mirth. To his surprise and shame, Felix felt himself blushing. He left the room unobtrusively, hearing, as he closed the door behind him,

Nigel Bathe plaintively demanding explanations.

"Look, come on, you chaps. Do stop it. How can anyone afford Normandy in high season on a captain's pay? That's what I want to know. Has the gel got money of her own or something?"

Felix paused outside the door. He thought about going back into the dining room but decided against it. He walked instead up the passageway to the main hall. There it was cool and quiet. Through the front windows was a glimpse of the lawn, lime-green in the afternoon sun.

Felix was annoyed to find that he still felt offended and ashamed: offended to hear the men talking like that about Gabriel; ashamed that he—who prided himself on his worldliness—should be offended. He shook his head and allowed a bitter little smile to pass across his features. He couldn't remember feeling so apart from his family. Not one of them understood him; not one had an inkling of how his mind worked. Not even Gabriel, who—

"Hello, am I wanted or something?"

Felix looked round. It was Charis. She had just emerged from the large drawing room to the left of the hall where the presents were being displayed.

"No," Felix said, indicating the front door. "I thought I might snatch a breath of fresh air."

Charis smiled. "We haven't had much of a chance to get acquainted, I'm afraid," she said. "It's all been so hectic. In fact, we must be off soon or we'll miss the boat. . . ." She paused. "Gabriel said I should get these." She held up two silver hip flasks. "They might be useful, he thought, if we went on a picnic."

"Don't let me keep you," Felix said. The thought of Gabriel and Charis on a picnic filled him with an irrational jealousy. He felt a spasm of intense dislike for this dark slim girl pass through his body. What did she know of Gabriel? he asked himself scornfully. How could she possibly know what he was really like?

"Still," Charis continued breezily, "I expect we'll get to know each other better. Later." She paused, clearly a little put out by Felix's lack of response. "We won't be far away," she went on. "The cottage." She smiled again warmly. "It'll be so nice to get to know you properly. Gabriel's told me so much about you."

She talked on, but Felix was no longer listening. His face felt hot. Gabriel and this girl, talking about *him!* Gabriel sharing confidences . . . But Charis had stopped.

"I say, is everything all right, Felix?"

"Yes. Yes, of course." He gave her a light, frozen smile, little more than the pursing of his top lip.

She looked at him concernedly. For a second he stared back, noticing her features with a microscopic intensity: her white powdered skin, the faint down of hair in front of her ears, the moist redness at the corners of her eyes, the shine of saliva on her teeth, the blue veins in her throat.

She touched her forehead. "It's been a long day," she said with a final effort to be friendly. Then she looked down. "Well, I mustn't . . . I suppose I'd better see if Hester's finished the packing." She looked up, seeming to have regained her cheery composure.

"I *will* look forward to living here," she chattered on. "We'll have half the summer left, nearly. The three of us. Gabriel, me and you. Now I must run along. See you later, before we go."

She turned and left. Felix watched her go.

Felix stood with Dr. Venables among the other guests outside the front of the house. They were waiting for the departure of the bride and groom. On the gravel before the front door stood the large Siddley-Deasey, its motor running and Cyril sitting in the front seat wearing his chauffeur's peaked cap. Four heavy pigskin cases had been brought out by servants and strapped to the rack at the rear of the car. The gusty wind had cleared the sky of clouds and a warm afternoon sun shone on the bare heads of the guests and thickened the smoke of the post-prandial cigars.

Felix had composed himself after his "fit" in the hall and had re-established a mood of jaundiced cynicism with which to see out the rest of the day. Nothing Gabriel or his "wife" could do now would affect him in the slightest.

The front door opened and the twin objects of his indifference appeared, flanked by the major and Mrs. Cobb. There was a burst of cheering and applause from the guests. As they stepped down onto the gravel, Hattie, Dora and Charles ran up with paper bags of rice and confetti. Little Dora, whose aim was erratic, threw in the stiff-armed lobbing way of young children and hurled a handful of rice full in the major's face.

The major, who had been on the point of addressing a remark to his wife—and who had his mouth half-open for this purpose—found his eyes, nose and mouth suddenly stung and filled with a scatter of rice grains. He staggered back, whirling round in shock, shaking his head, blinking and spitting, but two or three grains had lodged themselves in his throat and a bout of severe barking coughs was found necessary to dislodge them. Felix watched in pitying amusement as his mother energetically thumped the major's back while he hawked and retched—purple-faced—onto the gravel.

The oblivious crowd, meanwhile, swarmed past them and gathered round the motor car into which Gabriel and Charis had clambered.

Dr. Venables offered Felix a handful of confetti from the paper bag he was holding.

"I won't, if you don't mind," Felix said.

Dr. Venables looked at him quizzically. "Are you sure everything's all right?" he asked.

Felix looked exasperated. "Everyone seems particularly concerned about my health today."

"Suit yourself," Dr. Venables said, and pointedly tossed a handful of confetti at the car.

Gabriel and Charis sat in the rear seat, smiling radiantly at everyone and shouting their goodbyes. Felix heard his name called.

"Bye, Felix!" Gabriel shouted.

Felix coolly raised a palm in response, struggling to keep the emotions that had suddenly begun to turmoil within him in check. He was happy to back away as a path was cleared to allow the major—dizzy, streaming-eyed and breathless—to make his farewells. Then the gears were engaged, Cyril tooted the horn and the car slowly pulled away to renewed cheers from the guests, the smiling faces of the happy couple framed together in the small rear window, their hands waving goodbye until a turn in the drive and a dense clump of rhododendrons eventually obscured the view.

CHAPTER SIX

26 JULY 1914

Trouville-sur-Mer · France

Charis loved Gabriel. Of that fact she was absolutely sure. But there was no doubt that he was behaving most oddly.

They walked now along the crowded promenade at Trouville above the bright and frantic bathing beaches. It was eleven in the morning, they had been married for twenty-four hours and her virginity was still intact.

The journey from Stackpole to Trouville had been a frustrating history of delays. Cyril drove them down to Folkestone smoothly and expertly enough, but for some reason the steamer left the harbour an hour late, thereby ensuring that they missed their train to Paris. In Paris their planned stop for an evening meal had to be cancelled, and they rushed from the Gare du Nord to the Gare St. Lazare and only just managed to catch the Amiens–Trouville express. The journey to the Normandy coast took four and a half hours and they arrived at Trouville/Deauville station at half past midnight. Charis was extremely disappointed. Trouville Casino held a ball every Saturday night and she and Gabriel had counted on attending it, even if only for an hour. Worse was to follow. When they eventually reached the Hotel d'Angleterre it was found that one piece of their luggage was missing.

Charis also noticed, as they approached their destination, a distinct, uncharacteristic increase of tension in Gabriel's manner. Curiously, this seemed to be relieved by the loss of one of their cases, rather than exacerbated. He saw her established in their suite of rooms, wolfed down a sandwich and a glass of milk and went directly back down to the station to see if he could get any sense out of the night porters. "Back soon, darling," he had said. Charis undressed, put on her night-clothes, got into bed and lay patiently waiting for him to return.

She thought it a little peculiar that the missing case should prove so important to him. But Gabriel knew best. When he returned an hour and a half later it was with the case, but she was asleep, exhausted by the long day. She woke up as he climbed into bed beside her, her heart suddenly beating faster and a faint sense of panic over what she knew must next take place. But all Gabriel did was to lean over and kiss her affectionately on the cheek.

"Got the case, Carrie old girl. Let's get some sleep, shall we? Honeymoon starts tomorrow," was all he said, and turned away from her, pulling the sheets over his shoulder. He was asleep within minutes, or so his even breathing seemed to indicate. Charis lay awake for a while longer, savouring the unfamiliar experience of sharing her bed with a man. She thought vaguely about the morning and her "initiation into womanhood." Aunt Bedelia had solemnly and ambiguously informed her about Gabriel's nuptial duties. Gabriel was right, she reassured herself again. It was too important an event, too sensitive to risk while they were both tired and a bit irritable.

But in the morning Gabriel was up before her, standing on the balcony outside the bedroom.

"Wake up, Mrs. Cobb," he said with his familiar wide grin when he saw her sitting up in bed. "Far too nice a day for sleepyheads."

He seemed in a very good mood and did not disturb her when she put on her clothes in the dressing room. She selected a V-necked blouse from the once-missing valise and reflected that, after all, he *had* been correct to spend half the night searching for it; it would have spoilt things not to have all her clothes with her on her first full day as Mrs. Gabriel Cobb.

On their way down to the dining room, on the landing outside their rooms, Gabriel put his arms round her shoulders and gave her a kiss. His good humour was infectious and dispelled any lingering doubts she had about the events—or rather the lack of them—of the preceding night.

During breakfast they laughed and joked about the other guests in the hotel, trying to guess their identities. "A German Hebrew financier," Gabriel said of one.

"A millionaire from Dakota," Charis suggested.

"A pork-packer with his front-row tottie."

"Two boudoir boys."

The Angleterre was, they both agreed, rather a "smart" hotel, even if most of the fashionable crowd went to the Roches Noires across the street.

Later, they sat for a while on the hotel's terrace. Gabriel read a copy of *The Times* that was two days old.

"It seems funny," he said, "to think we weren't married then." He reached over and squeezed her hand. "It seems as if we've been married for ages."

Charis wasn't sure what he meant—she hardly felt married at all—but he said it so warmly that it seemed like the deepest compliment. Her eyes prickled with tears for a moment, so intense was her feeling of love for him. Dear, good Gabriel! She lowered her head to flick through the magazine she was holding. She heard Gabriel reading something out to her from *The Times*. She caught something about "Austria" and "Russia," but she wasn't really paying attention.

A patch of sun inched across the terrace. She watched its slow progress towards her feet, happy for a while to be idle and still with her husband. She felt an unfamiliar pride in her new status and for a few minutes luxuriated in her contentment. But soon the sunbeam was warming her feet and she began to sense an irritation at Gabriel's stolid absorption with the newspaper. He would have lots of time to read later. Why did he have to take up so much of the first morning of their honeymoon? She saw him take out a cigarette from his cigarette case without his eyes leaving the page. He patted his pockets absent-mindedly for matches, eventually locating a box, and lit his cigarette.

Charis swallowed. The taste of breakfast coffee still in her mouth. How she longed for a cigarette! But Gabriel had told her more than once that he disapproved of her smoking. Ridiculous, silly old Gabriel. It was that family of his. He could be stuffy sometimes. Gabriel looked up.

"Everything fine, darling?" he asked.

"Of course," she said. "Is the paper so terribly interesting?"

"It is, actually," Gabriel said, not detecting the implied complaint. "Didn't have a chance to catch up with the news, what with the wedding and all." He frowned. "Serious business." He looked back at the front page again.

"Shall we bathe?" Charis suggested, prompted by the sun on her ankles.

"Mmm," Gabriel said, still reading. "If you like."

"I'll go and get my costie."

"*Darling*." Gabriel jokingly rebuked her slang.

In the hotel room Charis smoked a cigarette out of a feeling of mild rebellion. She packed her swimming costume in a cotton draw-string bag. As she walked back down the stairs she chided herself for her irritation. It was Gabriel's honeymoon, too, she reasoned, and if it made him happy to linger over a newspaper after breakfast, then he should do exactly as he pleased.

Now, as they walked along the promenade, Charis linked her arm through his and felt the cosy feelings of love—and self-congratulation at her own good fortune—return. He stood so tall above her, his shoulders as high as her head. They passed another couple from the hotel and Gabriel tipped his boater.

The beaches and the promenade were thronged with people, even though it was Sunday. If anything, the crowds seemed better dressed in honour of the Sabbath. The promenade, her Baedeker said, "has been pithily described as the 'Summer Boulevard of Paris.'" It was one reason why she had chosen Trouville for her honeymoon.

"Shall we go across to Deauville?" Gabriel said. "They say the beach is quieter there."

"Oh, no," Charis said. "Baedeker says the beach is distinctly inferior. That's why everyone's here. Besides, it's such a long way," she said. "And I'm roasting."

"As you require, Mrs. Cobb," Gabriel said with mock deference, and led her down the steps onto the beach. They walked carefully across duckboards to the Hotel d'Angleterre's striped changing tents.

"See you *dans la mer*," Gabriel said as he turned towards those reserved for men.

Inside the tent it was dark and very warm and at first Charis could see nothing.

"Bonjour, Madame," came a surprisingly loud and hoarse shout from one corner. Charis looked round in some alarm. The speaker was a very small old woman in black who was struggling to get out of a sagging wicker chair flanked by a mound of fresh towels and swimming costumes. With operatic gestures she ushered Charis into a canvas cubicle. She helped Charis undress, hanging up her clothes with great care and much fastidious smoothing of creases.

"Maillot?" she yelled as Charis slipped her camisole top over her head.

"What? Oh . . . sorry," Charis said, self-consciously covering her breasts with her arms. *"Non,"* she said, pointing towards the draw-string bag. *"J'ai . . . dans le sac . . ."*

The old woman shuffled out and Charis quickly pulled on her costume—knee-length knickerbockers, flouncy tunic and bathing hat, in red piped with yellow. Outside, she blinked at the brightness of the sun and the sand. Down here on the beach it was much noisier than it seemed to be from the esplanade. There were shouts from beach vendors, bathers and children playing, and the regular soft crash of waves on the beach. People sat in deck-chairs reading. A game of cricket was in progress a few yards away. A man in a rubber bathing cap and a huge towelling beach robe flapped up the sand towards the men's tent. "Splendid!" he shouted at her as he stumbled past.

Charis couldn't see Gabriel anywhere, so she assumed he must already be in the water. She picked her way, gingerly at first and then with more confidence, down towards the breakers. The sand was loose, deep and warm on the upper reaches of the beach. Charis was glad she hadn't worn her bathing shoes; she liked the feel of the sand beneath her bare soles.

At the water's edge stood a group of men in uniform black swimming costumes. They were very sunburnt and their hair and bodies were sleeked with water.

"*Guide baigneur, Madame?*" one of them asked as she approached. "*Soixante centimes.*"

"No thanks . . . *non,*" she said. The waves didn't look too big and besides, she didn't need these men to support her in the water now she had her husband, wherever he might be.

"There you are," Gabriel called, wading laboriously out of the surf. "Come on in; the water's lovely."

He walked up the beach to join her, shaking his head and wiping the water from his arms. Beside the bodies of the *guides baigneurs* Gabriel's arms and shoulders looked very white and pink. She saw drops of water glistening in the wiry curls of chest hair that were visible above his costume top. The dark wool of his costume was shining and heavy from the water, sticking closely to his body. Charis didn't dare let her eyes wander lower than his chest.

"Oh, yes," Gabriel said, admiring her bathing costume. "Very ultra-modern. Come on, let's get it wet."

He seized her hand and pulled her, protesting, down the beach. They ran into the waves, Charis gasping with shock as the water splashed on her warm skin, letting out a half-stifled shriek as the first sizeable wave thumped into her midriff, rocking her back on her heels.

"Gabriel!" she cried, catching hold of him for support. She felt his hands grip her waist. Beneath her palms the skin on his shoulders felt cool and fine.

"Steady, old girl," he shouted, his square face smiling happily into her own, settling her on her feet. "You're on your own now," he said. Then he turned and plunged into the throat of an incoming breaker.

That night as she dressed for dinner, Charis thought about the perfection of the day. The swim, luncheon, a visit to Deauville racecourse to see the horses training, tea at the Eden-Casino, then back to the hotel and a delicious bath. It had been marvellous fun, Gabriel joking and laughing, giving her surreptitious kisses and hugs whenever they found themselves unobserved, calling her "old Mrs. Cobb."

She checked her reflection in a looking-glass. Her hair was up, an ivory satin band around her head, her hair brushed low across her brow. She took a tiny spot of rouge on the tip of her little finger and rubbed it into her lips. She was wearing a new dress for the first time, part of her trousseau, an ankle-length dress in black velvet with silver beadwork on the bodice and sleeves. She walked out into the main room of their suite. Gabriel stood there in his evening suit, smoking a cigarette.

"Good Lord," he said. "My, you look a swell, Mrs. Cobb. Ain't I the lucky chap."

Charis smiled, a little automatically, she realised. She half-wished Gabriel didn't feel he had to keep up this relentless joking and gaiety. It wasn't necessary; they didn't always have to be laughing and playing about. But Gabriel would persist. Now he clicked his heels and offered his arm as if he were a Prussian officer.

"Shall we see what's for grub?" he said.

People looked round as they walked into the dining room. It was busy but not full up. August was the most popular month in Trouville, coinciding with the race meeting. It was Paris-by-the-Sea then, she had read.

During the meal Gabriel ordered champagne, which she noticed he drank considerably more of than she. Indeed, his mood grew steadily more subdued as the meal progressed; he spent a lot of time gazing around the room as if unwilling to catch her eye. Charis understood. She felt the same sensations in her chest: a kind of breathlessness, as if foreshadowing the onset of a panic. To calm them both down, she started talking about the times they had had when they first met in India.

Charis had been born there. Her father was a railway engineer. Her mother had died of some fever or other when Charis was very young, so young that she retained no memory of her whatsoever. Charis had been promptly sent back to England to stay with a family who took care of "Indian children." From there she had gone to Bristol to live with her Aunt Bedelia (her father's sister) and attend the small private school for girls she ran. However much she had loved Aunt Bedelia, she had been "bored blue" by life in Bristol, and consequently at the age of eighteen went out to India to live with her father. For a year her father was based in Bombay, which she had thrived on, with its exotic cosmopolitan life—its yacht club and taxi-cabs, natives in European clothes, its box-wallahs and millionaire merchants.

But then he was posted up the line to a small garrison town, and if anything, Charis was bored even bluer than she had been in Bristol. Like it or not, she became one of the Railway People—no matter how elevated her father's position as chief engineer—and therefore distinct from Canal People, Army People or Government People. It was true that senior Europeans in the four groups happily intermingled at tennis parties, sales-of-work, polo matches and regimental sports days, but Charis soon grew aware that try to ignore or overcome it as she might, she carried the categorization with her wherever she went.

The only time she felt she left it behind was when the European population moved up from the garrison town on the plains to the popular hill station of Mahar Tal. There were no Railway People in Mahar Tal, as the railway stopped at the foot of the hills. Charis stayed with a friend, Eleanor, the daughter of a District Commissioner, and attained, by association, Government People status.

It was during her second summer at Mahar Tal that she met Gabriel. He had been seconded from his regiment to be a "bear leader" to the son of a local rajah. This involved teaching the young boy how to ride, how to play cricket, tennis and badminton, and generally inculcating all the social airs and graces of an English gentleman.

Charis met Gabriel at an "At Home" given by one of the senior officials' wives. Some tennis was played; tea and lemonade were drunk. The hill garden in which the At Home took place was devoid of turf but full of English flowers and surrounded by oak and pine trees. Gabriel had been quite a "catch." Since then, Eleanor and she had never been quite such close friends.

Charis shook herself out of her reverie and looked across the table at him. Gabriel was cutting up a peach with meticulous surgical care, his head bowed over his plate. In India everything had possessed a wonderful dreamlike quality. Somehow, back in England, it proved hard to sustain. Perhaps it was meeting Gabriel's curious family: all those sisters and brothers-in-law, his batty Aunt Mary and his eccentric mother, the very peculiar little major, and Felix, "clever" Felix, of whom Gabriel spoke most fondly, but who had seemed to her, if she were honest, an odious little prig.

No, she told herself, don't criticise. Not tonight, of all nights. It was an ordinary family, just like most people's. Only Gabriel's perfection showed them up rather.

Gabriel looked up at this point and caught her smiling at him. He smiled back, a little uneasily, she thought.

"Fancy the Casino, Carrie?" he asked, pouring the remains of the champagne bottle into his glass. "Shall we see if we can make our fortune?"

The Casino! she thought. What on earth was he talking about? "I don't think so, Gabriel," she said. "Perhaps tomorrow night."

"Fine," he said, "fine," and drained his glass.

They went into the hotel lounge, where Gabriel ordered brandy and a cigar. When he finished these he suggested a walk, but Charis again demurred. He had another brandy before they went upstairs to their room. Once there, Charis found Gabriel's lack of composure beginning to affect her too. As she sat before her dressing table in the dressing room, her hands shook slightly as she removed the pins from her hair. In the bedroom Gabriel cleared his throat loudly and said he was going down the corridor to the bathroom.

Charis wondered for a moment why he wouldn't use the one attached to their small suite but realised that this was a kind of ruse to give her a moment or two of privacy.

She felt a pulse beating in her temple and a tightening of her throat. She pulled a night-dress over her underclothes, without putting her arms through the sleeves, and removed her corset and knickers beneath it, as she had done all her life. It was curious, Charis suddenly thought, but she had never seen her naked body in a mirror. She put her underclothes away and climbed into bed, lying on the left-hand side. That was where she had lain last night. She didn't know if Gabriel had any preference.

In two minutes Gabriel returned.

"D'you know, I think the water's hotter down there," he said artlessly and ducked into the dressing room. Charis lay stiffly in the double bed. Dear Gabriel, she said to herself, as if it were a prayer, dear Gabriel, how I love you. Suddenly she reached over and extinguished the light by the bed. Then she realised that the central ceiling light was still burning. Did she have time to switch it out before Gabriel came back into the room? Would he switch it out? Ought she to remind him to do so? She slid out of bed and scampered to the door.

"Everything all right, Carrie?" Gabriel said.

She whirled round. He stood in the doorway of the small dressing room. He wore pyjamas with a blue and green stripe. For some reason she noticed he was wearing slippers.

She gave a shrill nervous laugh. "I thought I should lock the door." Her hand moved towards the key. There was a cardboard sign hanging from the doorknob. *"Priez de ne pas déranger, SVP,"* it said. They should really hang that outside, too, she thought in a moment of rationality. But no, she couldn't, not with Gabriel watching. But the light? What about the light? She turned the key in the lock and looked round again. She caught Gabriel edging noiselessly sideways towards the bed with little shuffling steps.

"Hah," he said nonsensically, his hands foolishly trying to slide into non-existent pockets in his pyjama trousers.

"Yes." She marched briskly, more briskly than she intended, across the carpet and round to her side of the bed.

Gabriel wandered back to the door, where he turned off the light.

"Yes," she heard him say in the sudden darkness, "Mmmm."

Charis got into bed for the second time. As she slid her legs down between the sheets, the hem of her night-dress rode up above her knees. Checking her automatic move to pull it down, she experienced a mild thrill of illicit pleasure. She lay back on the pillow and put her arms by her side. Her heart was beating quickly, but not wildly, she thought. That was good. The room was dark. The chambermaid had closed the shutters but left the windows open for coolness. She waited. Where was Gabriel?

"Gabriel?" she said quietly.

"Yes?" he said. He hadn't moved from the door.

"Are you all right?"

"I'm just letting my eyes get used to the dark. Fiendishly dark in here . . . with the lights out."

"Oh. I see. Yes, you're right, it is dark."

"I think I can make things out a bit clearer now."

"Good."

He came uncertainly over to the bed. She felt it give as he sat down. A spring creaked.

"Just taking my slippers off."

"Fine." Charis congratulated herself on her calmness. She knew exactly—from a physiological point of view—what was going to happen. She felt it was a woman's duty to know. Or at least that was what Aunt Bedelia had said. Aunt Bedelia could be a rather fierce person, and, Charis now realised, she had "advanced" ideas. She had given Charis ambiguous, wordy books to read and had explained certain things to her. But her aunt, who had never married, couldn't tell her what it would feel like. Charis was in genuine doubt about this. Eleanor had implied it was extremely unpleasant, though Eleanor had had no more opportunity to test her theories than Aunt Bedelia.

Finally Gabriel eased himself into bed beside her.

"Hello," he said. She felt his hand grip hers.

"Hello," she replied, her voice suddenly thick in her throat. She felt him roll towards her. His nose touched her cheek. She smelt the mingled scents of tooth-powder, brandy and cigars on his breath. He threw his right arm haphazardly across her body, just beneath her breasts. His left hand still squeezed her right hand. He kissed her, and Charis tried to abandon herself to the mood of romance that she felt must be welling up somewhere inside her. But instead she was only conscious of a mounting sense of curiosity and alarm. What was Gabriel going to do next? What, if anything, should she be doing to help him?

Suddenly, with his lips still applied to hers, Gabriel heaved himself on top of her, his weight driving the air out of her lungs. She broke off the kiss and inhaled as quietly as she could. Gabriel's face was now buried in her neck. She felt him shifting and her legs obediently widened. The hem of her night-dress rose still farther up her thighs; she seemed to be excruciatingly conscious of its passage against her skin. She felt it being tugged gently higher. Gabriel's right hand! His left still faithfully clasped hers. And now her heart did begin to thump and echo in her chest. The hem of her nightgown was now above her pubic hairs. Dear Gabriel, she said to herself again, dear Gabriel. She felt the thick cotton of his pyjama trousers against the inside of her thighs. He made tentative thrusting movements. Lord! she thought. Now his "erect member" should penetrate her "vagina." She had seen naked men, in statues and pictures—even swimming in rivers; glimpses of a white sausage thing hanging from a dark clump of hair. Now she felt something squashy pressing intimately against her, but there was, she was sure, no penetration of any kind. The weight of his body between her thighs was pleasant; so, too, was the way his nudging, thrusting movements rocked her. But she knew it had to be hard, and there was nothing hard there, or so she thought.

Then Gabriel rolled off her. Charis lay immobile with astonishment.

"Are you all right?" Gabriel whispered.

"What?"

"You're all right? I didn't . . . upset you?"

"No," she whispered. "No."

"Good," he said. "I'm glad. I didn't want to, you know, upset you too much, the first time."

"No, I'm fine, really. Fine."

"Good, good." He kissed her on the cheek. "Night-night, Carrie," he said, his tone buoyant with relief. "We'll go to the château tomorrow, shall we?"

Charis lay back in bed. Tonight, she said to herself, Sunday the twenty-sixth of July 1914, I, Charis Cobb, née Lavery, became a woman.

The next day they hired an excursion-brake and went to the Château d'Hebentot, about ten miles away from Trouville. They stopped on the way for a picnic—provided by the hotel—in the Forest of Touques. Gabriel was in a good mood again, and after their picnic offered Charis one of his cigarettes. The day was hot and cloudless. Charis sat with her back against a tree and Gabriel stretched out on the ground with his head in her lap. She puffed her smoke up into the branches above her and her uncertainties about the previous night disappeared under the onslaught of Gabriel's relentless good humour. She was left, though, with the abiding thought that something had gone wrong last night; that in fact very little had occurred which should have, and this she found lingeringly discomfiting.

That evening Gabriel again indulged heavily in wine and post-prandial brandies. The undressing and getting into bed was achieved with less fuss but with no real alteration in the subsequent events. Gabriel did spend more time kissing her, and for a while hugged her close before rolling heavily on top. Charis, having only a little second-hand knowledge to rely on, and having to use her imagination more than she liked, couldn't work out what was happening with Gabriel's anatomy, whether it was functioning perfectly or whether—a worrying idea this—it was some defect in her own make-up. She wondered if she ought to be doing something herself and Gabriel was being too polite to ask it of her, but he never uttered a word, nor conveyed any hints she was performing inadequately. Once again, the presence of Gabriel between her thighs and such shoving and heaving as went on provided ghostly sensations of pleasure, notions of potential enjoyment. But, she wondered, perhaps this was all anyone ever felt? She knew, from Aunt Bedelia's instructions, that there should be an issue of semen during the act. When Gabriel lay once more beside her she carried out a covert examination, but all seemed to be as it always had. But then she had no real idea what semen would be like, should she encounter it, and so her bafflement remained constant.

Gabriel, as on the Sunday night, was extremely solicitous, asking her several times if she felt all right and expressing his earnest desire not to cause her any harm or emotional discomfort.

They went bathing again on Tuesday, Charis braving the bellowing old crone in the bathing boxes, then splashing about happily in the crowded shallows. In the afternoon they walked down to the harbour and fishmarket to watch the fishing fleet come in.

That evening Gabriel drank two whiskies and soda before the meal, most of a bottle of claret and two brandies afterwards. Charis's preparations took the form of a fresh night-gown. As she pulled it over her head she heard Gabriel blunder into a chair. She felt a surge of irritation that he had to drink so much in order to "perform" in so unsatisfactory a way. For a moment she looked forward to the end of the honeymoon, to the time when the nightly obligation to behave as honeymooners would be over.

She lay obediently in bed as Gabriel sheepishly emerged from the dressing room and went over to the door to switch off the light. On his journey back to the bed, his hesitant, inebriated course caused him to collide heavily with the bedside locker.

"*Ouch!* Damn it!" he swore petulantly, hopping about on one foot. "*Ow.* Good grief, that's *sore.*"

Charis sat up in exasperation.

"What's happening?" she said angrily.

Gabriel collapsed on the bed. "I cracked my knee on that wretched cupboard-thing," he moaned in a sulky voice.

"Let me see." Charis reached out for him, something in his little-boy tones making her less yielding, more firm. Gabriel levered his way across the bed to her.

"You great goose," she said, relenting. "Who's had too much to drink tonight, eh? Where's your knee, you silly boy?" She grabbed hold of his proffered leg and started vigorously rubbing his knee. Gabriel rested his head on her shoulder, moaning.

"And stop moaning," she said. "Serves you jolly well right."

"Oooh," Gabriel said, pretending to wail, carrying on with the joke. "Not so hard." He put his arms round her. "Kiss it better. Go on."

"No, I will *not*," Charis laughed, trying to push him away. He resisted. "Silly, drunken boys get spanks, not kisses." She tried to slap his wrist and they struggled on the bed. Charis felt the ribbons untie at the throat of her night-gown.

"Naughty," she said warningly. Gabriel's arms were tight around her.

"Mummy'll be cross," she said, without thinking. Gabriel's lips were on her neck. Then lower. Suddenly his hand was cupped round a small breast; then, with a shock of horrified surprise, she realised his lips had slid down her chest and fastened on to a nipple. She felt the wet warmth of his mouth and tongue, and the tug on her breast as he sucked.

My God! was her first reaction. What in God's name does he think he's doing? She felt the pressure and nuzzle again, and unthinkingly put her hand on the back of his head. Gabriel, she thought . . . she didn't really understand. She leant slowly back against the headboard, feeling the unfamiliar length of his erection pressed against her thigh. "Who's a naughty boy," she said softly, unreflectingly easing her position. "Who's a very naughty little boy?"

When she awoke in the morning, Gabriel was already up and dressed. Charis's first thoughts were of the previous night. Now at least she knew what an "issue of semen" was. Pale yellowy, cloudy, sticky stuff, that required vigorous sponging to remove from cotton night-gowns. Gabriel had apologised for his precocity as Charis changed. But they had slept in each other's arms. When she got back into bed Gabriel had snuggled up close to her, resting his head on her breasts, kissing her throat and hugging her, telling her of his love for her, and promising fantastic happiness and bliss in the manner of a seventeenth-century poem.

Charis had stroked his fair hair, happy at least that their marriage had attained some kind of normality. But she was, nonetheless, confused. Gabriel was big and strong, so proud and handsome. She didn't want to mother him. But then, with a flood of charity she thought, why not? Every man needed simple comfort in his private moments. It wouldn't have surprised her if Gabriel had been denied, in his peculiar family, the normal care and affection a child should receive. All those sisters—and sisters can be so bossy, resentful of little brothers. And Felix was the real baby of the family too. Mrs. Cobb seemed to dote on him to a foolish and exclusive extent. Under the circumstances, she reflected before going to sleep, it was an entirely reasonable, natural thing for Gabriel to seek that sort of affection from his wife.

She ushered these thoughts through her mind again as Gabriel came over to the bed and sat down. He smiled tenderly at her and took her hand.

"Are you all right, darling?" he asked.

"Yes, of course," she said with some irritation. Why was he always asking her this, as if she were some kind of invalid? Surely *she* should be the one being solicitous? But she checked herself. "Of course, darling," she repeated.

"What do you feel like doing?"

"Oh, I don't know. Is it a nice day?"

"Super. We could bathe."

"What about taking the steamer to Le Havre?"

"Or there's a concert in the Casino this afternoon."

"Oh, not stuffy concerts, Gabriel. Please."

He laughed. "All right. There's a ball there on Saturday. Hope you won't find that so stuffy." He stood up. "Look, lazybones," he said. "I'll see you downstairs. We'll have a confab over breakfast."

Charis lay in bed for a few minutes after he had gone. She thought about the summer months ahead of them. The West Kents were still in India. Gabriel wasn't sure whether to re-join them or be temporarily re-gazetted to another regiment in England. Henry Hyams had said he could probably find Gabriel something in the Committee for Imperial Defence where he worked. Gabriel said it was tempting.

Charis wondered what it would be like living at Stackpole in the little cottage, wondered how much they would have to see of the other Cobbs. But no, she thought, she had ten whole days of her honeymoon left; she should concentrate on that. For the moment, the future could take care of itself. Perhaps *everything* would be perfect now, now that she knew what to do.

When she walked down the stairs into the large hall of the Angleterre she saw Gabriel bent over the reception desk reading a newspaper with the assistance of the reception clerk. He broke off abruptly when he saw her and escorted her into the breakfast room with a frown on his face.

"What's wrong?" she said, as she took her place at the table. "Can't we get the steamer till this afternoon or something?"

"No," he said, "it's nothing like that." He ran both hands over his hair. "That was a French newspaper. That chap was giving me a hand at translating. It's just as well I spotted the headline. You know we don't get the English papers until two days late."

"Why? What's going on?"

"Austria's declared war on Serbia."

She laughed with relief. "Serbia! Is that all? Another silly Balkan war?"

Gabriel looked grim. Really, she thought, never marry a soldier.

"We've got to go home," he said firmly. "I knew it would happen. There's nothing else for it. It's the European war, Charis. We've got to go back. Right now. Today."

PART TWO

The War

CHAPTER ONE

9 AUGUST 1914

Smithville · British East Africa

The Finnegan and Zabriskie Sisal Decorticator thumped and banged away with an immense din, shaking and rattling, throwing up clouds of dust, smoke belching from its exhaust stack. Walter Smith watched it with the delighted satisfaction he always experienced when his cherished machine was in operation. At one end Saleh and some farm boys fed in the spiky faggots of harvested sisal leaves. At the other, damp, chewed, pale-yellow strands were flung out, were collected in loose bundles and taken away to hang in the sun on drying racks.

Walter approached the thundering machine. The huge spinning drive-wheels and flapping belts fanned the fibrous air around him. He could feel the powerful vibrations running through the concrete floor, causing his legs to tremble visibly. He reached out and placed his hand on a steel plate. The thrum and shudder set up a tingle in his fingertips. He shut his eyes. He was at the centre of his world, every functioning sense claimed by his machine.

Then, as though from a great distance, he heard a faint shouting noise. He turned round. Some six feet away stood Wheech-Browning, his arms raised protectively as if to ward off a blow. Walter saw his mouth opening and closing. He couldn't make out what the man was trying to say.

"What?" Walter roared back. "WHAT DO YOU WANT?" He was exasperated to see the Assistant District Commissioner here. Wheech-Browning had been trying for weeks to get him to pay customs duty on the coffee seedlings he'd bought in Dar. Seedlings that were now so many tinder-dry, shrivelled weeds, despite the fanatical care and attention they'd received. The last time Wheech-Browning had called, Walter had taken him out to the patch of hillside where he'd envisioned his field of coffee bushes and shown him the forlorn, wasted rows.

"Defective goods," Walter had said. "Diseased, useless plants. You can't make me pay duty on these."

Wheech-Browning, on his part, apologised and assured him he could. As a result Walter was not predisposed to welcome further visits. Wheech-Browning was now pointing at the shed door and mouthing "outside." Walter reluctantly followed him out.

In the open air, the noise of the Decorticator was still considerable, but it was possible to speak. Wheech-Browning removed his sun-helmet and mopped his sweating face with a handkerchief. Then he swept his white jacket free of the shreds of sisal fibres. Walter noticed his boots and trousers were thick with dust. Looking back up the hill, he saw Wheech-Browning's mule tethered outside the house, guarded by two native policemen. Surely the man hasn't come to arrest me? Walter thought wildly for a moment. Surely the British wouldn't clap a man in prison for the late payment of customs duties?

"I don't know how you can stand it," Wheech-Browning said, delivering crisp blows to his thighs with the brim of his topee. Small clouds of dust rose up.

Walter waved away a couple of buzzing flies. "What?" he said. "Stand what?"

"The noise. The din. The hellish din." He pointed his hat at the Decorticator shed and the clouds of smoke issuing from the engine stack.

"Oh, the Decorticator. You get used to it. You don't even notice it after a while."

Wheech-Browning replaced his hat. "Bad news," he said, looking sternly at the Pare Mountains. Walter felt a flutter of panic in his chest. He could arrest me, too, he thought. It's exactly the kind of thing the English would do. You can't break the rules and get away with it.

Wheech-Browning switched his gaze back to Walter. "It's war," he uttered prophetically.

This was ridiculous, Walter said to himself. The man's taking it far too personally.

"It's all right," he said. "I'll pay."

A brief look of incomprehension crossed Wheech-Browning's face. Then it cleared.

"Ah, yes," he said. "I see what you mean. Yes, yes, you're absolutely right. We'll all pay." He looked down at his large feet. "In the end," he added gloomily. Then, "*Bloody* flies!" he suddenly exclaimed, swatting the air about his head with his hands.

"We'll *all* pay?" Walter repeated slowly. He was lost.

To Walter's surprise Wheech-Browning suddenly leapt four feet sideways, leaving the two flies circling aimlessly in the space he had occupied a second before. It took them a moment to find him again.

"Telegraph came three days ago," Wheech-Browning said. "I've been riding round the district since then, letting everyone know. It seems we declared war last week, on the fourth. The news has just taken a little time to reach us out here in the sticks."

Walter began to comprehend and relax. This had nothing to do with him.

"You mean the British are at war?"

"Of course. What do you think I've been talking about?" Wheech-Browning looked angry.

"Who with?"

"Good Lord, man, who do you think? Our German neighbours over there." He waved at the Pare hills. "The Huns, jerries, squareheads. The bloody wa-Germani, that's who with. With whom," he corrected himself.

"Why?"

"Oh, God. Um . . ." Wheech-Browning looked puzzled. "They didn't actually spell that out in the message." He drummed his fingers on his chin. "Something to do with mobilising and declaring war on France, I think. Anyway, whatever it was, it was nothing we could possibly ignore."

"I see. Damn." Walter was thinking that this state of affairs might make it difficult getting reimbursement for the coffee seedlings from the *Chef der Abteilung* in Dar.

"How's that going to affect us?" Walter asked. "I guess they'll close the border for a while. But wait, aren't the colonies staying neutral?"

Wheech-Browning gave a harsh ironic laugh. "Good God, Smith, what do you think's going on here? We're at war with Germany. And that includes those swine across the border." He looked scornfully at Walter. "We're expecting an invasion any day. Taveta's bound to be the first object of an attack. I've come here to tell you to evacuate your farm. Same as I've been telling everybody close to the border—"

"Hold on one second," Walter said forcefully. "Just hold on. There's going to be no evacuation here. I've got my sisal harvest to process. What am I going to do with no Decorticator?"

"Look here, Smith," Wheech-Browning began.

"No, you look here," Walter said. "You British have declared war on Germany. It's got nothing to do with me. I'm an American. Neutral. I've got no quarrel with the Germans."

"Well, you're a damn fool American," Wheech-Browning replied angrily, his face getting redder. "My God, if you'd heard the stories going round. Think of your wife and children, for God's sake. Your wife's English. If you get a company of German askaris in here, they won't stop to check your nationality."

Walter pursed his lips. "What about the British Army?" he asked. "Where are the troops?"

"We've got three battalions of the King's African Rifles, that's all. Half of them are up in Jubaland; the other half will have their work cut out defending the railway. You can't expect them to go running after every crackpot American—"

"Now, just a minute—"

But Wheech-Browning was in full flight, clearly rattled by the prospect of Taveta being overrun by thousands of bloodthirsty native troops. "I've got my orders to pull back to the railway at Voi at the first sign of attack. That's my advice to you. I'm staying with my police askaris at Taveta, but . . ." Wheech-Browning controlled himself. "Smith, believe me, this is official advice. It's just not safe."

"I'll be fine," Walter said easily. "Don't you worry."

Wheech-Browning made a despairing grabbing motion at the air. "Very well." He closed his eyes for two seconds. "I've told you. I can't order you. Anyway, I've got to get on. Think it over, Smith. It's not some kind of a game." He came closer. "There are stories going round. When they attacked the line at Tsavo—yes, already— it seems they caught one of the Indian station managers." He blanched. "Cut off his . . . you know. Horribly mutilated, by all accounts. They're savages." He paused. "Look, it'll only be for a few months at the most. They say there are troops coming from India. Once they're here they'll tie everything up in no time. But just at the moment we're a bit stretched."

Walter patted Wheech-Browning's thin shoulder. "I'll give it some thought," he said, deciding on conciliation. "Let me think it over."

He walked back up the hill and saw the ADC off on his mule before returning to the Decorticator and his sisal harvest.

Walter did take Wheech-Browning's advice seriously enough to inform Saleh and his boys and told them to keep their eyes open. He also firmly locked the doors and windows of the house at night and took his guns down from the wall. He told Matilda everything Wheech-Browning had said, adding that he thought it was unreasonable panic. Matilda's sanguineness remained as constant as ever. She felt sure that no one would want to bother them at Smithville.

As the days went by and nothing occurred to disturb the normal routine of their lives, Walter's little apprehensions disappeared.

One night he thought he heard an explosion in the distance. On another he made out a noise which just might have been taken for gunfire. But it was impossible for him to verify this. He sent Saleh into Taveta, and he reported that, although O'Shaugnessy's shop was closed, Wheech-Browning was still there with his company of police. The Indian bazaar was trading as normal, nobody had heard of any trouble, of any massing of troops along the border.

Walter busied himself with work on the sisal harvest. The Decorticator clattered and belched smoke most of the day as Saleh and his workers hacked the leaves from the plants in the fields, trundled them up the trolley lines to the "factory" and fed them into the voracious machine. Steadily the mounds of dried fibre grew higher. They spent a day roping them into loose bales, enough to fill two large wagon loads which Walter would eventually take down the road to Voi, where the Afro-American Fibre Company was based. There they had a scutching machine and hydraulic balers. The general manager, Ward, was an American, too, but he and Walter did not get on. Ward's charges for scutching and baling were too high, Walter considered, especially for a fellow countryman. However, he quite enjoyed his trips to the company's factory at Voi. He got good ideas for the future expansion of Smithville from looking at the way Ward ran the place. He'd bought the Decorticator from Ward, and had his eye on a scutching drum. On this coming trip he intended to buy another two hundred yards of trolley line; he was going to extend the sisal plantations in 1915.

As he worked on in this way and considered his plans for the future, the slight feelings of alarm generated by Wheech-Browning's words disappeared. The price he was getting for his sisal seeds, let alone the fibre, guaranteed him a prosperous year. If he planted another four acres he would have doubled his turnover in three years. It was unfortunate about the coffee seedlings; he had thought that particular idea was a master-stroke. He wondered vaguely about the possibility of rubber. There was a German at Kibwezi, near Voi, with six hundred acres planted. But rubber took even longer to grow than sisal, and however much Walter liked the image of Smithville surrounded by profitable acres of rubber trees, he wanted to move faster than that.

On the morning of the eighteenth of August, just before he left for Voi with the sisal fibre, he had his brainwave. He sat across the breakfast table from Matilda. Glenway was crying because he claimed he didn't like his porridge. Matilda, to Walter's annoyance, was ignoring the boy. She was reading a book, a cup of warm tea pressed to her cheek. She seemed to be growing more oblivious to the demands of her family. Walter reached for the butter tin. There was only a smear of the oily orange butter left.

"Matilda," Walter said, "do we have no butter?"

"What, dear?"

"Butter. It's finished." He put down his knife. "Would you see what the boy wants?" he added crossly.

Matilda put her book face down on the table. "What is it, Glennie?"

"It's not sweet," Glenway said, letting porridge plop from his spoon onto the enamel plate.

"Joseph," Matilda called to the cook, "did you remember to put vanilla essence in the porridge?"

Vanilla. That was it, Walter suddenly realised. The cash crop of the future . . . Someone had planted an acre near Voi. No machinery, no processing plant, just pods to pick. His mind began to work. He'd plough up the abortive coffee plantation, yes. Perhaps he could even get seedlings on this trip to Voi.

"No vanilla," Joseph announced from the kitchen doorway.

"No vanilla and no butter," Matilda reported. "Can you get some in Taveta on your way back?"

"What?" Walter said, his mind preoccupied with visions of vanilla fields, the brittle pods rattling soothingly in the breeze off Lake Jipe. "Sure. Oh, no, I can't. I'll get them at Voi. O'Shaugnessy's left. Shut up shop."

"Of course," Matilda said, picking up her book. "It's the war. I forgot."

Saleh appeared at the dining room door. He looked worried.

Walter stood up. "All ready?" he asked. Saleh had been hitching the oxen to the heavily laden wagons.

Saleh leant against the door frame. Walter realised it wasn't worry distorting his features, but fear.

"Askari." Saleh gestured feebly down the hill towards the factory buildings. "Askari are here."

Walter ran to the door, a sudden feeling of pressure building up in his chest. Matilda followed close behind. Sure enough, drawn up in a ragged line in front of the Decorticator shed was a column of black soldiers. For a moment, Walter thought they were British. They wore the same khaki tunics and shorts, the same felt fezzes as the King's African Rifles he'd seen. But then he caught sight of two Europeans who, just at that moment, were walking out of the Decorticator shed. They wore the thick drill jodhpurs and knee-length leggings, the long-sleeved jackets buttoned to the neck, of *Schutztruppe* officers. The leading man looked up the hill to the house and waved.

"Hello, Smith," he called cheerily. "How nice to see you again. May we come up?" It was Von Bishop.

"Look, it's Von Bishop," Walter said to Matilda as the two men walked up the hill. "You know, Erich von Bishop. I met him and his wife when I was in Dar. Very pleasant man."

"What happens now?" Walter asked as he watched his empty trek wagons being driven off towards Taveta. The large heap of deposited sisal bales was already beginning to crackle and smoke. Sixteen hundredweight, he thought. Two months' work gone. He saw his vanilla plantation swept from the land as though by a blast from a hurricane.

"I *am* sorry about all this," Von Bishop said equably. "We have to commandeer any transport and destroy all crops."

"What? Even those in the fields?"

Von Bishop shrugged. "Orders, I'm afraid." Then he laughed. "Don't worry, Smith, I won't try too hard in your case. After all, we are almost next-door neighbours."

He seemed quite unconcerned, Walter thought. He tried to summon up a rage or a sense of injustice, but Von Bishop's easygoing manner made it appear somehow inappropriate, an over-reaction, even a discourtesy. He looked away and saw his two boys dancing merrily around the pyre of sisal fibres.

"GET AWAY FROM THERE!" he bellowed, taking out his frustration on them. "Go and help your mother pack." They ran off obe-diently. Von Bishop had obligingly left them an old buggy and two mules in which they were to travel to Voi. Von Bishop said that, theoretically, he should have interned them, but as Walter was an American citizen he'd let them go. Matilda and Joseph were hastily getting their personal possessions together and a squad of farm boys was relaying them from the house to the buggy.

Von Bishop told Walter about the capture of Taveta. The in-vading Germans, about four companies strong, had crossed the border and had sent a note to Wheech-Browning and his police askaris telling them that they intended to occupy the town and that he had one hour to evacuate. In fact they waited overnight, and in the morning marched down the road into Taveta. Wheech-Brown-ing's men opened fire and the Germans reassembled for a frontal attack. But when they cautiously advanced they discovered that Wheech-Browning and his men had disappeared.

Walter thought this highly characteristic of Wheech-Browning and was about to tell Von Bishop a few home truths about his adversary, when a loud clanging noise came from the Decorticator shed.

"My God!" Walter cried and ran forward. Von Bishop made no attempt to restrain him. Inside the shed he found the other German officer banging experimentally at the Decorticator and some of the steel girders supporting the roof with a hammer.

"Hey! Stop it!" Walter shouted, snatching the hammer away. "What in God's name do you think you're doing?" But the man didn't speak English. Von Bishop said something to him in German and he shrugged and wandered off.

"Nobody touches that machine, Erich," Walter said warningly to Von Bishop. "Everything is tied up in that machine, one way or another. Burn the crops if you must, but leave this alone."

Von Bishop looked around the shed. "So this is the factory you told me about. Very impressive, I must say. Is it economically via-ble, though? With such a small acreage?" For a few minutes they talked about the pros and cons of independently producing your own sisal fibre, Walter searching his machine for any dents and scratches caused by the hammering. They were interrupted by

Saleh, who told them that everyone was ready and the buggy was loaded.

Von Bishop and Walter left the shed, Walter taking a final fond look at the Decorticator. Outside he saw his wife and children gathered in a small group curiously watching the German askaris ripping up his trolley lines, supervised and directed by the other European officer.

"For God's sake!" Walter exclaimed. "What's wrong with that man? Is he some kind of vandal? Got this urge to destroy?"

This time Von Bishop did place a restraining hand on Walter's arm. "I'm sorry," he said. "Trolley lines are required. So is fencing wire. You're lucky—I see you have no wire fences."

"Oh, yes," Walter said sardonically. "I'm a lucky man."

"Well," Von Bishop said, his breeziness returning, "fortunes of war and all that."

Walter shook his head and kicked angrily at a stone. "I suppose you're right," he said. Fortunes of war, he thought. It didn't feel in the least bit like a war, yet there were enemy soldiers with loaded weapons forcibly ejecting him from his property. Von Bishop was behaving like a man who'd come round to reclaim a book he'd once lent. Walter watched sections of his trolley line being prised from the dusty and unyielding ground. Then he had an idea. Reparations, he thought. I can demand reparations. He started doing quick sums in his head. Often this sort of disaster could be turned to your advantage. It should be seen as an opportunity for a fresh start: a chance to rethink and replan. He'd always regretted not laying the trolley lines closer to Lake Jipe. . . . Now, with his reparations, was the ideal time to redirect them. He turned back to Von Bishop.

"You're right, Erich. Fortunes of war. Could you provide me with a . . . I don't know, an affidavit or something? Just so I can prove things have been commandeered."

"Yes, of course," Von Bishop said. "With pleasure." He called the other officer over and told him to make out a careful note of everything that had been taken or destroyed.

"What about the house?" Walter asked.

"I suppose I might billet some men here," Von Bishop said. "It commands a good position on the hill. We can't pay you rent," he laughed. "Doubtless there'll be some minor breakages, wear and tear. Who knows, we might even finish building it for you."

Walter smiled. Even the sight of a thin plume of smoke rising from the linseed fields didn't give him pause. Von Bishop signed the piece of paper and tore it out of the officer's notebook. Walter looked it over.

"Imperial German . . . Erich von Bishop, Major. That's excellent, Erich. Excellent." He patted him on the shoulder. "Just don't touch the Decorticator, that's all. My future's in that machine. I'll come all the way to Dar to get you otherwise."

The two men laughed heartily.

"We have our own decorticators, Smith," Von Bishop said. "We don't need yours. Krupp's Decorticators. Very efficient. One hundredweight of fibre an hour. Much better than your American machines."

They were walking back to the buggy which now contained his family as well as their possessions.

"I don't know about that," Walter said. "Finnegan and Zabriskie are renowned—" He paused. "Krupp's, did you say? Is there an agent in Mombasa, do you know?"

Saleh and the farm boys were ranged beside the buggy. They all wore uniform expressions of deep misery, glancing uneasily about them at the armed askaris.

"Don't worry, Saleh," Walter said quietly, confident that he wouldn't. "Keep an eye on the place. Look after the farm and the Decorticator. We'll be back in two months." He gave the man an encouraging slap on the back and climbed up onto the buggy. Matilda sat beside him, still reading her book. The children nestled in the back among the trunks and bundles of clothes and bedding, protected from the sun by a makeshift canvas shelter. The ayah sat on the back, her feet hanging down, crying piteously. She was the only one who seemed obviously affected by the occasion.

"Well, goodbye, Smith," Von Bishop said. "Mrs. Smith. I'm so sorry we had to meet under these circumstances." He touched the brim of his sun-helmet in a casual salute.

Walter shook the reins and the mules moved forward. "Remember," Walter called back to Von Bishop, "look after the machine. I'm holding you responsible."

Von Bishop laughed again and waved. Seeing him do this, all the farm boys laughed politely and waved too. This is most strange, thought Walter. It's as if we're being seen off on holiday.

At the top of the rise, just before Smithville was lost to sight, Walter looked back. Smoke still rose from the sisal bonfire and at least half his linseed fields seemed ablaze. The gang of askaris had uprooted some fifty yards of trolley line and were piling the rails in neat bundles. Von Bishop was leading half a dozen soldiers up the hill to the house.

Walter felt suddenly disorientated and confused. Von Bishop's matter-of-fact behaviour, his genial appropriation of his goods and chattels, the total absence of threat, hardly made it seem like a criminal act.

"Criminals," Walter said experimentally, more out of a sense of duty than outrage. He felt the same. "Criminals!" he repeated more fiercely.

"What's that, my dear?" Matilda asked, raising her eyes from her book. If she was going to read all the way to Voi, Walter said to himself, he would get very angry. He shook the reins viciously and the buggy moved forward with a lurch. The ayah gave a squeal of alarm as she fell off the back. Walter reined in.

"When are we coming back?" Glenway called out as the whimpering ayah clambered back on board.

"Soon," Walter said with grim confidence. "Very soon indeed."

It was about a forty-mile journey from Smithville to Voi along an old caravan track that led through particularly arid and dusty scrubland. The Smith family in their buggy made slow but steady progress without seeing any further signs of the Germans. Walter briefly savoured the cruel irony of the fact that he had intended to make this journey today anyway—but with two valuable loads of sisal instead of his placid wife and increasingly fractious children. For the first time and for a brief moment he experienced a feeling of rage and frustration which seemed to do some justice to his new refugee status, but it didn't last long. The track was too bumpy and the wagon jolted too much for Matilda to read, he noted with selfish pleasure. But she seemed as unperturbed as always, gazing out over the thorny scrub, which shimmered and vibrated in the haze, at the distant hills and mountain ranges, fanning herself with her book. She also, in an effort to amuse the children, played interminable word games which seemed to consist of building ever-longer lists of groceries and vegetables, repeated ad nauseam, and which drove Walter wild with a kind of rampaging boredom, until he ordered them to cease forthwith. They stopped once to water the mules, for an hour and a half, at midday, and ate some sandwiches which Joseph had prepared before they left. Walter looked back up the road to Taveta, squinting into the glare, wondering if he could see the smoke from his burning fields.

It was nearly dark as they approached the small village of Bura, still some eight miles from Voi. The mules were plodding very slowly, the children and Matilda were asleep, curled up in the back, and Walter himself nodded dozily over the reins.

"Halt!" came a sudden shout. "Who goes there?" followed immediately by a ragged volley of shots. Walter saw the flash of the muzzles, but as far as he could make out, no bullet came anywhere near.

"Get down!" he yelled at his screaming, terrified family, and then bellowed "Friends!" up the road in the direction the shots had come from.

"Cease fire! Cease fire, you bloody fools!" came a familiar voice. A lantern came bobbing down the track towards them, casting its glow on long thin legs protruding from flapping shorts, and improbably shod in black socks and very large tennis shoes.

"Thought I recognised your accent, Smith," said Wheech-Browning. "Sorry my men were a bit premature. 'Trigger-happy' is the expression in your part of the world, I believe. Gave the children a fright, I expect." He held up the lantern. "Evening, Mrs. Smith. Sorry about all this fuss. Wheech-Browning here, late of Taveta. Ha-ha!"

"You stupid . . . stupid dumb *idiot!*" Walter seethed. "You could have killed us."

"Steady on, old chap. You could have been the wa-Germani for all we knew. No harm done anyway, thank goodness—that's the main thing." He gave a nervous smile. "Come across any Huns, by any chance?"

"Yes," Walter said, too exhausted to remonstrate further. "They threw us off the farm this morning. Set fire to the crops."

"My God, the swine," Wheech-Browning said, his voice hoarse with loathing. Walter wondered where the man got his antagonism from. "Can't say I didn't warn you," Wheech-Browning added, a little smugly. "They didn't take you prisoner, though. That's a bonus. We clapped old Heuber in irons for the duration, p.d.q. You know Heuber? Chap with the rubber at Kibwezi. He was most put out. Listen, are you going on to Voi? Can I get a lift back with you?"

On the way to Voi, Wheech-Browning gave him his version of the attack on Taveta. He claimed he'd received no message from the Germans to surrender and was extremely surprised one morning to see about three hundred of them marching down the road "bold as brass." It would be too undignified to leave without firing a shot, he thought, so he ordered his men to open fire. Nobody, he was sure, had been hit, but he was extremely surprised at the way in which the German askaris had scattered and had proceeded to lay down a furious fire on Taveta's flimsy defences. Wheech-Browning and his men wasted no time in setting off down the road to Voi. Luckily, Wheech-Browning said, considering the amount of bullets shot in their direction, they had suffered only one casualty.

"Unfortunately, he was my bearer," Wheech-Browning said. "Got a round in the throat. I was standing right beside him. Fountains of blood—you wouldn't believe it. I was covered, head to tail—dripping. Of course the fellow had been carrying all my personal gear. I had to leave everything behind in the retreat; everyone was hotfooting it out of town, I can tell you. Which explains"—he pointed to his footwear—"this unorthodox regalia."

Walter was glad enough to have Wheech-Browning beside him as an escort. He felt it was only his due anyway, considering he'd had his farm seized and his crops burned in the cause of an Anglo-

German war. Wheech-Browning could see them all right, he reasoned, make sure the authorities cared for them properly.

He was surprised when, as they reached the outskirts of Voi, Wheech-Browning leapt off the buggy, saying he'd better report to the King's African Rifles officer who was in command.

"But, hey," Walter called. "What about us?"

"What *about* you, old man?"

"What are we meant to do?"

"I should put up at the dak bungalow at the station," Wheech-Browning advised. "Pretty reasonable rates, and jolly good breakfasts."

The next morning, forgoing his jolly good breakfast, Walter went in search of the K.A.R. officer to see what the British Army's plans were for transporting the Smith family to Nairobi. He found the man in the Voi post office, which was being used as a temporary command headquarters.

"My dear fellow," said the K.A.R. officer, "no can do." He was smoking a pipe which he didn't bother to remove from his mouth. As a result, all his words were delivered through clenched teeth which made them sound, to Walter's ears, even more heartless.

"But I'm a refugee," Walter protested. "I'm a victim . . . of, of German war crimes. Surely there's something in your rule book about care of refugees?"

The man took his pipe out of his mouth, pointed its saliva-shiny stem in Walter's direction and closed one eye as if taking aim.

"Ah. Ah-ha. But, you see, I'm not so sure you are a refugee. According to Reggie Wheech-Browning, you were warned to evacuate your farm over a week ago. I'm afraid you can hardly expect us to take the consequences of your"—he stuck his pipe in his mouth again—"what shall we say? Your recalcitrance."

Walter marched back to the dak bungalow viciously cursing the British Army in general and "Reggie" Wheech-Browning in particular. He felt more irate and hard done-by now than when he'd been watching Von Bishop destroying his livelihood. At the dak bungalow he discovered that the train from Mombasa to Nairobi, which had spent the night at Voi, had departed half an hour previously. The

Smith family would have to wait until the next morning before their journey could continue.

Walter's anger swiftly died down but he insisted that his family get and keep a receipt for everything they spent or consumed. He was fully determined to present the largest bill possible in his reparations claim. He sold his American buggy and two mules to a thieving Greek merchant for a fraction of their true worth, and added this deficit to his rapidly growing column of figures.

The boys and Matilda seemed far less put out than he was. The dak bungalow was efficiently run and they enjoyed—as Wheech-Browning had promised—wholesome meals. In the afternoon Walter read his way through a pile of newspapers and illustrated magazines that had recently arrived from England. The news from Europe was two weeks old and was only of war declared and of the German invasion of Belgium. Talking to other travellers, Walter pieced together some idea of what had been going on in East Africa while he had been innocently gathering and decorticating his sisal harvest. Dar-es-Salaam had been bombarded by HMS *Astraea;* Taveta had been captured—as he was by now well aware—and instructions had been sent to India for the despatch of troops to East Africa. Indian Expeditionary Force "C" was believed to be on its way at this very moment and was expected at the beginning of September. "Should be over soon after that," his informant confidently told him. "Crack Indian troops. Fine body of fighting men."

Walter's spirits rose considerably at this. September, he thought. Let's not be too hasty . . . say, two months before it's all over. That would give him several weeks before the rains to lay the new trolley tracks down, possibly even plant out the first of the vanilla fields. . . . Conceivably, this enforced stay in Nairobi could turn out to be more beneficial than irksome. He could examine different strains of vanilla seedlings at his leisure; there might even be someone—the idea was appealing—who could tell him a little more about Krupp's Decorticators.

CHAPTER TWO

20 AUGUST 1914

Nairobi · British East Africa

Walter looked out of the window as the train approached Nairobi. Compared to the stifling heat at Voi, the cooler, drier air up here on the plateau felt almost chilly, even though it was mid-afternoon.

Nairobi in 1914 presented a curious sight. Built on a flat plain, with gently rising hills to the north and south, ten years before it had been no more than a cluster of tents and tin shacks around a rudimentary railway depot. Now there were many imposing stone buildings among the galvanised iron and wooden shops; motor cars bumped up the dirt streets, two of which—Government Road and Sixth Avenue—were illuminated at night by electric street lamps. On many occasions Walter was forcibly reminded of small American townships. The same single-storeyed wooden shop façades with hand-painted signs, the same wooden awnings over the sidewalks, but with bicycle racks outside instead of hitching posts. There was a half-mile of macadamised road leading to the centre of town from the station; otherwise all the thoroughfares were dirt or, slightly better, gravel and dirt.

As the train pulled into the station—new, stone, and quite impressive, Walter had to admit—he saw the distinctive bald-headed, slope-shouldered figure of his father-in-law, the Reverend Norman Espie, of the Friends of Africa Evangelical Mission. Walter had telegraphed ahead the day before—the mission was some ten miles outside Nairobi—and arranged for them to be met. He was going to send Matilda and the children to stay with her parents while he remained in Nairobi to see what the government was prepared to do about the loss of his farm.

So it was with less reluctance than usual that Walter allowed his father-in-law to grasp his hand and shake it vigorously for a full minute. The Reverend Norman Espie was of average size and was a wiry, fit-looking man considering he was in his fifties. But his lack—his almost complete absence—of shoulders gave him an un-alterably puny appearance. From the back his silhouette resembled a pawn in a game of chess, his arms tapering smoothly up onto his neck with no interruption and his round bald head teed up on top of it. Indeed he was the sort of man, Walter often thought, whose weakness was a kind of challenge: it made you want to punch him in the chest, just to prove you weren't affected by it.

"My son, my son," Espie was saying, "we have been praying for you." He released Walter's hand and fell to his knees—to Walter's extreme embarrassment. Walter assumed his father-in-law was about to offer up an impromptu prayer for their deliverance, but in fact he was only positioning himself the better to sweep his grand-children into his arms and smother them with kisses. From this humble posture he looked up at Matilda, who at this point had just stepped off the train. Espie clambered to his feet crying, "My child, my child," and wrapped his arms about her.

"Now, now, Father," Matilda said. Her father was the only person who could provoke a show of irritation in her. "Don't fuss so. We were in no danger."

"The barbarians!" Espie exclaimed. "If you knew the stories that have been coming out of Belgium. To think that in Christian Europe we can harbour such—"

"Shall we get along?" Matilda said in a business-like way. "The baby is very tired."

"The baby, the baby," Espie intoned. Walter went off in search of the baggage.

He saw his family loaded into Espie's—or rather the mission's—motor car (the ayah was sobbing plaintively for some reason) and waved them goodbye. Then he climbed into a rickshaw and gave orders to be taken to the Norfolk Hotel.

The rickshaw moved steadily away from the station up the long stretch of Government Road. Walter saw the new stone post office standing alone in a great field of grass looking quite incongruous. A red flag was flying from the roof to signify the arrival of the Mombasa train and to alert any letter writer who wanted mail sorted and carried on up to Entebbe in Uganda.

He looked curiously about him as they reached the built-up areas and jogged past the astonishing number of shops and stores Nairobi possessed. For such an out-of-the-way place it was truly incredible what goods were on sale. There were large general stores, taxidermists, jewellers, tobacconists, chemists, photographic studios, wine merchants, milliners and tailors selling all the well-known brand names from Britain. He passed Cearn's Outfitters, boasting proudly in their window that they possessed "all the luxuries and necessities of the colonial gentleman." He saw advertisements for Burberry and Aertex, "K"-shoes and Frank Cooper's Oxford Marmalade. He passed the wooden and corrugated iron two-storey building of the Stanley Hotel, one of eight hotels in Nairobi. The Norfolk was half a mile farther on.

At this stage the flow of traffic was considerable: some motor cars, lots of rickshaws and bicycles, bullock carts and horse-drawn buggies. Walter hadn't been in Nairobi for months and the throng and bustle always made him feel a little excited, the country boy come to the big city. All this traffic raised clouds of dust, which hung in the branches of the small tattered casuarina pine trees that lined the dry mud road and gave it a ludicrous air of pretending to be an avenue.

The Norfolk was Nairobi's best hotel. It was an unassuming single-storey stone building with a tin roof and a large verandah running the length of the Government Road frontage. It was not nearly as grand as the palatial Kaiserhof in Dar, but it did have electric light throughout and hot and cold running water, and was the meeting point and social centre of the town.

Although Walter became excited by his visits to Nairobi, he very quickly grew irritated by the place. Just as the tattered spindly trees in Government Road seemed to indicate ideas above its station, so too did Nairobi's newly won international renown as a big-game shooting resort allow the town to affect a similar inappropriate grandeur and sophistication which it could never possess in reality. And the presence of the British made that affectation almost insupportable. There was the Turf Club with its race meetings. The gymkhanas and polo matches, the Maseru Hunt, the golf club, the Masonic Lodge . . . all the trappings of an English provincial town. Many times Walter had listened to discussions about who would win the Governor's cup; about the cross-breeding of wanderobo hunting dogs with foxhounds for the hunt's pack; whether Somali ponies were better than Abyssinian ones; if it wasn't really about time that "shirt-sleeve order" was banned at race meetings.

He would shake his head in rueful wonder at the shouting incongruities that presented themselves daily. The immense mock-Tudor Government House, with its leaded lights and half-timbered upper floor; lady golfers in boaters and long white dresses driving off into a wilderness on a first tee where the air was dark with thousands of buzzing flies; the piping shouts of tally-ho as the Maseru Hunt took off after some hapless hyena, and above all the snobbish hierarchies that existed, symbolised by the Nairobi Club on the Hill for senior officials and the Parklands Club on the plain in Parklands for junior officials. Being an American, and one who, lately at any rate, had some money in his pocket, meant that he was always something of an outsider and that he was naturally excluded from the phenomenally exact social rankings that obtained in polite Nairobi society. He had no complaints on either count.

Walter occupied his room at the Norfolk, had a bath and went to sleep for a couple of hours. Later in the evening, feeling much refreshed, he walked through the hotel to the bar. To his surprise the place was crowded with men, spilling out of the room onto the verandah and even down the front steps onto Government Road. They were all dressed, moreover, for the bush, as if they were going on safari. Many wore crossed bandoliers of cartridges, and rifles and shotguns were propped in corners or leaning against the backs of chairs.

Walter recognised a group of fellow Americans: Ward, from the Afro-American farm enterprise at Voi; Paul Rainey, a millionaire big-game enthusiast; and others he knew from the American Industrial Mission. Although the bar was crowded and nearly everyone was drinking heavily, the mood was one of boredom and irritation. Walter joined the group and ordered a whisky and soda. The sight of a new face acted as a catalyst to their flagging spirits and great commiseration was soon being lavished on him over the loss of his farm.

There was also real interest. All these men had streamed into Nairobi at the outbreak of war to volunteer their services in the defence of the country and as reinforcements to the hard-pressed battalions of the K.A.R. Walter found himself something of a celebrity for actually having been a victim of *Furor Teutonicus* and he was prevailed upon several times to repeat his account of the seizure of his farm and of Wheech-Browning's heroic stand at Taveta. By unanimous assent it was agreed that Wheech-Browning's luckless bearer was the first casualty of the war, a war which everyone fervently expressed the hope would last long enough for them to "have a bash" at the squareheads. Walter was encouraged to join two of the volunteer units that had been swiftly formed to defend British East Africa. He could choose between the more prosaic Nairobi Defence Force or the East African Mounted Rifles—an aristocratic and cavalier crowd, requiring the ownership of a horse or polo pony. This particular outfit had claimed most of the Americans, as it was a polyglot assembly of nationalities containing also Boers, Swedes and three Italians. Members around the bar that night included a musician, several publicans, an ex-circus clown and a Scottish lighthouse keeper.

Walter didn't commit himself, as he had no intention of getting involved in the fighting, though he wasn't averse to being bought drinks as an inducement to join up. The fact was that the initial enthusiasm and war-fever had died away. The military had as yet no use for these volunteer forces and they were being encouraged to return to their farms and jobs. The group in the Norfolk Hotel that night represented a hard core, but one whose resolution was fast on the wane, considering that they'd been idling in Nairobi for two weeks and it was clear that it was unlikely they'd ever be deployed. Learning of the departure of the Indian Expeditionary Force "C" had been the most depressing news and had fully doused their ardour.

For his part Walter spent the next few days in an increasingly frustrating attempt to find someone who would admit he was a "problem." He was, he soon discovered, the only person in the whole of British East Africa who had had his land overrun and occupied. He tried to see the Governor of the colony, the notional commander-in-chief, but got no farther than the hall of Government House, where he was politely but firmly turned away and told to go and see the Land Officer. The Land Officer informed him that it was not a civil but a military matter and that he ought to take up any complaints with the officer commanding the K.A.R.

"And where is he?" Walter asked.

"Somewhere in Uganda."

As for the question of reparations, that would have to wait until the war was over, but in the meantime he could file a claim with the Registrar of Documents, Mr. Pailthorpe. Mr. Pailthorpe, in his turn, said he had received absolutely no official instructions about reparations ("For God's sake, man, the war's only been on for a fortnight!") and suggested he consult the Attorney General. Until Mr. Pailthorpe had received official notification from the Attorney General's office, nothing further could be done.

Walter decided to let the question of reparations rest for a while. All the government offices he had visited were housed in a terrace of corrugated iron shacks. Over the past three days Walter had been passed from one to another and he had no desire to wait out the duration of the war in a succession of sweltering ante-rooms. In the meantime he planned to visit his insurers and see if he could extract some interim payment for his burnt sisal, his smouldering linseed fields and uprooted trolley lines.

His insurers, the African Guarantee and Indemnity Co., occupied a small office above a butcher's shop on Sixth Avenue. Walter pushed past several sheep and antelope carcases and entered the dark interior. The close heat, the subdued murmur of sated flies and the rich, gamy smell of offal made his stomach heave and saliva squirt into his mouth. He was breathing heavily—inhaling the musty but fresher air on the first floor—when an Indian clerk ushered him into the office of Gulam Hoosam Essanjee Esquire, general manager of the African Guarantee and Indemnity Co.

Mr. Essanjee stood at a single window looking down at the traffic on Sixth Avenue. He was a dapper plump Indian of about Walter's age with black, well-oiled hair and the straightest, most clearly defined parting Walter had ever seen. He wore a washable rubber collar with his tie and coarse linen suit and was perspiring heavily. He had a very thin, neatly clipped pencil moustache. The room was oppressively hot and unusually dark. So dark that Mr. Essanjee had a lit hurricane lamp fizzing quietly on his totally bare desk. The darkness was explained by the fact that the other window in the room was obscured by a thick handwoven blanket, which was soaking wet and dripping steadily onto a mushy copy of the *East African Standard* placed beneath it.

Walter sat down heavily, still nauseated from negotiating the charnel-house below. "Can't we open the curtains?" he asked weakly. The stifling atmosphere was worse than the government offices.

"Not a curtain, my dear sir, Mr. . . ?"

"Smith."

"Mr. Smith. Not, I repeat, a curtain." Mr. Essanjee strode forward and lifted the bottom of the blanket to reveal what looked to

Walter like a miniature copy of the paddle wheel of a Mississippi river boat, placed on the ledge of the open window.

Mr. Essanjee let the blanket drop.

"A thermantidote. Very popular in my own country. The wind blows the rotating fan, which in turn casts a stronger breeze onto the tattie—which you will have observed has been soaked in cold water—*ergo,* a cool moist breeze penetrates the intolerably dry and hot room. Most efficient." Mr. Essanjee wiped his damp hands on his linen jacket. "The Essanjee Thermantidote. This is my own im-provised version. Patent pending." He smiled broadly at Walter. "The S. and G. Thermantidote." He sketched an "S" and a "G" in the air with his finger. "You follow? I am Gulam Hoosam Essanjee. My machine is the S and G—"

"Yes, yes," Walter said, feeling faint. "I see."

"My brother controls the agency in Mombasa. If you're inter-ested?"

"But what happens if there's no breeze to rotate the fan? Like today."

"Ah, yes. I regret an exterior breeze is essential. But the drip of the water from the tattie has, I find, a cooling effect of its own. No?" He sat down at his empty desk. "Now, my dear Mr. Smith, what can I do for you?"

Walter explained about the loss of his farm, while Mr. Essanjee sat nodding his oiled head. He presented Von Bishop's affidavit and said he was claiming for the loss of various goods. Mr. Essanjee went to a wooden filing cabinet and extracted a copy of Walter's policy. He hummed and hawed, tapping his fingernails on the desk.

"Yes," Mr. Essanjee said. "There seems to be no problem. We shall regard it as theft."

Walter couldn't believe what he was hearing. "Oh. Well, that's excellent."

"'We aim to please.' Is this not what they say in your country? I see here it says you are a citizen of the U.S.A."

"Indeed it is, and indeed I am." Walter felt full of irrational affection for this plump little man.

"Reimbursement shall be effected as soon as we receive our assessor's report."

"Oh," Walter said. "An assessor's report." He stroked his moustache.

"Of course," said Mr. Essanjee, touching his own with the little fingers of each hand. "Simply procedure. It's not a question of doubting you, Mr. Smith. But you can hardly expect us to take the word"—he held up Von Bishop's affidavit—"of our sworn enemy."

"You're right, I suppose," Walter said. "But my farm is now occupied by this same enemy. It is, as you might say, behind enemy lines."

"Alas." Mr. Essanjee spread his damp palms. "This war; it causes endless inconveniences."

Walter had a mad idea. "At least I *think* it's behind enemy lines. Von Bishop might just have taken what he wanted and left. Supposing the enemy have withdrawn. Would your assessor be prepared to come with me? Who is your assessor, by the way?"

Mr. Essanjee bowed his head. "It is I. We are very short-staffed at the moment. The international situation, you understand."

"Would you come?" Walter asked.

"Naturally," Mr. Essanjee said suavely. "At the African Guarantee and Indemnity Co., we aim to please."

CHAPTER THREE

30 AUGUST 1914

Voi · British East Africa

"Don't you think you're going a bit far?" Wheech-Browning said two days later. He was sitting in a dilapidated cane chair outside his tent in Voi. The slightest move he made set up a filthy screeching noise.

"I mean, good God, there is meant to be a war on, you know. You can't just swan up to Heinrich Hun and say, 'Look here, old chap, any chance of a cease-fire while we carry out an insurance assessment?'"

"Normally," Walter said patiently, "I'd agree." He paused while Wheech-Browning noisily shifted his weight. "But I *know* Von Bishop. He was practically a next-door neighbour. He's British too."

"*Was* British," Wheech-Browning corrected fiercely. "Damned bloody traitor."

"He's a farmer. He'd understand, I'm sure. If, that is, he's there.

For all I know the place may be deserted. After all, Mr. Essanjee and I aren't soldiers. We won't be there long. Mr. Essanjee says its only a formality."

"Precisely," Mr. Essanjee confirmed. "A mere formality." He was standing behind Walter, dressed in an immaculate white drill suit with matching solar topee.

"Well, I don't know," Wheech-Browning said, standing up. "I mean, we are meant to be at daggers drawn. . . . Mind you, there hasn't been a shot fired in this area since my old bearer got it in the neck." He paused, cocked his head to one side and smiled. "Got it in the neck. Not bad." He paced up and down. "Tell you what," he said. "We've got these volunteer chaps with motor bikes: East African Mechanical Transport Corps. I take one out and drive up the road to Taveta once in a while. Bit of scouting." Wheech-Browning had been seconded to a battalion of the K.A.R. as an intelligence officer. "If all three of us tootled off up the road, I could drop you off a few miles away. You might even do a bit of spying while you're about it."

"Sure we will," Walter said.

"Capital," echoed Mr. Essanjee. "Capital."

"Right," Wheech-Browning said. "First thing tomorrow morning."

The motor bike was a Clyno 6 h.p. with a side-car. Wheech-Browning drove, Walter rode pillion, while Mr. Essanjee sat in the side-car with Wheech-Browning's rifle. All three of them wore goggles. Dawn was breaking and the air was quite cool. Mr. Essanjee had tied a silk muffler round his throat. His white suit seemed to glow eerily in the bluey light. They stopped at the K.A.R. lines at Bura where Wheech-Browning informed a sleeping picket where they were going. Then they motored off along the caravan trail, bumping along at fifteen miles an hour across the flat scrubby desert that separated them from Taveta. Soon the rising sun picked out the snowy top of Mount Kilimanjaro, towering out of the shadowy foothills up ahead. They drove on across the plain beneath a placid gulf of sky, the tinny sputtering of the engine breaking the silence, towards the beautiful mountain, watching the sun creep down its side.

"Splendid view," Wheech-Browning shouted.

They had to stop after half an hour to allow Mr. Essanjee to be sick. He said he found the motion of the side-car most unpleasant. Wheech-Browning and Walter waited patiently, warmed now by the sun rising in the sky, while Mr. Essanjee retched and spat fastidiously a few yards off the road, leaning over at an angle to avoid besmirching his spotless suit. He and Walter changed places, which seemed to solve the problem. Walter's weight in the side-car, Wheech-Browning observed, cut their speed down considerably.

They stopped after a couple of hours while Wheech-Browning consulted the map and tried to plot their position. Walter peered over his shoulder. The caravan track was a dotted black line across a perfectly white, unmarked piece of paper. Wheech-Browning pretended to scrutinise the surrounding countryside for landmarks.

"Not the most efficient map in the world," he said with a nervous laugh. Walter, who reminded them that he'd been travelling the Voi–Taveta road for the last four years, said that he thought they were about five miles from the Lumi River bridge. Salaita Hill, a smooth mound that rose a couple of hundred feet out of the flat scrub, was a mile or so ahead. Before they reached the hill they should come across a rough path that led to Smithville and Lake Jipe.

"Good," Wheech-Browning said, taking a swig from his water bottle. "Let's make a move." He offered the bottle to Mr. Essanjee, who politely declined. "You see," Wheech-Browning said, "it's like I told you: not a squarehead in sight. Probably find your farm's deserted."

"If they've touched my Decorticator . . ." Walter said, his eyes narrowing vengefully.

"Never fear, Mr. Smith," Mr. Essanjee said. "You are covered by the African Guarantee and Indemnity Co. Have no fear."

They came to the track that led to Smithville. Ahead was Salaita, and beyond that they could just make out the darker line of trees that marked the Lumi River. Swinging his gaze to the left, Walter could see the rise of small hills amongst which Smithville nestled.

"Huns in those trees, I'll be bound," Wheech-Browning said. "I don't think I'll come any closer if you don't mind. How far is it to your place from here?"

"About four miles. It'll take us an hour to get there, a quick look over, then an hour back. Shouldn't be too long a wait."

"Absolutely no trouble. See that outcrop there? I'll stroll over with my binoculars." He pointed to an untidy tumbled clump of boulders some six hundred yards off. "See what the old Germani are getting up to."

Walter and Mr. Essanjee looked in the direction he indicated. Walter saw the rocks, warm in the morning sun.

Then suddenly they seemed to explode in puffs of thick black smoke. A second later came the loud report of rifles. The thorn bushes around them seemed to be plucked and shaken by invisible hands.

"Bloody hell!" exclaimed Wheech-Browning. "Damn Germans! Not even a warning."

"Oh, my bloody God," Mr. Essanjee said and sat down with a thump. He looked in horror at his thigh. The starched white drill was being engulfed by a brilliant red stain.

"Oh, shit!" Walter said.

"Ouf," Mr. Essanjee sighed, and fell back to the ground. Walter and Wheech-Browning ran over and knelt by his side. Another stain had appeared in the middle of his chest.

"Good God!" said Wheech-Browning, holding his hand up to his mouth. The rattle of firing ceased.

"Let's get out of here," Walter said. They leapt onto the motor bike. Wheech-Browning attempted a kick-start, but banged his ankle on the foot rest.

"Christ!" he wept, tears in his eyes. "That's agony!" Wincing, he kick-started again and the engine caught. Walter glanced back over his shoulder. He saw small figures scrambling down the rock pile and running up the tracks towards them.

"Hold on!" Walter shouted. "We'd better get Essanjee."

"Fine. But look sharpish!"

They dragged Mr. Essanjee over to the side-car and toppled him in head first, leaving his legs hanging over the side. Then Walter and Wheech-Browning jumped on the bike and, with rear wheel spinning furiously, they roared off back down the track to Voi.

Some miles farther on, when they felt they were safe, they stopped. They confirmed that Mr. Essanjee was indeed dead. His suit and jacket were soaking with blood, rendered all the more coruscating by the contrast it made to the patches of gleaming white. They rearranged his body in a more dignified position, so that it looked as if he were dozing in the side-car, his head thrown back.

"Damn good shots, those fellows," Wheech-Browning observed as he wedged his rifle between Mr. Essanjee's plump knees. "He was a plucky little chap for an insurance salesman. What did you say the name of his company was?"

"African Guarantee and Indemnity Co."

"Must bear that in mind."

Walter wondered who would process his claim now. How long would it take to find a replacement for Mr. Essanjee? And would he be as amenable? He heard Wheech-Browning say something.

"What was that?" he asked.

"I was saying that, if you ask me, the only way you're going to get back to that farm of yours is to join the army and fight your way there."

Walter tugged at his moustache. "You know," he said resignedly, "I think you may be right."

CHAPTER FOUR

SS *Homayun* · *Indian Ocean*

Gabriel Cobb stood in a patch of shade on the aft officers' deck of the SS *Homayun*. The sun beat down out of a sky so bleached it seemed white, scalding the gently swelling surface of the ocean. The smoke from the *Homayun*'s twin stacks hung in the air, trailing behind the ship, a tattered black epitaph marking its ponderous eight-knot passage from India to Africa.

Gabriel had been standing in the same position for nearly an hour, mesmerised by the wake streaming out behind. He was sunk in a profound lethargy, a sense of depressed boredom that seemed to penetrate every corner of the ship, if not the entire fourteen-vessel convoy of Indian Expeditionary Force "B"—Force "C" had arrived a month earlier—eight thousand men, steaming off, as far as he knew, to invade German East Africa.

He leant back against a bulkhead and exhaled, feeling his shirt press damply against his back. He was lucky to find this corner of the deck unoccupied. Every bit of shade had been claimed by sprawling supine soldiers, desperate to escape from the balmy clamminess of their tiny cabins. God only knew, Gabriel thought, what it must be like for the other ranks, the Indian soldiers and regimental followers quartered below decks, sleeping in hammocks slung only a foot apart. He took off his pith helmet and used it to fan his face. God only knew what it was like for the stokers shovelling coal into the furnaces in the belly of the ship. He tried to cheer himself up. At least he was better off than the stokers and the miserable, ill-disciplined men he was supposed to lead into battle.

Gabriel sat down on the deck and stretched his legs out in front of him. It was small consolation. He'd never known life deal him such a succession of cruel disappointments. His ambitions had been modest. He wished only to fight in France with his regiment, but even that was to be denied him. He paused. The effort of swishing his hat to and fro was enervating in this heat. He allowed his head to roll to one side. Everywhere he looked he saw ships. Tramp steamers, reconditioned liners, troopships. He saw the battleship HMS *Goliath,* its four stacks belching smoke as for some reason it got up steam. It raised only a flicker of interest. The German commerce raider *Emden* was known to be loose in the Indian Ocean. So too was the cruiser *Königsberg,* recently on display to the inhabitants of Dar-es-Salaam, now believed to be roaming the coastal waters in search of prey. He didn't really care; anything would be preferable to the numbing monotony he'd been experiencing for the last four weeks. He saw the battleship slowly wheel round and head back in the direction of India. Just another straggler, Gabriel thought, falling behind.

It was now the middle of October. The war had been going on for nearly three months. For at least two of them, Gabriel calculated with some sarcasm, he'd been on board ship. Anyone would have thought he'd joined the navy.

Gabriel and Charis had returned from their shortened honeymoon on the thirtieth of July. Gabriel had gone at once to London in search of instructions but had been told to go away, as there was nothing anyone could tell him. They then spent an uncomfortable few days at Stackpole—no one was expecting their return; the cottage was not ready; Cyril was still distempering the bedroom walls—watching the slide into war. He and Charis had been unhappy. Charis had been cool and distant. Every day she pointedly reminded him that they could be walking along the promenade at Trouville. Every day, that is, until the fourth of August, when war was declared, thereby vindicating what had seemed like precipitate caution on Gabriel's part. On the night of the fourth they had also been able to move into the cottage, and as if by magic, some of the happiness and intimacy they had experienced in Trouville returned. But it was clouded by the knowledge that Gabriel would soon have to go away. Diligently he telephoned to London every day, keen to get his orders. On the sixth he was instructed to report to Southampton, where he would find a berth on the SS *Dongola*, a P&O liner, which would take him to rejoin his regiment in India.

The *Dongola* left Southampton on the thirteenth, crammed with officers re-joining regiments in Egypt and India. Sammy Hinshelwood and a few others from the West Kents who had been on leave were also on board, and the first days of the voyage out were passed in frenzied speculation about the possible length of the war and what role the West Kents would play in it, assuming it lasted long enough. As they sailed slowly across the Mediterranean, the now familiar boredom began to infect them all. Interminable games of contract bridge were the main diversion, sessions starting at breakfast and lasting long into the night.

From time to time the odd wireless message brought snippets of news of the progress of the war in Europe: the German advance through Belgium, the fall of Liège, the disastrous French attack in Lorraine, the battle of Mons. The sense of frustration at missing out was acute. But there were no mails at Gibraltar (they were not even allowed off the ship) and none waiting at Port Said either. As they neared Port Said the weather became noticeably hotter. Awnings were stretched over all available deck space and most of the officers forsook their cramped cabins to sleep on deck during the night. Gabriel, fortunately, had a cork mattress that he could lie on and so passed the night in some comfort. The others had to make do with blankets, or at best a deck-chair. One break in the routine occurred when they were all inoculated against smallpox and yellow fever. Gabriel was incapacitated for two days with a high temperature.

It took the *Dongola* a week to chug through the Red Sea. The thermometer rose to 114 degrees (140 degrees in the stokehold) and everyone went about stark naked at night in an attempt to keep cool. "Just as well there are no ladies on board," Gabriel said to Sammy Hinshelwood one evening as they picked their way through naked bodies towards their mattresses.

"On the contrary," Hinshelwood laughed, "it's a great shame."

That night as they lay side by side Hinshelwood talked for a long time about sex. About a girl he knew, a tart he'd picked up at the Adelphi Theatre. Gabriel lay beside him, uneasy and embarrassed. Hinshelwood made some coarse jokes about his interrupted honeymoon, and described Charis as "a truly charming girl." Gabriel made no response, but the muted talk of women made him excited and he had to roll onto his stomach to conceal his arousal.

One of the stewards died of heat-stroke in the Red Sea. Gabriel attended the small religious service and watched as the weighted body was tipped into the water with a forlorn splash. The death depressed him unusually. Gabriel found his thoughts continually on the armies in Europe and the war ahead. One night somebody said that a quarter of the troops would surely be killed. That gave each individual a one in four chance, Gabriel thought. Even when it was figured as personally as that, Gabriel discovered, to his vague surprise, that the idea of war seemed even more exciting.

After the Red Sea the Indian Ocean was cooler. However, the *Dongola* caught the tail-end of the monsoon season and rolled and pitched the rest of the way to Bombay. Everyone on board suffered terribly from seasickness. Often there were two hundred or more men leaning over the leeward side of the ship being sick into the sea. The sides of the *Dongola* became streaked and spattered with dried vomit, and the faint acid smell of sick hung in every corridor and companionway.

They arrived in Bombay after a twenty-six-day voyage. Gabriel and Hinshelwood were given instructions to proceed directly to the regiment at Rawalpindi. "I'm damned if I'm getting straight on a train after a month in that accursed ship!" Hinshelwood swore. He and Gabriel booked into the Taj Hotel for a night. They bathed, had two enormous meals and went shopping. The next morning they boarded the train at Bombay Station and spent a dusty, but tolerably comfortable, fifty hours crossing the Punjab to Rawalpindi.

For two weeks life regained its sense of composure. News of the German retreat to the Aisne caused great belligerent excitement. Gabriel returned to a means of existence that he had known before his marriage. Except on this occasion there was no Charis nearby. Nor was there much time for entertainment of any sort, as the Regiment was busily preparing itself for embarkation. The main Indian expeditionary force for the European theatre was in the process of being despatched, and in addition two subsidiary forces were being raised. One was for the Persian Gulf and one for the invasion of German East Africa. Rumour had it that the West Kents would be embarking for Europe in early October, but no one was sure. Gabriel thought it was typical of the army's Byzantine reasoning to send him all the way to India just to send him back to Europe. It was, he later realised, equally typical of the army to decide that, of all the officers in the regiment, he was the one chosen not to accompany it. The fateful Movement Order telegram arrived from headquarters in Simla. It informed him that he was being "attached" to the 69th Palamcottah Light Infantry, who were due to embark for East Africa in mid-October as part of Indian Expeditionary Force "B."

East Africa! The Palamcottah Light Infantry! Gabriel's disappointment was bitter and acute. A third-rate Indian regiment from the little-regarded Bangalore Brigade in Madras. His prompt protestations and appeals had no effect. His colleagues sympathised but their patience over his relentless moaning and complaints was limited. Sammy Hinshelwood reminded him that the West Kents could end up guarding the Suez Canal and that at least Gabriel could be sure of some action before the war ended.

So for the second time in a month Gabriel recrossed the Punjab, but on this occasion, as if cruelly to remind him how his plans had gone awry, the journey took ninety hours. He shared the train with a hospital unit full of Indian sub-assistant surgeons and with dozens of coolies and bearers. They, it transpired, were also going to East Africa, but the British doctors seemed quite content with their lot. A place called Nairobi, they said; apparently the climate was superb. Gabriel spent most of the journey in a corner of the crowded compartment (the fan wasn't working) trying to read a book. The doctors repeatedly congratulated themselves on their good luck. All they seemed to care about, Gabriel reflected, was the weather. One day they spent a full ten hours motionless in a railway siding with nothing to eat or drink except some *petit beurre* biscuits and warm soda-water.

Gabriel's spirits had been set in a decline ever since he'd received the news of his transfer. At the barracks in Bombay they took another plunge when he was united with his new battalion. The 69th Palamcottah Light Infantry hadn't seen active service since the Boxer rebellion in 1900, and the battle order for that campaign hung proudly in the mess. A little enquiry on Gabriel's part provided him with the information that the Palamcottahs had in fact got only as far as Hong Kong. There they had been pressed into service with a regiment of Army Pioneers and had made roads for nine months, an activity for which they had shown a surprising efficiency and which had earned them an official commendation from the Governor of the colony.

It was small consolation also when it turned out that the Palamcottahs were so undermanned and ill-prepared that six other officers, apart from Gabriel, had been separated from their official regiments to bring the battalion up to something like operational strength. The seven new boys swiftly formed a circle of malcontents in the mess, ignoring and being ignored by the regulars. Gabriel was the last to arrive and was happy to contribute his own grumbles to the dark mutterings that continually preoccupied the disaffected group.

There proved to be virtually no chance to get to know the men under his command because the day after his arrival embarkation orders were received. The *Homayun,* the ship that was to transport the Palamcottahs to East Africa, made the *Dongola* look like a luxury liner. The *Homayun* was a dirty little steamer which before being drafted into war service had plied the route between Bombay and

Arabia, conveying pilgrims to Mecca and back again. About a thousand men were finally crammed aboard: the Palamcottahs, a detachment of sappers, the Punjabi Coolie Corps and about thirty mules and four dozen sheep, which had to be tethered on one of the decks.

Gabriel found himself sharing a small cabin with two other officers, a doctor from the Indian Medical Service, and a tall thin major from the Welsh Guards called Bilderbeck, who had been at the staff college at Simla but was now attached to the expeditionary force's headquarters staff as intelligence officer because he'd served in East Africa before the war.

Embarkation was completed by the thirtieth of September. The last mules were winched on board; the last lighter had deposited its load of excited coolies and had returned to the wharves. The *Homayun* got up steam and moved slowly out of Bombay harbour until she was some three miles offshore. Then, with a rattle of chains, the anchors were released and she stopped once more. Gabriel assumed, as he looked over the railing at the distant shore, that they were waiting for the rest of the fleet to form up.

The days went by with an inconceivable slowness. Two, three, four, five. The *Homayun* rolled heavily at anchor in the ocean swell, and to a man, it seemed, the coolie corps went down with seasickness. A widening slick of human effluence polluted the sea around the immobile ship. Gabriel inspected his company twice a day, just to give himself something to do. They were thin-faced, resentful men in baggy uniforms and thick khaki turbans. The Indian officers—the jemadars and subadars—seemed too old and slack, and treated Gabriel with caution and suspicion. On the seventh day new Maxim guns were ferried out and each company supplied with two. Seizing the opportunity, Gabriel held machine-gun drill every afternoon, teaching the lethargic sepoys how to strip down, load and fire the bright, shiny weapons. They fired at empty barrels thrown over the side, kicking up the scummy surface of the sea with a flurry of bullets.

Ten days went by and still the *Homayun* swung listlessly at anchor. Gabriel fell into a state of thoughtless passivity of which he would never have believed himself capable. After breakfast he would make a cursory inspection of his troops, send the sick men to the surgery and then retire to the shadiest part of the ship and try to write letters. His life was so empty that once he'd got beyond "Dear Mother and Father, here we are still on the *Homayun* . . ." there seemed little point in going on. He tried several times to write to Charis on more personal matters, but to his consternation he found that even harder. He did think about her a lot, and the emotions he experienced were genuine, but when it came to giving them some shape, pinning them down in a few heartfelt words, he found it impossible to identify and name correctly what were in actuality only the vaguest and most nebulous sensations.

"My Darling Charis," he would write. Then he would pause. What could he say? That he loved her? But surely she knew that. It wouldn't do to state things so bluntly; he needed a more elegant turn of phrase. . . . And he would drift off into a doze until it was time for luncheon. In the afternoon came yet more sleep, or else vacant staring at the shoreline. Sometimes he would plunge into the sail-bath that had been rigged up and for ten minutes feel more alive. In the evening he'd mix uneasily with the other officers, but nobody really knew each other and the talk was desultory and formal. No orders had been issued and Lieutenant-Colonel Coutts, the portly, ageing commanding officer, had nothing to report at the few briefing sessions called. As on the *Dongola* most officers ended up passing the time by playing cards or deck quoits. Gabriel played a few hands of whist, but he didn't know how to play contract bridge and couldn't be bothered to learn.

Eventually, sixteen days after they had embarked, the *Homayun* finally weighed anchor and took its place in the convoy that sailed out of Bombay harbour. No explanation for their wait offshore was ever forthcoming; it was assumed that someone had forgotten about them. As India gradually disappeared from view, Gabriel was possessed briefly of a thrilling and venomous anger at the nameless staff officer whose order had condemned them to the two-week purgatory they had lived through. Sixteen days, roasting motionless offshore. Sixteen entire endless days of petty irritations, extreme discomfort and near-fatal boredom. Gabriel felt his face go taut with frustration and his eyelids twitch with angry tears. He felt sure that he could have killed the man responsible without a qualm, slowly, intricately and with excruciating pain. . . . Calm down, he told himself, calm down; at least they were on the move.

Just before they left, a launch delivered mail from Europe. There were three letters: from his mother, Felix and Charis. The news was six weeks old. He opened his mother's first.

My dear Gabriel,

The news from France is most depressing. Your father says we have lost a battle at a place called Mons. He has pinned a large map on the library wall where the entire household is invited each day to hear the latest news of the fighting.

Charis is well, despite a slight cold. She was so sad after you had gone, but has buckled down with a will helping us organise collections of provisions for the poor Belgians. She has decided to stay on in the cottage even though there is so much room in the house. However she comes to us for most luncheons and dinners.

Felix received a letter from the War Office telling him to go to the OTC recruiting office at Oxford. But it now seems they can't take him because of his eyes. I always knew that boy read too much. Your father refuses to speak to him so he has gone up to London to stay with his friend Holland. I think it's for the best, for the meanwhile, anyway.

Henry is up to his ears in work at the Committee for Imperial Defence. He told Albertine not to worry; he will see Greville gets a staff posting (Greville is not to know about this, it seems). Nigel Bathe, however, is going to a place called Mesopotamia. Henry says there is nothing he can do. Poor Nigel is most disappointed: he so wanted to go to France. . . .

His mother's letter continued in this vein for several more pages. Felix's was briefer.

. . . you will have heard I am not to be called to the colours. Such a disgrace. Father practically accused me of arrant cowardice. It was pointless to remind him that there are so many volunteers that anyone not 100% fit is turned away. Cyril, of course, was snapped up. I've never seen anyone look so pleased. . . .

Your dear wife has wisely decided to remain in the cottage. She seems well, running about the country with Dr. Venables collecting blankets for the Belgians. Life at home is more intolerable than ever, what with Father's nightly (compulsory) briefing on the course of the war.

I am going to stay with Holland, also rejected by the army. We will be going up to Oxford together in October, though goodness knows what the place will be like with everyone off at the war. Nigel Bathe has been sent to guard some desert wastes. He thinks the war is some vile and complicated plot to thwart and discomfit him. . . .

Gabriel saved Charis's letter until last. He sat and looked at her handwriting on the envelope trying to conjure up an image of her face in his mind. They had had three nights in the cottage before he had left for Southampton. Three nights in which they had managed to repeat the solitary success they had enjoyed in Trouville. Gabriel leant back on his bunk and shut his eyes. He could feel his heart beating faster at the uncomfortable, somehow embarrassing memories. He opened the letter.

My Darling Gabey,

How I miss you! Our little cottage seems so quiet and empty. I want my big strong boy back beside me, and to take me in his arms. You will be careful, won't you, darling? I want my Gabey back in one piece so don't go trying to be a hero. . . .

Gabriel found it impossible to read on; he could hear Charis's voice echoing through each word. He put the letter down and thought back to their last nights together and the pattern of arousal that each one seemed instinctively to follow.

Each time as he had changed into his pyjamas he felt almost sick with mounting apprehension. He would go through the door into the tiny upstairs bedroom which was almost entirely filled by their soft double bed. And there Charis lay. Her long wavy dark hair down, her white night-dress crisp and fresh. Then she would scold him, gently, for some misdemeanour. One night it was for not brushing his hair, another night for a mismatched pyjama top and bottom. "You naughty boy!" Charis would say and sternly resist his imploring pleas for forgiveness and understanding. "No! You may *not* give me a kiss and I'm *very* cross with you." The tone of voice, the situation, worked like a magic charm on him, Gabriel realised. All the fumbling apprehension, the shaming absence of arousal—the fear, even, of slipping into bed—disappeared.

They played out their parts with the instinct and assurance of professional actors. Charis strict but ultimately forgiving, Gabriel alternately fawning and sulky. The teasing, coyly bullying Charis of those nights had his erection pressing against his pyjama trousers within seconds. He would lay his head on her small breasts, kissing her throat, plucking at the cords that held her bodice together. "Stop it!" she would cry with fake horror. "You dreadful, dreadful boy! What are you doing?" But somehow the cords always came undone and he would uncover her small white breasts, smearing his face over them, dabbing at the tight nipples, hunching himself into position between her parting thighs. Then clumsy thrusting, a feeling of heat, moistness, a glove-like grip.

Such transient sensations, Gabriel thought. No more than a few seconds, that was all. Then she would cradle his head in her arms, stroking his hair, cooing endearments, calling him their private names, "Gabey, my big boy . . . Gabbins, my naughty boy . . . my terrible lovely Gabey," and Gabriel would drift off to sleep.

On their last night Gabriel woke up and found her gone. Half awake, he stumbled out of bed and along the little passage to the bathroom. He pushed open the door and she was standing there naked, a face-flannel in her hand, in front of the basin. "Oh, sorry," Gabriel said, and backed out of the room. That was the only time he'd ever seen her naked. Her slim pale body like a boy's, her breasts very small, almost flat, her little dark bush. Her body, he had to be frank, was not what he had expected. Before that night on the honeymoon, he had imagined women to be very soft and yielding, with large soft breasts like pillows. She didn't come back to bed for a while and he fell asleep. They didn't refer to their midnight encounter again.

All these memories returned as Gabriel read her letter. But to hear these endearments and phrases, to have the roles conjured up for him when she wasn't there, made him feel confused. He felt a heavier sweat break out on his upper lip. He felt his face grow hot. He realised he was experiencing shame. He was embarrassed. Ashamed and embarrassed at his own intimacy with his wife! He felt suddenly appalled at himself. And this realisation brought guilt and self-contempt in its train. What kind of a person was he? he asked himself. What kind of a person was he to feel so ill-at-ease, so uncomfortable with the truth?

Gabriel never reread her letter. Now, some ten days into the voyage, it still lay deep in his small case in his cabin. He didn't want to think about it, or about their married life. He found he was becoming almost prudish as a kind of reaction. Some of the other officers on the *Homayun* were dubious types, coarse and much given to risqué conversations. Gabriel never joined in their discussions.

One day someone had passed him an old copy of *Nash's* magazine, folded open to a page covered with photographs of a French dancer—one Mademoiselle Sadrine Storri. She was very pretty, Gabriel saw, in a plump, coquettish way. Her dark hair was tousled. She wore her dancing costume, a scant toga strewn with garlands. She had heavy thighs, and in one photo leant forward to expose the swells of a nicely rounded bosom. Because she danced with bare legs, the caption said, the censor had determined that on-stage she should be lit only by a blue light.

"Nice little filly," the man had said on passing the magazine over. Gabriel had given a taut smile and glanced at the photographs for form's sake.

"My Grecian dance is absolutely artistic," Gabriel read. He turned the page. There were more photographs of her posing in velvet shorts and a skimpy top that showed her midriff.

"I say, look at Cobb," the officer called. "We've certainly got the newly-wed interested."

Gabriel had blushed deeply. He had been interested. But almost simultaneously he hated himself for being so. What kind of husband was he, poring over photos of a French tart?

He looked out now at the convoy. He had been on the ship for twenty-six days, and it was beginning to affect him. The crushing,

annihilating boredom. The constant noise from the bickering coolies. The braying mules and the bleating sheep. His fifth-rate resentful men. His uncouth, unfamiliar fellow officers. Thank God, he
thought, for the two men he shared his cabin with. He never really
saw the doctor, who was the busiest man on board, constantly
tending the coolies and other ranks who were coming down with all
manner of ailments—but mainly dysentery and malaria—at the
rate of seventy a day. But at least Bilderbeck was a decent sort, if a
little strange.

Bilderbeck spent a lot of time drawing up information sheets
and maps of German East Africa, compiling official intelligence
notes on the climate, population and terrain based on journals and
records he'd kept while serving in British East some seven or eight
years previously. He was a lean, ascetic-looking man in his mid-
thirties with a slightly weak chin. He spoke very quickly with a low
voice, delivering his words in short bursts, as if from a Maxim gun.
He would sometimes laugh or smile at stages in conversation which
didn't seem to warrant any such response at all, as if he saw jokes
and ironies invisible to others all the time. Talking to him was
extremely disconcerting, as his wry smiles and cynical looks seemed
to imply that these observations were shared. Rather than seek for
an explanation, Gabriel had decided that the best thing to do was
simply to copy Bilderbeck's expression as it changed: smile when he
smiled, roll eyes and sneer when he sneered. The other officers
were not so accommodating and clearly thought Bilderbeck a little
mad. Consequently, as time moved on, he and Gabriel spent more
time in each other's company.

They talked about the war. Bilderbeck asked Gabriel if he'd
ever been in action. Gabriel admitted he hadn't. Bilderbeck said
he'd personally killed upward of thirty people during his service in
Africa. "But they were all natives," he added, as if this somehow
wasn't so remarkable.

Gabriel looked curiously at him. "What . . . ? I mean, what was
it like?"

"Just shot 'em," Bilderbeck said. "I shot three of my own men
once. Native soldiers. A fine lot of men, in fact, but these ones had

killed a woman and outraged a girl. I shot them there and then. I had to set an example, you see. To the others." He smiled broadly. Gabriel smiled automatically in return.

"Actually I did kill a Russian once," Bilderbeck mused. "In Constantinople." Bilderbeck paused. "What do you think of this lot?" Bilderbeck jerked his thumb in the direction of the officers' quarters.

"I haven't really got to know them," Gabriel said.

"Sportsmen," Bilderbeck sneered. "If they're not senile, all they think about is ponies and women." He darted a look at Gabriel, smiling weirdly again.

"I shall find my girl," he said suddenly. "I know I will."

"Your girl?" Gabriel repeated, mystified at this turn the conversation had taken.

"One day I shall find her."

Gabriel wondered what he was talking about. "Yes," he said safely. "I expect you shall."

"You're married, aren't you?" Bilderbeck said. "Love your wife?"

"What . . . ? Yes, I do, yes."

"My God," Bilderbeck said, shaking his head in wonder. "Is she your girl, then?"

Gabriel thought it best to agree. "Yes," he said simply.

"Hah!" Bilderbeck gave a cynical laugh. "Sportsmen! Treat the army like a social club."

Indian Expeditionary Force "B" sailed on steadily towards Africa. Sheer desperation eventually forced the troops on the *Homayun* to search for some form of distraction. When they crossed the equator they had a crossing-of-the-line ceremony. The captain of the ship was Neptune. All the officers under thirty were initiated. Gabriel was copiously lathered, shaved with a three-foot-long wooden razor and was then thrown into the sail-bath.

This effort seemed to stimulate the others, and one night shortly after, they had a concert—a piano and two mouth organs. A downpour drenched them half-way through but the men played on and the audience remained heedless of the rain.

As they sailed south, the weather grew hotter and hotter. The doctor spent his days moving among the crew with pitchers of lime cordial. Every three days they had to drink a glass of quinine dissolved in water.

Lieutenant-Colonel Coutts fell down a flight of steps, was concussed and broke one of his ribs. The news drew a loud snort of disgust from Bilderbeck. Gabriel felt quite sorry for Coutts, who was a kindly and lazy old chap in his late fifties. Gamely enough, he was up and about after a couple of days but was clearly in some pain and discomfort. However they were nearing their destination and a slight air of tension was beginning to percolate through the ship, so expressions of sympathy were few and far between. Bilderbeck made a trip over to the *Karmala,* a P&O liner, to pass on his maps, notes and opinions to General Aitken, the commander-in-chief.

The final distraction of the voyage was less happy. One of the sailors on the *Homayun* had, it appeared, been found guilty of plotting mutiny. For this crime he was sentenced to six months' imprisonment and twelve lashes from the cat-o'-nine-tails. All the officers on the *Homayun* were invited along as witnesses. Gabriel went with some misgivings and stood uneasily beside Bilderbeck. The whipping was to be administered by the boatswain of the *Goliath,* a large man with a bulging ruddy face. In his hands the cat-o'-nine-tails looked very small and curiously inoffensive. The culprit was brought out, bare-chested, and tied to a wooden triangle, hastily constructed by the ship's carpenters, his hands at the peak and his feet spread to the other two points. The sentence was read out and the boatswain whipped the man very quickly. The prisoner's back turned bright pink before their eyes and the skin broke by the seventh or eighth lash. At the end the boatswain was panting heavily from his exertions. Gabriel felt more shocked than sickened.

"This is 1914, not the Crimea," he protested to Bilderbeck as they walked back to the officers' quarters. "It's barbaric."

"No," Bilderbeck said firmly. "Mutiny in time of war." He flashed a quick smile. "I'd have had him shot."

On the thirtieth of October the convoy halted about a hundred miles off Mombasa. Gabriel felt a pressure steadily build up in his lungs, a sense of nervous anticipation that he couldn't shake off and that left him feeling permanently slightly breathless. He paced about the decks all day experimenting with impromptu breathing exercises: holding his breath, breathing shallowly, inhaling deeply and letting the air out of his lungs as slowly as possible. But none of this worked.

He saw another battleship steam out from the direction of land. Shortly after, Bilderbeck was summoned over to it and a boat was lowered for him. That evening the battleship—the *Fox*—steamed away with the *Karmala*.

The convoy sat off Mombasa for another two days. Gabriel inspected his men. They were weary and disgruntled, many of them having been seasick for a full month. He got some of them up on deck for PT but the resulting shambles was so embarrassing that he dismissed them after five minutes.

The *Karmala* returned to the convoy and Bilderbeck came back to the *Homayun* to pick up his kit. He was to be permanently attached to General Aitken's staff. Gabriel stood in the doorway of the cabin watching Bilderbeck pack.

"Where are we going?" Gabriel asked. "Dar-es-Salaam?"

"I shouldn't really tell you," Bilderbeck said. "But no. It's Tanga."

"Oh," Gabriel said. He'd seen Tanga on one of Bilderbeck's maps. A port to the north of Dar, starting point for the Northern Railway that ran up to Kilimanjaro.

"Got a pillow?" Bilderbeck asked, holding up his own.

"Yes," Gabriel said. "I have. Why?"

"And a basin? Pillow and a basin. The two most essential pieces of equipment to have on active service. Get some decent sleep and have a chance for a wash and a shave. Always make sure you've got them with you. Best advice I can give."

"Thanks," Gabriel said distractedly. "Yes, I've got both." He paused. "Are we invading Tanga?"

"That's the idea," Bilderbeck said, a look of withering cynicism on his face. "It's the first invasion of a hostile beach for forty years or thereabouts, and they pick this lot." He put his hands on his hips and shook his head sorrowfully. "There's another problem, though.

It seems the navy made a truce with the German governor in Tanga at the very beginning of the war. Now the navy are insisting that we must inform the authorities there that 'belligerent hostilities' are going to be resumed. They feel their dignity demands an official abrogation of the truce." Bilderbeck's face lit up in one of his most beaming smiles.

"Good Lord." Gabriel sat down on his bunk. "Isn't that a bit . . . ? I mean, won't they know then that we're going to attack?"

"Of course they will." Bilderbeck gave a great hoot of laughter. "Of course they will. But try telling that to the navy." He rubbed his hands together like a fly. His mood seemed one of profound satisfaction, as if he'd just had some hotly disputed fact confirmed in his favour. "Remember," he said, looking up, "whatever happens, don't forget your pillow and basin."

CHAPTER FIVE

2 NOVEMBER 1914

Tanga · German East Africa

Gabriel stood at the rail of the *Homayun* and gazed out at the shoreline a mile away. It was six o'clock in the evening. He looked down at the map in his hand and then back again at the shore. What he was looking at, he calculated, was the headland called Ras Kasone that jutted out on the southern side of Tanga bay. Behind the lee of the headland, about two miles distant, lay the town of Tanga, which from his position was invisible. At the tip of the headland was a signal tower, and nearby that was a white stone house. Five hundred yards down, to the left of the white house, was a red house. All of these buildings seemed deserted, though the German flag flew from the signal tower. From what he could see through the thickening dusk, the shore facing him was composed of cliffs, at the bottom of which was dense and tangled vegetation, and curious twisted trees which he had been told were mangroves. Beneath the red house, however, was a beach some two hundred yards long. This, according to Lieutenant-Colonel Coutts, was where the Palamcottahs were to land later tonight: Beach "A."

At the briefing he'd just attended, and where the map had been issued, Lieutenant-Colonel Coutts (still in pain from his broken rib) had read out Major-General Aitken's orders. The first sentence had been immensely reassuring. "From reliable information received," it read, "it appears improbable that the enemy will actively oppose our landing."

Gabriel watched his company edge down the gangway into the huge wooden lighters that had been towed from Mombasa to provide transport from the ships to the beach. All around the headland he could see the ships of the convoy moored in line. Earlier that morning, Lieutenant-Colonel Coutts had informed them, the *Fox* had steamed into Tanga harbour, had officially abrogated the truce and demanded the surrender of the town—which was not forthcoming. Tanga, it appeared, was deserted.

Gabriel followed his second-in-command, Second Lieutenant Gleeson, down the gangway. Gleeson was gazetted to the Palamcottahs, a young man, just twenty-two, with pale-blue eyes and a blond moustache that reminded Gabriel of Nigel Bathe. He had very yellow teeth. Gleeson seemed not to have the slightest objection to a newcomer being placed in command over him. Gabriel had made some attempts to strike up some sort of a friendship with him during the voyage, but with little success. He suspected Gleeson of being a little "simple."

Lieutenant-Colonel Coutts was not fit enough to take part in the invasion of Tanga, and the adjutant—Major Santoras—was now in temporary command of the battalion. In the lighter, Gabriel looked around for the subadar of his battalion, Subadar Masrim Rahman. To Gabriel it seemed that every second man in the Palamcottahs was called Rahman. Unfortunately, Subadar Rahman was one of those most prone to seasickness, and the pitching and wallowing of the lighter had already rendered his brown skin a pale-beige colour.

"Everything in order, Subadar?" Gabriel asked, having to raise his voice above the babble of conversation.

"Sir," the subadar replied, removing his hand from his mouth to perform a shaky salute.

"Do you think you could shut the men up?" Gabriel said, and pushed his way through the press of soldiers to the stern of the lighter, where Major Santoras and six of the other officers were gathered, all peering at copies of the map of Tanga by the light of torches. The Palamcottahs could muster only three full companies—illness during the voyage having taken its toll. Two companies were to land and a third was being kept in reserve.

"What's this mark?" someone asked.

"It's a railway cutting," Major Santoras replied. "Between the landing beaches and the town." He went on less confidently: "There'll be bridges over it, I think. . . . Should be, anyway."

"Anyone know what the country's like beyond the beach?"

"Someone's put 'rubber' down here. I assume that means rubber plantations."

"Are the North Lancs landing on our beach?" Gabriel asked. These were the only regular British troops in the entire invasion force. Gabriel thought he would feel more secure, somehow, if he knew they were nearby.

"Don't think so," Santoras said. "They're round on the other side of the headland—Tanga side. Beach 'C.' No, sorry, Beach 'B.'"

"Actually it's Beach 'C,' I think," another volunteered. "In fact, aren't we meant to be landing with them?"

"Are you sure?" Santoras asked. "I thought the colonel said Beach 'A.'"

"Look! There go the Rajputs!"

Everyone looked over towards the transports to their right. A small tug was towing a string of three lighters towards the shore. It was nearly dark, but they could just be made out. About three hundred yards offshore the tow lines were slipped and the lighters drifted in towards the beach on the surf until they grounded. As the first men jumped into the water a flat crackle of shots rang out briefly; then there was silence. About two minutes later the *Fox* fired a salvo of shells. Everybody jumped with alarm. The shells exploded impressively around the red house. Gabriel realised he'd just witnessed his first shots fired in anger.

The Palamcottahs remained in their lighters for another five hours. Seventeen men in Gabriel's company collapsed from exhaustion and chronic seasickness and had to be helped back on board the *Homayun*. It was about one o'clock in the morning when the lighter finally crunched into the sand about eighty yards offshore. It had turned into a brilliant moonlit night and the beach below the red house was thronged with dark figures.

"Right, Cobb," Santoras said. "Get 'A' company ashore. Report to the beach officer for our assembly point."

"Who's the beach officer, sir?" Gabriel asked.

"Um, some major in the Fifty-first Pioneers, I think," Santoras said.

Gabriel and Gleeson, followed by their men, struggled to the bow of the lighter. Gleeson led the way. He jumped into the water and disappeared completely from view. He emerged, spluttering, a few seconds later. The water came up to his neck.

"Bloody deep," he said cheerily. "Better warn the men."

Gabriel jumped in. The water was deliciously warm. He was furious, though, to be completely soaked. He told Gleeson to see the rest of the company off and splashed his way slowly through the moderate surf onto the beach. With a pang of melancholy he recalled that the last time he'd been in the sea was at Trouville. Telling himself to concentrate, he looked back and saw a line of his men, rifles held above their heads, following him ashore. He felt his sodden uniform cool in the breeze coming off the sea. The beach was crowded with disembarked men, some of whom were being marched up a gully that led to the red house on the cliffs. Crowds of native porters and coolies shouted and milled aimlessly in large packs, waiting for the stores and ordnance to arrive.

When most of "A" company was ashore, a man with a torch stumped over and shone the beam in Gabriel's face.

"And who in God's name are you?" he was asked.

"'A' company, Sixty-ninth Palamcottah Light Infantry," Gabriel said.

"God Almighty!" the man swore. "You're not meant to be landing until tomorrow morning." He consulted the clipboard he held. "Beach 'C.' There's no room here for another battalion. Stop!

Stop!" he shouted as the remnants of "A" company emerged dripping from the waves. Gleeson went splashing back to the lighters to pass on the beach officer's instructions. A signalling lamp was set up and messages were exchanged with the *Homayun*. After an hour's wait a tug appeared and towed the rest of the battalion away from the beach and back to the ship.

"What about us?" Gabriel said.

"Attach yourself to the Rajputs for the night. We'll sort you out in the morning. See Lieutenant-Colonel Codrington. He's in the red house."

Gabriel formed up his muttering and perplexed troop. Two men were missing, leaving seventy-six in all. They had either drowned or else had never left the lighter. "A" company moved off the beach and up the gully to the cliff top. Here in the moonlight, Gabriel could see a great mass of men, many of them engaged in digging trenches. He stationed his men by a clump of palm trees, told Gleeson not to move, and went in search of Colonel Codrington. As he strode across to the red house he realised he was walking on dry land for the first time in a month. Other impressions added themselves to this: it was enemy soil too; out there were men he regarded as foe. And he was in Africa. The African night was cool, though that might have been due to his damp uniform, and he could hear all about him the strange persistent noise of the crickets and cicadas. He shivered with a kind of exhilaration and stamped his feet as he walked, happy not to hear the hollow sound of wooden decks returned to him. The land around the red house seemed to have been cleared for cultivation, but beyond that was a darker, higher mass of what looked like thick forest. Everywhere he could see columns of men being marched to and fro, and others settling down as best they could for the night. There were a great deal of shouted orders being exchanged and somewhere someone was blowing furiously on a whistle. It certainly didn't look like an invasion force, and there was a complete absence of danger.

Gabriel passed unchallenged into the red house. Staff officers hurried to and fro with papers in their hands. Engineers were installing a telephone line which had been run up from the beach. Gabriel asked for Lieutenant-Colonel Codrington and was directed upstairs. There he found a room filled with officers, most pressed around a table covered in maps. He saw Brigadier-General Tighe, a small man with a doleful, flushed expression. The force attacking Tanga had been divided into two brigades: on the left was Tighe's; on the right was the one the Palamcottahs were attached to, commanded by Brigadier-General Wapshare.

Gabriel paused, suddenly feeling a bit foolish. What should he do? Inform Tighe that he was reporting for duty to the wrong brigade? In the meantime he saluted the row of backs that was presented to him. In one corner of the room a major was energetically cranking the handle of a field telephone and shouting, "Hello hello hello hello" endlessly into the mouthpiece. Gabriel looked about him: there appeared to be half a dozen lieutenant-colonels in the room, all identically dressed in topees, khaki jackets, jodhpurs and knee-length brown leather boots. Then he saw the tall figure of Bilderbeck.

"Hello, Bilderbeck," Gabriel said, tapping him on the shoulder.

"Cobb!" Bilderbeck said loudly. A few people looked round. "What are you doing here? You should be on Beach 'C.'"

Gabriel explained about the wrong landing and his lost company of troops.

"God," Bilderbeck said, dropping his voice. "Between you and me, this is what I call a fiasco. I should sit tight till tomorrow, get some sleep and then wander over in the morning. Beach 'C' is only about a mile away."

He walked back down the stairs with Gabriel. The scene of noisy disorder outside prompted a bark of ironic laughter. "Think the Huns know we're here?" he asked rhetorically. He glanced up at the sky, which was lightening perceptibly in the east, out over the ocean. He looked at his watch. "The Rajputs are advancing on the town in half an hour," he said. "I'd better get back." He grinned, his teeth gleaming in the strong moonlight. Gabriel smiled back uneasily.

"I'll look by to see how you're getting on later," Bilderbeck said. "See if I can get a call through to Santoras. Let him know the score."

"I say, thanks, Bilderbeck," Gabriel said sincerely, but Bilderbeck was already striding back to the red house, which now had lights blazing from all its windows.

Gabriel wandered back through the columns of grunting coolies bringing up ammunition and supplies from the beach. He felt strangely depressed, not having had any instructions, and curiously impotent. "A" company was not meant to be where it was; therefore the purposes of strategy and logistics declared it to be non-existent.

He found Gleeson leaning up against a palm tree looking out at the anchored convoy. The men were lying beneath their unrolled turbans and looked ominously like rows of sheeted dead. No rifles had been stacked; packs and provisions had been dropped anywhere.

"Any luck?" Gleeson asked.

Gabriel told him they'd have to wait until the morning.

"What's going on?" Gleeson asked incuriously. "I saw machine guns being taken up to the perimeter."

"The Rajputs are attacking Tanga," Gabriel said listlessly.

"Rather them than me," Gleeson said. "I'm shattered. Fancy some tea? I've got a flask here."

Gabriel accepted. "How are the men?" he said, knowing he ought to be passing among them, issuing words of calm and comfort. But they weren't like his company in the West Kents. They seemed total strangers. Gleeson seemed to have some sort of peculiar rapport with them, but that was because he spoke the language. Gabriel supposed he should at least let the Indian officers know what the latest news was, but they all seemed asleep. It wasn't surprising, he reflected, after five hours in a tilting, swaying lighter.

He heard the whine of a mosquito in his ear. His uniform was nearly dry now. He strolled to the edge of a knoll and looked down on the landing beach. The coolies and native bearers were still hard at work; they formed straggling lines, moving stores up from the beach to the cliff top. Farther out, the convoy of ships was silhouetted against the gash of grey and citron-yellow that was the dawn sky. Gleeson's tea had left a metallic taste in his mouth; cheap flask, he thought. He turned round and looked in the direction of Tanga.

He heard a cock crow. Out there in the bush, he thought, there are columns of men "marching unto war." He hummed a few bars of the hymn tune, trying to take his mind off the sudden pressures and cramps he was feeling in his bowels. He tapped the rhythm on his holster. "Onward, Christian so-oh-oh-oldiers . . ." General Aitken expected no resistance. . . . He laughed at himself. What was so wrong with needing to perform a natural function? He walked over to a clump of bushes, lowered his trousers and squatted down.

Gleeson woke him up at six. He'd managed to get only a couple of hours' sleep.

"The show seems to be on," Gleeson said airily.

Gabriel looked around him at the unfamiliar scene. The early-morning sun bounced off the red tiles on the roof of the red house. The terrain looked quite different in daylight. The patch of cleared ground was dusty and covered by straggling clumps of sun-bleached knee-high grass and low thorn bushes. Waist-deep trenches had been dug around the perimeter and from them Indian troops looked out into the comparative lushness of coconut groves and rubber plantations that lay between Ras Kasone and Tanga. By the red house three reserve companies of Pioneers were drawn up. Scattered everywhere were great mounds of boxes, crates and sacks. Gabriel saw brand-new signalling equipment, bundles of stretchers and, to his alarm, ranks of coffins. There were also a dozen motor bikes.

From the direction of Tanga came the cracking and popping of rifles and machine guns. It sounded like a fire blazing in distant undergrowth.

"Good grief," Gabriel said. "That's damned heavy. I thought this landing was meant to be unopposed." Everybody around the house had stopped what he was doing and was looking in the direction of Tanga.

"The Rajputs set off about an hour and a half ago," Gleeson said. "They must be at the town by now. Probably a rearguard."

But the noise of firing didn't stop. Soon everyone went nervously back about his business, as if evidence of lack of concern might work some magic. Gleeson took some men down to the beach and came back with a box of ship's biscuits and fresh water. Gabriel didn't feel like eating but happily accepted a mug of warm water and rum. The alcohol made him relax.

From time to time, runners would appear from the forest of coconut trees and sprint into the red house. The noise of firing continued and Gabriel reflected that the "rearguard" was certainly putting up something of a fight. He saw General Tighe himself come out of the house and order the three reserve companies to march off in support of the Rajputs.

Gleeson went back to sleep, but Gabriel felt agitated. He wandered over to one of the perimeter trenches. The sepoys guarding it looked edgy and fearful. He noticed that there were no English officers. Suddenly about a dozen African porters bolted out of the trees and raced past the outpost guards, whimpering and gibbering with fear. Gabriel turned and watched them disappear over the rise and down onto the beach. Everyone looked at each other in astonishment; then a murmur of alarm spread through the men in the trenches. Some loud arguments ensued and Gabriel saw some native officers raising their swagger sticks to restore order.

"Who were those men running away?" Gabriel asked a jemadar with a fierce moustache.

"Machine-gun bearers, sir. From the Rajputs."

Gabriel swallowed. Where were the machine guns in that case? A commotion farther up the line attracted his attention. It was the first of the stretcher parties returning from the fighting. He ran over. There were four stretcher cases, all white men. Orderlies and doctors fussed over their bodies. Three of the men were very still, their mouths open and their eyes staring. The man on the fourth stretcher was groaning and trying to say something.

"My God," Gabriel said to no one in particular. "They're all officers." He noticed that the groaning man was a lieutenant-colonel.

"Who's that?" Gabriel asked one of the doctors leaning over him.

"Lieutenant-Colonel Codrington, Thirteenth Rajputs."

Gabriel turned away and walked back towards the red house. He felt alarmed and confused at the sight of the wounded men. What was going on? If Bilderbeck were here, he thought, he'd be able to tell me. He took away with him a jumbled, hazy impression of the men on the stretchers: he hadn't noticed any blood; he'd been looking at their faces, their bare heads with once neatly brushed hair now mussed and tousled.

Gabriel re-joined Gleeson and they watched another half battalion, fresh from the beach, march off at once into the coconut groves. Runners arrived at and departed from the red house in ever-increasing numbers. A heliograph was set up and soon messages were being flashed from shore to ship.

It grew hotter. By 9:00 A.M. the sun was sufficiently powerful to force Gabriel into the shade. He looked at his company of men, all of whom had now claimed their rifles and packs and were sitting in small silent groups in whatever patch of shade they could find. Gabriel wondered if he should have reported to Brigade HQ in the red house but decided that the last thing they'd want to deal with now was his errant company.

At about half past nine the report of heavy guns could be heard from somewhere in the bay. About six salvos were fired.

"Probably the *Fox*," Gleeson said, exposing his yellow teeth in a wide grin. "Shelling Tanga," he said. "That'll show 'em."

Shortly after, they heard bugle calls and a distant yelling. The sound of firing, which hadn't stopped since Gleeson had woken him at six, seemed to be drawing closer.

"Are those our bugles?" Gabriel asked.

"Think so," Gleeson said.

"They don't sound like them, though."

Gleeson cocked his head. "No, they don't, do they?"

A staff captain came out of the red house, looked around and loped over.

"Are you 'A' company, Sixty-ninth Palamcottahs?" he said languidly to Gabriel. Gabriel said they were. "Good. We've had a message about you. Seems you're to stay put for the time being."

"Stay put? What? Here?"

"That seems to be the idea." The staff captain removed his sun-helmet to reveal a bald and shiny pate which he mopped with a handkerchief. "Filthy hot," he said.

"How are things?" Gabriel asked. "I mean, what's the picture?" There were more bugle calls as he spoke.

"Stiffish resistance at the railway cutting," the staff captain said. "We're retiring. In good order," he added hastily. "We'll wait for the main landing today. . . . Look, I must dash."

Gabriel watched him bound back to the red house. He went back to Gleeson.

"They've had a message about us," he said authoritatively. "Seems we're to stay put."

Gabriel and Gleeson kept their distance as the Rajputs and Pioneers straggled back into camp. The men were either talking with hysterical excitement or else were cowed and dejected. They watched dozens of wounded being carried and helped down to the beach. Soon the area around the red house was thick with exhausted troops.

"Doesn't look so good," Gleeson said, "does it?"

At lunch-time Gabriel went up to the red house to see if he could get any more information. It seemed that the landing of the main force at beaches "B" and "C" round the headland was proceeding as normal, but the beaches were so congested with men and equipment that the Palamcottahs were still on the *Homayun* and probably wouldn't be disembarked until the next day.

"Seems we're still to stay put," Gabriel reported back to Gleeson.

In the afternoon it rained for two hours and everyone was soaked again. Normally the men of the Palamcottahs had regimental bearers and servants to cook and care for them, but as these hadn't been landed with them they had to fend for themselves. Gabriel found he still wasn't hungry, though he drank some fresh coconut milk—of which there was a plentiful supply—with some relish. Unfortunately, an hour later this brought on a severe attack of diarrhoea. As a result, as evening approached at the end of his first day on enemy soil, Gabriel was feeling weak and rather seedy as well as damp and dirty. He did, however, manage to have a shave before he went back to the red house to inquire if there had been any further news for "A" company.

"My Christ! Are you all right?" Bilderbeck asked him. "You look dreadful."

"Tummy upset," Gabriel confessed. "But listen, what happened today?"

"A bloody shambles, that's what," Bilderbeck said fiercely. "A bloody shambles."

"What have you got there? If you don't mind my asking," Gabriel said. Bilderbeck was standing half-way down the stairs that led to the upper floor of the red house. His arms were full of what looked, to Gabriel, like ladies' underclothes.

"Ladies' underclothes," Bilderbeck said. "Courtesy of our absent hostess. They're going to provide me with a soft bed tonight. You won't believe this"—he glanced right and left to make sure he wasn't overheard—"but I've lost my pillow." He gave a great shout of laughter. Gabriel responded nervously. "Help yourself," Bilderbeck offered, unloading half his bundle. "No sense in sleeping on the ground."

Gabriel followed him out to the patch of piebald lawn on the landward side of the house and watched him construct a bed of palm fronds and petticoats.

"What happened today?" Gabriel asked again. "It didn't look as if things went as planned."

"To put it mildly," Bilderbeck said, adjusting his makeshift couch with the toe of his boot. "Bloody damn fool navy, that's what," he said. "This idiotic truce business. When the *Fox* sailed into Tanga harbour yesterday morning to abrogate the thing, they gave the Germans twenty-four hours' warning of our attack. Just enough time for Von Lettow-Vorbeck to get his troops down from Moshi by rail."

"So Tanga *was* deserted."

"It was."

"And now it's well defended."

"Getting stronger by the hour." Bilderbeck's face was lit up for an instant by a seraphic smile. He dug his tobacco pouch out of his pocket and offered it to Gabriel.

"Pipe?" he said.

"No, thanks." Gabriel took out his cigarette case and lit a cigarette while Bilderbeck got his pipe going.

"We'll be attacking tomorrow then," Gabriel said, aware of a slight hollow feeling in his chest. "Are the North Lancs ashore?"

"Oh, yes. They'll be on the left."

"Good," Gabriel said. He felt that a battalion of British troops would make all the difference.

"But what about the right?" Bilderbeck asked, voicing Gabriel's fears. "Who in God's name will be on the right? A crowd of bloody catch-me-quicks, that's who."

CHAPTER SIX

3 NOVEMBER 1914

Tanga · German East Africa

The next morning, the bald staff captain sauntered over and told Gabriel that his company was to be attached to the 13th Rajputs in the centre of the attack on Tanga. Gabriel formed his men up and checked their equipment. He asked Subadar Rahman to do his best to instill some fighting spirit into the listless troop. At approximately ten-thirty they were told where to take up their preliminary position. This was the first time Gabriel had moved away from the red house and he was amazed to see thousands of men standing about in rough columns in the assembly area between the white house and the red house.

Dirt tracks led away from the beach-head and disappeared into the coconut groves.

"A" company took up their position. Looking back at the white house Gabriel could see the three generals and their aides clustered in a group. Orders were clearly being issued and staff officers were running around checking on the placings of different units.

After standing for an hour in mounting heat, Gabriel's company and the Rajputs in front of them were ordered to advance three hundred yards into the bush. Gabriel followed the backs of the Rajputs, and they left the open ground and moved into the welcome shade of the coconut plantations. As they marched off, Gabriel looked back and saw what looked like an entire battalion of the North Lancs wheeling round behind them to take up position on the Rajputs' left. The British soldiers were in shirt-sleeves and looked very red-faced and sunburnt, but Gabriel found it an immense comfort to see them. His own men still seemed taciturn and nervous. Subadar Rahman's pep talk had done little good. Gleeson seemed quite jaunty, though, to Gabriel's surprise. He was whistling quietly to himself through his yellow teeth.

As they moved into the trees and the denser undergrowth that grew between the pale-grey trunks, Gabriel lost sight of everyone except his own men and the tail-enders of the company in front. Somebody called halt and they all stopped. It was a genuine relief to be in the forest and out of the sun. At the Rajput briefing, which he had attended, their instructions had been to offer support to the Kashmir Rifles (who, Gabriel supposed, were somewhere in the trees up ahead) and capture and secure the jetty and customs sheds on the dockside. Tanga town, so they had been informed, was about two thousand yards ahead of them. Between them and the town were the coconut and rubber plantations, a native cemetery, a ditch and a deep railway cutting. Yesterday's attack suggested that the far side of the cutting was the enemy's first line of defence.

Gabriel looked at his wristwatch. Twenty to twelve. The advance was ordered for midday. Over to his right and left he could hear orders being shouted and whistles and bugles blowing as the two brigades were cumbersomely formed up. Announced by a cracking of vegetation, a young staff officer thrashed his way out of a thicket and walked up to Gabriel. His tunic was covered in sweat and dust. He consulted a small notebook.

"Are you the One Hundred-and-first Grenadiers?" he asked.

Gabriel·said no and told him who they were. The man looked at his notebook again.

"Lord," he muttered. Then, "I don't suppose you've seen the North Lancs?"

Gabriel said he thought they were somewhere to his left. The Rajputs were ahead, and as far as he knew, the Kashmir Rifles were in the vanguard.

"Oh, good," the staff officer said. "That seems about right."

"Have you any idea where the Palamcottahs are?" Gabriel asked.

"Beyond the North Lancs, I think," he said without much confidence. "By the way, could you form up in line rather than column? We've decided to advance in line." He plunged off into the bush as Gabriel and Gleeson effortfully ushered their hot and bothered men into line abreast.

At ten past twelve the bugles sounded the advance. Gabriel waved his men forward and almost immediately the line began to undulate and break up as the men encountered denser vegetation and had to skirt impenetrable thorn thickets and clumps of bamboo. Gabriel and Gleeson, in the centre, found a rough path which took them in the right direction but this soon petered out. After a strenuous half hour they broke into the clearer ground of a rubber plantation. Up ahead Gabriel could just make out the disappearing backs of the Rajputs. "Come on," he shouted to his men. "Faster."

A perspiring native runner panted up and handed him a note. It was from a captain in the North Lancs who said a gap was opening between them and the Rajputs and he would be obliged if the Rajputs could wheel slightly to the left. Gabriel sent the runner ahead to the Rajput columns and wondered if he and his men should alter course too. He looked about him as they made faster progress through the rubber trees. He couldn't even see either wing of his own company. He sent Gleeson off to check that all was in order. He realised he was striding along as if he were on a country hike instead of marching into battle. A little self-consciously he unholstered his revolver and held it at the ready.

After the rubber plantation came more thick forest with high

grass, creepers and bushes at ground level, and their progress
slowed again. Gabriel tried to visualise the advance as if from a
bird's-eye view—three thousand men moving on Tanga—but
found it impossible. By now he was dripping with sweat. His leggings and trousers were thick with dust and torn from the many
thorn-bearing plants he'd had to push his way through. He took off
his sun-helmet and wiped his forehead with a palm. His hair was
wet through, as if he'd just plunged it in a basin of warm salty
water.

The thought of a basin of water, even warm and salty, reminded
him that he was extremely thirsty. He was about to call for a water-
chaggal when he realised the company didn't have any, as the
water-carriers had not been landed with them. He looked at his
watch. Two o'clock. They'd been struggling through the bush for
nearly two hours. He had no idea how far away they were from
Tanga. It struck him that ordering the attack during the hottest
time of the day wasn't the brightest of ideas. Gleeson came up to
report that the company was maintaining some sort of order. Five
men had collapsed from heat exhaustion and he'd sent them back.
He saw Gabriel had his revolver in his hand and took out his own.

"Think it'll go off all right?" he asked with a nervous smile.
"The attack, I mean, not my gun."

Gabriel realised that Gleeson, like himself, had never seen active
service. This was their first fight. He was pleased to note in himself
no sensations of fear. He glanced at the men on either side of him.
They looked tense, but that was scarcely surprising. They held their
rifles loosely across their chests, the fixed bayonets flashing in the
odd beam of sun that came through the canopy of leaves.

Suddenly they heard the sound of firing from up ahead and a
confused shouting and cheering broke out. At this point Gabriel's
company was forcing its way through particularly dense bush, and
no view of what was going on could be gained. He could hear
sniggering bursts of fire from machine guns, more regular and controlled than the indiscriminate popping sound of the rifles.

"Over here," Gleeson shouted. "There's a sort of track."

"This way," Gabriel called to the native officers. He waded
through thick grass to the track. As he stepped onto it he heard a

crashing and trampling noise, the sound of men running. Suddenly, round the corner came a great mob of Indian soldiers, dozens it seemed, running at full speed away from the firing. Gabriel spun round. All at once, everywhere, he could make out figures struggling to escape through the undergrowth, darting beneath the trees, flashing through the clearings of sunlight and dappled patches of shade. To his horror he saw some of his own men join the stampede, pausing only to fling away their rifles.

He crouched down behind a tree and aimed his revolver up the track, expecting a charge of German askaris to be hard on the fleeing men's heels. The firing up ahead continued with the same intensity but there seemed to be no pursuit. He stood up. He and Gleeson exchanged mystified glances. What was going on? They gathered the remaining men together and advanced on up the track. Soon the trees began to thin. The track ended at a large field of fully grown maize which looked as if it had been smashed and trampled on by a giant pair of feet. Here they saw their first dead bodies, which set up a chatter of alarm amongst "A" company's remaining sepoys.

Enough of the maize stalks were still standing to obscure their view. Gabriel looked to his right. The Kashmir Rifles should be there. On the left were the Loyal North Lancs. Where were the Rajputs? Surely they couldn't all have run away? He wondered if they'd wandered off course in the coconut plantations. But what lay beyond the maize field? Gabriel waved his men down into a crouch and got out his map. It made no sense at all. He looked aimlessly about him, trying not to let his gaze rest on the numerous dead bodies. Firing was continuing to his right and left, but all seemed quiet up ahead.

Gleeson crawled up behind him. "Runner from headquarters," he said. Gabriel thought Gleeson didn't look very well. The runner handed over the note. It was from Brigadier-General Wapshare. It said, "Your men should bring their left shoulders up and march towards this point so as to envelop the enemy's right." What point? Gabriel asked himself. He raised his left shoulder experimentally but it seemed no clearer. He turned it over and saw a crude map with a bold arrow on it. There was no addressee. Surely the note couldn't be meant for him? He turned round to question the runner but found that the man had gone.

There was nothing for it but to advance. Waving the men forward, Gabriel, followed by "A" company, moved cautiously through the maize field. It seemed to be well provided with a harvest of corpses and the thought crossed Gabriel's mind that machine guns must have been previously sighted and fixed on this point. At the edge of the field he fell flat on his belly and peered out at the view ahead. The land was clear: dried grass dotted with a few acacia trees and completely flat. Fifty yards ahead he could see the ditch, fringed with greener grass and straggling bushes, and beyond that the railway cutting. To his right was a slight rise and he saw some British troops there, and a machine-gun section firing short bursts in the direction of the town. Beyond the railway cutting the neat white buildings of the town were visible between trees. He could see the sea, away to the right, and two of the transports standing offshore. His view to the left was obscured by a plantation of young rubber trees. But a great deal of firing was coming from that direction. The North Lancs, he guessed, in the thick of things.

"What do you think?" he said to Gleeson, who'd snaked up to join him.

"The Rajputs seem to have cleared out completely," Gleeson said. "Bad show."

"Yes," Gabriel agreed. He wondered what they should do. "I suppose we should press on into the town. They must have fired on the Rajputs. Why aren't they firing on us?"

"Good question," said Gleeson with a shaky smile.

"Let's go," Gabriel said and stood up. He gave a long single blast on his whistle. "Come on!" he shouted to his men.

He set off running in a half crouch towards the ditch, not making the best of progress through the knee-high grass. He dodged round a spindly acacia tree. He thought he saw puffs of smoke beyond the railway cutting. He was being shot at! Suddenly, to his utter astonishment the air was "thick with bullets." The expression leapt unbidden into his mind. It was a cliché, he was aware, but he never expected it to be literally true: black dots and specks whizzing erratically through the air. He felt a sudden burning pain in his neck. He was hit! Oh, God, he thought, not in the neck. He stumbled, but ran on, clapping a hand to his wound to staunch the blood, bullets buzzing and darting past. But wait, he thought, they weren't bullets—they were bees!

He stopped and turned round. His men were leaping about or writhing on the ground like epileptics as the swarming myriads of bees attacked. He saw Gleeson frantically swatting the air with his sun-helmet. The atmosphere shimmered and danced with the irate black objects. With dismay he saw the demoralised remnants of his troops pick themselves up and run hell for leather back to the maize field. Gabriel inflated his lungs and blew the longest, shrillest blasts he could on his whistle, in an attempt to check the rout, but they were gone, pursued by the furious bees.

"My God," Gleeson whimpered as he staggered over. "I've been practically stung to death!" The backs of his hands looked lumpy and swollen; his cheeks and neck seemed thickened with incipient carbuncles, making him look stupid and loutish. "Look." Gleeson pointed up. In the acacia tree Gabriel saw what looked like several slim elongated barrels. A few bees still hovered around them. "Bloody native beehives," Gleeson wept, holding his puffy hands in front of him like a lap dog. They were swelling up at an alarming rate.

Gabriel suddenly realised they were standing in what was meant to be the middle of a battlefield. He looked over to the mound and saw the troops who had been manning the machine gun wildly striking out as if they had been attacked by invisible assailants. Across the railway cutting he could just make out a few German askaris fleeing for shelter in the railway workshops. He looked back at Gleeson, who was whimpering in agony over his ravaged hands, which now resembled a pair of well-padded cricket gloves. Then little clouds of dust began to kick up out of the grass.

"Come on, Gleeson," Gabriel said. "Into the ditch." They rushed the remaining few yards and leapt into the ditch, which was about four feet deep. Gabriel sank up to his ankles into the brackish slimy water that lay in its bottom.

With a moan of relief Gleeson plunged his boiling hands deep into the mud. "Put mud on my neck!" he cried, and Gabriel slapped handfuls of the foul-smelling stuff on his cheeks and neck. His own sting was throbbing painfully but he seemed to have escaped lightly.

While Gleeson soothed his hands, Gabriel inched up the wall of the ditch and peered back to the maize field. Not a sign of his men. He noticed that the machine gun on the mound had started firing again.

"No trace of them," he said to Gleeson.

"The swine." Gleeson swore bitterly. "The cowardly swine!"

"Feel you can move on?" Gabriel asked. "Let's go on down the ditch. We'll never cross the cutting here."

Gleeson nodded his assent, his eyes shut, his bottom lip caught between his yellow teeth.

Bent double, they made their way along the ditch in the direction of the sea, stepping gingerly over the few dead bodies they encountered or rolling them out of the way. Gleeson held his mud-caked hands in front of him as if he'd just made them out of clay and they were still fragile. Soon they came to a place where bushes and thorn trees lined the parapet of the ditch, and Gabriel took the chance to peer out and get their bearings.

Cautiously he raised his head. From this position he had a better view of the town. He saw a large stone building with steep tiled roofs and the words DEUTSCHER KAISER HOTEL written on it. As he watched, the German flag which was flying from the flagpole was lowered.

"We're in the town, I think," he called to Gleeson. "What time do you make it?" Somehow, somewhere, he'd lost his watch.

"Almost four, I think," Gleeson said. "I can't see my watch face. It's covered in mud."

Gabriel scraped it off. Gleeson's watch had stopped at ten past three. "I'm afraid your watch has stopped," he said.

Gabriel looked to his left. He saw white troops moving beyond the railway cutting, dashing from house to house. "The North Lancs are across the cutting," he reported. Gleeson elbowed himself up to join him.

"What should we do?" Gleeson said. He held his enormous

hands before his face, like some grotesque surgeon waiting for his rubber gloves.

"Let's go on in," Gabriel said. He couldn't think of anything else.

"Right."

They scurried across the patch of ground to the railway cutting and slithered down one side, then stepped across the rails and toiled up the opposite thirty-foot incline, Gabriel with an arm locked in Gleeson's elbow. Once at the top they ran on through some vegetable plots and fell to the ground heavily in the shelter of a mud-brick house.

"Hoi!" they heard someone shout. "You!" They looked up. Crouched behind a stone wall up ahead were half a dozen men of the North Lancs.

"You speak Indian?" a corporal was shouting in a thick Lancashire accent. Gabriel and Gleeson crawled over to join them.

"Oh. Sorry, sir. It's, er, them fooking niggers in t' Kashmir Rifles. Just down road there. Every time we shows our faces they bloody shoot at us."

"I speak Hindi," Gleeson offered. He looked most odd, Gabriel thought, with half his face covered in mud. Gleeson crawled into a nearby house with the corporal and soon Gabriel heard him shouting instructions. Gabriel peered over the wall. He found he was looking up a pleasant street of single-storey, white mud and stone houses. Dead bodies, with their already familiar indecent splay-legged posture, lay in the middle of the road. He couldn't tell if they were friend or foe.

"Quite a fight here," he said.

"Yes, sir. We had the signal to fall back. They got jerries in every bloody house. But those daft monkeys keep shootin' at us. They're guarding the bridge back across the cutting. None of them speaks English." He paused. "What happened to the lieutenant, sir? If you'll excuse me asking."

"He was stung by bees. My whole company was attacked and driven off."

"By bees?"

"Yes, millions of them."

The man shook his head in admiration. "Squareheads, eh? Amazing. They think of everything."

Gabriel looked over the wall again. The afternoon sun was low in the sky and strong shadows were being cast across the road. Then he saw figures slipping in and out of the houses, moving down the street towards them: three Europeans and about thirty askaris with bayonets fixed to their rifles.

He saw one of the officers—who seemed unaware of their presence—stand for a moment in front of the gable end of a house. Without thinking further, Gabriel levelled his revolver and fired. He saw a big chunk of plaster fall off the wall behind the officer's head before the man flung himself into a doorway. In immediate response there was a great fusillade of shots and Gabriel ducked down under cover. He cursed his feeble aim: he had had a splendid target. He found himself trembling with excitement; his heart seemed lodged somewhere in his throat. He heard the whup of bullets passing over his head and the chatter of a machine gun. Ricochets hummed and pinged off the stonework.

"We want to get out of here, sir," one of the North Lancs said. "Don't want to get caught by them jerry niggers." All the men kept their heads well down.

The corporal scuttled out of the house. "It's clear now, sir. We can go."

"Hold on," Gabriel said. "Where's Lieutenant Gleeson?"

"He's been hit, sir. Got him with that last volley."

"Wait here," Gabriel ordered and darted into the house. He peered into a couple of rooms. He saw a brass bedstead, cheap wooden furniture. In an end room he found Gleeson lying face down beneath the window from where he'd been shouting to the Kashmir Rifles. The wall behind was pitted with bullet holes. Gabriel was suddenly appalled by the thought that he might have been responsible. If he hadn't shot at that German . . . Keeping his head down, Gabriel carefully turned Gleeson over and almost collapsed in a faint. One or several bullets had removed Gleeson's lower jawbone in its entirety, but somehow his tongue had been untouched. It now lolled, uncontained, at his throat like a thick fleshy cravat, pink and purple. Gleeson's upper lip was drawn back revealing his top row of yellow teeth; his fair moustache was spattered with dried mud and blood. What was most horrifying was the way his eyes boggled and rolled, and his tongue twitched feebly at his neck. With a little moan Gabriel realised Gleeson was still alive, blood welling and pumping gently from the back of his throat. It was extraordinary, Gabriel thought in a daze, how large the human tongue actually was, when its entire length was revealed. He crawled out of the room on his hands and knees and was sick in the passageway. Poor Gleeson, he thought, poor old Gleeson.

After a few moments Gabriel got to his feet and went back to the side door. There was no sign of the North Lancs. They had all gone without waiting for him. He wondered where the Germans were. He went back inside to the end room, trying not to look at Gleeson. Gabriel lowered himself out of the window. He crossed the backyard and eased himself through the garden hedge. An immense noise of gunfire was coming from the direction of the wharves, but as far as he could see he was alone again. He ran across a dirt road and slid down into the railway cutting. Here and there lay the bodies of sepoys, not all of them dead—he could hear moans and cries coming from some of them.

He scrabbled up the opposite side. He saw tree-dotted scrub between him and the safety of the forest and the coconut plantations. Head down, he ran across the two-hundred-yard stretch of clearer ground at full speed, leaping undulations and bushes and the large numbers of dead and dying scattered about. Almost idly he noted how a dead body seems part of the ground, as if the earth were in a hurry to claim it. . . . He told himself he was in shock; poor Gleeson's horrible injury had unsettled him. He would calm down in the forest, gather his strength and then go back and try to help him. Try to carry him to a casualty clearing station.

He fought his way through the first welcoming thickets, broke through into an open space, tripped and went sprawling. He found a depression in the ground and crawled into it. He lay back, an arm over his eyes, his chest heaving as he struggled to get his breath.

He sat up with a start. He couldn't believe it, but he seemed to have fallen asleep for a few seconds. He had a pounding, vicious headache. His mouth tasted foul with dried saliva. His throat was parched. Still the relentless popping of gunfire came from the direction of the town. He put his head in his hands, suddenly overcome with weariness and the emotions rampaging through his body. He pulled his knees towards him and rested his head on them. He rubbed his forehead on his kneecaps.

He unholstered his revolver. His hands looked like a stranger's. Black with dirt, scratched, a badly bleeding knuckle (how had that happened?). They felt thick with blisters and callouses. He heard the booming reports of naval guns, and decided to try and make his way in that general direction. Most of the fighting seemed to be coming from the seaward edge of the town. He set off. After some time he came to one of the many rough tracks that led east to west along the headland from Ras Kasone to Tanga. He debated for an instant whether to return to the beach or go back towards the town. With some reluctance he turned towards Tanga. He hadn't gone more than twenty yards when he met Bilderbeck running down the path towards him.

"Cobb!" Bilderbeck shouted. "Just the man!" It was as if he and Bilderbeck had met on the steps of his club. Bilderbeck grabbed him by the arm. "This way," he said and led him a little distance off the track. There, in the shelter of an earth bank, were seven Rajput sepoys cowering together.

"Tell them to get up," Bilderbeck said. "Tell them to take up firing positions up the road."

"I'm afraid I don't speak the language," Gabriel said apologetically.

"What? Oh, never mind." Bilderbeck strode forward and started roughly pulling the sepoys to their feet, yelling "Get up!" and pushing them in the direction of the town and the firing. Two reluctantly obeyed, picking up their rifles and slouching dispiritedly off. The others crouched where they were, wailing and moaning softly. Bilderbeck drew his revolver and threatened them. Then he fired into the bank and there was a flurry of movement as the men leapt panic-stricken to their feet, milling around confusedly in evident terror at this mad Englishman with a gun.

But one man had not moved. He sat in a hunched squatting

posture, one arm raised vaguely in protection, muttering distractedly to himself.

"Get up, you filthy coward!" Gabriel heard Bilderbeck roar. But
the man wasn't hearing anything. He was gibbering like a lunatic,
high and piping, a loop of saliva hanging from his chin.

"I warn you," Bilderbeck said. Gabriel couldn't believe what he
was seeing. Bilderbeck levelled his revolver at the sepoy's head. The
gun was only six inches from his head.

"I am ordering you," Bilderbeck said in an eerily reasonable
voice, "to get to your feet and take up a firing position at the end
of the road."

The man stared bleakly at the gun.

"Right," Bilderbeck said angrily and fired. Gabriel flinched un-
controllably at the noise.

The bullet hit the sepoy just in front of his left ear. The man's
head jerked sharply to one side and he slumped back as if in a deep
swoon. There was a delicate spattering sound as bits of expressed
brain hit the leaves of the bushes behind the man. Immediately the
other sepoys rushed up the track with cries of fear, Bilderbeck
running behind them waving his revolver and shouting.

Gabriel looked down. On the toe of his boot was a greyish pink
blob, like a wet, peeled shrimp. With a shudder he wiped it off on
the earth and ran after Bilderbeck.

Soon they arrived at a semblance of a front line on the more
open ground by the sea. Groups of men crouched behind trees and
rocks, two machine guns covering a dirt road.

Bilderbeck seemed quite unmoved by his summary execution.
He told Gabriel it was his third that day. Gabriel felt his body
tingling and trembling, as if any moment he might drop from accumulated shock and exhaustion.

They took up a position behind a jumble of rocks and watched
a company of North Lancs drawing back in reasonable order from
the customs house and the sheds around the jetty which were just
visible. Peering forward, Gabriel could just make out German
askaris darting across gaps in the alleyway to reoccupy the abandoned buildings. Ragged covering fire broke out from the British
lines and one of the Maxims stuttered into life.

"Bloody day," Bilderbeck said gloomily. "Everybody ran for it. You should see the beaches. Mass panic. People swimming out to the lighters. *Disgusting!*" He gave Gabriel a fierce smile. "Where are your men?"

Gabriel explained about the bee attack and most of the bizarre and erratic course his day had taken. "What's going on?" he asked, trying not to think about Gleeson.

"Well, we've been well and truly cut to pieces on the left. Fifty percent casualties in the One Hundred-and-first Grenadiers. The line's in tatters, thanks to all the bloody cowards who ran away." He went on. The town had been far more heavily fortified and defended than anyone had expected. Every building was like a blockhouse. With no organisation, with huge gaps in the attack, with the left wing being pushed farther and farther back, the few gains made in the town had to be yielded.

"It's all gone *wrong,*" Bilderbeck said, as if it were a personal insult. "Even our general's got no spunk for a fight."

Gabriel felt suddenly overwhelmed by a desire to sleep. "I suppose I should try and get back to my men," he said vaguely.

"They'll be on the beach by now," Bilderbeck sneered. He took out his map from his pocket and smoothed it on the ground. Gabriel thought maps should be banned. They gave the world an order and reasonableness which it didn't possess. COCONUT GROVES, it said in large letters. The phrase sounded pleasant, restful. It gave no indication of the tangled choking undergrowth they had clawed their way through at noon.

Bilderbeck's finger traced a crescent on the map from the native graveyard up to the ditch, then back to the coast. "We're here now." Bilderbeck tapped a point ahead of a building marked HOSPITAL. "The hospital's just back there, overlooking the sea. You might find some of your men on the left of the line by the cemetery. There's a mixed lot of North Lancs and Grenadiers around there. Go back down the road and take the first track on the right that's marked with a red and white stake. It'll take you along to the cemetery."

He and Gabriel crawled away from the front line until they had lost sight of the town. Then they stood up.

"I'd better get back to headquarters," Bilderbeck said, looking glum. "See you later, Cobb." He went behind a large tree and emerged with a bicycle, which he mounted and rode off down the track.

Gabriel walked slowly down the road behind him, now filled with troops making their unauthorised way back to the beach and the morning's assembly point. As he cycled past each group, Bilderbeck delivered a volley of insults and abuse, but the dishevelled and exhausted men ignored him completely.

Presently Gabriel came to a track branching off to the right which was marked by a red and white striped pole. The staff officers at least were doing their job. He walked along a narrowing path, half-heartedly brushing creepers from his face. The sun was sinking lower in the sky and there was an orangey light hitting the tops of the trees. The incessant noise of firing grew louder as he approached the left wing of the British lines, but he scarcely gave it any thought. It seemed as much a part of the natural landscape now as the chirping of crickets or the calls of the birds.

Soon he came to the graveyard, no more than a large patch of cleared ground with a few graves dotted about it, most of them marked by plain cement plinths or crosses, but with the occasional more elaborate Moorish headstone.

He saw an outpost of the British line in the far corner and began to pick his way towards it. Nothing today had been remotely how he had imagined it would be; nothing in his education or training had prepared him for the utter randomness and total contingency of events. Here he was, strolling about the battlefield looking for his missing company like a mother searching for lost children in the park.

He looked up. The outpost was composed of native troops in khaki uniforms and tarbooshes. They seemed to be bent over some wounded men. King's African Rifles, Gabriel thought; they were the only African troops in the British Army. Then he realised there had been no K.A.R. in the expeditionary force.

At once, instinctively, he turned on his heel and started to run, a ghastly leaping fear in his heart. He heard shouts come from behind. He started to run like a sprinter, as he'd been taught at school, arms pounding and pulling at the air, lifting the knees high. He thumped heavily across the uneven ground, throwing his sun-helmet off his head. Faster, he told himself, *faster,* get to the forest, just get back to the forest. He shut his ears to the pursuit, the drumming of feet behind him. "Don't want to get caught by those jerry niggers," the North Lancs soldier had said. So: faster, faster.

They caught up with him about twenty yards from the shelter of the trees. They even ran alongside him for a pace or two, far speedier than he in their bare feet, even when encumbered by their rifles and bayonets.

Gabriel ran on regardless; it was all he could do. Then he felt the first bayonet slice into his leg, a slashing, tearing stroke that severed the big rectus femoris muscle in the middle of his thigh. He crashed to the ground, squirming and rolling over and over to avoid the pronging, skewering blades. They missed once or twice but they eventually got him. He saw the bayonet coming as he spun round. Watched it spear through his tunic. Felt an icy coldness which wasn't really painful travel the length of his coiled intestines. He saw the blade withdraw, with a squirt of his own dark blood, looked up in horrified disbelief as another man stepped into place for his turn, felt his mouth fill with hot, salty blood. He wriggled desperately in an attempt to get out of the way, saw the second blade slice in just above his hip bone, glancing inward off the pelvis, feeling the rasp and judder of the point on the bone. He thought he heard faint cries of *"Halt!"*

And that was all.

CHAPTER SEVEN

6 NOVEMBER 1914

Tanga · German East Africa

"The North Lancs put up a good fight. So did some of the Kashmir Rifles," Von Bishop heard Hammerstein say to the English officer Bilderbeck. Hammerstein was Von Lettow's chief of staff. They were all riding on mules towards Ras Kasone, two days after the battle. Hammerstein spoke just as they were passing a burial party heaving British corpses onto a wagon. It seemed, Von Bishop thought, a tactless thing to say. But Bilderbeck appeared not in the least put out.

"Thank goodness," he said. "At least someone did." He gave a cackle of laughter. Hammerstein exchanged a covert glance with Von Bishop.

It was half past nine in the morning. The day was growing hot and humid. Bilderbeck was the officer sent by the British to supervise the removal of the wounded and to hand over the large quantities of abandoned stores. Von Bishop rode a few paces behind him and Hammerstein, who were chatting away about the war like old friends. Hammerstein's English, Von Bishop had to admit, was really of quite a high standard.

Von Bishop took off his peaked cap and shook his head. On the afternoon of the fourth, shortly after the *Schutztruppe* had driven the British out of Tanga, the battleship *Fox* had bombarded the town for half an hour, doing great damage. Von Bishop had been knocked senseless for a few minutes when a six-inch shell exploded nearby. He had suffered only mild concussion but it had left him with a high-pitched singing sound in his ears, soft but persistent, and it refused to go away. This morning he had bent down, placed his hands on his knees and had shaken his head to and fro so severely that he had fallen over from the effort. But still it remained: a quiet *eeeeeeee* going on in the background.

He looked at the thick undergrowth in the coconut groves on either side of the road and thought it little wonder that the British had taken so long to attack. He himself had arrived by rail from Moshi shortly after noon on the fourth and had ordered his company of askaris into the attack on the British left flank against the Indian troops of the 101st Grenadiers. It had been exhilarating to see the machine guns cut down the advancing troops and then to follow in with the charge. That exhilaration had been sustained throughout the day as the British had been routed, until the unfortunate incident with the exploding shell. Now all he could think about was this noise in his ear. *Eeeeeeeee.* It was driving him mad.

Soon they emerged from the coconut groves and into the trampled open spaces above the beaches. The British fleet lay at anchor about a quarter of a mile offshore, tugboats, launches and lighters plying to and fro between the transports. The red house had been converted into a hospital and was full of British wounded. They were to be evacuated to the fleet under conditions of parole: namely, that none of them would serve again for the duration of the war.

Von Bishop let Hammerstein and Bilderbeck go into the red house to administer the parole. He left the mules with the askari guard and walked over to the headland to get a better view of the

English ships. There was a pleasant breeze blowing off the sea and he allowed himself to experience the complacent satisfactions of a victor as he surveyed the vast piles of abandoned stores stacked among the mangroves on the beach. Sixteen machine guns, someone had said, half a million rounds of ammunition—even new motor bikes—all left behind by the British when they hastily re-embarked yesterday morning.

However, Von Bishop was extremely surprised to see a British officer, clipboard in hand, emerge from behind a pile of packing cases. Hurriedly Von Bishop ran down to the beach. The man, who was a major, looked up casually as he approached.

"Hello there," the major said.

"Who the hell are you?" Von Bishop said excitedly. "And what the hell do you think you're doing here?"

The major, an elderly man, was very neatly dressed in gleaming Sam Browne and riding boots. He had curious sagging, fleshy cheeks which trembled when he spoke.

"The name's Dobbs," he said, a little nervously now, as if he sensed he shouldn't be where he was. "Quartermaster General, Expeditionary Force. I'm making an inventory of all these stores we're handing over. For my records," he added plaintively. "I've got to make a report, you see."

"But this is ridiculous!" Von Bishop said, waving his arms about. "Stay here!" He ran back to the red house, past the long lines of stretcher cases that were now being taken down to lighters on the beach. Von Bishop reported the matter to Bilderbeck, who rolled his eyes in exasperation and accompanied him back down to the beach.

"Quite extraordinary," Von Bishop explained to Hammerstein, who'd strolled down to join them. "The man was just walking around, calmly making notes."

Bilderbeck apologised to Hammerstein and ordered Dobbs to get off the beach and back to the fleet at once.

Hammerstein shook his finger at the very red-faced Dobbs. "No flag of truce," he chided. "By rights you should be taken prisoner." Dobbs hung his head and meekly went to board one of the lighters.

Hammerstein took out some cheroots and passed them round.

They stood smoking on the beach watching the wounded being loaded on board the lighters. This job was nearly complete when Hammerstein spotted two lifeboats full of men rowing into shore from one of the transports. The boats grounded a little way down the beach and the men on board took off their clothes, jumped into the shallows and began to swim and splash about in the surf. Some of them had cakes of soap and began to wash themselves.

"Look, I'm dreadfully sorry," Bilderbeck said. "I don't know what they think they're playing at." He ran down to the boats. "Who's in charge here?" he called angrily.

A very white naked man sloshed out of the water and saluted. "Sergeant Althorpe, sir. Loyal North Lancs. Ablutions detail, sir."

Hammerstein and Von Bishop joined the group. "I really must protest, Bilderbeck," Hammerstein said suavely, flicking his cheroot stub into the sea. "If they don't go back at once I shall have to order my men to open fire. Really, you know, this is a war. It's not some kind of sporting event."

Bilderbeck, looking—Von Bishop thought—extremely ashamed, ordered the men back to the transports. The naked men complied, but with extreme reluctance. There was much resentful muttering, and as the two lifeboats pulled away from the shore, Von Bishop heard foul insults being shouted at them.

Once the last of the wounded men had been taken offshore, Hammerstein invited Bilderbeck for breakfast at the German hospital. They rode back through the hot and steamy forest to the large white building of the hospital. The fighting had raged round this building during the battle on the fourth, and for most of the day it had been behind British lines, sheltering wounded from both sides. The imposing stone building was set in its own beautifully laid-out park of gravel pathways and low clipped hedges. Wooden benches were set in the shade cast by two huge baobab trees.

On the ground floor was a wide verandah where a long, linen-covered table was laid and where they all enjoyed breakfast in the company of Dr. Deppe, the senior physician, and some other *Schutztruppe* officers. They had iced beer, eggs, cream and asparagus, and talked amicably about the previous days' battles, trying to work out if Bilderbeck had been opposite any of them during the fighting. Von Bishop remained silent; he wasn't entirely sure if he approved of this sort of fraternisation. After all, wasn't it exactly the sort of thing Hammerstein was criticising on the beach? Von Bishop had his reservations about Hammerstein, too, even more so when he saw him exchanging addresses with Bilderbeck, promising to get in touch after the war.

Hammerstein eventually took his leave and asked Von Bishop to see Bilderbeck to his boat (moored by the shore just below the hospital) when he was ready. Von Bishop didn't hear at first, as he had his little fingers thrust down both ear holes in an attempt to alter the pressure in his inner ear. A whispered consultation with Dr. Deppe had produced this as a possible diagnosis of the irritating whine.

Bilderbeck, however, didn't want to leave before seeing those British officers and soldiers in the hospital who were too seriously wounded to be moved.

"Come up to the wards," Deppe invited. "You too, Major von Bishop. I can have a look in your ear."

"What's wrong with your ear?" Bilderbeck inquired with a wide smile.

"I've got a whine. *Eeeeeee*. You know, going on all the time in my ears." He found the man's mannerisms most strange. It was nothing to smile about.

"Pour some oil down them," Bilderbeck advised, now narrowing his eyes suspiciously, as if he suspected Von Bishop of malingering.

They arrived at the ward. It was on the first floor, very high-ceilinged with large French windows giving onto a generous balcony. Everyone in the beds was lying ominously still. Many bandaged limbs were in evidence and nobody spoke except in whispers.

Deppe handed Bilderbeck a list of names which Bilderbeck began to copy down.

"Let me look in your ears," Deppe said to Von Bishop and shoved the cold snout of an auriscope into the nearest moaning orifice. Von Bishop winced.

"Ah," said Deppe. "Um. Ah-ha. Yes, I can see nothing."

Bilderbeck interrupted. "Captain Cobb," he said to Dr. Deppe, pointing to a name on the list. "How is he?"

Deppe looked at the list. "Captain Cobb. Oh, yes. Very bad. Two bayonet wounds in the lower abdomen. And a severely injured leg. In that bed over there."

Deppe inserted his instrument in the other ear. Out of the corner of his eye Von Bishop watched Bilderbeck go over to a bed and speak to the injured man lying in it.

"See anything?" Von Bishop asked Deppe, who was now making clicking noises with his tongue.

"Your ears are full of wax," Deppe said. "I can't see anything. Come back tomorrow and I'll clean them out. Maybe I can get a better view."

Von Bishop walked with Bilderbeck down to the small launch that was moored at the jetty below the hospital. Four very bored naval ratings were sitting in the stern smoking, oblivious of the two German askaris that stood guard over them.

"Goodbye," Bilderbeck said, and shook hands. He grinned.

"Goodbye," said Von Bishop, annoyed to find that he'd smiled back. He watched the launch pull away. He tugged at his right ear lobe. That fool Deppe's probing seemed to have made the whine go up a tone or two. He had no intention of allowing the man to clean out his ears. He would ask Liesl to have a look; after all, he thought, she used to be a nurse, she might as well put her training to some use.

He walked thoughtfully back to Tanga thinking of his wife. The trip to Europe had been a great mistake. She had changed utterly, in almost every respect, and what was worse, she seemed to be in a permanent bad mood. She was getting so fat, too. All she wanted to do was eat. As he had boarded the train in Moshi, fully armed, off to repel an enemy invasion, she had kissed him briefly goodbye and made him promise to buy her some Turkish Delight in Tanga.

"Tanga!" He had forced a laugh, extremely irritated. "It may be a smoking ruin for all we know. And you want me to buy you sweets."

"Promise," she said. "Try to get some."

He had eyed her broadening figure, the well-padded shoulders, the horizontal creases in her neck, the freckled creaminess of her cheeks. He found it almost impossible to imagine her as she had been before: tall and lean from the hard work they put in on the farm.

"Don't you think you had . . . ?" he began, then thought better of it. "As you wish, my dear," he said.

Now he shrugged his shoulders in resignation as he strolled through the mined town, kicking at a stone, trying to ignore the noise in his head. Where would he get Turkish Delight in Tanga?

CHAPTER EIGHT

16 MARCH 1915

Oxford · England

The first thing Felix remembered when he woke up was that he'd failed Pass Moderations in History. He turned over in his narrow bed and looked at the gap of sky he could see between his badly drawn curtains. Dark. And the pattering on the window told him that Oxford was experiencing its fifth day of continuous rain. He turned on his side and looked up at his De Reske poster, which he'd had framed and now hung on the wall in his bedder.

"Morning, darling," he said, as he had done on waking each day of his two terms at Oxford. Holland didn't approve of the De Reske poster. Well, that was one thing he was not going to abandon for Holland.

"Morning, darling," he said again, stretching. "Tipping down as usual."

"Morning, sir," came an unexpected reply from his sitter—the sitting room that made up his quarters in college. The voice was loud and possessed of a rich Oxfordshire burr. It belonged to Sproat, his scout. Felix heard the rattle of cutlery as Sproat laid out his breakfast on the table. He heard the sitting room door open and there was a dull watery clang as his tin bath, containing two inches of water and lugged up three flights of stairs by Sproat's boy Algy, was set down.

"Get that foyr lit, Algy," Felix heard Sproat say, then louder: "Foyr blazin' in a minute or two, sir. Eight o'clock now. First chapel at half past the hour. If you've a mind, that is."

"Thank you, Sproat," Felix shouted. He and Sproat hated each other, a feeling no less intense on Sproat's side than Felix's. What he couldn't understand was the way Sproat contrived to see as much of him as possible. He had a whole staircase of rooms to attend to but somehow he seemed to organise his rota so as to spend most of his time with Felix.

Felix got out of bed, put on his slippers and pulled on his dressing-gown. He went over to the window. It was still dark, the rising sun making little impact on the thick, pewtery clouds. His bedder window looked onto the kitchen of a neighbouring college. He saw a kitchen skivvy dash out and empty a pail of slops into a dustbin. Felix drew the curtains closed. Time to face Sproat. He went into his sitter.

"Morning, sir," said Sproat again, smiling broadly. His servility was his most effective goad. He was a thin, balding man with wispy gingery hair. He had very large teeth, like a horse's, with prodigious gaps. These were now on display between parted lips. For some reason the sight of Sproat's teeth each morning removed Felix's appetite for breakfast. He looked out of the sitter window at the sodden college quad. He saw a dressing-gowned figure holding an umbrella dash across from a stairway entrance towards the college lavatories.

"Morning," Felix said. "Morning, Algy," he added automatically. Algy was crouched in front of the recently made-up fire, holding a sheet of newspaper over the chimney in an attempt to get the fire to take. He was reputed to be Sproat's son, a spindly, taciturn lad about twelve years old with a permanent cold. He never spoke in Felix's hearing, and Felix suspected that Algy had sent him to Coventry. The boy had only uttered one question in Felix's two terms. One morning he'd said, in Sproat's absence, "Woi in't you fightig, zur?" and received a cuff about the ears for his insolence. On the chimney-piece Felix had a small vase, pointedly displaying the five white feathers the good ladies of Oxford had seen fit to present him with over the weeks. Holland had been handed only two and professed himself extremely jealous.

Sproat, however, had no such qualms about conversing. "Doesn't seem much better this morning, sir," he said.

Felix glanced out of the window. "Typical March weather," he said.

"Oh, no. I wasn't talking about the weather, sir. I was meaning your sore, sir."

Felix's hand leapt up to the corner of his mouth. He winced. He had a large cold sore on his bottom lip, about the size of a sixpence. It had started off on the bottom left-hand corner of his lower lip. An itch, then a blister, then a crop of blisters that soon spread onto the skin below. These had burst, crusted and formed a scab which never seemed to heal. He'd had it for over two months. It had sprung up within days of the news of Gabriel's capture. No matter how dutifully he applied lotions and ointments and resisted the urge to pick at it, it refused to disappear.

"Seems to 've had some kind of suppurations in the night," Sproat observed, rising on his toes and leaning forward to get a closer look. "Some sort of transparent oozings, I would say."

"Would you, Sproat," Felix said, and went immediately back to his bedder to confirm this diagnosis in his looking-glass. Sproat was right. Felix now recalled that he'd spent a troubled, restless night after drinking a great deal of whisky punch in Holland's rooms.

The dark crust had broken and now gleamed with fissures of fresh blood. The furze of bristles that surrounded it—Felix had to be careful while shaving—made it seem even more of a disfigurement.

"I've got a friend who swears by this lotion, sir," Sproat called through the door. "Says he could get it for me cheap, like. Round about two shillings for a small bot—"

"No, thank you, Sproat," Felix interrupted firmly. The man had persistently cheated him since the day Felix had arrived in Oxford—hence their enmity, though it was now fuelled by every potential disagreement. Sproat had sold him a commoner's cap and gown, "new" curtains, fire-irons, a dozen sporting prints and a kettle within ten minutes of showing a nervous Felix up to his rooms, and all at vastly inflated prices. Furthermore, he claimed to be on especially good terms with certain Oxford tradesmen who would grant Felix a discount if he did all his ordering through Sproat. Felix bought a thousand cigarettes, a case of claret and one of hock, tea, jam, tobacco and half a dozen pipes before he'd grown wise. The ensuing row, bitter accusations and wounded protestations of innocence had soured things irreparably. Felix's Fabian leanings would not allow him to prosecute Sproat any further, but he counted it sufficient punishment to let Sproat—a devout Tory—know that in future he would be supplying himself from the new co-operative stores in the High Street. Sproat, though, had ardently sustained the feud and derived great satisfaction from any discomforts that came Felix's way—gatings, JCR fines, poor academic performance and the like. The cold sore had been like a gift from the gods.

"No, thank you, Sproat," Felix repeated as he walked back into the sitter, a false smile on his face. The fire was now lit and burning and a large brown kettle had been placed on the hob to boil up water for his bath and his teapot. Felix lifted the tin cover from the plate that contained his breakfast and saw two gelid, rapidly cooling poached eggs on a piece of toast.

Sproat removed a copy of the *Oxford Magazine* from his jacket pocket. Felix pinched the bridge of his nose. Here was another Sproat torment: the "butcher's bill," as Holland termed it. Pointed reproach directed at Felix in the guise of pious reminiscence.

"Bad weeks, sir," Sproat said, opening his magazine. "Harold Albert Talbot. Exhibitioner of the college. Nice chap. Quick, thoughtful sort of person. Died of wounds at a place called Neuve Chapelle." Sproat shook his head sadly. There was nothing Felix could do; to interrupt the college roll of honour would be playing into Sproat's hands, the ultimate sacrilege. He nodded in commiseration.

Sproat read on. "Noel Muschamp. Dear dear dear. Died in an accident at the aviation school. Fine man, fine man. Staircase six. Lord, here's another. Thomas Percy Gruby. Rowed in the First Eight in 1904 if I'm not mistaken. Got a fourth in Literae Humaniores . . ."

Sproat continued. Felix sat and listened and felt the depression settle securely on him. Sproat closed his magazine.

"Well, sir," he said, not bothering to conceal the note of triumph in his voice. "If that'll be all?" He left.

Felix opened his coffee jar and found it empty, so contented himself with a pot of tea. He looked distastefully at the two inches of water in the tin hip-bath and decided to forgo the dubious pleasures of a wash this morning. He stood at the window with his cup of tea and looked down on the deserted quad. In a normal term of a normal year it would have been full of bustling figures on their way to lectures or off to breakfasts with friends, but due to the war the college was now half-empty, and even those numbers had been supplemented by men from other colleges which were being used as temporary barracks for various army units of yeomanry and territorials.

Felix sat down in front of his staring poached eggs and blinded one with an aggressive stab of his knife. The wound in the congealed yolk reminded him of his cold sore and he felt the familiar sensations of what he now termed his Oxford mood descend on him.

Oxford had been a terrible disappointment. It wasn't so much Oxford's fault, though, as the war's. By the beginning of the first term two thousand undergraduates had volunteered for service. Felix and Holland—both turned down at the OTC recruiting office, Felix for his weak eyes, Holland for chronic myopia and a bronchitic chest—had arrived to find a university filled only with the very young, old or infirm. Life went on, lectures were taken, exams were sat, but there was no trace of the spirit they expected to find. It was made worse at the turn of the year when a black-out was imposed and all the bells in the clock towers were silenced after dark. Only a few dim red lights glowed at important junctions. If

Holland hadn't been there, Felix was sure he would have revolunteered out of a sense of sheer self-pity and disillusionment.

Holland was disappointed with Oxford, too, but it didn't affect him so badly. The war would be over in a matter of months, he said. The European powers simply couldn't afford to fight on any longer; economists had established this. They had done their duty in volunteering; it wasn't their fault if they weren't required. They should make the best of the opportunities Oxford presented. In the first term Holland had formed a group called *Les Invalides,* consisting of himself, Felix, Taubmann—another consumptive—and two of the more agreeable American Rhodes scholars. They met once a week to discuss anything that was unconnected with the war. But despite the energetic debates on futurism, emancipation of women, the Ballet Russe and Strindberg (Holland's new idol) and the copious amounts of alcohol they consumed, it was clear that all their efforts amounted to little more than a despairing gesture.

Then had come the news of Gabriel's capture. First a telegram with black borders saying he was missing in action. This had thrown the entire household into total hysteria, Cressida told him later. Happily, it was swiftly followed by a cancelling telegram. A state of ignorance persisted for a further ten days before the news came that Gabriel had been taken prisoner. Henry Hyams, through his connections at the War Office, managed to ascertain that Gabriel was in fact in a German hospital. During the Christmas vacation a letter arrived from one Major Bilderbeck GSO II (Intelligence), informing them in minute and immaculate handwriting that Gabriel had been severely bayonetted in the abdomen and would have to spend many months under intense medical care if he was to pull through. There was something about the tone of the letter that convinced everyone at Stackpole that it contained nothing but the truth: no hopes raised, none dashed. At least they knew Gabriel was alive (just) and where he was. But for some reason, discovering the details of Gabriel's plight had an adverse effect on the major. His shock at what he thought was the death of his son was transformed by the news of his wounds into a bleak despair, rather than relief. Life in the house became well-nigh intolerable. Many sullen and poisonous looks were directed at Felix, as if he were somehow responsible for Gabriel's dreadful plight.

As a result Felix had chosen voluntarily to return to Oxford a week before the start of term, and there he'd paced the damp January streets in a mood of some depression himself. One morning he numbly accepted two white feathers from a group of stern old ladies in the High without even a glance. He found himself standing some ten minutes later in the Botanic Gardens looking moodily at the swollen brown river, the white feathers still clutched in his hand as if he were posing for some late Victorian painting entitled "A Coward's Remorse." An old gardener had woken him from his dream when he edged up and reassuringly said, "Don't you go minding them daft women, sir."

Holland's return had boosted his spirits, but by then the cold sore had fastened its mysterious but implacable grip upon his face. However, this term Holland seemed less preoccupied with Oxford life, as his London one had acquired a new dimension in the shape of a "mistress." She was, according to Holland, an artist's model, a *morphineuse* in addition, and someone who made his life hell. She didn't give a damn for polite society, Holland said, and he was writing some excellent poetry.

With a sigh Felix pushed away his untasted poached eggs. Nothing in his life was going as planned; all his hopes of the past summer had proved vain and ephemeral. University was boring and lifeless, Gabriel was at death's door in an enemy hospital, the girl he loved didn't care for him, he was heavily in debt, he had no interest in his studies, he had failed his exams, his family regarded him as a subversive malingerer and his face was disfigured by a loathsome suppurating ulcer.

Dwelling on these misfortunes in turn, Felix slowly got dressed. He had a tutorial at ten with Jock Illiffe, his tutor, an ancient and decrepit don whose rooms were unbearably overheated and stank of cat. There were two of these creatures, fat and fluffy, who had scattered their hairs over every seat and cushion in the room. One week, as an experiment, Felix read to the dozing Illiffe, and the cat that warmed his lap, the same essay he'd declaimed the week before. As on the prior occasion, when Felix had finished reading

Illiffe had opened his eyes, leant back and said, "Well, yes, that seems pretty much to be the ticket."

Felix still had half a translation to do for the morning's tutorial but decided there and then that he was going to cut it. Illiffe only realised he was due to take a tutorial if the tutee actually went to the trouble of presenting himself. It was the sole blessing that the war had conferred, Felix admitted: the college had become very slack. It was not difficult to ignore the innumerable petty regulations that cluttered up and interfered with one's life.

What should he do then? There was a leccer—he corrected himself—*lecture* in All Soul's. Holland deplored Oxford slang. He had ridiculed Felix one day when he'd inadvertently talked about going to a debate in the Ugger, as the Union was commonly known. But the lecture was as unappealing as Illiffe's tutorial. He could read a novel in the Junior Common Room? Very dull. He'd been doing that all term anyway. What about a walk? Up the Banbury Road to Marston. There was a barmaid there in a pub who had caught his and Holland's eye the other week. But no, it was still raining. Perhaps he could go and stare at the nurses who were billeted in Merton? Perhaps he should pack up his gear? Term ended the day after tomorrow. This thought depressed him even further. Reading between the lines of his mother's regular letters, it seemed that his father was taking Gabriel's capture very hard indeed. God alone knew what kind of Easter vac he would have.

He belted his overcoat and stood undecided at his door. He walked slowly down the staircase. On the first landing a voice called out. "Hey, Cobb. Hang on a tick. Want a word." Felix waited outside the room from where the summons had issued. It belonged to a man called Cave-Bruce-Cave, who had joined up immediately war was declared and had his left hand blown off within hours of arriving in France. Reluctantly he'd returned to Oxford to complete his degree. Cave, as he was known for convenience's sake, was a large fresh-faced man who, with limited resources, did his utmost to preserve the atmosphere of mindless ragging and frivolous high jinks that had thrived in Oxford's pre-war days. His missing hand had been replaced by a crude wooden one, and his favourite trick was to set fire to it in restaurants.

"Yes, Cave," Felix said.

"Look what I've got," Cave said. On his table was a wire cage containing what looked like half a dozen rats squirming and cheeping.

"Rats," Felix said. "So what?"

"Rat hunt, Cobby. Bit of fun for the end of term. Let 'em loose in the quad and hunt them down with hockey sticks. I've got some of the chaps from the OTC coming over. Fancy a bash?"

"No, thanks," Felix said. "I'm busy."

"Oh. Where are you off to?"

"Going to see Holland," Felix improvised.

"Great stuff. Can I come along too?"

"No," Felix said. Holland liked to use Cave as butt and victim of his jokes. Cave seemed to enjoy being teased by him. "See you later."

He stepped out of the college doorway and wandered down to Broad Street. The rain had stopped but it was a cold, raw day. At the cab stand in the middle of the Broad the cab horses stood with heads bowed and manes dripping. The small wooden stand was covered in posters. IF YOU CANNOT JOIN THE ARMY TRY AND GET A RECRUIT. Felix felt a guilty unease which he knew Holland would scoff at. He agreed with Holland's views on the war; he just didn't have his single-minded conviction about them. In the past he had found that a strong belief in something had proved no impediment to a sudden recantation if and when it proved more convenient. It wasn't his fault that the army was being so fussy. He only had a slight astigmatism in one eye that manifested itself whenever he was tired or read for more than ten minutes without the aid of his glasses. Hardly a major disability, but it was enough to disqualify him. He had done his duty but he still felt his family's suspicion: his father's hatred—it wasn't too strong a word—and the doubt of his brothers-in-law.

He turned morosely away and walked back up the Turl. The earth that was regularly strewn over Oxford's paved streets had, over the last few sodden days, turned into a fluid mud that spattered up the back of his trouser legs as he walked. He turned left into Brasenose Lane and thrust his hands deep into his pockets as he moved down the narrow alleyway between Brasenose and Exeter colleges. At the bottom lay Radcliffe Square, the squat bulk of the Camera guarded by its high, spiked iron railings. Felix crossed the square and came to the High. By now the street was busy with horse-drawn drays and carts serving the shops. The gutters ran with frothy brown water; the road was covered in two inches of mud. Felix picked his way carefully across it and went down another alley to the rear gate of Christ Church, to which college Holland had been recently moved, since his own had been occupied by officer cadets. As it was, half of Christ Church had been given over to a battalion of Oxford yeomanry. Felix passed through the gate and into Peckwater quad. Like almost all of Oxford's buildings, the stone was now black and scrofulous with crumbling decay. The steady rain and the dark clouds heightened the impression: the colleges looked as if they were suffering from some particularly unpleasant wasting disease. Felix looked up to the top windows. The light was on in Holland's room. Uniformed soldiers seemed to be everywhere.

Felix knocked and walked into Holland's rooms. They had been stripped of all decoration, a new purity and austerity which Holland thought better suited his character. The wooden panelling on the walls had been painted white, on the floor was a plain grey carpet, and the settee and armchairs were covered in black cretonne. At the window overlooking the quad stood a baby grand piano on which was set a bowl of narcissi—the room's sole decorative touch—on the point of coming into bloom. Here Holland sat picking out a tune from the score propped in front of him. He waved Felix to a chair.

Since coming up to Oxford, Holland had grown a small Van-dyke beard and exchanged his gold-rimmed, almond-shaped spectacles for a pair of the fashionable new tortoise-shell ones. This had the effect—deliberately sought—of removing his air of boyish absent-mindedness and replacing it with a strong sense of a formidable, uncompromising intellect.

Felix watched him struggling with the score. Holland was, without doubt, the most remarkable person he'd met. Felix reminded himself of this fact regularly, as Holland's edicts and advice had such a heavy, and usually infelicitous, influence on his own life;

there had to be a good reason, he thought, why he so persistently got himself into trouble by following them.

"On the table," Holland called, not looking up from his music. "What do you think?"

Felix went to the table and glanced through the pile of papers scattered there. He looked at the title-page: "After Strindberg: whither the English stage?" It was evidently for *The Mask*, a quarterly magazine on the theatre to which Holland had recently begun contributing: another accomplishment Felix envied him. He pretended to read the article, but he didn't feel like concentrating on Strindberg this morning.

"Jolly good," he said.

Holland's sway over Felix had been established in their final year at school, and Felix had accepted it with the zeal of a disciple acknowledging the messiah. It gave him a vital focus and expression for his own half-thought rebellious instincts and discontents, but he had come to realise, even while they were at school together, that he did not want to emulate Holland. In fact he had no great desire to be like Holland at all. What he really envied about his friend was his home life, its almost unbelievable difference to his own: the social circles Holland's family moved in, the exciting freedoms and opportunities that didn't have to be secretly fought for but which were rather served up to him on a plate, almost as if they were his birthright, and not seen, as they were *chez* Cobb, as depraved and seditious habits.

Holland's father was an illustrator, a corpulent and lazy man whose talents were sought by magazines like *Nash's*, *The Strand*, *Pall Mall* and *Vanity Fair*. They lived in Hampstead in a large untidy house which was always full of the most interesting people, old and young, of very "advanced" views, mainly belonging to the literary and artistic worlds.

There was another reason why Felix allowed himself to be dominated by Holland: his sister, Amory. Felix was in love with Amory, passionately in love. As far as he knew, he was the only person who was aware of this fact. Not even Amory, he was sure, guessed at the ardour she had prompted. She was twenty years old, an art student. She had a thin face and a slim, bony body. But it wasn't so much her appearance that attracted Felix as her opinions: she was very modern. She shared a small flat with a girl-friend, she smoked, she drank alcohol (Felix had seen her do both—under the eyes of her parents!), there seemed to be a distinct possibility that Amory would be modern enough to take a lover. Sex no longer existed in some vague, unrealisable, dreamlike state. Amory was the first girl he'd met, the first he could claim to know, with whom it became a potentiality, something tantalisingly feasible.

Holland crashed a discord on the piano. "Damn Dohnányi," he said and closed the lid. "Did the militarists bother you, Felix?"

"No," Felix said. "I think they're used to me by now. I'm not interrupting, am I, Philip?"

Holland had decreed that on entering university they should abandon the public-school habit of addressing each other by their surnames. However, "Philip" still sounded uneasy on Felix's tongue.

"I was bored rigid," he said. "I cut Jock's tutorial; couldn't stand the thought. I wondered if you felt like a walk."

"Why not?" Holland said. "Marston? Shall we oblige the wench with our presence at luncheon?"

Holland put on his overcoat, selected a walking stick, and they set off. Back to the High Street, along Cornmarket and into the broad but lopsided avenue of St. Giles—young plane trees on the left, fully grown elms on the right. As if to compensate, the plane-tree side was balanced with row upon row of parked army lorries.

Holland took off his glasses. He was almost blind without them but hoped that by displaying no obvious infirmity he might attract accusations of cowardice from passers-by. This did occasionally happen and gave Holland an unrivalled opportunity for a violent exchange of views. Felix, on his own, often went to the other extreme, wearing his glasses all the time, sometimes slipping a pebble in a shoe to promote a bad limp. When he passed through London he often wore a black eye-patch, to place his non-combatant status above question, or else a silk mourning band on his sleeve, another useful way of avoiding embarrassing remarks. Holland, of course, remained ignorant of these ploys.

"Cave-Bruce-Cave is organising a rat hunt in the quad this afternoon," Felix said. "He invited me to join in."

Holland laughed. "He's priceless, that man. He'll be debagging you next or ragging your rooms. Shall we have him round for tea?"

"Let's not," Felix said. "I don't think I'm up to Cave today."

They walked on up the Banbury Road. The horse chestnuts showed some tiny green buds but it still could have been the middle of winter. There were few people out on the road, so Holland put his glasses back on.

"Thank God for the vac," Holland said. "I can't wait to get back to London." This gave rise to talk about Enid, Holland's *morphineuse*. Holland was worried in case she was having an affair with the artist she was currently posing for. "In the nude," Holland added. "You can see it would be difficult to fight off any advances."

"Doesn't she mind?" Felix asked. "About, you know, taking her clothes off in front of a complete stranger?" Felix found it impossible to imagine how an artist could simply stand there calmly drawing or painting while a naked woman posed six or eight feet away.

"She gets paid for it, Felix," Holland reproached him. "It's her job."

"I know. But I still can't see . . ."

"My dear Felix"—Holland laughed a little patronisingly—"not everyone is as frustrated as you."

"Are you sure about that?" Felix replied sharply. Then he grinned. "No, perhaps not."

"It's a point, though." Holland frowned. "It's almost the done thing for an artist to have an affair with his model. Oh, yes," he said, "talking about artists, I got a note from Amory this morning." He withdrew a crumpled letter from his pocket. "Yes, she's having an exhibition at her art school and she's giving a little party, at her flat and then on to a club. Why don't you come along? Twenty-ninth of March. Come and stay. You've been bellyaching about your dreadful family. Come up to the bright lights—or rather, come up to the black-out."

Felix found it hard to imagine better news. It was remarkable how quickly the future could change. "Thank you, Philip," he said, his voice thick with gratitude. "I'd love to. In fact, it'll be wonderful. The twenty-ninth? Are you sure?"

"Of course. You can meet Enid."

A thought crossed Felix's mind, a glowing coal of a thought.

"Did, um, Amory, actually, you know, ask you to, to invite me? In particular, I mean?"

"What? Oh, no. No, she wrote to ask *me,* in fact. But don't worry. I'm sure she won't object if I bring a friend—she has met you before, after all, hasn't she?"

CHAPTER NINE

1 8 MARCH 1915

Stackpole Manor · Kent

Felix took off his eye-patch and stepped out onto the platform at Ashurst Station, blinking furiously in the weak early-afternoon sun. His compartment had contained two lieutenants and a major all the way down from Charing Cross and he'd had no opportunity to remove his disguise. He had also buried his head in a book to forestall any embarrassing questions (where and how was he injured?) and the effort of reading with one eye unaided by spectacles had given him a dull headache. He had heard, nonetheless, a lot of talk about a victory at Neuve Chapelle and yet again felt annoying stabs of guilt, until he assuaged them with some of Holland's arguments which had been directed at Cave-Bruce-Cave. "But surely," Cave had once said, "we're fighting for our freedom?"

"Wrong, my dear Cave," Holland had said. "We are fighting for our golf and our weekends. We went to war to prevent an

Austrian and German pacification of Serbia, that's all. The French allied themselves with Russia because they were terrified there would be a revolution and Russia would default on all the money they owe to France. Now we're fighting to keep a tyrannical Czar on his throne. Now you tell me. Are those causes worth dying for?"

Holland's logic seemed incontrovertible. Even Cave had gone off troubled and perplexed. Felix ran through the arguments again as he waited for his right eye to adjust to the unaccustomed light. He called a porter over.

"There's a cabin trunk in the guard's van. Would you get it for me, please?"

"Sorry, sir. I'm a parcel porter, sir. Can't fetch luggage."

Felix unloaded his trunk himself, then went in search of another porter who, when found, wheeled his trunk into the station yard. Felix had cabled the time of his arrival to his mother, but as usual, there was no one to meet him.

He had smoked three cigarettes before he recognised the Humberette turning into the yard. He was extremely surprised to see Charis at the wheel. She stopped the car and got out.

"Hello, Felix," she said cheerily. "I had to go into Sevenoaks and your mother asked me to collect you. I do hope you haven't been waiting long. Oh"—she pointed to the cigarette butts—"you have. I am sorry. Anyway, welcome home."

She put out her hand and leant forward automatically as if for a kiss. Felix took her hand, but hadn't thought of kissing her, or anybody, come to that, because of his cold sore, so held back for a moment. By the time he thought, really he should kiss her, she *was* family, and leant forward himself, she had withdrawn her face. They see-sawed this way for a brief while until their cheeks eventually brushed. Felix kissed mid-air and felt the touch of her lips on his ear. It made him shiver but he covered it up with a nervous laugh. They both got into the car with red faces, then got out again because they hadn't loaded the luggage. Felix found that the Humberette was too small to take everything and realised that he'd have to leave the cabin trunk.

"Don't worry," he said as he packed in his two suitcases.

"Leave the trunk here. I can pop back down to the station and pick it up later."

To his consternation he saw a look of intense grief cross Charis's face and her eyes fill with tears.

"Good Lord," he said, "what did I say?"

Charis rubbed her forehead. "No, it's silly me. You just reminded me of Gabriel then. Something you said. It was when we were in Trouville. I am sorry. I just can't help it. It happens all the time. People think I'm an awful noodle."

They got into the car, Felix taking the wheel, and drove off.

"Has there been any news?" Felix shouted over the noise of the engine. "About Gabriel?"

"No. But all his things have been sent back. They arrived last week. There's a letter for you." She paused. "I've got everything at the cottage. Would you like to come down and have tea later?" She shot a glance at him. "I wanted to ask you something. About Gabriel."

He could see she was about to go sad again. "Of course," he said quickly. "About half four?"

Charis's spirits picked up and she prattled on in what Felix recognised as her usual bright but fairly mindless way for the rest of the drive back to Stackpole. Felix dropped her at the cottage and drove on up to the house. The bare trees and the untended lawns and borders amplified the familiar depressing effect the sight of his home had on him. His mother had heard the car and came running to the front door and folded him in a powerful two-minute embrace.

They went into the hall, where he greeted Cressida. A boy whose face seemed vaguely familiar took his cases up to his room. They were walking down the passageway to the inner hall when a squat figure in a dressing-gown came hurrying towards them.

"Hello, Father," Felix said, offering his hand. "Good to see you. You're looking well." It wasn't true. His father's face was as sallow as ever, but the flesh seemed to have lost its firm rotundity and now hung from the bones. His side-whiskers were long and untrimmed, his dressing-gown carelessly tied. He looked like some demented Victorian cleric, Felix thought.

His father stared at him, ignoring his proffered hand. "I know your type," he said malevolently. "I suppose you think this is . . . this is some kind of *health spa!*" he shouted, and hurried on his way.

"What on earth is he on about?" Felix said, astonished, as his mother ushered him into the inner hall. "Is he all right?"

"He's been terribly upset, my darling. About poor Gabriel. I think it's to do with the nature of the wounds . . . you know. The bayonets seem to bother him awfully. Says he dreams about it—can't get it out of his mind. Anyway, here we are, home again." There was a huge fire roaring in the hearth. "Sit down, darling. Now, tell me. Are you well? What's that dreadful sore? Don't you think he looks a bit pale, Cressida? Darling, promise me you're eating properly."

Felix stepped over the eve-gate, crossed the bridge above the stream that led to the fish-ponds and set off through the beech wood towards the cottage. He carried a torch with him for the walk back. There was a gloomy, metallic quality to the late-afternoon light and a cold wind had sprung up that made the heavy branches sway and thrash above his head.

Charis opened the door and showed him in. The small sitting room had been nicely and neatly furnished, though there were rather too many bits of brass and pewter around for Felix's taste. There was a photograph of Gabriel in his uniform on the window ledge. Laid out along the settee as if for kit inspection were bundles of clothing, a pillow, a thermos flask, a collapsible canvas sink and other items that Felix recognised as belonging to Gabriel. The sight of these brought an unfamiliar pressure to his throat. The thought of Gabriel without these bits and pieces of his made whatever ordeal he was currently undergoing seem poignantly immediate.

"He left all this on board his troopship," Charis said. "I've not . . . I've not got anything that he actually had with him."

"I see," Felix said.

"Do sit down," Charis invited. Felix smiled at her. She was wearing an apple-green dress with a darker-green cardigan over it. She had a long string of pearls around her neck with a knot tied at the end. Her dark hair was held up loosely by a finely worked tortoise-shell comb. Felix sat down at the table on which the tea service was already laid out. Charis took a kettle from in front of the fire and set about making tea in a large silver teapot. She held it up.

"Wedding present," she said and gave a rueful smile.

Felix noticed a pile of letters beside her place. Presently Charis sat down and they drank their tea. Felix toasted some buns in front of the fire, and they ate them with thick strawberry jam. They chatted inconsequentially about this and that. Felix told her he'd failed Pass Moderations in History. Charis provided details of her work with Belgian refugees. Eventually she picked up the letters.

"Have a look at these, Felix," she said. "I don't mind. One of them is addressed to you. They were all loose sheets. None had been posted." She handed him the first sheet.

Felix took it. A pale-blue leaf of writing paper. The letter-head said SS *Homayun*. The date was the twenty-first of October 1914. He read.

> *Dear Felix,*
>
> *We are on our way! Do you remember our talks about the European war? I never thought I would be fighting on the "dark continent." I've been at sea for weeks. We had to sit sixteen days in harbour before the convoy sailed. Life on a troopship is extremely boring but I have become quite an expert at deck quoits!*
>
> *I was sorry to hear that your eyesight let you down with the OTC. Never mind! Keep trying. As the war in Europe progresses we are sure to need every "man jack." I hope to see you soon. We should sort everything out here by Xmas.*
>
> > *Love to all at Stackpole,*
> > *Your affec. bro.*
> > *Gabriel Cobb*

Felix felt unaccountably moved by this bland letter. He remembered Gabriel the day before his wedding, swimming in the willow pool. Felix kept his eye off the photograph. He forced a chuckle.

"Old Gabe wasn't exactly the world's greatest letter writer, was he?"

Charis didn't reply. She handed him the other sheets. Felix

accepted them with sudden misgivings. He had always made a point of not thinking of Gabriel and Charis as man and wife, had never speculated on the nature of their relationship. He wasn't sure if this invitation to share their privacy was something to be welcomed. There were a dozen sheets of paper, all from the *Homayun,* all undated.

> *My darling Charis,*
>   *Our ship is still in Bombay harbour. Sorry not to have written before but if*

That was all. Felix turned to the next.

> *Darling,*
>   *How I miss you! This war.*

And the next,

> *My darling darling Charissimus,*
>   *I do hope*

Felix quickly riffled through the others. They were all the same. The greeting, the beginnings of a line, and then blank. On one sheet the "g" of "darling" had been slashed down the length of the page.

"What do you think it means?" Charis asked quickly. "I wrote to him every day. I never had a single letter in reply."

Felix felt himself stiff with embarrassment. This was exactly what he wanted to avoid. He tried to be light-hearted.

"You know Gabriel. He . . . he probably couldn't express himself. He may have been terribly busy. You just can't tell."

"But he wrote to you. Your father had a letter. Sammy Hinshelwood got a postcard from Bombay. Why couldn't he write to me?"

"He wanted to, clearly," Felix said. "At least he *started* to write. He probably wasn't sure of—" To his alarm he saw Charis had covered her face with her hands. Her shoulders began to shake. Felix made a grimace. The stupid girl; she should have spoken to his mother about this, or Cressida. He had no idea what the proper procedure was on this sort of occasion. He rose from his seat. Hesitantly he placed his hands on Charis's shoulders. He felt them trembling and shivering beneath his palms, felt the hard line of her collar-bone on his fingertips. Now he was close to her he smelt the same odour of rose-water that he'd noticed at the wedding.

"There, there," he said, feeling foolish, wishing she'd stop sniffing. He noticed, almost absent-mindedly, the nacreous inlay on her hair-comb, the small mole in front of her right ear, the shininess of her fingernails.

"Gabriel wasn't the most articulate of people," he improvised. "He'd probably never given thought as to how to express his feelings—in written form," he added. "If you're going into battle and you're not used to organising your, your innermost thoughts on paper, that sort of letter can be, well . . ." He left the sentence unfinished. It was the best he could do at short notice.

Charis looked round at him. She wiped away a tear with a knuckle. "I'm sorry," she said more brightly. "I'd sworn I wouldn't cry." She sat up. Felix removed his hands from her shoulders and wondered, absurdly, what to do with them. He shoved them in his pockets and went over to the fire.

"Thank you, Felix," Charis said.

He spun round. "Oh. Nothing."

"You're right about Gabriel. That's what I thought too. But you know how it is: you need to hear it from someone else."

"Yes, quite." Felix looked down at his shoes. He wanted to squirm under the assault of her sincerity and gratitude. Why on earth should *he* know why Gabriel couldn't write? He couldn't even understand why he'd *married* this girl.

"He was extremely fond of you. *Is.* Is extremely fond of you," Charis said.

"I'd better be getting back," he said uncomfortably. Any talk like this about him and Gabriel stirred up his emotions. He found himself suddenly wondering what it must have been like for Gabriel. A bayonet. Bayonet wounds in the abdomen . . .

Charis saw him to the door. "I'll see you tomorrow probably," she said. "I'm always over for luncheon." She put her hand on his arm. "Thanks again, Felix. I've been so miserable, you know. I feel a bit better tonight."

"Ecclesiastes!" Major Cobb shouted. "Chapter six, verse twelve."

There was a rustle of paper as the assembled servants found their places in their Bibles. The major stood in front of a large map of Africa. Red and black pins faced each other across the borders of British and German East.

"'For who knoweth what is good for man in this life,'" the major called out in a clarion voice, his eyes fixed on the library ceiling. He obviously knew the text by heart. "'All the days of his vain life which he spendeth as a shadow?'" Here the small eyes descended and his gaze danced round the room. Felix pretended to be reading over his mother's shoulder. "'Spendeth as a shadow,'" the major repeated. "'For who can tell a man what shall be after him under the sun?'" As he read the last line the major's voice got simultaneously slower, deeper and harsher. Despite himself, Felix shivered. What a horrible old man, he thought.

"He's obsessed with this East Africa place and Gabriel," his mother had whispered as they filed into the library for morning prayers. "He's been like this for weeks now. He keeps reading the same lessons from Ecclesiastes and Job. The servants have complained to me, but there's no telling him."

"Let us pray," commanded the major.

Afterwards Felix went out into the garden for a walk to calm himself down. He'd only been back twenty-four hours and already he felt like leaving. Thank God, Amory's exhibition wasn't far away. He wondered how soon he could leave for London. Holland had said he should stay. Amory . . .

He walked down the avenue of pleached limes. They were looking a bit out of control, green twigs and new shoots springing up all over the place. He cut across the lawn towards the fish-ponds and met a small boy who was lugging a bucket of corn and breadcrumbs in the same direction. It was the same boy who had carried his cases up to his room when he arrived.

"Hello there," Felix said, trying to recall his name. His face was smooth, bullet-shaped.

"I remember you," Felix said. "You're Cyril's boy."

"Thas right, sir."

"What're you doing?"

"Feeding the carp, sir. In the ponds."

They walked down to the ponds together. The boy slung the grain out into the middle, and almost immediately the water began to boil as the heavy fish powered up from the depths to fight for the food.

"Some big ones there, eh?" Felix said. He smiled to himself. Fuckin giants, was the way Cyril had described them. Big fuckin beggars.

"Thas right, sir," the boy said.

"How's your Dad?" Felix asked, taking out a cigarette and lighting it.

"Oh, my Dad's dead, sir."

Felix felt the hairs on the back of his neck prickle. He dropped his cigarette and bent to pick it up. It was soaked from the dew in the grass. He threw it away.

"What happened?"

"Don't rightly know, sir. Killed in the war. For King and Country, my mam says. In France, like." He picked up the bucket and walked off back across the lawn to the kitchen.

Felix watched the big fish cruising slowly to and fro just below the surface, searching for any remaining grains.

"Hello." He heard a voice and looked round. It was Charis. "Just been fed, have they?" She looked up at the clouds. "Not much of a day. Where's the spring? That's what I want to know."

"Did you know Cyril was dead?"

"Cyril? Who's Cyril?"

"The gardener. Chauffeur at your wedding. Used to live in your cottage."

"Oh, yes. About a month ago, I think. Um, Arras. No. Ypres, wasn't it?"

"Why in God's name wasn't I told?" Felix exclaimed angrily. "He was a friend of mine."

He saw the look of surprise on her face. "Sorry," he said. "I've just found out. It's come as a shock." He shook his head in bitter disbelief. He apologised again. "Mother should have told me. But I expect she had a lot on her mind. Poor old Cyril. God, he was excited about going." He paused. "Is it all right if I smoke?"

Charis said yes and he lit another cigarette.

"Oh, God, God," Felix said, running his hand around the back of his neck. "Holland's right."

"Holland?"

"He's a friend. You remember? I stayed with him last summer."

"You were at school together."

"Yes." He turned away from the pond and they walked back up the ramp of lawn to the house. "I shall be seeing him soon, I'm glad to say. He's asked me up to London."

"Oh." Charis stopped walking.

"Is there something wrong?"

"Didn't your mother write to you? No, she couldn't have. It's my birthday on the twenty-ninth. She's having a dinner party for me, perhaps a little dance." She suddenly sounded very downcast.

"I, we, were expecting you'd be here. I think a lot of the family are coming." She looked him directly in the eye.

"Couldn't you postpone your visit to your friend?" she said. "Just until after the party?" She was making a direct appeal, he saw, and a personal one.

She had a nerve, he thought. He felt thoroughly uncomfortable. Why were people always forcing duties on him?

"We thought," Charis said, "that you could act as my partner. Gabriel not being—"

"I'm so sorry," Felix said firmly. "But I can't. I'm afraid it's impossible for me to change my plans."

CHAPTER TEN

29 MARCH 1915

The Café Royal · London

The Domino Room at the Café Royal was full to capacity. All the seats around the marble-topped tables were occupied. The babble of conversation was deafening. The rich gilt and plaster mouldings of the ceilings and pillars were almost invisible through swirling clouds of cigarette smoke. Condensation formed on the huge mirrors that lined the walls. A warm fug of beer, cheap perfume, wet overcoats and cigar smoke enfolded the excited patrons.

Felix leant back and puffed on his cigarette. He was trying to look extremely relaxed, but in reality he was entranced. He'd never seen so many *louche* women. Had never sat beside couples who embraced and caressed each other in public. Had never counted so many red lips and blackened eyes. The entire room seemed to tingle with the electric potentiality of sex.

"I can't think where Enid is," Holland said. "Look." He pointed out a tall man with a bushy beard and crumpled suit. "That's the artist chappie who's painting her." He shrugged. "Maybe she'll turn up at Amory's."

"This is an extraordinary place," Felix said. "Who are these women?"

"Oh, art students," Holland said nonchalantly. "Models, *quelques putains.*"

"Lord," breathed Felix. The night before they had been to a show at the Criterion. Coming out into Shaftesbury Avenue, Holland had pointed out, one by one, all the prostitutes wandering among the crowds of theatre-goers. They had counted more than three dozen by the time they reached the underground station at Piccadilly Circus. With an air of world-weary languor Holland told him about London's more notorious thoroughfares: the Strand and New Oxford Street commanded the highest prices, Bloomsbury and Charing Cross were distinctly less reliable, and as you went farther east, price and quality dwindled way to desperation level.

"Shall we go?" Holland suggested. They rose and edged their way out through the mass of bodies. After the heat and press of the café, the night air outside was deliciously cool and fresh. A fine drizzle was falling. The black-out made it hard to distinguish anything and at first all Felix was aware of was the astonishing noise of London's traffic.

A cab tout procured them a four-wheeler which took them down to the Embankment via Piccadilly Circus. The inside of the cab smelt of polish and old leather. Felix gazed out of the window—rubbing a face-sized porthole in the condensation—at the crowded streets.

The cab stopped outside a rather drab tenement in Cheyne Walk. Holland paid off the driver, and Felix stood on the pavement outside a grocer's shop. His cheeks felt hot and he held his face up to the cool spray of the drizzle, closing his eyes for a moment. His pulse seemed to be beating unreasonably fast and he wanted to make sure he was calm. He heard the clip-clop of horses' hooves as the cab moved away. He felt himself swaying and opened his eyes again, before he lost his balance. Perhaps the three brandies and water in the Café Royal had been a mistake. He touched his cheeks and forehead with the back of his hands. Still hot.

"Where's Amory's flat?" he asked Holland, who was wiping drops of rain from his spectacle lenses.

"Two up," he said. "Above the grocer's."

They went through the small door beside the shop. There were no lights on the stairs and there was a strong smell of apples and decaying vegetable rinds. They climbed up two flights. From behind a door they could hear the noise of conversation and what sounded like a guitar.

"Here we are," Holland said, and made to knock at the door.

"Just a second, Philip," Felix said, moving to the grimy landing window. "Over here." Holland came over. "What does my cold sore look like?" Felix asked, presenting his face to whatever faint light managed to sidle through the dirt and cobwebs on the window pane.

"It doesn't look too bad, does it? Not too obvious?" To his joy the sore showed some signs of clearing up. A dark and crusty scab had formed. At least it didn't look like some moist and repulsive canker, even though the scab had been a dominating feature in the looking-glass earlier that evening.

"Hardly see it," Holland said. Felix wasn't sure if this referred to the absence of illumination or the insignificance of the sore, but was happy to stay with the ambiguity; he couldn't afford to over-burden the frail raft of his confidence any further.

Holland knocked on the door. It was opened by a burly young man with a heavy pipe dragging down the corner of his mouth. "Ha, ha," he shouted over his shoulder. "*Le petit frère* has arri-vayed." Holland moved past him without a word; Felix bestowed a nervous half-smile.

Like the Café Royal, the small sitting room of the flat was crowded with people in a fog of cigarette smoke. Felix noticed a dangerously sagging ceiling blackened at one end with old soot from the fire. One window gave onto a view of untidy back lots. The other overlooked the Embankment gardens and the Chelsea Jelly Factory across a glimmering stretch of the Thames. The room was dark (Felix breathed a sigh of relief), lit only by a few candles. In a corner on a wooden chair was a girl with a guitar, with a small audience sitting raptly at her feet. Other shadowy people perched on a horsehair settle or leant against the walls and spoke to each other in very loud voices. An open door revealed a room with two beds which was occupied by the overflow from the sitting room. On a gate-legged table—half open—in front of the Thames window were a cut-glass punch-bowl, a basket of oranges, plates of nuts and a half-dozen straw-cupped flasks of Chianti. There was no sign of Amory.

Holland and Felix moved with some difficulty towards the table, stepping over legs, ducking between conversations.

"Chianti or punch?" Holland asked.

"Ooh. Chianti, please." Felix felt his eyes stinging from the smoke. He lit a cigarette and took a gulp of wine. It tasted harsh and vinegary.

"Hey! Filippo!" came a great shout. Felix whirled round in alarm. He saw Holland being embraced by a large, bearded man dressed entirely in black. Behind this person stood Amory. *Entirely naked.* The shock lasted a second or two until Felix realised she was wearing a skimpy dress of flesh-coloured tulle. Her brown hair was piled on top of her head in a complex fir-cone effect and secured by a thick jewel-studded ribbon. Her thin face was heavily powdered, her heavy-lidded eyes touched with kohl. Felix felt his legs tremble with desire, love and anticipation. The tulle dress hung from thin satiny straps, revealing a large expanse of her hard chest. Her bosom was noticeable by its absence, but Felix didn't care. It was those half-closed eyes that drove him wild, as though the effort of keeping them open was proving too much for her.

The dark, bearded fellow was still pounding Holland's back and uttering cries of "Hey!" "Wah!" and "Yes!" Amory brushed past him and refilled her glass with punch. She smiled at Felix.

"Hello," she said. "Have you come with Philip?"

"Yes, I—" Felix began but she had already turned away.

"Philip, I think it's most rude of you not to introduce your friends. Oh, do leave him alone, Pav."

Holland broke away from Pav's embrace. "This is Felix Cobb. But you've met him, Amory. And, Felix, this is Pavelienski something or other. The great artist. We all call him Pav."

"Wahey!" exclaimed the great artist and punched Holland in the arm.

"Hello, Pav," Felix said. He exhaled cigarette smoke in what he hoped was a firm, nonchalant-looking stream.

"Hello," he said to Amory. "We met last summer once or twice."

"Oh, yes?" Amory said, pouring more Chianti into his glass. "We did?" She moved away, summoned by a distant conversation. Felix gulped more Chianti. Pav accepted one of his cigarettes. The artist had long black hair and a thick beard with spirals of grey in it. And all the more revolting for that, Felix added to himself uncharitably. He sensed he was in the presence of his rival. He gazed at the wine in his glass. A single hair floated on the surface. He wondered if it was one of Amory's. He decided not to fish it out; he'd drink it down, digest this small particle of her being.

Pav made a sudden movement, a grab at Felix's face, and he flinched reflexively, his wine splashing over his sleeve, taking the hair with it.

Pav's extended fingers were inches from Felix's eyes, and the man was scrutinising him intently. He turned his hand to and fro, as if he were unscrewing the lid from a large jar.

"You hef a spendid sroat," he said in his heavily accented mid-European voice. "I am liking to draw it."

Felix shot a glance at Holland, but he was staring at other people in the room.

"Oh," Felix said, embarrassed. "Yes. Thank you very much."

"Look, there's Enid," Holland said. "Come and meet her, Felix."

Felix forced himself to be attentive. He had been speaking to Enid for the last half hour. He could safely say that the fabled *morphineuse* was one of the most boring people he'd ever met. Holland said she was twenty-eight but she looked at least a decade older. She was a small, broad woman with a great shelf of bosom and wild straw-dry black hair. She wore a jarring futurist dress and was draped with beads and jewels. Her face was haggard and her eyes were ringed with purple. Felix switched his attention back to the monologue.

". . . He's got mumps, believe it or not. Yes, he's got mumps. Terrible mumps. And he had a horrible discharging from one ear. *Horrible*. Eugh! One side of his face was all swollen from the mumps. . . ."

Felix looked distractedly about the room. Where had Holland and Amory got to? The guitar player had quite a singsong going— "My Little Grey Home in the West"—and consequently only a near shout ensured that one's half of a conversation was heard. Some of the guests actually had sketch-books out and were drawing each other. Perhaps Pav would like to attempt his throat this evening, Felix thought scornfully. But these were artists, he reminded himself; they weren't burdened with his self-consciousness.

"I must get some more wine," he shouted at Enid, and swiftly weaved his way through the packed room to the table. There was no Chianti left, so he moved on to the punch. He stood by one of the now opened windows and breathed in the night air. He leant against the wall and ran his fingers between his neck and his stiff collar. As far as he could make out, only he and Holland were wearing evening dress.

Beside him was the door into the bedroom. Some people were standing just inside it having a heated discussion. The singers were now giving a full-throated rendition of "Give Me Your Smile" and it was some time before Felix realised that the two speakers were Amory and Holland and that they were talking about him.

". . . he's *not* coming to the Calf," he heard Amory insist.

"He *has* to," Holland asserted plaintively. "I told him he could."

"Well, you jolly well should have told *me* first. I've got a table for sixteen. Where's he going to sit, for heaven's sake?"

"He can squeeze in," Holland said. "I can't tell him to go away."

"Oh, God! You and your wretched friends!"

Felix told himself he'd misheard the last remark. He launched himself off the wall and made straight for the punch-bowl. The final chorus of "Give Me Your Smile" was in full swing. Under such noisy conditions it wasn't surprising that your ears would play tricks on you, he reasoned. Anyway, he thought, as he drained a glass of punch, hostesses always panicked about seating arrangements, numbers and that sort of thing.

By the time they arrived at the Golden Calf, as he'd heard the night-club referred to, Felix was—he recognised—fairly seriously drunk. Unsteadily he handed over his coat, scarf and gloves in the tiny vestibule. He aimed himself at, and cautiously descended, three or four steps and looked about him. The dark cellar was filled with round tables at which people were eating late suppers. Waiters weaved to and fro with trays of food, ice buckets and bottles. At one end was a small dance floor in front of a low stage on which sat an immaculately turned-out Negro band. The ceiling was supported by huge white wooden caryatids carved in the shape of hawks, cats and serpents, with details—a tongue, a beak, eyes or scales—picked out in scarlet. The clientèle, though it contained many uniformed men, seemed raffishly elegant and lively. The atmosphere, to Felix's befuddled mind, oozed licence and vice.

Amory was greeted by a cadaverous-looking woman in a black fur coat, loosened to reveal pale shoulders and décolleté. The group was led through the cluttered tables to a pink alcove, a *cabinet particulier,* in which was set a large round table. Felix had been staring fascinatedly at the orchestra—he'd never seen so many Negroes grouped together before—and was the last to arrive. No place had been set for him and he stood smiling foolishly while one waiter fetched an extra chair and another set a new place between Enid and a young man in khaki uniform whom Felix had not met. He sat down. Amory and Pav were across the wide table from him. His arrival had caused everyone to be squeezed uncomfortably together.

"Hello," said Enid, her plump arm squashed against his side. "I don't think we've met. What do you think of this coon music? I *adore* it."

Felix looked wistfully across the table at Amory. Hairy Pav was whispering in her ear and she laughed at whatever it was he was saying, throwing her head back and exposing her long throat. Now *there* was a splendid throat. He'd give anything to cover it in kisses, Felix thought, the pain of his impotence suddenly spearing through his chest. He shut his eyes and immediately his head began to spin. He opened them and seized the glass of Moselle that he had just been poured, as if it were some crucial handhold. Waiters were arriving with food. Felix realised that he was by now dangerously drunk. A plate of prawn sandwiches was deposited in front of him. The faint fishy smell wafting up made his stomach heave. He plugged his mouth with his napkin, leapt to his feet and raced to the cloakroom.

Felix offered up a silent prayer to the inventor of the tango, as he and Amory glided jerkily about the dance floor. His hand was pressed into the small of her back. From time to time the movements of the dance obliged him to lean up against her or roll his pelvic area across hers. He thanked God also for providing him with the foresight to learn the hideously complicated steps the summer before.

Amory was slightly taller than he and looked fixedly over his right shoulder as they danced. Every now and then a soft collision or clumsily executed turn would cause their eyes to meet and she would flash him an automatic smile. Felix's spine was humming like a tuning fork with ecstatic love and adoration, but it was clear to him that Amory wasn't enjoying herself as much as he was.

They bumped into Holland and Enid.

"Feeling better?" Holland called.

"Fine," Felix answered airily, hoping no trace of his vomit lingered on his breath. In fact he did feel better. Infinitely more so. He wondered if Holland knew how stupid he appeared with his ridiculous little beaver. He looked like a bargee, dancing with that ludicrous woman. This novel sense of superiority elated him and he whirled Amory round with more gusto, exerting extra pressure with his hand on her back, bringing his face entrancingly close to hers.

"Shall we sit down?" Amory said into his ear, the warm breeze of her words causing that side of his body to erupt in goose-pimples. He allowed his fingers to touch her elbow as he "guided" her to the table, which was deserted, all the other guests being fully employed on the dance floor.

The pink lamp cast a glowing rubescent light, softening Amory's hard features, which had reminded him forcibly—he now banished the uncharitable thought from his mind—of one of the more predatory caryatids supporting the ceiling. They sat down beside each other. Felix poured out two glasses of wine. He had long ago exceeded his limit, but the zenith of confidence to which the alcohol had driven him made this prudent observation seem laughably unimportant. He took out his cigarette case. It was electroplated nickel-silver, one of the more useful products of the family enterprise in Wolverhampton.

"Will you smoke?" he asked. A waiter approached with matches and lit their cigarettes. Felix gazed at Amory and ordered one half of his mouth to turn up in an intimate smile.

"This has been a marvellous evening," he said, lowering his voice.

"Can you see who Pav is dancing with?" Amory snorted thin smoke streams from her nostrils.

Felix leant forward, supporting his chin with one hand, allowing the other—with his cigarette—to rest on the chair back behind him, exactly like the man in the De Reske poster, he calculated.

"You have a charming . . . ah, *pied à terre,*" he said.

"What?" Amory's cigarette was tapped sharply. Ash fell obediently into the marble ashtray.

"*Pied à* . . . your flat. It's charming." Felix allowed smoke to coil and wreathe from his mouth.

No reply. Her fingernails marshalled breadcrumbs on the pink damask table-cloth.

"I've been looking forward to this evening for a long time." Felix's hand left his chin and disappeared beneath the table.

"Honestly! Where can that man have got to?"

Felix glanced down at the slim length of tulle-clad thigh inches away from his own. He felt a sudden breathless—almost insupportable—excitement take hold of him. His hand descended on Amory's knee.

"Oh, Amory," he said, more feebly than he'd intended.

"Oh, for *God's* sake!" She got to her feet with tired exasperation. "You silly, boring little boy!"

When he got outside into the street, the first thing Felix did was actually punch himself in the face. He made a fist and struck himself a blow in the face, such was his self-loathing and bitter frustration. It wasn't particularly hard, but it caused him surprising pain.

"Bloody hell!" he swore. He followed this up with some of Cyril's richer vocabulary. He felt disgusted with himself. He looked down at his clenched and trembling fist and was surprised to see one white knuckle spotted with blood. Exploring fingers soon established that his cold sore was now scabless. He laughed scornfully but silently into the night sky. That effectively removed any chance of re-joining the party. He dabbed at his weeping sore with his handkerchief, printing it with red polka dots, as he wandered miserably off down the dark street.

Amory had stalked away from the table, presumably in search of Pav. Felix had remained immobile, head hanging, for a few seconds, his hand resting forlornly on Amory's abandoned seat until the faint sensation of warmth that rose from her imprint in the recently vacated cushion died away. Felix tried to get his burning cheeks and the fun-fair of emotions that jangled in his body under control. This partially achieved, his one thought had been to flee, and without further deliberation he strode out of the night-club, pausing only to collect his things from the cloakroom.

Now as he walked down the road he sardonically vilified himself, his puny love-making, his grossly inflated sense of his own worth. He called himself an ignorant schoolboy, a naïve conceited fool, a scrofulous impostor. How could he hope to attract anyone with this huge sore perched on his bottom lip? He walked on unheedingly, going through the night's scenes again with punitive disregard for his badly damaged self-esteem. His self-laceration halted, however, when he looked about him and realised he was lost. Where was he? How long had he been aimlessly walking? He turned a corner. Fitzrovia? Bloomsbury? Night workers were hosing the streets down. Other gangs of men shovelled the dirt and horse shit into glutinous, yard-wide mud pies.

Felix crossed the road to a coffee stall and joined the queue of customers. He looked at his watch. Five past one. The public houses had been shut for half an hour. Standing in front of the coffee stall was a mixed bunch of soldiers, navvies and cabmen. There were two tarts with the soldiers and all of them seemed the worse for drink. Clearly he wasn't in the city's most salubrious district. Felix handed over his penny ha'penny and received his mug of steaming coffee. He warmed his hands around it and moved a little way off to the side.

"Hot potato, sir?" came a voice. Parked beside the coffee stall was a costermonger's barrow carrying a glowing brazier. Felix bought a hot potato, suddenly ravenously hungry, remembering also that he'd deposited his supper in the cloakroom basin at the Golden Calf. He wolfed down one potato, then bought another which he ate more slowly, salting it liberally with the potato man's salt shaker. He began to feel slightly less disgusted with himself, enjoying the sensation of being out so late in London's dark streets. He felt alone, pleasantly sad, but secure and somehow terribly wise.

"Where are we?" he asked the potato man.

"Just off Bloomsbury Square, guv," the man said.

Felix saw a woman in the queue looking him up and down. She wore a loose green coat and a tatty fox fur round her neck. A large picture hat with brown artificial roses stuck in it cast a shadow over her features. She left her place in the queue and wandered over. Felix stared at her.

"Hello, darling," she said flirtatiously. "I can tell you're a naughty boy."

Why not? Felix suddenly thought. Why on earth not?

Felix followed the woman's broad hips up a dark flight of stairs. A hot burning feeling—not unlike acute indigestion—filled his throat and chest in anticipation of the transaction that was about to take place. His bravado overrode any sense of reluctance that had attempted to interpose itself in the course of their brief walk from the coffee stall to this gloomy Bloomsbury tenement.

The woman opened a door off a landing and went into a small bed-sitting-room. A gas lamp on the wall was turned down low. Felix's nervous glance took in a single unmade cast-iron bed, a table with a jug and ewer on it, a small fireplace. In front of the fire was an orange box over which was laid a pair of trousers.

"Get the spuds?" came a voice from the bed.

Felix jumped with alarm. A man sat up in the bed. The woman said nothing.

"Oh," the man said. "I see. Right you are, then."

"Is it——?" Felix began.

"He'll be gone in a minute," said the woman. Felix wondered if she was referring to him or her partner. He stood close to the wall while the man, who had been sleeping in a collarless shirt and combinations, pulled on his trousers. Felix stood motionless, watching the man lace up his boots. He looked like a waiter, Felix thought. The man unhooked his coat from the back of the door and put a faded bowler hat on his head.

"Enjoy yourself," he said as he went out of the door.

Felix looked at the rumpled bed. The woman removed her hat. Her face was heavily powdered, her dull hair secured in a loose bun.

"What do you want?" she said.

"What? Oh. Just, em, ordinary sort of——"

"That'll be two pound," she said. "Put your clothes on that box."

Felix struggled to breathe. He handed over two notes. It left him with a handful of change. Holland had told him that a pound was the most he'd have to pay, but somehow he didn't feel like haggling. Anyway, he told himself in compensation, it wasn't the sort of thing you could fix a price on.

The woman went to a wardrobe that stood in a corner and opened it. She put the money inside and started taking off her clothes. Felix felt his entire body begin to tremble and shake. It felt as if his lungs had been filled with scalding steam. He turned away and began numbly to undress, laying his clothes deliberately on the orange box. He undressed down to his long-sleeved woollen vest and knee-length drawers. He wondered if he should take off all his clothes. As a compromise he removed his vest. Should he ask her name?

"Gas up or off?" the woman said.

Felix turned round. This was the first naked woman he'd seen. She stood by the gas tap, one arm raised. Small flat breasts with curious bulbous nipples, a plump, creased stomach and heavy buttocks and thighs, a thick triangular bush of dull brown hair. His astonished gaze fixed on the hair. He'd known of its existence, of course, but he'd never given it much thought; it had never really played a part in his fantasies. There was so much. She had more than he did. A great turfy clump.

"Up," Felix said. The woman climbed into the bed, pulling the blankets up to her chin. Felix joined her. His knee bumped her thigh.

"Sorry," he said, wondering what to do. He felt paralysed with ignorance.

Her face was unpleasant, with puffy cheeks and a thick nose. Tense with apprehension he bent his head to kiss her on the lips.

"None of that," she said harshly.

"Sorry," Felix said again.

He brought his hand up to her shoulder and quickly ran it down the length of her body until it touched the extraordinary crinkly brown hair. It was wiry, not as soft as his.

"Just a minute," she said. "What you got on yer mouth? Ain't diseased or anythink, is yer?"

Felix recoiled suddenly, his movements pulling the blankets away from her body.

"Sorry," he said for the third time, as she snatched them back. He *had* to stop apologising, he told himself.

"No," he said. "It's just a cold sore. You know. A cold sore."

"Oh . . . yes," she said dubiously. The hissing gas lamp illuminated the wrinkled sheets and set greasy highlights in her hair. Felix thought uncomfortably about the nameless man who had been occupying the bed minutes before.

Urging himself on, Felix lay down and hunched his body up against the woman. She shifted her weight and he found himself lying on top of her, her legs spread wide. He could feel the prickling furze of her hair against his belly. For some reason itches sprang up all over his body in response. There was a faintly damp feel to the woman's skin, and various smells, not unpleasant but unsettlingly alien, assaulted his nostrils. He wished vainly he were down in the street eating a third potato.

He felt the woman's hands tugging at the fly buttons on his drawers. His cock, he realised, was wholly inert.

"Gawd, bloody hell," the woman muttered. She pushed him off and thrust her hand into his drawers. He felt a surge of prim outrage at the touch of a strange hand.

She grabbed his cock in her fist. "Get you hard," she said and began to pump it vigorously up and down. Felix looked up at the ceiling, feeling his stubborn anatomy at once respond to such forceful stimulation. The woman was still muttering to herself. Felix shut his eyes. It was better, he found, if he couldn't see anything.

"Ach, you dirty little bugger!" she swore. She sat up, holding her sticky hand out distastefully, as if she'd just been clearing a blocked drain. "All over the bloody blankets. Go on. That's yer lot. Go on, fuck off out of it!"

Felix crawled out of the bed and crouched over to his warm clothes. He put them on quickly, shutting his ears to the insults that were coming his way. He fumbled with his stiff collar, his fingers mysteriously transformed into stubby, strengthless growths. A collar stud dropped to the ground and rolled away somewhere. He thrust his collar and bow tie into a pocket and tied his scarf around his neck. He hauled himself into his overcoat, flinging a last glance at the woman, who was rubbing at the blankets with a cloth.

"Can you tell me how I get to Charing Cross from here?" he asked in a high, hoarse voice.

"Fuck off, you dirty little squirter," she said vengefully. "Clear off out of it."

A fine wet mist hung over the Kent countryside. A uniform grey dawn light emphasised the absolute stillness of everything. It seemed to Felix that he was the only moving object in the landscape. The only sound was the squelching his sodden shoes made as he trudged up the lane towards Stackpole Manor. It had been a mistake to cut across the fields. The dew was so thick he might as well have been wading through water. An early-morning mail train had taken him to Ashurst Station but the price of the ticket had used up the last of his money. There had been nothing for it but to walk home.

He opened the main gate at the bottom of the drive and closed it behind him quietly. He didn't want to wake anyone in the lodge. They would naturally be surprised to see him out and about at this time of the morning in evening dress. He sloshed up the drive. He couldn't really understand why he'd come back to Stackpole. A vague attempt to flee the scene of his mortifications, to put the maximum possible distance between himself and London. He still had his clothes at the Holland house, he realised. He'd have to send for them or else go back. Go back? *Never,* he thought, never. What would Holland think of him now? Would Amory tell the company about his appalling behaviour? Would they all laugh and condescend? "You silly, boring little boy!" He groaned out loud. He could hear her voice in his ears now. And then the tart . . . At least nobody but himself knew about the tart. What a disastrous night: disaster on a truly epic scale. This realisation caused his soggy pace to slow. He stopped. He passed a shaking hand over his eyes. He sank down on his haunches and rapped his forehead with his knuckles. He knew why he had come back to Stackpole. There was nobody in London whom he could turn to. At least here they knew nothing of his shame.

He got to his feet again. He saw the turning that led down to Gabriel and Charis's cottage and, for no particular reason, went down it. To his surprise he saw a light shining from a downstairs window in the cottage. He went up and looked in. Charis sat on a low footstool in front of a newly lit fire. She was wearing a long navy-blue dress and her hair was down. She held a steaming cup of something in her hand.

Felix rapped on the window pane. Charis turned round so sharply she almost fell from her stool. Then she recognised him and looked up in relief, a hand over her heart. She got up and moved out of his vision to open the front door.

"Felix! Gracious. I practically died of shock. What on earth are you doing? Come in, come in."

Felix went into the small sitting room and warmed his hands in front of the fire.

"I've just walked from the station," he said.

"Oh. London not all you expected?" she asked sympathetically.

"You could put it that way."

"Have some tea," she said. "You look miserable."

"If you don't mind, I'll take off my shoes. They're sopping."

"Go ahead." She went to fetch another cup and saucer.

"How was your party?" he asked. "I wish I'd stayed."

"It was all right," she said. "I couldn't sleep. Which is why I'm still dressed, if you're wondering. I went for a walk."

"Who was there?"

"The Hyams. Some people from around and about. And Sammy Hinshelwood."

"Oh? How was Sammy?"

Charis handed him a cup of tea. "That's why I couldn't sleep. Sammy was . . . how shall I put it? I think the kindest way would be 'over-gallant.'"

"Good Lord," Felix said, genuinely shocked as he understood the implication. "Sammy Hinshelwood? I mean, he was Gabriel's best man!"

"He had a bit too much to drink. I think he just meant to be comforting. Anyway, no harm done. He apologised. Said he was fearfully sorry."

Felix shook his head in outraged mystification. He looked at his bare toes. They were very white from the wetness, the nails yellow, as he imagined a dead person's would be. Sammy Hinshelwood . . . who would have thought? Charis sat on the edge of the sofa. Felix glanced at her. She was wearing a shoulderless, very dark blue full-length gown. She looked as if she had been dipped in ink up to her armpits, so sharp was the contrast between her white skin and the blue. Her long hair fell almost to her waist. This informality suddenly seemed overpoweringly intimate. He could see little creases at her armpit where her skin bulged slightly over the reinforced top of the dress. She had a string of jet and amber beads around her neck. He tried to imagine her naked body. He imagined it firm and smooth, hairless like a girl's or a statue's. Nothing like the one he'd seen a few hours previously.

She looked up and caught his eye.

"Did you cut yourself?" she asked.

He touched his cold sore. "It's not a cut," he said. "It's that cold sore. You know, I've had it for months. Can't seem to get it to go away."

She got to her feet. "You stay here," she said. "I've got just the thing for it upstairs. TCP. You'll see, it'll be gone in no time."

She left. Felix heard her footsteps above his head. He sipped his tea and stared into the fire. A notion had come into his head, unbidden and nasty. Don't think that sort of thing, he commanded himself, but the order had no effect. Remember Gabriel, he said again. "Gabriel." He repeated the name out loud, as if it were some kind of shibboleth. A few coals collapsed on the fire.

CHAPTER ELEVEN

17 JUNE 1915

Nanda · German East Africa

"Thank you," the Englishman said, as Liesl von Bishop handed him his crutches. He smiled at her. He had a broad face. Square, as if his jaw muscles were overdeveloped.

"Danke schön," he repeated.

"Excellent, Mr. Cobb," cried Dr. Deppe. "An accent of first-class quality!"

Liesl suppressed the usual stab of irritation. Deppe was so smug about his English. Who did he think he was? She was *married* to someone who was half-English, after all. She had even *visited* the country. Deppe thought he was so wonderful.

Liesl watched the English officer totter to his feet. His arms and shoulders began to shake with the effort of keeping himself upright. Liesl and Deppe ran to his side and eased him back onto the bed again.

"Gosh," he said. "Still a bit rocky."

"It's not astonishing," Liesl said. "You are very weak yet." The Englishman was surprised to hear her speaking English.

"Frau von Bishop is a linguist too," Deppe said patronisingly as he propped the crutches beside the bed. "A good effort," he said. "Little by little, that's how we do it. Tomorrow, one step. The next day, two. And so on."

Liesl moved to the window. Life had been tolerable until Deppe had arrived from Tanga with his wounded and the sick Englishman. A double amputee, a man with one lung, and this one with the bayonet wounds. Remarkable recoveries, Deppe had said. He was keeping notes on them for some article he planned to write in a medical journal after the war. Liesl saw him now, sitting hunched over a book in the corner of the big ward, scribbling away. She sighed, pulling the damp, sweaty material of her makeshift nurse's uniform away from her body.

Outside the window her view consisted of a wide compound of stamped earth that sloped down to a fenced-off stockade containing the jumble of wooden and grass huts that was Nanda's prisoner-of-war camp. There were about eighty English and South African prisoners there who had been captured in the numerous small engagements that had made up the war in East Africa since the great victory at Tanga. Not that she knew much about it. When Erich came here on his rare leaves he would tell her how things were going, but she paid only scant attention. To be honest, she didn't care, now that she was denied the comfort of living in her own home. She was waiting only for it to finish.

She had been moved from the farm at Moshi soon after war had been declared; too close to the fighting, they had said. She had stayed in Dar for two months and out of sheer boredom had offered her nursing services to the large hospital there. But she had been sent farther south to Nanda, where a new hospital had been established for more seriously wounded men whose convalescence would be lengthy and who were unlikely to return to the fighting. Erich had encouraged the move. He didn't like her living alone in Dar, and besides, he said, Nanda was safer. The British were sure to bombard Dar before long, he claimed. Nanda was far in the south, a smaller hospital, generally more tranquil.

In that respect Erich had been right. Liesl had found herself in effective charge of the hospital until Deppe arrived. The building had once been an agricultural research station and was situated at one end of the small town. Liesl had a wood and tin bungalow to herself—and Erich, whenever he came on leave.

The prisoner-of-war camp had been set up shortly after her arrival, and there was a small garrison of troops based there to guard it. The rest of the population was made up of the wives and families of the rubber planters whose extensive plantations surrounded the town.

To Liesl's surprise she had found herself quite happy to take up her nursing duties once again. She was even secretly grateful to the war for making this possible. When she returned from Europe in 1914 the first few weeks had been among the worst of her life. Every morning on waking, she was instantly overcome by a mood of poisonous irritation that made her days a misery. Nothing satisfied her; nothing pleased her. She detested the country, the malevolent climate, the demands of the farm. She took out her unhappiness on Erich.

She couldn't say she was exactly happy now, but at least she wasn't miserable any more. That is, until the wretched little man Deppe had arrived with his textbook cases, turning everything upside down, altering tried and tested routines and rotas, busying about like some officious little bureaucrat . . .

She picked at the wooden sill, prising away a splinter.

"Excuse me. *Entschuldigen.*"

She turned round. It was the soldier Cobb, calling from his bed. *"Wasser. Kann ich,* um, *Wasser haben. Bitte."*

She brought him a glass. "I speak English, you know," she said. "You don't have to speak German."

She remembered when this Cobb had arrived. The journey from Tanga had been almost too much for him, Deppe's precious case history almost prematurely closed. He had a fever that lasted a week. She remembered sponging his body with damp cloths. He was very thin, his body unreally pale. There were knotted purple weals on his white belly and the huge gash in his thigh, still with its stitches in. Deppe said the dressings on the thigh wound had to be changed every twenty-four hours. More work for everybody. His double amputee as well, both legs gone almost at the hip. Deppe congratulated himself for keeping these people alive. At least Cobb was entire, even though he would always walk with a bad limp. She took the glass from him.

"Thank you," he said. "How come you speak such good English?"

"My husband's father was English. He lived in Leamington Spa, near Stratford-on-Avon. Have you been there?"

"No, I can't say I have. Where's your husband now?"

"He's fighting."

"Against the Germans?" A puzzled but sympathetic look crossed his face.

"No, no. He's a German now. For many years. He's fighting against you." Liesl made no attempt to excuse his embarrassment.

"Perhaps you could teach me German?" he suggested in an attempt to regain his composure.

Liesl looked down the ward. In the morning it was quite cool. Later in the day it became unbearably hot.

"Why do you want to learn German?" she asked. But she had already lost interest in his reply. She thought about the "bath" waiting for her in an hour when she went off duty. Every day she got her maid, Kimi, to pour buckets of cold water over her while she stood in a tin bath. Then she would eat. Then she would sleep.

"Well," Cobb said, "I might as well make some use"—he waved his hands about—"of all this. Get something out of it, at least."

Liesl wearily climbed up the wooden steps that led to the rickety stoop of her bungalow. It was small, with two rooms—a bedroom and a sitting room—and had belonged to one of the bachelor managers of one of the plantations. It was sparsely furnished. The manager had been called up by the *Schutztruppe* and was now in the

Kilimanjaro region, billeted, for all Liesl knew, in her own large and spacious farmhouse.

For ten months now the war had been little more than stalemate, but this, according to Erich, was exactly what Von Lettow wanted. He knew that the *Schutztruppe* could never finally defeat the British, but at the same time a well-fought and protracted campaign could ensure that more and more men and materials would have to be supplied, diverting them from the more crucial battlefields of the Western Front.

Now the German Army at Moshi and Taveta faced the British at Voi. There had been skirmishes at Jasin on the coast, the Belgians were advancing tentatively from the Congo, but little more. Since the débâcle at the battle of Tanga in November of 1914 the British had done nothing. Nothing, that is, Liesl corrected herself, apart from sinking the *Königsberg* in the Rufiji delta.

She remembered the *Königsberg*. It had been moored in Dar-es-Salaam harbour, bright with flags on the day she had arrived back from Germany. She tried to imagine it scuttled in some jungle tributary, and an image of rusting steel, river weeds and creepers slid obligingly into her head. She thought of their farmhouse, the neat garden and the banana groves all destroyed, razed and blackened by war and gunfire. . . . She shrugged and went over to a rear window. She saw her maid, Kimi, lounging against the kitchen shack chatting to the cook.

"Kimi," she shouted, "bring the water."

She went into her bedroom and sat on the bed while Kimi and the cook staggered in with four buckets of water. Outside the African dusk was nearing the end of its brief life. A red sun, just below the tree line, a smell of wood-smoke and charcoal fires, the first crickets beginning to trill and hum.

Kimi stood obediently in silence as Liesl undressed. As her clothes came off, Liesl began to feel pleasantly relaxed. Kimi stepped behind her and unlaced the worn cotton corset. Liesl told her to wash it. She needed new clothes but they were becoming impossible to buy. She stood there for a moment, quite naked, slumped in an archetypal pose of tiredness and resignation. Ten hours in the hospital. She weighed her heavy breasts with a forearm and, holding them out from her body, wiped beneath them with the corset, then used it to rub her armpits. She did nothing but sweat in this country. She looked down at her creamy freckled body. Freckled all over. Pale as an abbess, Erich had once said a long time ago. Only now the paleness was marred by red rashes of prickly heat: a belt beneath her navel, smears at her sides, too, where her clothes chafed. She arched her back, stretched and stepped into the galvanised-iron bath that lay in the middle of the floor. Kimi climbed onto a chair that stood beside it. Liesl reached down and, with a grunt of effort, passed her one of the brimming buckets.

"Where's the soap?" Liesl demanded.

"No soap left," Kimi said.

Liesl sighed. She would bring some over from the hospital tomorrow. Never mind—it was the water that mattered. A few seconds of delight.

"Go on," she said.

Slowly Kimi emptied the pail over Liesl's broad white shoulders. The coolness of the water made her gasp, but the shock wore off disappointingly quickly. The water slid down her body. Absentmindedly Liesl went through the motions of washing herself, her hands guiding the trickling water to every nook and crevice, passing over her arms and belly, raising one leg and then the other. Kimi's face was locked in a frown with the effort of keeping the heavy buckets aloft. As one emptied, Liesl would pass her another.

Finally clean, Liesl dried herself with a thick cotton towel, very patched and frayed, and put on fresh clothes. Then she ate and went to bed. Unless she was being visited by one of the other women in Nanda with whom she had made casual acquaintance, for a game of cards, some coffee or speculation about the course and consequences of the war, she always went to bed early.

This routine had been quickly established and had not changed for the five months she had been in Nanda. It had altered only on Erich's two brief leaves, when he set up his camp-bed in the narrow bedroom, and was always there on the stoop to greet her when she came home from work.

CHAPTER TWELVE

21 NOVEMBER 1915

Voi · British East Africa

Walter stood outside the post office at Voi, checking and re-checking his uniform. He felt slightly ashamed at the way his gleaming new Sam Browne belt defined rather than restrained his paunch. Another hole had been pierced at the very end of the belt and the short tip now refused to stay beneath the buckle. The slightest movement caused it to flip out.

Patiently Walter waited for his summons to meet Brigadier-General Tighe, commanding officer of the brigade currently massed at Voi in preparation for the impending attack on the German Army, just a few miles across the plains at Taveta.

Walter pulled at his moustache and looked at the ceaseless pro-cession of troops, donkeys, mules and motor vehicles, carts and wagons of every shape and size, that passed up and down the main street of Voi in front of the post office, now acting as forward HQ for Tighe's brigade. Walter thought back to the time a year before when he and his family had arrived here as refugees, early victims of this "war." Mentally he added the quotation marks. He'd done nothing since he'd joined the East African Mounted Rifles after Essanjee's tragic death. Nothing except gradually acquire, over the months, separate pieces of his uniform, and endlessly drill and canter across the countryside around Nairobi. From time to time, small units went out on scouting parties and sneaked across the border with German East but they rarely encountered any Germans.

In Walter's case even this surrogate form of action had been denied him, as he'd been cross-posted to the 3rd Battalion of the King's African Rifles as a scout, where his local knowledge of the ground in the vicinity of Taveta was held to be of considerable use.

Arriving at Voi six months ago, he had been astonished to find the tiny railway junction and administrative centre transformed into a massive army camp. Neat rows of tents stretched out in every direction as huge contingents of troops from South Africa arrived to swell the battered remnants of Indian Expeditionary Force "B." Indian sepoys, local Africans, South African Cape Coloureds and Whites and British troops only just maintained cordial relations in the makeshift garrison town.

Walter had watched the army assemble, first with fevered anticipation, then with wild hope followed by deepening disappointment, culminating in utter boredom. They waited and waited, as the vast motor pool grew, mountains of stores piled high, cavalry regiments wheeled and manoeuvred, mountain batteries drilled and fired blank shells, and the men grumbled and bickered at each other.

The thought of Smithville just an hour or two's ride away made Walter want to weep with frustration. Many times he'd been out along the road he'd taken with Essanjee and Wheech-Browning until he came in sight of Salaita Hill, and many times he'd peered through his binoculars at the rise of ground that obscured his home and the farm buildings.

He wondered what condition the farm was in, whether the Germans had demolished everything he'd worked so hard to build up. The house, the barns, the drying racks, the crops, the Decorticator . . . But somehow his imagination refused to picture the

Decorticator as a wreck: a rusted, broken-down shell. It seemed too large and potent, too massy and fixed to be destroyed. Perhaps the webbing drive-belts would need replacing, the steam engine decaulking and overhauling, but somehow the Decorticator itself, the mighty iron wheels, the grinding teeth, the threshing chains seemed as permanent as any man-made object could be.

It was a source of some pain to him that his family seemed not to share his anguish and concern. They were happily ensconced in a bungalow at the Reverend Norman Espie's mission. Matilda had been delivered of a healthy baby girl, and even the other children, to Walter's disgust, referred to the mission as home.

"Smithville's your home," he had rebuked them angrily one day in Nairobi when they had been tired and said they wanted to go "home" to the mission. He had been astonished at their blank looks. "Smithville. The farm. The Decorticator."

"There, there," Matilda had said. "Don't confuse them, dear."

"Home is where the heart is," intoned the Reverend Norman Espie piously.

"Yes," Walter agreed. "You bet. *Exactly.*" Espie looked hurt for a second but then hastily assured Walter that he understood precisely how he felt.

Walter rubbed the toe of his boot on his neatly wound gaiters. Tighe had kept him waiting outside now for over half an hour. His stomach was beginning to rumble in anticipation of lunch. He took off his sun-helmet and inspected the brim. He flicked away some specks of dust.

An orderly appeared at the door. "Mr. Smith? You can go in now."

Walter was led through into what had been the postmaster's office. Tighe and his brigade major stood in front of a table on which was laid a large map. Tighe had an empty glass in his hand, and as he turned to greet him, Walter saw the marginally unfocussed gaze of someone in a well-advanced stage of intoxication.

"Ah, Smith, isn't it?" Tighe said. "Want"—he swallowed air—"benefit of your local knowledge. Expertise, what have you. Take a gander at the map."

Walter stood beside him. Tighe was a small man, bald, with a round, rosy, cherubic face that made his little toothbrush moustache seem wholly inappropriate. Brandy fumes exuded from him as if he'd been marinated in alcohol.

Walter looked at the map. Voi, then the blank space until Taveta. The long line of the Usambara hills running west from the coast and ending at the magnificent full stop of Kilimanjaro.

"Broadly, it's going to go something like this," Tighe said. "We attack south and north of Kiliwhatsit. Meet up on the other side, then trundle down the Northern Railway to Tanga pushing the Germans in front of us. That should just about do it.

"Now, General Stewart with the First Division is taking the northern attack, while we want to move through the pass behind Taveta." He drained his glass. "Splash a touch more in that, would you?" Tighe said to the brigade major.

"Colonel Youell of the K.A.R. told me you'd farmed around Taveta. He thought it might be useful if we could get through the Usambara hills a bit farther down. He seemed to think we could cut through from Lake Jipe to Kahe directly. What d'you say? Oh, thanks." He accepted his drink from the brigade major.

"Can't be done, sir," Walter said, suddenly consumed with homesickness on hearing Lake Jipe mentioned. He pointed to the map, at the pass between the end of the Usambara hills and Mount Kilimanjaro.

"On this area here, sir, there are several small hills. There's Salaita in front of Taveta; behind the town the road goes between two hills called Latema and Reata. They command the ground completely. It would be very hard to move people off those hills."

"Oh." Tighe looked surprised. "Are you sure? Are you expecting any problems there, Charles? What do our people say?"

"I doubt it very much," the brigade major said. "Remember, we've got Stewart and the First Division coming down behind Kilimanjaro. They won't want to make a stand at Latema-Reata. No, we're pretty sure they'll pull back down the railway to Tanga."

"Well, Smith," Tighe said cheerfully, "looks like you're wrong. Thanks anyway."

"Yes, sir," Walter said. He put on his sun-helmet and saluted.

"By the way," Tighe said, "curious accent you've got. Where are you from? Devon? Cornwall?"

"No, sir. I'm from New York City. United States of America."

"I see." Tighe looked at his drink. "Smith. Seems an unusual name for an American. Long way from home, eh?"

"No, sir," Walter said, pointing to Smithville on the map. "My home's there."

Tighe shot a glance at his brigade major. "Yes. Mmm. Right you are. Well, jolly good to have you chaps alongside us. Good luck."

Walter stepped out from the porch into the sun, adjusted his sun-helmet and sighed audibly. The British. He shook his head in a mixture of rage and admiration. A general who was an alcoholic, an army resembling the tribes of Babel, and everyone milling around on this arid plain without the slightest idea of what they were meant to be doing . . .

He walked slowly up the road towards the area of the huge camp where his tent was pitched. He undid the top buttons of his tunic and, with a gasp of relief, unbuckled his Sam Browne. Happily, uniform regulations in this theatre of war were lax, to say the least. Shirt-sleeves and shorts had become the order of the day.

Walter skirted a company of drilling sepoys and moved down behind an immense open stable of mules and donkeys. The rich smell of manure was carried to him on a slight breeze. The air above the tethered animals juddered with a million flies. He watched some sweating, half-naked syces drag away a dead pony. The death toll among the horses and mules was staggering, tsetse fly claiming dozens of victims each day, but there seemed to be an inexhaustible supply of pack animals; fresh train-loads were constantly arriving.

Beyond the lines of tethered mules lay the sprawling, tatterdemalion encampment of what were euphemistically called support troops, meaning all the thousands of bearers, coolies and servants, and their wives and families, required to keep this swelling army in anything like working order. Walter imagined that this must have been how the Israelites appeared after wandering around the Sinai desert for forty years. A huge, heterodox mass of people, a sizeable township, without houses, institutions or sanitation but with all the mundane dramas—births, deaths, marriages, adulteries—that any town contained. He had never been into the bearer camp. Initially, some soldier had attempted to impose a semblance of military neatness and order on the mob, making them erect their shambas, shanties, thorn shelters and rag tents in neat rows, but it disappeared without trace in days. Looking down on the bearer camp from a slight rise, one could just make out the original grid plan, like medieval strip fields since covered by a layer of scrubby vegetation. But from ground level it appeared merely a swarming, pestilential mess.

Walter crossed a flimsy wooden bridge that had been laid across a wide gully. Facing him was a sizeable open space, recently cleared of its thorn bushes and boulders and trampled flat by the feet of thousands of coolies, which now did duty as Voi's aerodrome. On a spindly, varicose pole a wind-sock hung like an empty sleeve. Over to the right were temporary hangars, little more than canvas awnings that provided some shade for the two frail biplanes—BE2C's—which at the moment constituted the presence of the Royal Flying Corps in East Africa.

As he watched, Walter saw one of the machines being pushed out onto the strip. Curious, he walked over to get a better look. He had seen aeroplanes twice before. Once in Nairobi and once—a seaplane—at Dar-es-Salaam. It wasn't the fact that such machines could fly that astonished him so much as their fragile delicate construction. He was an engineer and the mechanical contraptions he had dealt with—locomotives, Bessemer converters, threshers, the Decorticator—were robust, powerful artefacts, somehow asserting their right to function well through the very strength and size of their components. Forged iron, steel plate, gliding pistons. When you saw the Decorticator at full steam, you saw a symbol of the potential in human ingenuity. No task, however fantastical, seemed impossible when this kind of strength could be created, this kind of energy generated, harnessed and controlled. But the aeroplanes . . . Patched canvas, broken struts, loose rigging wires. Walter felt he could pull one apart with his bare hands, punch it into rags and kindling.

As he approached, Walter recognised, to his dismay, a familiar lanky figure: Wheech-Browning. He wore a faded khaki shirt, loose knee-length shorts and plimsolls without socks. On his head he had a tweed cap—reversed—and aviator's goggles pulled down over his eyes. Wheech-Browning was the last person Walter wanted to see. He couldn't stand the man. It was Wheech-Browning who had recommended his posting to the 3rd K.A.R. at Voi, for which action Walter bore him a potent grudge. But the sad demise of Mr. Essanjee had, as far as Wheech-Browning was concerned, established between them a bond which Wheech-Browning felt was now impossible to sunder. He treated Walter as a dear friend, a comrade-in-arms whose shared exposure to enemy fire had brought about an indissoluble union. This amity might just have been tolerable if Wheech-Browning had not at the same time pursued the matter of the unpaid duty on his coffee seedlings with the same vigour as he sought Walter's friendship. Temporarily relieved of his duties through military service, Wheech-Browning had put the matter in the hands of the District Commissioner—one Mulberry—at Voi. The latest meeting with Mulberry had ended with Walter being threatened with prosecution for non-payment of debts. Walter turned on his heel and began walking in the other direction.

"Smith! I say, come and have a look."

Reluctantly Walter returned to the aeroplane, now being fussed over by mechanics. Wheech-Browning stood by the side of a very young blond-haired pilot who looked, to Walter's eyes, to be about twelve years old.

"Do you know Flying Officer Drewes? He's going to fly me over to Salaita. See what jerry's up to. Good idea, yes?"

Walter thought. "Say, could you fly over to Smithville? It's not far. You could—"

"Sorry, old boy." Wheech-Browning smiled. "Fuel problems. That's right, Drewes, isn't it? But I'll tell you what: I'll have a squint through the old binocs. See if the place is still standing." Wheech-Browning tapped the stretched canvas side of the aeroplane. "Amazing machines. Wonderful sensation when you're up in the sky. Feel like a god. You should try it, Smith."

"You've been up before?" Walter asked.

"Who, me? No, no. First time. First time for everything, eh,

Drewes? No, I read about it in some magazine. Drewes here was going up on a flight so I asked if he'd take—"

There was a farting sound as a mechanic swung the wooden propellor and the engine caught. The aeroplane began to shake and shudder.

"All aboard the Skylark," piped Drewes in a high voice.

Wheech-Browning pushed his goggled face up to Walter's. "See Mulberry?" he bellowed above the noise. Walter nodded. "Jolly good," Wheech-Browning shouted. "He seemed in a bit of a wax about this customs duty business." It never ceased to astonish Walter how Wheech-Browning failed to see that the customs-duty business might jeopardise their "friendship."

Wheech-Browning gave him a thumbs-up sign, pulled his cap down and clambered with difficulty into the small observer's cockpit behind the pilot. Drewes revved up the engine, throwing up a towering plume of dust behind the aeroplane. Two mechanics at either wing-tip pushed and heaved the plane into position for take-off.

Walter suppressed his irritation at the news of Mulberry's "wax" and moved to a sheltered position at the side of a hangar where he could get a good view without being blinded by dust. He saw Drewes look at the limp wind-sock; then he saw Wheech-Browning stand up in his seat, lick his forefinger and attempt to hold it above the propellor's back-draught. Some decision must have been reached, because the biplane then moved very slowly over the uneven ground to the other end of the runway. Wheech-Browning leapt out of his seat, grabbed a wing and dug his heels into the ground to allow Drewes some purchase to pivot the plane round so it was facing the way it had come.

Wheech-Browning resumed his seat in the cockpit and the tinny note of the engine grew angrier as it was accelerated. Then the plane began to run forward, imperceptibly picking up speed, dust billowing behind it, the tail skid kicking up stones and gravel. As it passed the hangars, Walter saw Wheech-Browning give a cheery wave. Suddenly the tail lifted, and with a bump or two the little plane was in the air, three feet, six feet, twenty feet. It climbed with agonising slowness.

"Too hot," somebody said in the watching group. "It's too hot today. They'll never get up."

As if in response to his words the plane began to descend, even though the engine seemed to be straining harder. Ten feet, eight feet, two feet. There was a cloud of dust as the trolley undercarriage hit the ground.

"Told you," the knowledgeable voice said. "They'll have to wait till the evening." Nobody seemed concerned.

"Oh, my Christ," someone gasped. "The gully!"

The aeroplane sped merrily along the ground, the tail cheekily lifted, until it seemed suddenly to stand on its nose and plunge beneath the level of the earth. There was a crumpling sound, as of a flimsy chair giving way. For an instant the tail plane pointed vertically in the air; then it slowly keeled over.

Walter and the others sprinted over towards the site of the crash, coughing and choking as they ran through the clouds of dust that hung in the air. Because of his girth, Walter was soon outpaced by the others. By the time he arrived, Drewes' broken body had already been lifted from the splintered and torn remains of the aircraft, and he had been laid on the floor of the gully. Wheech-Browning, Walter assumed, must be trapped in the mangled wreckage. It served the stupid bastard right! Walter swore. The damned fool. But then he saw a plimsolled foot stamp its way through the canvas side of the fuselage. Willing hands soon tore a larger gap and Wheech-Browning slithered and eeled his long frame out onto the ground. His cap was missing but he still wore his goggles, one lens starred crazily where the glass had been shattered. A trickle of blood ran down the side of his face from a cut.

"Good God," he said, "that was hairy. Forgot about the damned gully. Thought we'd made it."

"Are you all right?" Walter asked.

Wheech-Browning gave an experimental wriggle, as if a cold penny had been dropped down his back. "No bones broken," he said. "Bit wobbly though. Drewes kept shouting something about it being too hot. How is he, anyway?"

"He's dead."

"Oh." Wheech-Browning took off his goggles and rubbed his

eyes. "Oh dear. I am sorry. Great shame." He looked directly at Walter. "What is it about us, Smith?" he said, with a kind of mystified sadness. "Every time you and I get near a machine, it seems some poor so-and-so dies."

Walter looked at him in blank amazement. He was too astonished to reply.

CHAPTER THIRTEEN

10 DECEMBER 1915

The King's Arms · Aylesbury · Buckinghamshire

Charis watched Felix swing himself to the side of the bed. The pale expanse of his pyjama jacket glowed in the dark room. She felt the bed vibrate as he shivered. She reached out and pressed the palm of her left hand against his back.

"You're awake," he said. "Sorry." He leant back and kissed her on the cheek. "I didn't mean to wake you."

"You didn't." She heard him fumbling for his glasses on the bedside table.

"It's early," he said. "Just gone six." He stood up and put on his dressing-gown. He smiled at her. "It's hardly worth going back to sleep, is it? We have to be at the station in a couple of hours. I'll just be a minute." He left the room.

Charis got out of bed and walked over to the window. A pale silvery light shone on the boring winter fields in the distance. Tasteless colours, she thought. Dark-brown and green. Like the chocolate sauce and pistachio ice cream she and Gabriel had one afternoon in Trouville. She noted, with mixed feelings, that the thought of Gabriel made her feel as guilty as ever. She wasn't any more accustomed to betrayal. Was that good or bad? She tried a hard, grim smile but it felt affected and wrong for her, like too much red lip-salve. She rubbed her arms through her night-dress, beginning to sense the chill in the hotel room. She crouched before the ashy fire and poked at the remains of the charred logs with the fire tongs. No embers left.

She went to the dressing table and took some things from her Gladstone bag and placed them on the top. A saucer, a small bottle with a clear liquid inside, and a tiny piece of sponge—slightly larger than a lump of sugar—to which an eighteen-inch length of cotton thread was securely tied.

With a little grunt she lifted up the ewer of water from its basin and splashed a few drops in the saucer. Then she added a little fluid from the bottle. She mixed the two together with her finger, wishing the water were warm. Then she dipped the sponge in the solution, letting it soak there for a while.

She pulled up her night-dress and put one foot on the chair; then, wincing from the cold, she pushed the little piece of sponge into her vagina as far as it would go. The thread dangled between her thighs. Felix, she was sure, had never noticed it in the eight times their "bodies had mingled" since that first evening in August.

She replaced the saucer and bottle in her bag and offered up a silent prayer of thanks to Aunt Bedelia with her little handbooks and pamphlets and their commonsensical advice. Did Felix ever think of taking precautions? she wondered. Was it something that ever crossed his mind? Did he ever wonder what would happen if—?

But this train of thought made her feel suddenly weak—almost faint—at the risks they were taking. She shut her eyes and breathed in deeply through her nose. Why was she so weak? Why couldn't she obey the dictates of her reason? She saw everything with utter clarity and understood with no ambiguity the absolute wrongness of what she was doing. That should have been sufficient, she told herself. If these things were so evident, self-restraint should be automatic. But even as she ran through the catalogue of her sins, in her mind some perverse illogic exerted a more powerful impulse. The answer was simple. She wasn't deluded; she wasn't out of control. In some sort of way she must *want* to do what she did.

"The flesh is weak," she said to herself, in partial expiation. As if to prove her point she slipped off her night-dress and stood naked in the cold room for an instant. She felt her body break out in goose-pimples. Glancing down, she saw her nipples redden and pucker.

"Brrrr!" she exclaimed and jumped into the still-warm bed.

Felix came back.

"Nobody stirring," he said. He saw her night-dress on the bed-post and his smile broadened.

"Have I kept you waiting long?" he asked facetiously as he took off his dressing-gown and pyjama jacket. "Ooh, it's cold," he said and hurried in beside her. They huddled close to each other.

"I should resist you," Charis said, half-seriously, "but I'm so weak."

"Don't blame yourself," he said, making a joke of it. "I'm irresistible." She thought his smile was a little forced. They tried never to talk about Gabriel. She had no real notion of how Felix felt, if he felt as she did or not. By a kind of unspoken agreement they had arrived at a position where they didn't mention his name if they could help it. It was safer. On the few occasions when some reference was made, Charis felt the feelings of shame and guilt burn through her, her mind flood with images of their last days together. She would tremble with the effort of self-control; it seemed almost impossible to breathe. Felix showed nothing as far as she could see; he just became silent for a while. Was he wrestling with his feelings? Or just respecting hers? She felt she desperately needed to know sometimes, but she didn't dare ask for fear of what might be unleashed, of what would be for ever spoiled.

As she lay now in his arms she knew, though, that sometime soon they *had* to talk about Gabriel. They had to. It seemed to her they only got by because their meetings were so infrequent. When they were together for any length of time, the spectre of Gabriel inevitably intruded on them, like Banquo's ghost.

"Charis?"

"Oh, sorry, Felix."

"You're not falling asleep on me, are you?" He kissed her neck. She ran her hand down the back of his head, her fingers seeking the top bump of his vertebrae.

"Just dreaming," she said. She felt his hand on her breast above her heart, taking the nipple between thumb and forefinger.

"Dreaming of your demon lover," he said.

"Thinking about last summer," she lied.

"Oh. The ponds."

Charis reached down and took his cock in her hand, holding it lightly, as if weighing it. It was very soft, like that, surprisingly so, she thought. She squeezed it gently, feeling it slowly thicken and firm, filling out her fist. Felix rolled on top of her. Her hand went back to his shoulders searching for a small mole, rubbery, slightly raised above the surface of his skin, a familiar map reference on his body, like the small scar on his thigh, the baby softness of his underarms.

In the summer of 1915, during fine evenings Charis often left her cottage and went to a stone seat by the middle fish-pond, which was obscured from the big house by a large clump of Portuguese laurel and rhododendron.

It was a little classical arbour that had been constructed by Felix's mother. There was a sizeable piece of broken fluted column set in a border, and beside the marble bench was a bust of the Emperor Vitellius on a slim octagonal plinth.

As the evening cooled the water, the big carp would come up from the dark and weedy bottom of the pool and nose at flies, or cruise slowly to and fro. Charis began to take some breadcrumbs with her to feed them and soon, she fancied, they came to expect her arrival, the first crumbs thrown bringing a dozen or more fish up from the depths.

One evening Felix joined her; he had seen her from his room, he said. They had become more friendly since their meeting after her party when, unaccountably, he'd turned up at her front door in his dripping evening dress. The distrust and caution on his part that had seemed to lie between them disappeared, and consequently, when Felix was at Stackpole, life there became noticeably more enjoyable. The bizarre gloom that emanated constantly from the major had been added to by the return of Nigel Bathe from Mesopotamia. During a bomb-throwing instruction course he'd been attending, a bomb had exploded in his hands, and both arms had been amputated at the elbow. He came with Eustacia to convalesce at Stackpole. The air of lugubrious tragedy that permeated the house became almost palpable. Felix's return from Oxford for the summer vacation brought welcome relief.

The evening meetings by the fish-pond began naturally and easily to extend themselves, weather permitting. Some days Charis found him there before her, waiting. He told her about his life in Oxford, how boring it was, and about his friend Holland. They argued about pacifism, Charis attacking Felix's antiwar stance out of a sense of loyalty to Gabriel rather than through any firm conviction of her own. The presence of Nigel Bathe and news of disasters at the Dardanelles and Suvla Bay made her arguments harder to establish, but she persisted, and in talking this way with Felix came to understand something of his hatred for the soldiers in his family, the powerful need he felt to be different from his father and brothers-in-law. But what about Gabriel, she would ask, playing her trump card. Ah, Gabriel was different, the exception that proved the rule. But slowly Gabriel's name came up less and less frequently. Sometimes they simply sat and looked at the cruising fish, not talking for minutes at a time.

One evening it was unnaturally hot. A dull static heat that seemed to promise thunderstorms a day or so ahead. Clouds of midges dithered above the pool. There was no breeze and the air was clinging and felt over-used, as if, Felix said, it was composed of exhalations only. All the people of the world breathing out at once. Charis wore an old straw hat in which she'd stuck cornflowers and poppies. She took it off and fanned her face, looping damp tendrils of hair back behind her ears. She glanced at Felix but he was staring fixedly at the pond, tapping out a rhythm on his knee. Confident he wasn't looking at her, Charis pulled forward the V of her blouse and fanned air down her sticky front, shutting her eyes and throwing her head back. When she opened her eyes Felix was looking at her. She blushed.

"Phew," she said, "it's so hot. Beastly hot. Do you think it's as hot as this in Africa?"

"Charis," Felix said, with visible effort and a strained formality, "I have to say. I can't . . ." And to her utter astonishment he lurched forward, put his arms around her and kissed her. For a moment she did nothing, stunned, perplexed and amazed to feel the pressure of his hands on her shoulders and his lips squashed against hers. She pushed him away.

"Felix," she cried. *"Really!"* She picked up her hat, which she had dropped. To her vague discomfort she didn't feel outraged or disgusted, as she had with Sammy Hinshelwood.

Felix then seemed to curl up inside himself on the seat. He covered his face with his hands, then snatched them away and stared up at the hazy evening sky.

"I'm so sorry," he said fiercely. "I'm sorry, I'm sorry. I know it's disgraceful. Please forgive me. I couldn't help myself."

"Well," she said. "Well"—noticing that her cheeks were now hot and her heart was thumping noisily in her chest—"let's forget it. All about it. Too much sun." She laughed with too much gaiety. "Too much i' the sun. Driving you mad." She threw some bread into the pond and there was a swirl and burble of water as the carp fought for the pieces.

"Look at those fish," she said a little wildly. "Wouldn't it be lovely to be a fish today, all cool and wet at the bottom of the pond? Swimming around without a care in the world."

Charis opened her eyes and looked at the electric light fixture in the ceiling. Felix still lay on top of her, his weight pressing her spread-eagled body down into the soft mattress. The whole of the lower half of her torso seemed to be humming still, a feeling of delicious sensitivity at the base of her spine. She heard Felix's breathing slowing down. He gave a small groan.

Nine times now. With Gabriel it had really happened only twice. But nothing like this. She clenched her fists.

The embarrassment of that first lunge passed away in a day or so. Felix returned, she thought, to his normal self, friendly and amusing. But all the changes had been wrought in her. Try as she might, she couldn't reconsign him to his old role of companion and welcome distraction. Feelings had been unleashed, emotions aired; she found these facts impossible to ignore. In a subtle way everything had changed. The past became different too. All through the summer, she now realised, he had been looking at her in ways she was innocent of: seeing her not, as she thought, as sister-in-law or new friend, but as someone desirable. She started reliving the months of their friendship, going back to that dawn visit in late March, running through her innocuous memories for signs and clues that would explain his amazing outburst. Felix, of all people. How extraordinary! Felix harbouring these thoughts about me through all these months . . .

She was—she had to be honest—pleased in a way, and vaguely flattered. And, suddenly aware, she became conscious of the effect her presence and appearance had on him: covert glances, inexplicable tensions and strange expressions on his face that she would have missed before. It was nothing serious, she told herself. Very young men like Felix often indulged in these "crushes." It was amusing, something to smile about privately and tolerate, not condemn or proscribe.

But then, another evening at the fish-pond, he seized her hand and pressed his lips to her palm. An absurd romantic gesture that she supposed he must have seen in a play or some musical revue.

"Felix," she rebuked jokingly, pulling her hand away, "someone might see. Now stop it."

It was the wrong thing to have said, she realised later, in the wrong tone of voice. His adoration now moved into a new phase. From being something private and inconceivable, it became now an enjoyable secret that they both shared and acknowledged. Their flirtation was something that they could both allude to and that she could tease him about.

On another day she suggested a walk and a picnic.

"Ah," Felix said, "but I might not be able to control myself."

"You shall come only if you promise to behave."

"I swear, I swear."

The fact that it all took place beneath the innocent eyes of the Cobb family made the summer weeks tinglingly illicit. There was nothing that anyone could find remotely improper about brother and sister-in-law finding some harmless pleasure in each other's company, and for the first time since Gabriel had gone away she found that life at Stackpole held something for her.

Then late one evening Felix came round to the cottage with some old blankets which he said his mother had asked him to deliver. Charis offered him a cup of cocoa and they sat and chatted in the small parlour for an hour. When Felix took his leave it was in the tones of mock-medieval romance which he sometimes employed to ridicule his infatuation but which also allowed him to air it.

"I must to horse," he said, striking a dramatic pose. "Farewell, sweet maiden."

"Fare thee well, gentle knight," Charis laughed, dropping a curtsy. She showed him to the door. It was nearly dark. Felix melodramatically turned up his jacket collar.

"Egad, the night is wondrous wild," he said. "When shall we two meet again?"

"Ah, me," Charis said, clasping her hands on her heart and expiring against the door jamb. "Luncheon tomorrow?"

They both laughed at the bathos. But then suddenly Felix was kissing her again, and reflexively Charis had her arms round his neck for an instant before she came to her senses and struggled herself free.

"Felix," she said seriously, "you must stop. You mustn't do that."

He looked very unhappy. "I know," he said. "I should. But it doesn't seem to make any difference. Somehow, because it's Gabriel, it seems to make it all right." He looked at her. "Does that make any sense?"

It didn't, but she ignored him. "But you must stop. Don't you see? You have to. You've got to."

He went away but came back later, after eleven, "to apologise." Charis had been in a state of real agitation after he'd left, angry with herself for not censuring him more and for not having checked this state of affairs before. Felix started to kiss her again, and her attempts at resistance only seemed to make his ardour more intense. Nothing she said had any effect. It was easier, she found, to give in. He left after midnight. He half-heartedly beseeched her to let him stay, but she bundled him out of the door.

Charis watched Felix knot his tie. He was whistling to himself, "Lily of Laguna," she recognised.

"A happy man," she said, hunching the blankets over her shoulder. He caught her eye in the glass.

"Of course," he said. "You too?"

"Of course."

"Want breakfast?" he asked. "They'll be serving by now."

"No. I'll just have a pot of tea."

"Sent up?"

"No, I'll be down soon."

After that first night Charis suffered some remorse. But she still couldn't understand how it had all come about. The facts were irrefutable: she and Felix were having a love affair. Everything would be all right, she told herself, if it could be maintained at this level of kissing and hand-holding. She knew that many women—respectably married women like herself—indulged in this sort of thing. It was no more than a flirtation, a pastime, nothing serious. If only Gabriel, she told herself in moments of irritation or when her conscience bothered her unduly, had acted more like a husband. If only she'd had more of a married life before the war claimed him, then she was sure she would never have yielded. It was hardly her fault, after all. What could anyone expect: married for a week, then a year of separation? And who knew how long that would last? It was like giving a child a bag of sweets, watching her open the bag and then snatching it away. She couldn't be blamed for wondering what they would have tasted like.

Her casuistry satisfied her temporarily. She put Gabriel out of her mind as she and Felix stole moments for kisses and caresses and enjoyed the complicity of being lovers, while the world sighed its approbation and happily surveyed them in its ignorance.

But Felix soon began to chafe under the restraints that living at Stackpole imposed. He began to introduce the idea of getting away for a day or two, just to be "free" and "natural" together for a span of longer than a couple of hours. Besides, he reminded her, the new term was starting at Oxford in a matter of weeks. The summer was nearly over.

And so the plan had evolved with a mysterious momentum of its own. Felix was to go to London, ostensibly to visit Holland. Charis would go to Bristol to spend a few days with her aunt. On her way back she would stop at a small hotel that Felix knew in Aylesbury. He would meet her there. Under the guise of husband and wife they would spend a weekend at the hotel. Then Charis would return home. Felix would go back to Holland's for another brief visit. His return to Stackpole would occur some days after Charis's to allay all possible suspicions.

The plotting and the anticipation, Charis had to admit, had been exciting. No reference was made to what would happen that weekend in Aylesbury.

Charis dressed slowly. She felt unusually agitated and troubled. This was their second visit to the King's Arms in Aylesbury, a pre-Christmas visit to Aunt Bedelia coinciding with the end of the Michaelmas term in Oxford. A shaft of unkind watery sun shone through the windows onto the crumpled bed. Felix seemed more sure of himself, more composed this visit. Certainly the pleasure had been more acute. . . . She held her hand out in front of her and watched it tremble. By contrast, her nerve was going alarmingly fast, she felt. The same questions rose up inexorably in her mind. How was it, when she loved Gabriel so, that she could become the mistress of his brother? The same answer came as inexorably in return. She had not been driven to anything; she was not under compulsion; she could exercise her free will. Somewhere inside her, somewhere hidden, she must have *wanted* it to happen.

It was this thought that made her miserable. She felt confused and baffled. For a second she experienced a shocking sensation of leaping, jostling panic in her chest. Was this true guilt? she asked herself. Were these the symptoms? Trembling hands and breathless turmoil? But it wasn't so much guilt that she was feeling as a kind of fear. She felt dazzled and giddy from the pressures she was under. She went over to the bed, pulled back the blankets and looked at the still-damp stains on the sheets. But it was so nice to be loved, she told herself, to be held by someone, not to sleep alone all the time. She needed that.

Feeling slightly stronger, she went downstairs to the hotel dining room. It was a cheerless room at the best of times, walls a pale mustard-yellow with waist-high wooden panelling. It was almost empty at this early hour; apart from Felix there were only two other guests at breakfast. Commercial travellers, she thought, by the look of them. One sleepy waitress was on duty.

"Hello," Felix said as Charis sat down. "Everything fine?"

She smiled. In public he lost some of his assurance, became more boyish and anxious. "Of course." She reached out and patted his hand in what she imagined was a wifely way.

Felix was eating a kipper. She poured herself a cup of tea and watched him finish it. He had his spectacles on, the better to fillet the fish, she supposed. He wore a tweed suit. He looked older with his glasses on, certainly old enough to be her husband. But she needn't worry, she told herself; no one at the hotel had ever seemed remotely suspicious.

"Sure you won't have something?"

She shook her head. He really was so different from Gabriel. Thin-faced where Gabriel was broad, dark not fair. He had none of Gabriel's unreflecting, stolid contentment. Felix seemed always bothered with life, suspicious of the cards it was dealing him, always weighing things up and criticising. In many ways he was rather a ruthless person, she thought, but not in the ways *he* imagined he was. A good person to have a love affair with, she concluded, a little ruthlessly herself. At least one person should be impatient with moral conventions, have no time for social norms, be able to scoff at the predictable judgements of conscience.

Felix put his knife and fork together. "What time's our train?" he asked.

"A quarter past eight."

He glanced at the clock on the wall. "I suppose we should be getting along to the station."

The London train was running late. Charis and Felix stood on the deserted platform and watched a thin sleet fall on the railway lines. Behind them the waiting room windows were fogged with condensation.

"I don't mind if it's cold," Charis said, rubbing her gloved hands together. "It's when it's cold *and* wet that I can't stand it."

Felix nodded gloomily, and stamped his feet to restore the circulation.

"Cheer up," Charis said. "I know the weekend's over but you are going to be home for six weeks."

"I know," Felix said. "But it's not the same. Christmas last year was bloody. Now, what with Nigel and Eustacia, too, I . . . oh, I don't know."

Charis slipped her arm through his. After all, they were husband and wife until Marylebone.

"But it'll be different this year," she said. "Last year we weren't together."

"Yes, I suppose so," Felix agreed. "It's not just this filthy weather. Oxford's ghastly these days. It's empty. Or rather, the colleges are full of soldiers. Drilling in the parks, nurses wheeling wounded men about in the college gardens. OTC this, yeomanry that. And this wretched war going on and on." He looked down at his feet. "Philip's changed too. He's talking about joining an ambulance unit in France. He wants me to come too. Something he read in Nietzsche, about subjecting the soul to all possible torments." He gave a wry smile. "I read Nietzsche *last* year. Philip dismissed him: 'a salon philosopher.' I ask you. And the train's late."

Charis laughed and squeezed his arm. "Oh, gloomy old thing. Don't worry, it'll be spring before you know it. And this war won't go on for ever—"

She wished she hadn't said that. She knew that the thought of the end of the war meant only one thing to both of them. Gabriel's return. Sometimes she forced herself to think about what would happen when peace arrived and Gabriel came back. Her mind acknowledged the broad truths: that he *would* come back, that he would be ill or maimed, that he might be changed in some way. But it refused to go into details, such details as how it would be possible for life to return to normal.

When the train arrived, they managed to find an empty compartment at the front. Felix sat with his back to the engine; Charis sat opposite him. The train chuffed off. Felix opened a newspaper. Charis watched the passing countryside, the mesmeric peak, trough, peak, trough, of the telephone wires, and tried to tangle and lose her thoughts in the rhythmic clatter and rumble of the wheels on the railway lines. But gradually she felt her early-morning panic return. She picked a thread loose from a seam on her glove. The end of the war. It seemed an appalling nemesis, not a moment for rejoicing. How could she live with both Gabriel and Felix at Stackpole? She knew instinctively and confidently that this current state of affairs would never have arisen if Gabriel had been present. Felix had once implied as much to her, joking that in the beginning he had resented her for stealing Gabriel's affections away. Felix would have to leave—that was all there was for it, she told herself, conscious of the note of hysteria. She could never dissemble in front of Gabriel. Something would happen. He would know; she'd be sure to give herself away. She felt her mouth go dry, heard her pulse resounding in her head.

Felix put down his newspaper, took off his glasses and leant forward to take her gloved hands. Charis smiled at him, his serious face, the pink marks on his nose where his spectacles had rested. She felt a love for Felix of a different order from the one she felt for Gabriel. It was a kind of gratitude, really. A gratitude for showing her alternatives. In his own very different way, she thought, he is just as strong a person as Gabriel.

"Charis," Felix said, staring at their linked hands, "do you mind if I ask you something?"

"Don't be silly," she said. "Ask away."

"About. About Gabriel."

It was as if the train were suddenly speeding along the edge of a precipice. She felt the sucking, empty feeling inside her that happened when a motor car went too fast over a humpbacked bridge.

Felix glanced at her face, then looked back at their hands. Then he took his hands away and rubbed his forehead.

"I get these terrible dreams, you see," he said, screwing up his eyes. "About Gabriel. Nothing threatening. No . . . no accusations. It's as if everything is normal. Like we were before the war. We're just doing things together. Ordinary things. In a very normal, natural way. Quite happy, too, in an unreflecting way.

"And then when I wake up, you see, I feel terrible. I feel this awful—I feel I'm . . . *wrong*. That I'm disgusting and corrupt." He looked out of the window, but carried on speaking. "I know I *shouldn't* feel this. I know I'm not ashamed about us." He paused. "But then I think: what if Charis feels this? What if *she*'s tormented too? And I'm somehow forcing her? You see, if I felt that was true, then I don't think I could somehow go on. That it would be terribly wrong to carry on."

He looked back at her for an instant. "I need to know how you feel, I think. I think that's what I'm saying."

Charis forced herself to reach forward and take his hands. Tons of evasions seemed to sit on her shoulders. Through the shrill ringing noise in her ears she heard her calm, reassuring voice saying, "I think about it too, Felix. Dear Felix. But Gabriel's not here; that's the difference. He's away. He doesn't know what's happening. He never will. We'll never hurt him. He's not a part of our world. It's only because he's away that our own world came into existence, that we created our world." She checked herself momentarily; she was beginning to babble. "Our love," she said slowly, "is a separate thing. It's not," she improvised wildly, "it's not part of the world we knew before the war. It's on its own. Enclosed. Quite distinct."

She saw his features relax. She'd said enough. A deep, infinite sense of disappointment gripped her like clinging ivy. "Don't worry any more, Felix darling. I don't worry. I don't even think about it." Fleets of regrets hemmed her in.

He was smiling. "Thank you," he said. He leant forward and kissed her gently on the lips.

CHAPTER FOURTEEN

11 MARCH 1916

Salaita Hill · British East Africa

On the twelfth of February 1916 the British Army in East Africa finally opened their offensive against the Germans. Walter watched two thousand brawny South Africans assault the gentle slopes of Salaita Hill after a four-hour artillery barrage. He sensed the depression and disconsolate moods of the last eighteen months lift miraculously from him as the innocuous hill was pounded with high explosives. He felt sure he'd be at Smithville within a matter of days. The South African troops had loudly vowed to sort out any "bleddy Kaffirs" they found that happened not to have been blown apart. Two hours later, six hundred of them were dead as they ran away from the withering fire coming from the German trenches.

On the twenty-first of February the German Army of the Western Front—in a completely unconnected response—attacked Verdun, thereby initiating a four-month siege.

Walter had to wait only three weeks until a second attempt on Salaita was made, but he found the delay cruelly frustrating nonetheless. In the interim the British Army was presented with a new commander-in-chief in the shape of General Smuts. Smuts modified the British tactics. Headlong attacks were to be abandoned. The advance on Taveta and the German border was to be co-ordinated with a series of flanking movements through the foothills of Kilimanjaro as well as the previously planned drive from the north under General Stewart. The Germans would be trapped in a pincer at Moshi, their escape routes down the Northern Railway cut off.

But this time Walter found his mood alternating between elation and scepticism. Staff-officer friends of Wheech-Browning told him that the war would be over in a few weeks. The possibilities of returning to the farm provided many hours of enjoyable speculation. But whenever Walter looked at the rag-bag army that was meant to bring this about, at the vain and bickering generals, his innate pragmatism would advise him not to raise his hopes too high.

So on the ninth of March, Salaita was attacked again and found to be deserted, the Germans having stolen away in the night. Two days later Walter rode his mule down the main street of Taveta, back in the familiar little township after an absence of eighteen months. Thus far, everything had been achieved without too much difficulty (the six hundred dead South Africans excepted), the Germans content to pull back without offering a fight whenever it looked as if the forces massed against them were overpoweringly superior. But up ahead lay the Taveta gap and the twin hills of Latema and Reata. Walter rode out of Taveta to scout them for the K.A.R., who were due to be involved in the first attack. At the foot of the hills the ground was thick with a dense, shoulder-high thorn scrub, which seemed to continue all the way up to the top. Walter dismounted and moved a few yards into the scrub. Soon he could see nothing, not even the summit of the hill he was meant to be climbing and upon which the Germans were well entrenched.

He reported as much to his battalion commander, Colonel Youell, a brave, weather-beaten man who felt he'd been personally let down by the Germans' refusal to contest Salaita Hill. Walter said it was his considered opinion that the two hills would be extremely difficult to take without massive casualties; that it would be a good idea to wait until the flanking movement made its way round Kilimanjaro, at which point the Germans, seeing the danger of being cut off, would surely yield their ground.

Youell ignored him. "It may sound sensible to you, Smith, but with respect, it's obvious that you're not a professional soldier. We don't want them to fall back. We must force Von Lettow to stand and fight. We've got to engage him here precisely so that he doesn't realise he's being cut off until it's too late."

Walter acquiesced, and asked for permission to visit his farm, just to see how everything was. Permission was refused.

"I need you with me," Youell said benignly. "You're to be attached to battalion HQ. This is your country around here, Smith. I need your advice."

Why don't you take it, then? Walter thought. Nobody in this army listened to a word he said.

On the eleventh of March, Walter stood uneasily with Youell's battalion staff as the first wave of troops drew up on the flat plain some three miles beyond Taveta. There was Youell's K.A.R. battalion and the 2nd Rhodesians who were going to attack Reata Hill, and the 130th Baluchis whose objective was Latema. The sky was clear and the morning haze had dispersed around Kilimanjaro, whose incurious snowy summit shone brightly in the distance.

General Tighe was supervising the battle from a grove of trees on the outskirts of Taveta. He sat in a deck-chair in a patch of shade with his boots off, feet propped on an empty ammunition box in front of him. Walter watched the troops marching off across the plain of corn-yellow grass towards the smooth contours of Reata Hill. Youell and battalion headquarters followed some way behind.

As soon as the advancing files of men entered the brush at the foot of the hill, the German machine guns opened fire. Youell soon caught up with his men who were pinned down on the lower slopes, huddling and crouching at the roots of the thorn bushes. Progress was impossible. A runner was sent back to ask for an artillery bombardment, and soon the field batteries began to pound the slopes in front of them.

Walter knelt beneath the flimsy shelter of the thorn bushes as the sun rose higher in the sky. About fifty flies seemed to be buzzing around him. Perspiration dripped from the ends of his moustache. The constant crash and boom of explosions filled his ears. Battles, he thought, were unbelievably noisy places.

Youell and his adjutant had a map spread on the ground and were trying to work out the positions of the battalion's other companies and the 2nd Rhodesians. Walter felt an urge to perform a natural function but thought Youell might object to his lowering his trousers in what was in effect temporary battalion HQ. He certainly had no intention of crawling off into the bush for the sake of privacy.

Presently the barrage lifted and the advance continued, making somewhat better progress through the openings and pathways cleared by the heavy shelling. Walter stuck close to Youell as they clambered, puffing, up the slope. All around him Walter could hear the pop-gun reports of rifles, and the yelling and shouting of the K.A.R. askaris. The noise of gunfire was continuous and Walter assumed that at least some proportion of it must be coming in his direction, but so far there had been no sign of the enemy.

They halted, gasping for breath, at a rock outcrop. Some K.A.R. soldiers occupied the uppermost boulders. Walter calculated that they couldn't be far away from the summit. He felt exhausted from the climb. Youell took off his sun-helmet to reveal surprisingly boyish wavy hair.

"Are we near the top, Smith?" he asked.

"I think so, sir," he said.

"Let's take a look." Youell began to clamber up the rocks. He glanced back. "Come on, Smith."

Walter followed him up. They crouched behind the boulders. The firing seemed to have died down somewhat on their section of the hill. Youell spoke some words of encouragement to the askaris.

"Have a look, Smith," Youell said.

"Me, sir?"

"Yes," Youell said. "Find out where we are."

Walter took off his sun-helmet. Although it was only cork and canvas, it gave the illusion of affording some protection. Now he felt the sun warm the top of his head. His brains seemed to heat up. He had an unpleasant sense of the fragility of his skull, as if it could be as easily shattered as an eggshell. Cautiously he raised his head above the rocks. The summit was a mere fifty yards away. He could see a battered redoubt, crumbled earthworks, scattered sandbags and boulders. There was heavy firing somewhere to his right. It all seemed quiet ahead. Perhaps the Germans had pulled back again?

Walter told this to Youell in a whisper.

"Why are you whispering, Smith?"

"Sorry, sir."

"Can you see anyone at the summit? Are the Rhodesians there?"

"I couldn't say, sir."

"Well, have another look, dammit."

Walter looked again. He thought he saw some figures moving behind the earthworks. He ducked down and put on his sun-helmet.

"The summit's definitely occupied, sir."

"Us or them?"

"I couldn't make out, sir."

Youell called down to his adjutant to see if there had been any word from the Rhodesians. The adjutant said he'd heard nothing and sent off a runner.

Then they heard someone shouting from the summit. In English.

"Hey! You down there. The Germans have gone."

Youell smiled in triumph. "You see, Smith. We've done it."

He stood up. "Well done, you men!" he called. "K.A.R. here. Coming up to join you."

"Sir," Walter cautioned. "If I were you, I wouldn't—"

The fusillade of shots slapped through the air, pinging and buzzing off the boulders. Colonel Youell was spun round and toppled backward off the outcrop. Walter scrambled after him, the air suddenly loud with firing once again. The shocked adjutant turned his colonel's body over. Walter saw the blood pumping strongly from a wound below his ear, pouring down his neck and congealing in the dust.

"Oh, God," the white-faced adjutant said, looking up at Walter. "Do you think he's going to die?"

With the nelp of two askaris, Walter dragged and carried Youell's dead body down through the mangled thorns to the bottom of the hill. There they found a stretcher and tramped back through the knee-high yellow grass towards Taveta. The firing grew more distant as they moved away. A steady stream of injured men were stumbling or being helped across the plain. Walter looked back at Reata, its outline blurred by dust clouds, the firecracker sounds of the battle faint in the warm, pleasant afternoon.

At the casualty clearing station, the harassed medical orderly indicated a row of dead men laid out like game birds after a shoot. Walter felt he couldn't leave a colonel with the corpses of ordinary soldiers, so he had him taken back to Taveta in a motor ambulance. Once there, they joined the procession of stretcher cases being ferried towards the field hospital, set up in the stable block of the police barracks. Their route took them in sight of Tighe's brigade HQ. Walter ordered his stretcher-bearers to change course. Youell's death should be reported to the general.

Tighe left his group of staff officers, who were all surveying the hills through binoculars, and limped over. He was smoking a cigar.

"Yes? It's, um, the American chappie, isn't it?"

"Yes, sir. Smith, sir."

"Well, who've—" He started again. "Wha's th'mather. Matter."

"Colonel Youell, sir. He's just been killed on Reata Hill."

"*Good God!* Eddie Youell? How the hell did that happen?"

"Bullet in the head, sir. He stood up."

Tighe winced. He seemed to be swaying gently. He changed his stance slightly. "My God. Good God. Brave man, Eddie. God." He puffed on his cigar. "What's it like up there? Damned hard to make out. They've got the Baluchis well pinned down on Latema."

"They're still on the summit, sir."

Tighe nodded, waved his cigar vaguely in Walter's direction, turned round very cautiously and re-joined his staff.

Walter left Youell's body at the field hospital and dismissed the two askaris. He then went back to the K.A.R. tents and got his mule-handler to saddle up his mule. The town was milling with troops, wagons, ox-carts and motor lorries as three South African battalions were brought in as reinforcements for the beleaguered men on the two hills. No one challenged or questioned him as he rode out of town and took the track that branched off to Smithville.

It was three in the afternoon as Walter approached the familiar surroundings of his farm. Away in the distance he could see the placid peak of Kilimanjaro, the white snows reflecting back the afternoon sun. He could hear, very faintly, the distant pattering sound of gunfire as the assault on the two hills continued. Behind him rose clouds of dust on the road between Taveta and the new railhead as supplies and fresh troops were brought in. He seemed to be completely alone in the landscape. He had come across no pickets or patrols of either side. However, the thought crossed his mind as he drew near Smithville that it might still be occupied, being far enough away from the main British advance. He dismounted and tied his mule to a tree.

He left the track and struck out into the bush in a wide semicircle that would eventually bring him up behind the house. He realised that he had left his rifle somewhere on Reata Hill. He was unarmed, apart from a large penknife he always carried. He took it out of his pocket and opened the blade. He wasn't quite sure what he'd do if he encountered anyone, but he felt marginally less ill-at-ease now that he flourished some sort of weapon.

He crept through the tall grass as quietly as possible. Soon he saw the remains of the shamba that had stood behind the house. It had obviously been burnt down some considerable time before. He paused, crouching behind the knobbled bole of a euphorbia tree. Across a forty-yard gap of broken ground lay the house. He felt a sensation of enormous relief to have made it back to Smithville again. It was followed by an equally forceful sensation of tiredness; all the tensions of the day, which somehow he'd been holding off, descended on him. If he lay down and shut his eyes, he knew he would fall asleep immediately.

From his position the bulk of the house obscured most of the view. He could see nothing of the other farm buildings—hidden anyway by the rise on which the house stood—and nothing of the sisal fields beyond. From what he could make out, the linseed plots that led down to Lake Jipe were not the scorched wasteland he'd been expecting. He felt suddenly elated. Perhaps Smithville had escaped largely unscathed? Just the wagons and livestock, the trolley lines and the sisal crop the price he'd had to pay?

He stirred himself into action and scampered from his sheltering tree into a small grove of dead banana trees nearer the house. He noticed that the tops of the trees had been neatly cut off to prevent them bearing any further fruit. Someone had been thorough.

He peered through a gap between the fibrous trunks. He felt a little foolish, a fat, sweaty man trying to run as lightfootedly as he could, a tiny blade gripped in his fist. But nothing and no one stirred. He broke cover again and ran up to the house, flattening himself against the wall. He inched forward towards the kitchen door. The windows on this side were securely shuttered, a hopeful sign that the place was abandoned. He tried the kitchen door. It swung open. Still no sound. Everything was completely quiet in the afternoon heat.

He stepped in. And stepped out again immediately, hacking and coughing loudly. The *smell!* He felt his stomach heave. He spat on the ground, and wiped his brow. "Jesus," he swore. *Shit.* The house smelt like a giant's shit hole. It was humming with flies too. Millions of flies—the air seemed solid with them. One thing was certain though. There was nobody in the house. Nobody with a functioning nose could last more than a few seconds.

He calmed himself down. He took a huge breath and, holding it in, re-entered the kitchen. It was dark and all the shutters were closed. He blundered over to the windows and flung them open, then leapt outside to recharge his lungs. He peered cautiously in through the door. Every surface—shelves, table, chairs, cooking trough—was decorated with coils of human faeces, as was the floor. The air danced with black sated flies. Streaming plumes of them escaped through the newly opened windows. Taking a deep breath, and watching where he placed his feet, he went into the dining room and flung open the shutters there, before clawing his way outside again. He was like a swimmer bringing up treasure from a river bed. He could do it only little by little, as his breath lasted. It took him twenty minutes to open up the house. Not a single room had been spared. It looked as if a battalion had marched in, lowered their trousers and, on the given command, had shat where they stood.

Walter felt exhausted and mystified. What was going on? He felt his head throbbing and pounding from all the breath-holding he'd done. He took a few paces back and leant dizzily against a banana tree trunk, overcome from his exertions. Who had fouled his home? Why had it been done? Unanswered questions tumbled in his brain.

Somebody tapped him on the shoulder. He gave a bellow of alarm and flung himself madly round onto the interloper, his hands clawing for the stranger's throat, beating him to the ground.

"Bwana!" came a terrified croak. "It is me, Saleh!"

Walter released his grip. Sure enough, it was Saleh on whom he was now sitting. The little man seemed in unspeakable agony, his head jerking to and fro, his mouth gagging for breath.

"Saleh," Walter cried, "what's wrong?"

Saleh's hands plucked weakly at Walter's sleeves.

"Bwana," he gasped, "get off. I beg you. I can't breathe."

Apologising profusely, Walter got to his feet. Saleh lay motionless on the ground, limbs askew, as he fought to regain his breath. He sat up groggily. Walter helped him to his feet and stood patiently while Saleh dusted off his ragged tunic.

"Bwana," he said finally, "a terrible thing has happened."

"I know," Walter said. "I've just been inside."

"No, bwana," he said soberly. "This way."

He led Walter some way off to the side. As they walked away from the house, the farm buildings came into view. To Walter's relief they were still standing. A bit ramshackle but no serious damage was visible. The sisal fields had disappeared under weeds and grass but he could see the great spiky leaves poking through the vegetation. Reclaimable certainly, with some hard work. He was beginning to feel his luck had held out. Von Bishop, it seemed, had been as good as his word. He felt a pang of guilt over Mr. Essanjee's death. Had there really been a need to bring him all this way to make the assessment?

Thoughtfully he followed Saleh's thin body. Where was the man taking him? To his village? Perhaps the German askaris had laid it waste? But Saleh had stopped. With a sudden shock, Walter realised they had reached his baby daughter's grave.

It had been crudely opened. The mound of stones were scattered and the remains of the little coffin and its contents strewn haphazardly around, as though some large beast had been digging there. On the wooden cross was set a tiny skull the size of an apple.

Silently Walter and Saleh garnered the bits and pieces—brittle ribs like thin claws, vertebrae the size of molars—and replaced them in the hole. Walter picked up the skull. It was bleached and dried. It hardly weighed anything in his hand; a gust of wind might have blown it away. He laid it in the hole. With his boots he shovelled the earth in and then they rolled back the rocks.

"When did they do this?" Walter asked.

Saleh told him it was just before the soldiers left, two days ago. There were always soldiers billeted at Smithville, Saleh said, sometimes as many as a hundred. Two days ago they had all left. Walter felt his exhaustion returning. The sun was heavy in the sky. He thought it was time he was getting back.

"Don't worry, Saleh," he said, moved by the man's woebegone expression. "It's just bones." He tried to say something comforting. "The baby's soul has gone to heaven." He thought he sounded like the Reverend Norman Espie. "Anyway," he said, remembering, "Mrs. Smith has a new baby girl now." He patted Saleh's shoulder. "A new baby." He hitched up his trousers and let out a great sigh of breath.

"We'll all be back here soon," he said, talking in English. "You'll see, this war is nearly over. We'll get the farm going. Yes?" He tried to cheer up the morose Saleh, who was now struggling to comprehend. "Farming again, Saleh, farming. Plenty of work. Get the Decorticator going and—"

He turned abruptly on his heel and ran down the slope towards the Decorticator shed. Behind him he heard Saleh shouting, but he paid no attention. As he approached the wooden building, a feeling of ghastly premonition built up in his chest. He stopped short, gasping for breath before the large double doors. He paused for a moment, willing everything to be all right. Then he swung the doors open.

Walter walked disbelievingly into the large empty shed, his boots ringing out on the concrete floor. He moved uncertainly about the vacant space as if expecting any moment to make contact with some ghostly machine. Orangey wands of sunlight sectioned the floor, squeezing through slits and gaps in the plank walls. Walter looked at the archipelago of oil stains, the fixing bolts set in the concrete, a few inches of tattered canvas drive-belt.

"No!" he bellowed. *"Bastard!"* He shook his head, pacing out the four walls, trying to come to terms with the disappearance of something so immutable and massy, so incontrovertibly *there.*

Saleh arrived timidly at the door. "Bwana," he said apologetically. "They took it a long time ago."

"When?" Walter said.

"After you and the memsahib went away."

Walter whirled round. Saleh backed off.

"I could not stop them, bwana," he protested. "Many men came. For five days they were working."

"Who was it?" Walter demanded in a hoarse whisper. "Who took it?"

"Many men," Saleh repeated. "The Germani."

Walter swallowed. He knew who had taken it. Von Bishop. The man had tried systematically to defile his home. Erich Von Bishop had stolen his Decorticator. He would have to pay. It was as simple as that.

CHAPTER FIFTEEN

24 JUNE 1916

Nanda · German East Africa

Wincing slightly, Gabriel removed the grubby, worn bandages from his thigh. A pad of bloodstained lint was stuck to the scab. Gritting his teeth, he pulled it away. The six-inch scab that was revealed glistened and oozed. Gabriel's eyes watered with the stinging pain. Deppe couldn't understand why his leg was taking so long to heal. Gabriel smiled to himself. He hopped to the doorway of the lean-to shed he lived in at the back of the hospital. A piece of blanket hung from the lintel. Pulling it to one side, he could see the hospital kitchens and the dusty vegetable plots. There was no sign of Deppe or Liesl. If they ever found out what he was doing he'd be sent away at once, he was sure. Liesl might not send him away, but Deppe would. Deppe would never forgive him.

Gabriel limped back to his bed and sat down. The constant reinfection of his leg wound was easier to explain now that all the medical supplies were running out. They were washing and reusing all bandages now; most wounds got infected these days. Automatically he touched the puckered scars on his abdomen. He would always be grateful to Deppe; it was a shame he had to frustrate his best efforts with his leg.

Gingerly, with his fingernail, Gabriel prised up an inch of the scab. His eyes started to water again. With his other hand he took a pinch of dirt from the floor and sprinkled the grains onto the glistening wet wound beneath, like salt on underdone meat. He pushed the scab back into place, and carefully rewound the bandage on. In a day or so, if past performances were a reliable guide, the wound would become itchy, then inflamed and putrid. Liesl would have to clean it out, use some of the dwindling supplies of disinfectant, wash the bandages and replace them. He tied the final knot. It was a risk, of course. If it didn't get treated, the consequences could be most serious. But that was the advantage of working in the hospital: you were always well looked after.

He pulled the tattered hem of his shorts down over the bandage. He sat for a while staring at his thin knees. He had lost so much weight over the months of his recovery. He couldn't understand why; he ate as much as anyone else—better even than the other prisoners had. But he was just skin and bone now: skin, bone, muscle and cartilage. Deppe said that was another reason why his thigh wound was taking so long to heal.

Gabriel got to his feet and went outside. He squinted up at the sun trying to guess the time. Four o'clock, four-thirty maybe. Perhaps he should go back to the ward and see if there was anything Liesl wanted him to do. There was always work to be done. Usually it meant helping the dysentery cases. Sometimes he helped feed the very sick men, or wash them. When Liesl was on duty he did all sorts of fetching and carrying jobs. Deppe wasn't so happy about employing him. He said that it was against regulations to compel prisoners to do menial work. But Gabriel always reminded him that he wasn't being compelled. He wanted to help, he told Deppe, wanted to do his bit to relieve suffering. But Deppe wouldn't listen and always frowned heavily when he saw Gabriel giving assistance. Fortunately Deppe spent less and less time at the Nanda hospital. As the war went on and the casualty list inevitably grew, his expertise was required at other hospitals, makeshift clinics and convalescent homes. "Deppe's just an old woman," Liesl had said when Gabriel told her about the doctor's reservations. "Anyway, he is never here." It was this conspiracy against the fussy doctor that had encouraged their curious friendship, had broken down the formal restraints that exist between nurse and patient, captor and captive. Not, Gabriel smiled to himself as he went into the hospital, not that you'd expect Liesl to pay much attention to customs or conventions. He'd never met such a strong-minded woman.

It seemed that as the war dragged on, so Liesl's attitude had become more indifferent and resigned. In his months as her patient Gabriel had been well placed to notice this transformation. She did her job as thoroughly and efficiently as the conditions allowed, but she didn't seem particularly to care one way or another about anything. Only Deppe had the power to irritate her. She didn't despair, but she didn't hope either. When Gabriel put his plan into operation and made his first tentative offers of help—holding a man above an enamel basin while she attended to an emergency farther down the ward—she hadn't even said thank you. She seemed rather to take it as just another event in the undifferentiated flow that constituted her day. Gradually—almost without effort on his part—Gabriel's role in the ward increased. There were servants who worked in the ward but they couldn't be expected to do the more sensitive tasks, and also a lot of the soldiers resented any more intimate contact with them. So Gabriel bathed feverish patients, spread ointment on chafing stumps, supported the dysentery cases as they trembled and shuddered during their burning evacuations, and sometimes he changed the simpler dressings. Soon he was a familiar figure in the one long ward that made up Nanda hospital. He would chat to the English soldiers; he even learnt a smattering of German, enough for the rudiments of conversations with the German wounded who, steadily, came to form the largest portion of the patients.

But now there were no English prisoners in Nanda. A week ago the eighty men and their garrison had been moved near the coast. No one knew why. One theory was that the effort of guarding and feeding them was proving too costly and that they were going to be returned on parole to the advancing British. Gabriel was thankful he had discovered that after they'd left. If he'd known in advance, it would have been very hard to justify his staying on. As it was, his conscience was satisfied by a plea of ignorance.

He thought of this now as he stood at the end of the long ward. The heat was stifling. Over sixty beds had been crammed into the former store-room-cum-warehouse of the research station. The windows were open, cane blinds hanging in them to minimise the heat of the afternoon sun. An old African servant came past with two heavy slopping buckets. "*Jambo,* bwana," he said. Everyone knew Gabriel.

At the other end of the ward he saw Liesl taking a pulse. She looked up, saw him and made a smoking gesture with her hand. Gabriel turned and went into the small room that served as a dispensary. He sat down at the table in the middle of the floor and set about rolling two cigarettes from the crude, locally cured tobacco and their dwindling supply of paper. They were using a copy of Goethe's *Die Leiden des Jungen Werthers,* a small, nicely bound book that Liesl said belonged to her husband. One leaf was sufficient for a single cigarette. They had reached page forty-eight.

Gabriel had become quite an expert at rolling cigarettes. It was as if, as his hands got bonier and the knuckles more evident on his fingers, they acquired a new dexterity. He took time over it, packing the tobacco tightly, rolling the paper up in a neat, even cylinder. Often he'd spend a day making a dozen or so cigarettes and offer them to Liesl as a present. She smoked a lot. Fortunately there was plenty of tobacco. Paper was the problem. If the war continued, Herr von Bishop's small library wouldn't last very long.

Gabriel finished the cigarettes and waited for Liesl to return. Outside, the oppressive weight of the afternoon sun seemed to have stunned the world into silence. Gabriel stood up and looked out of the dispensary window whose view gave onto the deserted prison camp.

When the prisoners had been marched off, he had kept out of their way. Had he done the right thing? He consoled himself with Major du Toit's remarks. It had been Major du Toit who had initiated the plan. Major du Toit was the senior British officer in the P.O.W. camp; it was he who had encouraged him to try and stay within the hospital and who had urged him to give his parole, convinced that Gabriel's injuries would debar him from ever fighting again.

In the hospital, Major du Toit had argued, he was in an ideal position to smuggle items of food and medical supplies to the men behind the wire. Also, as he soon found out, he could pick up news of the war far more easily. Nanda was a military camp. In the civilian camps, prisoners who gave an oath not to try to escape were allowed to wander freely around whatever village or town the camp was set in. But for the captured soldiers, such an oath also contained the undertaking not to fight against Germany or her allies for the duration of the war. Du Toit had forbidden any of his men—apart from Gabriel—to take such an oath and consequently they spent their time behind the barbed-wire stockade. As it turned out, having Gabriel on the outside proved most useful. And this was what Gabriel told himself too. He pilfered professionally from the German stores—especially from the efficient quinine substitute they had developed—and was able to pass on the news of the attack on Taveta in March, the invasion of German East and the advance down the Northern Railway to Tanga. For the last few weeks the *Schutztruppe* had been in constant retreat and the fall of Dar-es-Salaam was expected any day.

But then the prisoners had left, a long straggling line of tattered troops with their little bundles of personal possessions, and with them had gone the garrison of native askaris—effectively emptying Nanda of three quarters of its population. Gabriel had watched the column go with decidedly mixed feelings. The hospital was now full exclusively of sick and wounded Germans. He was the only Englishman in Nanda.

Gabriel ran his fingers through his hair. The problem was that, now the prisoners had gone, there was really no excuse—no reasonable excuse—for his remaining in the hospital, for so selflessly reinfecting his leg wound. He rubbed his forehead. What reason could he give himself for staying on?

Liesl came into the room. Gabriel turned and smiled. She wore an old blue calico dress that had faded from navy to an uneven pale-blue. She had a white cotton scarf tied over her gingery hair. She sat down heavily on the wooden seat with an audible sigh, the thump making her large breasts shiver under the material, and Gabriel felt the familiar tugging in his guts.

"Deppe is coming back tomorrow," she said in English, lighting her cigarette. "But for only one day, thank you, God. Do you want your cigarette?" She held it up.

"No." Gabriel cleared his throat. "You have it."

"Thank you." She coughed. "It's so strong, this tobacco." She patted her chest and coughed again, pressing her breast with a forearm. Gabriel stood motionless by the window. He found it extraordinary how every movement this woman made—the slightest gesture—seemed loaded with sexual potential. He watched her now wiping her creamy freckled neck with a handkerchief, the action revealing the dark patches of perspiration in the armpits of her dress.

"Hammerstein is going," she said matter-of-factly. "An hour or two, I think."

"Anything I can do?" Gabriel asked.

"No," she said. "Nothing."

Hammerstein took longer to die than estimated, so Liesl didn't leave the hospital until quite late. Outside, it was dark and the familiar noises of the African night—the crickets, the bats, the hootings and the howlings—were everywhere about her. Gabriel watched her pause for a moment in the doorway and then set off down the main street of Nanda towards her bungalow. The street was dark, lit only by a few glimmering lanterns set outside the doorways of the mud shops and houses and the glow that spilled from some windows. Gabriel watched her go. Then he turned and went round the back of the hospital, through the kitchen gardens and into the rubber plantations beyond. He set off down an avenue between the trees. This was another, more discreet, route he had found to Liesl's bungalow.

He knew his way instinctively now, ducking under the low branch of a mango tree, squeezing through a gap in a thorn barrier, cutting through a dark copse of cotton trees. He paused as he came in sight of Liesl's bungalow, waiting until he saw her enter. Then he moved forward across a patch of waste ground and past the huge stand of bamboo that towered over the house at the back, the dried knife-leaves of the bamboo crackling softly under his feet. He moved more slowly now as he entered the thicket of bushes directly behind the house, praying silently to himself that the shutters would be open. It had been a hot day; surely the maid would have opened them in the evening in an attempt to cool the house?

He heard Liesl call "Kimi!" as he took up his position. The shutters were open; an oil lamp was already lit in the room, filling it with its damp yellow light. Gabriel stood there, breathing shallowly, his heart beginning to beat faster as he mentally rehearsed the routine he now knew so well.

He had stumbled on it quite by chance some weeks before. Liesl had left some cigarettes he had made her in the hospital. He had taken them round to her bungalow only to be told by her maid that Frau von Bishop couldn't see him, as she was busy. Gabriel said it wasn't important and had left the cigarettes. Going by the side of the house, he had seen the light cast onto the bushes from the back window. Guiltily he'd made his way into the thicket to spy, for some reason suspecting a lover. But there he saw the sight that had proved his undoing. A magnificent pale Bathsheba, heavy-breasted and full-thighed, glistening palely in the lamplight as the buckets of water were tipped over her, while he looked on, captivated, an impotent David in the shadows outside.

He stood there now, well screened by the bushes and hidden by the darkness, peering through the leaves into her bedroom. Liesl came into view, framed for a moment by the window. Then she moved out of vision while she undressed. He heard faintly the tinny scrape of the bath being shifted into the middle of the floor and the mutter of some words she exchanged with her maid. It was only a matter of moments now.

For some reason Gabriel felt the acid bite of his guilt more strongly that night than before. He lay on his hard bed in the fetid heat of his hut, unable to get to sleep, tormented and entranced by the remembered images of Liesl. Sometimes the desire he felt seemed to prove too much for him and he thought his chest would burst, his ribs springing apart like staves from an old barrel. The ache of his longing hit him with full force. He wanted desperately to bury his head in those pillowy enveloping breasts, set his forehead in the soft junction of her neck and jawbone, feel her strong arms about his body. . . .

He turned over. It was only since he'd started spying on Liesl that the other dreams had left him. The dreams of Gleeson's shattered face, of Bilderbeck's shot, the steaming brain on his boot. Then the horrific race through the graveyard, the thumping feet of his pursuers. The writhing on the ground, the skewering, pronging jabs of the bayonets. He always woke up with the one that had glanced off his pelvis: when he felt the nail grating of the metal point juddering on the fresh bone, skidding off into his vitals.

He told Deppe about these dreams, how they came almost every night. Could that be why, he suggested, he was so weak and emaciated? "Nonsense," Deppe replied confidently. "Dreams can't have that effect."

Gabriel touched his throat, felt his bobbing, trembling Adam's apple, then trailed his fingers down his chest, touching a nipple, then through the damp chest hairs. He dragged a fingertip over the ridges of his ribcage, like rattling a stick on park railings. Then he flattened his palm over his belly, pressing down on the weals and distorted flesh of his two scars. Lower still, he touched his penis, cupped and lifted his sweaty balls, feeling instantly more comfortable as he did so. It was curious, he thought, how the touch of your own hand on your genitals was so reassuring.

His mind began to wander. A soldier had been brought in with bayonet wounds the other day. Much worse than his, half his intestines on show. They had turned a peculiar carroty colour. He didn't last long, even though Deppe was up all night operating, with Liesl and two of the other nurses. He'd worked hard that night too; they had been glad of his assistance. When the man died, he brought everyone hot tea, got the cooks out of bed to make some food. Where had the dead man come from? someone had asked. From Morogoro, Deppe had said. The Central Railway. There's heavy fighting there. We're pulling back. It was surprising, Gabriel thought, how much you learnt about the war from casual conversation in a hospital. Injured men coming in from battlefields, cured ones going to new postings. Names were always being mentioned. He had quite a clear idea of the main troop dispositions, exactly as Major du Toit had said.

He sat up, shaking his head to wake himself. He suddenly saw what he had to do. Du Toit had been right all along. His position in the hospital *was* valuable. It was *still* valuable. He still had a job to do here. He would continue to gather information. He would conduct innocent conversations with the men in the wards, piece disconnected remarks together, build up a picture of the campaign. He felt suddenly elated by this. It was a kind of authorisation of his continued presence. He would stay on in his present role for as long as he could: unassuming, ubiquitous, unsuspected. He would become an "intelligencer," keep notes, plot positions on a map. And then? Then he would escape.

He lay back with a smile of satisfaction, and stretched his hands out to touch the sheet of butter muslin he used as a mosquito net. He wouldn't think about escape just at the moment, though. He would stay on a few weeks and allow his store of information to accumulate. He felt his wound itching slightly, and he scratched at it through the bandages. Good, he thought, it's beginning to fester again. He gritted his teeth and pressed his knuckles into the bandages, feeling the pain jolt along his leg. Deppe was coming tomorrow. It should look bad enough to get him back in the ward again.

CHAPTER SIXTEEN

25 JUNE 1916

Stackpole Manor · Kent

Charis wrote to Gabriel every month. They were chatty, inconsequential letters about life at Stackpole and the family, but they now suddenly became almost unbearably hard to write. She had no idea if he ever received them because she never got a reply. All they knew was that he was wounded and a prisoner. She had asked Henry Hyams about letters and he had told her to send them care of Divisional Headquarters, Indian Expeditionary Force "B," Nairobi. He said that supplies and provisions for the care of British P.O.W.'s were passed on to the Germans, who were trusted to distribute them along with any personal letters. "That's the general idea," Henry Hyams had said. "Not that you can necessarily trust the Huns to comply. But have a go, Charis my dear, have a go."

So she wrote every month with an increasing sense of unreality, staring at Gabriel's photograph, trying to summon up an image of him and their brief life together. It wasn't very successful, and she had to keep stopping as, all too often, she ended up thinking of Felix.

But she hadn't written for over six weeks now. For some reason she became suddenly convinced that all her letters had got through, that over the almost two years they had been separated, the letters had come to represent—for Gabriel—his sole contact with the world he'd left in 1914. And as the days passed and the terrifying prospects of the future closed in, it was this personal failure that manifested itself as the most shameful sign of her guilt, the one thing that would ultimately condemn her and, even worse, lead Gabriel to guess that there was something terribly wrong.

But equally appalling in its way was the fact that there was nobody in the world to whom she could turn or confess. Not even Felix. He had written from Oxford saying that, as usual, he had booked them into the hotel in Aylesbury. She had invented a cousin in London and a visit there that would coincide neatly with the end of the summer term in Oxford. But everything had changed. She had written to Felix saying she wasn't well and wouldn't be able to meet him. It was no lie.

But he wouldn't leave her alone. Because she'd missed Aylesbury, he had started coming to the cottage in the middle of the night. And for the first time they had sex at Stackpole. This, too, had been enormously upsetting. She couldn't use the bedroom—its associations with Gabriel were too intense—and so they made do with the sofa in the front room. But there was none of the conjugal intimacy of their hotel encounters. They couldn't lie in each other's arms and talk. When they finished they got dressed again, and Felix would sneak back to his room.

This improvisation—with its echoes of clandestine suburban adultery—proved doubly depressing. One night she'd broken down, crying into her hands. When Felix asked what was wrong, she blamed it on the shabbiness of the way they were now forced to carry on. It was his total inability to console her, to say anything beyond a feeble "Don't worry," or "It doesn't matter," that finally showed her Felix wouldn't be—couldn't be—any help. It wasn't his fault. There was nothing he could do. It was simply the dreadful, final nature of her predicament.

Yet a solution did suggest itself with a kind of quiet, childlike logic one afternoon as she sat by the fish-pond. She wasted no time. That evening she wrote to Gabriel. What she imagined would be the hardest letter of her life turned out to be simple and straightforward. She told him everything, only leaving out the name and identity of her lover, and begged his understanding and forgiveness.

She had sealed the letter and kept it in a drawer for several days, running through the futile options once more for form's sake. Then the previous afternoon she had walked briskly into Stackpole village, past the church where she'd been married, had bought sufficient stamps at the post office and, without any pause, had placed it in the pillar-box.

This done, a sort of cheerful calm had descended on her which was punctuated by brief moments of dreadful panic. These were quelled swiftly by an invocation to consider the future, which brought in its train such a sense of misery and guilt that the absolute rightness and inevitability of the course of action she planned to initiate established the comforting indifference again.

By such methods she had managed to get through the day. She had gone for a walk up the river and stood and gazed at the slowly flowing water for a long time. In the evening she had prepared a meal as usual, set it out and eaten it down heartily. Half an hour later she found she was hungry again. She had banked up the fire and sat in front of it on a low stool, hugging her knees to her, watching the dance of the flames and the collapse of the coals in a benign mesmerised trance.

Shortly after midnight Felix tapped on the window. She fixed a smile on her face and let him in. They kissed.

"Is everything all right, Charis?" he asked. "I missed you at luncheon."

"I went for a walk. I'm fine. I lost track of the time."

Satisfied, Felix launched into details of his latest plan. Oxford was so terrible that he and Holland couldn't face the prospect of another year there. Holland felt that it was perfectly acceptable for them to volunteer as ambulance drivers, as long as they were posted to France together.

"I say, Charis, are you listening?"

"Sorry. I was dreaming. You were saying?"

"I might be going to France as an ambulance driver. At the end of the summer."

"Oh."

"What do you think? Don't you mind?"

"I shall miss you." The deeper truth that this statement contained caused tears to brim on her eyelids. Felix was touched and put his arm around her.

"Don't worry about me, Carrie," he said. "I shall be miles from the front."

Their embrace led to a kiss and thence to a partial undressing and an uncomfortable union on the small sofa. They had become more adept and assured in making the necessary manoeuvres. Charis saw this confidence make itself daily more evident in Felix. He was twenty now; he seemed finally to be leaving the last traces of his boyishness behind.

He didn't stay for long. Shortly after one o'clock he started yawning and said he'd better get off to bed. Charis saw him to the door, remembering to switch off the light in the hall so he couldn't be seen leaving. His complete obliviousness to everything she was suffering was, paradoxically, her greatest support. If he had sensed anything badly amiss, if he had questioned and probed, she doubted if she could have sustained the minimal poise and control she possessed. As it was, it required very little effort on her part to convince him that everything was normal.

"See you tomorrow," he said, kissed her on the nose and was gone.

Charis sat for an hour running through her plan in her mind. She couldn't avoid causing grief and pain, she knew. But it would be nothing to the consequences that would fall on all their heads if the truth came out.

Eventually she sat down at the writing desk and wrote briefly to Felix.

My darling Felix,
I have been thinking things over and have decided to go away.
Under the circumstances it seems the only possible thing to do. Any
sort of compromise would be intolerable. I have written to Gabriel and
told him everything.

It seemed a bit terse and ambiguous, but that gave her a vague satisfaction. She thought of adding some phrase like "I am sorry" or "Don't have any regrets," but decided against it, signing only her name.

She sealed the letter in an envelope and addressed it. She felt determined and businesslike, she gladly noted, not morose or self-pitying. She was going to be rid of all the doubts and dilemmas, shames and disappointments, all the pains and griefs that stood ranked in the future waiting for her. An interminable hellish gauntlet that she would no longer have to run. Her skilful evasion seemed suddenly profoundly satisfying. The choice she made now was, she thought, as bold and intelligent as any stoical decision to endure.

She picked up Felix's letter and put on her heaviest tweed coat. It was a golfing coat with an attached cape and big buttoned skirt that came down to her ankles. She put her hand on the doorknob. She had everything she needed.

Outside, it was a dark, cool night, cloud-free, with the stars shining up above. She walked briskly up the drive to the big house. It was just cold enough for her breath to condense for a second or two. She slipped Felix's letter into the letter-box in the front door. A faint wind moved through the rhododendrons, causing the thick shiny leaves to clatter drily. She took a deep breath. All the worries and fears were dwindling into insubstantiality as swiftly as her condensed breath was hurried away by the breeze. It seemed to her that she faced only an avenue of bright tomorrows. She turned on her heel and set off down the path she had chosen.

CHAPTER SEVENTEEN

26 JUNE 1916

Stackpole Manor · Kent

"Job," cried Major Cobb, "chapter twenty-eight, verse twelve."

"Oh dear, no," breathed Mrs. Cobb, standing beside Felix. "Not again." She pressed her fingers into her cheeks as if her teeth were aching. "Not again."

Felix stared at the map of Africa, then squinted slightly so that the reds and greens went hazy and elided. The holiday before, he had deliberately missed family prayers one morning, thinking he was old enough to absent himself without having to ask permission. His father had gone, in Felix's opinion, raving mad. He had exploded with wrath at the breakfast table when Felix eventually appeared, accusing him of being a worthless atheist, a snivelling coward, a disgrace to the family name and, moreover, exhibiting a callous disregard of his brother's noble sacrifice. It was the last insult that had stirred his conscience and so now he thought it worth it—for the quiet life that everyone was after—to comply with his father's whims.

"'But where shall wisdom be found?'" the major intoned, "'and where is the place of understanding?'" His fat features had slackened, the puffy cheeks sagged, the double chins now bristly dewlaps which were never properly shaved. But he was as obsessive as ever, and Felix could see him shaking slightly as he loudly repeated the words of the daily lesson.

"'Where is the place of understanding? Man knoweth not the price thereof; neither is it found in the land of the living.'" He prodded the open Bible in front of him with a stubby forefinger. "'Neither is it found. In. The land. Of. The living.'"

His mother stopped Felix, with a gentle pressure on his arm, as he was filing out of the library to go to breakfast.

"Darling," Mrs. Cobb said, a worried look on her face, "I'm a little concerned about your father."

"I'm not surprised," Felix said. "Shouldn't he be in hospital?"

"Really! Felix. He's just so upset."

"We're *all* upset, Mother. That doesn't mean we have to behave like"—he indicated the map—"like *that."*

"Oh, dear," Mrs. Cobb said, taking her bottom lip between her teeth for a moment. "Oh, dear. What is happening with this dreadful war? It's most unfair."

Felix went into the dining room. His father was sitting at the end of the table reading a newspaper. Beside him was Cressida, trying to ignore his constant mutters and exclamations. Felix's empty place was next to hers. Opposite them sat Eustacia and Nigel Bathe. Nigel Bathe wore a tweed jacket, the two empty sleeves of which were pinned up just below his elbows. Beside him Eustacia cut up a plate of bacon and eggs, loaded up a forkful and popped it in his mouth.

"Morning," Felix said. "Nigel, Eustacia, Cressida . . . Father."

Felix felt as he always did these mornings a surge of pity for Nigel Bathe, whom he'd never liked. Nigel still grumbled and complained as of old—about the size of his disability pension, the inefficacy of the artificial limbs he was learning to use—but Felix didn't grudge him it now. The rest of the family seemed quite accustomed to his presence at meals, his being spoon-fed by Eustacia, but Felix found it a most unsettling start to each day.

"Aha!" shouted the major, causing everyone to look up sharply and a section of fried egg to jerk off Eustacia's extended fork and splat on the shiny table top.

"Here we are, here we are." The major cleared his throat. "'On June the nineteenth, British forces in German East Africa occupied the important town of Handeni.' Where's my map?" He sprang up from the table and marched out of the room.

Everyone pretended nothing had happened. Felix opened the chafing dishes on the sideboard and helped himself to a large plate of kidneys, scrambled eggs, fried bread, bacon and sausage. He found that keeping his head down while he shovelled in food was the best way of avoiding the pathetic sight of Nigel Bathe across the table.

He sat down. "Well," he said vacuously, "looks like it's going to be a pleasant day." He turned round in his seat and craned his head to see out of the window. His guess seemed accurate enough. The lawn was bright with sun, the fish-ponds were blue, and only a few small indolent clouds occupied the sky above.

There were three letters by his place. A catalogue from a book-seller, confirmation of an appointment with his optician, and one, unstamped, in a plain white envelope. He recognised Charis's writing at once, and with a frown of curiosity tore it open. Nobody paid any attention.

He read the letter.

"Oh, God. Jesus Christ," he said in a shocked voice, getting up from his place.

"Felix!" Cressida and Eustacia said in unison.

He ran out of the room, stuffing the letter in his pocket. He rushed outside, sprinting across the sunlit lawn, the heels of his shoes biting deeply into the dew-damp turf. He vaulted over the eve-gate, skidding on a patch of mud beyond and falling over. He picked himself up and pounded through the wood towards the cottage. The back door was locked. He ran round to the front and let himself in. He knew at once the cottage was empty. He stood in the little parlour, looking at the grate of the fire, the ashes of the night before still there. His eyes passed uneasily over the sofa and he saw that the lid of the writing desk was folded down.

He went upstairs. The bed was unslept in. He opened the wardrobe. It was filled with hanging clothes. On the chest of drawers he saw Gabriel's photograph. The strong square face, the simple smile. He felt an awful turmoil in his body, a sudden sickening awareness of just what he and Charis had done. He recalled the words of the letter: "I have written to Gabriel and told him everything."

He sat down on the bed and rubbed his eyes. His brain was refusing to work. He realised one trouser leg was thick with mud, also one sleeve of the jacket and his left hand. He stood up. The bedspread was smeared and dirty.

He walked shakily down the stairs. Think, he told himself, *think*. She seemed to have walked out of the house without taking anything. No clothes, no suitcase . . . He tried to ignore one explanation that was shouting persistently in his head.

Not Charis, he said to himself. She wouldn't. The sense of his own responsibility, so successfully evaded for so many months, hit him with full force. He sat down again, on the bottom stair, trembling all over. He patted his pockets for a cigarette, then realised he'd left them in his bedroom.

He got to his feet. The police would have to be informed. Perhaps she'd gone to Aunt Bedelia's, just fled in a panic for whatever reason? It sounded plausible. But what was wrong? he asked himself. Why should she do it? Why now? She said she hadn't been feeling well lately—perhaps that could have been a contributing factor. He turned a few more thoughts over in his head. But her note? He took it out of his pocket and spread it on his knee. It was so terse and final. Almost hostile. But why should she write to Gabriel too? This new factor made his head reel. He felt the blood thumping at his temples; he found it difficult to swallow. His stomach heaved and he gagged. He put the back of his hand to his mouth and leant against the wall for support. His mouth was full of fresh saliva, like thick water.

At once he pushed himself off the wall and rushed out of the house. Back through the wood, over the eve-gate, across the bottom of the lawn towards the fish-ponds. He saw his mother and Cressida standing agitatedly on the terrace. They called his name as he ran into view, but he ignored them.

He leapt down the steps to the seat by the middle pond. His first feeling was one of immense relief as he saw its vacant, glassy surface. The lilies, the reeds, the ornamental bulrushes, all as it always was, sunlit and undisturbed. He stood panting at the edge trying to peer beneath the reflections and the glare of the sun. He could see nothing. But the carp, prompted by his shadow on the water and expecting a feed, began to rise up from the depths. The water swirled; fish bodies coiled and swerved; thick lips and blunt snouts tested the surface.

"Blasted bloody fish!" he swore. He turned round to find a stone to throw—to make them scatter.

Then he saw the pedestal. The marble bust of the Emperor Vitellius was missing.

Felix kicked off his shoes and struggled out of his jacket. His mother and Cressida had reached the upper pond and were awkwardly descending the wide steps, their skirts held up in their hands.

"Felix!" his mother wailed in evident distress. "What's happening, my darling? What's wrong?"

He ignored them.

He jumped into the pool. It was deep, eight feet or more, and very cold. He allowed his momentum to take him down to the bottom, feeling the pressure in his ears, and the faint sound of his mother screaming. He opened his eyes, paddling furiously with his hands to keep himself down. Through the murk, all about him, he sensed the carp darting away into their hiding places.

Then one of his beating hands struck something soft. He spun round. Charis's body was close in to the side. He'd been looking too far out. She was in the attitude of a dive or plummeting fall, her feet trailing up behind her, her head held down, tied in grotesque familiar proximity to the Emperor Vitellius.

Felix felt his lungs were on the point of bursting, but he forced himself closer. A length of twine was tied round her neck, its ends in turn wrapped and secured with many knots about the marble head. Through the drifting clouds of mud and sediment he saw that her eyes and mouth were open, her face relaxed and expressionless. Her hair had loosened itself and streamed weedily about her features, stirred by the currents of water caused by his beating, flailing hands.

CHAPTER EIGHTEEN

1 JULY 1916

Sevenoaks · Kent

"It seems she tied herself—round the neck—to the bust. She just had enough strength to lift it off the pedestal on her arms, take two steps to the edge and fall in. The weight dragged her straight down to the bottom." Felix paused and took another cigarette out of his case.

"She had tied a lot of knots. She couldn't even have got free if she had wanted to. She didn't leave herself any room for second thoughts."

Felix lit the cigarette. He was sitting with Dr. Venables in the saloon bar of a hotel not far from the magistrates' court in Sevenoaks where the inquest had been held. Dr. Venables had been called to give evidence, too, as he had performed a post-mortem on Charis's body. Felix was the only member of the Cobb family who had attended. He was still feverish and agitated from all the lies he'd told.

The inquest had been a mere formality. Felix had told his edited story. He said he'd lost the letter in his panic and confusion. It had simply said, he swore, that Charis intended to go away. No reason had been given. A police constable from Ashurst read out his version of events and then Dr. Venables had been called to confirm the cause of death. "A tragic case," the magistrate had concluded. "Mrs. Cobb is as much a victim of the war as our young men who have bravely given their lives in France."

Afterwards, Dr. Venables had invited him for a bracing drink. Felix said he didn't want one but the doctor was very insistent. He sat opposite Felix now, his unnaturally dark hair shining damply in the gloom of the bar. He pulled regularly at his ear lobes while Felix talked.

Felix was acutely uneasy. For the last few days he had lived— he felt—constantly on the edge of a breakdown. The sense of his own appalling selfishness and lack of insight was a consistent tormenting rebuke. Sharp beaks of guilt stabbed at him. He felt a sense of overpowering, frustrating anger at her death. But somewhere deep inside, like an unfamiliar noise in a sleeping house, a more persistent trouble nagged.

He tried to focus on Charis's death, on the powerful sense of loss which he knew he felt, in the hope that some expression of grief might relieve or overwhelm the massive doubts and guilts that were building up explosively within him. But, try as he might, impugn himself as he might, it was Charis's dreadful legacy that obsessed him all his waking moments.

The letter. The letter to Gabriel. What in God's name had possessed her to send it? He felt grossly ashamed that this was all he could think of. He despised and utterly condemned his highly developed instincts of self-preservation. He could live with his guilt— just—as long as it remained a secret which he alone knew. The thought of Gabriel ever learning about Charis and him was horrific, the most potent of fears, and it left him weak and trembling.

He had telephoned Henry Hyams at the War Office on the

pretext of wondering how the news of Charis's death could best be conveyed to Gabriel. Did letters, he asked, ever get through? There was a reasonable chance, Hyams said, though it would probably take months, and now, with the British Army well inside German East, there was really no telling.

This was both good and bad news. Clearly there was a possibility nothing would happen. Who knew the potential accidents and delays that could befall a single letter on such a perilous journey? But, then again, Hyams had implied that some letters did arrive. . . . He forced himself to stop. His self-disgust was making a nerve tremor in his cheek.

He drained his brandy and soda. Dr. Venables called for another. Felix glanced at his epicene features. He looked very grim and serious.

"A terrible business," Dr. Venables said. "Such a charming girl. I'd grown very fond of her, you know, in our work together."

"I know."

"There's one thing I don't understand."

"Why she did it?"

"No. No."

"What's that, then?"

"Why did she write to *you*, Felix? I hope you don't mind my asking."

Felix looked up, startled. He stubbed out his cigarette, his mind racing. "We'd become good friends," he said slowly. "Of sorts. Since, that is"—he cleared his throat—"Gabriel's capture."

"What did her letter say?"

"Well, exactly what I told the magistrate, as far as I can remember. That, um, she was going to go away, and that she was sorry."

"Those were the words she used?"

"I think so. To be honest, I can't recall exactly. That's the general drift. I was shocked."

"Quite so."

"I've looked everywhere for the letter." Felix took a sip at his brandy. "But I was frantic, running through the woods like that.

Perhaps when I dived in the pond . . . ?" Felix left his sentence unfinished. What was Venables driving at?

"That's another thing."

"What?"

"Why you went straight to the pond. *That* pond."

"I didn't go *straight* there. I went to the cottage first."

"But when that was empty . . ."

"Yes."

"Why?"

"It was something she said once. I suddenly remembered. It was her favourite place. We often used to sit and chat there. I had this feeling. I don't know. I can't explain."

Dr. Venables leant forward. He placed the tips of his fingers together and looked at his large, clean hands. Felix stared at them too. He noticed they were quite hairless. "I want to ask you something, Felix," Dr. Venables said. "And I want your honest answer. Depending on your answer, I will then give you some information. Do you understand?"

"Yes." Felix glanced round the bar. It was almost empty and quiet. This wasn't like Venables at all.

"Total honesty, Felix."

"Of course." He felt dizzy with the pressure.

"This is what I *have* to ask you, Felix. Were you and Charis having a love affair?"

"What?"

"You heard me. Were you and Charis having a love affair?"

"No."

Dr. Venables caught his eye. The question was repeated telepathically.

"No," Felix repeated. The massive effort it took to force his gaze not to waver was exacting an immense toll.

"You were not having a love affair."

"That's correct."

Venables seemed to relax ever so slightly.

"Let me ask you another question, then. Do you know if Charis was having an affair with another man?"

"Another man?" Felix felt his head loud with clattering, unaskable questions. What was Venables trying to prove? "No," he said. "Not as far as I'm aware."

"I see." Venables placed his hands on the table. "Thank you, Felix. I had to ask."

Horrible suspicions seemed to be squirming in sockets of Felix's brain.

"Why do you think she was? Having a love, um, affair?"

"Simply seeking for a reason, Felix." The doctor's eyes were candid. "Trying to find an explanation."

Felix's fingers lightly touched his lips, chin, nose, as if discovering his features for the first time. He stood up, and said with absurd formality, "Would you mind if I took a breath of fresh air?" Venables moved his seat to let him get by.

Outside, the streets were busy. Motor cars tooted warnings as they reached the sharp bend in the road to the left of the hotel. A barefoot boy, wheeling a costermonger's barrow full of cabbages, whistled loudly as he trundled his load along the pavement, turning down an alleyway to the hotel kitchens. Felix stood on the little gravelled forecourt in front of the hotel, keeping his hands thrust deep in his pockets. He looked for a while at the passing traffic and sauntering pedestrians.

He went back into the saloon bar and sat down.

"You said," he began carefully, "that depending on my answer you would give me some information. What was that?"

"It's irrelevant now," Venables said. "You gave the right answer."

"But what if I'd given another one?"

"But you didn't."

"Yes." Felix looked at Venables. Did he know? Was he guessing? What made him ask now?

"I think we should forget about all further speculations," Venables said. "This conversation should not be reported or reopened again outside this saloon bar. There is no need to—what shall I say?—give rise to unnecessary suffering in your family. I think you'll agree that there are problems enough to deal with at Stackpole."

"Yes," Felix said, "you're right." A thought kept darting elusively through his head like a minnow. It didn't bear contemplation, or rather something would not allow it to be contemplated. Other more atavistic impulses seemed to be denying it access to his understanding. He let it go. Venables' sleek, waxy features gave nothing away.

"Can I offer you a lift home?" Venables asked. "I've left my motor by the court room."

"No, thank you," Felix said. "I've a return ticket for the train."

They left the bar and went outside. Somewhere, behind the hotel, the costermonger's boy was still whistling.

"Somebody's happy anyway," Dr. Venables said with a sad smile. "Not that many of us have got much to be happy about in this day and age." He held out his hand. "Well, Felix. Remember what I said."

Felix shook his hand. "I shall."

"And if you ever feel in the need of a talk, come and see me. I used to enjoy our discussions."

"Of course," Felix said. Dr. Venables still held his hand firmly.

"What are you going to do now, Felix?" The question seemed to be innocent, but Felix realised you could be sure of nothing with Venables.

He decided to be innocent too. "I shall get the train straight back."

"No. I meant with your future. What are you going to do with yourself?"

Felix had been wondering the same thing. He had come to some sort of decision.

"I've been thinking about that myself, Dr. Venables." He knew but he was not going to tell Venables. "I'm afraid I don't have an answer at the moment."

PART THREE

The Ice-Cream War

CHAPTER ONE

25 JANUARY 1917

Dar-es-Salaam · German East Africa

Felix looked out over the guard-rails of the *Hong Wang II,* a Chinese-crewed tramp steamer that had brought him slowly up the coast from Durban to the entrancing waterfront at Dar-es-Salaam. The widening sweep of the bay, the white buildings set in groves of mango and palm trees, and the cloudless African sky presented a scene of great beauty. Only the ruined shell of the Governor's palace on the headland and the wreck of a scuttled German freighter on a sandbank marred the general effect of peace and tranquillity.

Felix looked down at his knee-length shorts, khaki puttees and polished brown boots. He still felt a fool in this uniform. It was extremely odd, moreover, to be a second lieutenant in a native regiment which he had yet to encounter. This was not entirely true, as one unit of the regiment was on board the *Hong Wang II* with him. On the foredeck a four-gun mountain battery of the Nigerian

Brigade prepared to disembark. These were the stragglers in a large West African contingent that had arrived in East Africa a month or so previously. Felix's own battalion in this brigade, the 5th, was already entrenched in the front line at a place on the upper reaches of the Rufiji river, wherever that might be.

The *Hong Wang II* dropped anchor in the middle of the bay. Soon Felix and his kit and the English officers and NCOs of the mountain battery were being carried in a launch to one of the many wooden jetties that stuck out from the shore.

His kit was disembarked and laid in a pile on the ground. Felix stretched and stamped his feet. All around him was the bustle of the port, the cries of the rickshaw boys, the grinding and clamour of the steam cranes. The air was filled with smells of dust and fruit, dead fish and manure. The sun was lowering in the afternoon sky but still burned with a force that made his new uniform chafe. He felt a sense of exhilaration fill his chest. Gabriel was incarcerated somewhere in this country. They might be separated from each other by only a few hundred miles. The war could be over, by all accounts, in a matter of months, now that the Germans were well and truly on the run. Soon, he felt sure, he and Gabriel would be reunited and somehow everything would be resolved. For a moment he felt intoxicated by a sense of his own self-importance, the glamour of the role in which he had cast himself. Now that he was here in Africa he felt he could say that his quest had truly begun.

An Executive Service officer, a captain, approached the officers from the mountain battery and gave them instructions. Felix showed him the sheet of paper that contained his orders.

"Kibongo," the E.S.O. captain said. "Umm." He paused. "Fifth Battalion, Nigerian Brigade . . . Ah-ha. Mmm." He sounded like a schoolboy who didn't know the answers to a classroom quiz.

"Tell you what," he said. "There's a Movement Control officer at the railway station. He'll know. I think the headquarters of the Nigerian Brigade is at Morogoro. I'll get a boy to bring your kit. Yes, Morogoro, that's where you'll be going."

"No, it's Soga you want," the Movement Control officer said. Then added, "I think. Get off at Soga, anyway. They'll probably send someone to meet you there. Hang on, I'll get a boy to sling your gear on the train. Soga, remember."

Felix found a compartment and watched the boy stow his kit. Steadily the other seats were taken up by officers from an Indian regiment. Some of them knew about the Nigerian Brigade, but had no idea where Kibongo was. They told him to get off at Mikesse, not Soga.

Felix sat back and told himself to relax. He was sufficiently used to army ways by now not to worry unduly about such vagueness. In fact he was amazed at the way the organisation worked at all. He had received written orders; that was sufficient. At some point in the future he and his battalion would meet.

In the stifling heat of the small compartment he watched the sun turn orange and sink behind the railway workshops. There was a further hour's delay before the train pulled off with a lurch. In the brief dusk Felix saw the acres of coconut trees behind the town, and splendid, solid-looking stone houses set amongst them.

The twenty-fifth of January 1917: it had been nearly six months since he had set in motion this particular chain of events, which had resulted in his sitting now in a troop train chugging slowly across conquered German East Africa.

A week after Charis's funeral—a taut, stressful affair—Felix had gone up to London to seek out his brother-in-law, Lieutenant-Colonel Henry Hyams, at the Committee for Imperial Defence. Hyams was surprised to see him and commiserated briefly about Charis's suicide.

"Bad business, Felix. Terrible shame. Poor girl." He frowned. "It all got too much for her, I suppose. Gabriel and all that."

After some more awkward conversation on the topic, Felix stated that he wished to obtain a commission in any unit of the British Army that was currently fighting in East Africa. Henry Hyams didn't ask him why; it must have seemed to him a logical request, Felix thought, based on clear and commendable motives of duty and honourable revenge. Hyams considered that his earlier failure with the recruiting office would present no problems now. That was 1914, he reminded Felix, when—no offence implied—

they were taking only the very best. Now that there was conscription, they couldn't afford to be so choosy. He made some notes on a pad and checked a file.

"East Africa, East Africa. British regiments. You have no desire to go soldiering with the mild gentoo, I take it?"

"No, it must be a British regiment," Felix affirmed.

"Well, we've got the Second Battalion Loyal North Lancs and the Twenty-fifth Battalion of the Royal Fusiliers. The 'Legion of Frontiersmen.' Sound like a fine body of men."

"Yes. They sound ideal."

"That's the ticket then." Hyams beamed confidently. "I'll arrange everything. Leave it all up to me."

Two weeks later Felix was informed by telegram which Officer Training Corps he was to attend. He looked disbelievingly at the address: Keble College, Oxford. For the next three months he was back in Oxford, living in Keble's sooty redbrick splendour in the company of two hundred other young men seeking commissions. Throughout the end of the summer of 1916, while the battle of the Somme ground itself into a state of inertia, he received instructions on how to command men, drilled endlessly in the University Parks, fired rifles at the butts in Wolvercote and undertook textbook manoeuvres on the level expanses of Port Meadow. He assailed all these distasteful duties in a spirit of unreflecting determination, resolving to acquit himself adequately so there could be no impediment offered to the task he had set himself. In fact, he wasn't exactly clear what precisely the nature of this task was. It was born out of a mixture of near-intolerable guilt, unfocussed motives of purgation and a simple but powerful need to be doing something. The notion of the "quest," of somehow finding Gabriel, took a slower hold on his imagination. It was the most apt penance he could think of; he forced himself to concentrate on Gabriel and their eventual reunion and tried his hardest not to dwell on Charis.

And so the months of training—hurried and not particularly efficient—had gone past, and Felix found that instead of regret and melancholy, his moods had been primarily ones of deep boredom, loneliness and discomfort. On the day their postings were announced he had clustered round the notice-board outside the college lodge with the other cadets, searching for his name. "Cobb, F.R."—his eyes flicked across—"5th btn, Nigerian bde, German East Africa." The Nigerian Brigade? Who or what were they? He received commiserations from his fellow officers. Where was Nigeria? someone asked. Felix had to go and look it up in an atlas.

"Sorry, old chap," Henry Hyams said when Felix asked for a transfer. "No can do." The brigade was just being formed, Hyams said. It was the only unit in the East African theatre that wanted English officers and NCOs.

"Don't look so glum, Felix," Henry Hyams said, looking a little hurt. "At least you'll be in East Africa. It's a damn tricky job swinging these things, you know. They're crying out for men in France."

Felix peered out of the carriage window at the African night. What was it like out there, he wondered? The train moved with frustrating slowness, reducing speed to five miles per hour every time it came to the gentlest of bends. The Indian Army officers had all fallen asleep; one of them was snoring quietly. The oil lamp in the compartment had been turned down too low to read. Felix rubbed his eyes. Somewhere in his kit he had an inflatable rubber cushion which would have eased his stiff and aching buttocks, sore from the slatted wooden bench seats, but he would have woken the entire compartment searching for it.

The train moved sluggishly but inexorably on. Sometimes it stopped in the darkness for no apparent reason. The monotony was briefly relieved when they pulled into tiny stations with names like Pugu, Kisamine and Soga, where it took on more fuel and water.

At Soga, Felix managed to get out of the compartment and jumped to the ground to stretch his legs. The night was warm and very dark; clouds seemed to be covering the moon and stars. All around him Felix could hear the relentless "creek-creek" of the crickets, shrill and mechanical. He gave a slight shiver. There was a curious smell in the air, strangely intoxicating, a damp earthy smell of the sort sometimes encountered in old potting sheds or undisturbed dusty attics. Felix filled his lungs with it. He felt seized by a sudden nervous excitement.

Up ahead the squat little locomotive was being filled up with water, a faint hiss of blundering escaping steam was carried down the line. He watched other men jumping from the carriages and the cattle trucks that carried the native soldiers. He saw some men relieving themselves and took a few steps away from the train to do likewise. He found himself standing in a sort of coarse knee-length grass. Ahead of him he could just make out a dark line of trees and bushes. He urinated, the patter of his stream silencing the crickets at his feet. He shivered again, the excitement gone, replaced by an apprehensive fearfulness. As he did up his fly buttons the thought crossed his mind that the foaming, trembling darkness around him might be harbouring all manner of wild beasts. Lions, leopards, snakes, anything. Hurriedly he clambered back into the compartment. He was not in some country lane, he reminded himself; he was in Africa.

It was almost mid-day when the troop train crawled into Mikesse. The Indian Army officers obligingly threw down his kit to him and he stacked it beside the rails. To his vague worry he was the only person to get off. The train didn't stay long. Morogoro, General Smuts' headquarters, was another thirty miles up the line. Everyone, it seemed, was going there.

Felix looked about him. A featureless railway station with no platforms, the tracks laid across packed-down red earth. In the distance a thickly wooded range of high, mountainous hills. Under large, shady trees dotted here and there, motor vehicles were parked and porters slept or lounged. It was very humid. Solid continents of grey clouds loomed to the north. Felix was about to go in search of some assistance when a small white man in khaki uniform emerged from the station building. The man caught sight of him and marched over. He had a spruce, fit-looking body, but his head appeared to belong to a man twice his size. Felix saw he had a sergeant's stripes on his sleeve. The man had a poor, crude-looking face, as if it were an early prototype whose features hadn't yet been properly refined. It was utterly expressionless, as if this, too, were a faculty reserved for later, more sophisticated models. He had one of the heaviest beards Felix had ever seen. Although he had obviously shaved recently, his entire jaw was a metallic blue-black; indeed, the bristles seemed to need shaving up to within half an inch of his lower eyelids.

"Lieutenant Cobb, sir?" he said. He had a very strong but clear Scottish accent. Felix supposed him to be from Aberdeen or Inverness.

"That's right. Are you from the Fifth Battalion?"

"Aye, sir. I'm Sergeant Gilzean."

He then said something Felix didn't understand.

"I beg your pardon?" Felix said.

"I said, 'Fegs it's a bauch day,' sir," Gilzean repeated patiently, as if this was an activity he was accustomed to. "I'll just make siccar they beanswaup porters look snippert with your gear."

"Oh. Yes, fine."

Men were called from beneath the trees and Felix's kit was taken round the station building and stacked in the back of a dusty Ford motor car.

"Where are we going?"

"Kibongo, sir. South bank of the Rufiji."

"How far away is it?"

"About one hundred and twenty miles."

"Good Lord!"

They bumped down a track that led from the station, and drove past a sizeable native village and a huge transport camp. Crates and sacks were piled twenty feet high. Motor lorries and dozens of Ford motor cars of the sort they were driving were parked in long rows. Beneath palm-leaf shelters were makeshift engineering and repair workshops. On a hill was a large stone building flying a red cross. A lengthy column of bootless African soldiers in green felt fezzes and flapping khaki shorts were passed.

"Are there no English troops out here?"

"A few," Gilzean said. "But they're all sick. Peely-wally lot the English, ye ken. And they Sooth-Africans. You'll find we're unco fremt haufins out here."

"Ah," Felix said. "I think so." The man might as well be talking ancient Greek, Felix thought.

They drove on, a cloud of red dust in their wake. They passed a large tented camp and overtook a straggling train of porters, all with loads on their heads. Mikesse, Felix managed to discover from Gilzean, was the only supply centre for the troops on the Rufiji river front, a hundred and twenty miles to the south. They drove out of the hills around the town and motored through beautiful highland country, dense with trees, native villages on every slope, before they began to descend slowly towards what looked like a huge, rather tatty forest. The trees were of all types and grew fairly widely apart. The ground between the trunks was thick with tangled thorn bush. The road had been enlarged recently, judging from the piles of freshly cut vegetation and the occasional groups of Pioneers and sappers that they passed, engaged in levelling out deep ruts or strengthening the many small bridges they had to drive across.

The clouds that Felix had noticed at the station had spread out to cover the sky, and the light was dull and gloomy.

"Looks like rain," Felix observed.

"We'll get drookit the night," Gilzean said, then added, "It's the rainy season. We stop fighting when the rains come."

"Have you seen any action?" Felix asked in what he hoped was a casual way.

"Och, aye. We've been dottling aboot the jungle for a month. Fankled here, fankled there. Fair scunnert, but, eh, neither buff nor stye, ye ken."

"Oh, about two months," Felix said.

After five hours of bumping along through the scrubby forest they came to another camp. Felix supposed he'd been travelling along what he'd come to know as "lines of communication," not that he and Gilzean had established many. At this new camp Felix was provided with a hot meal in the transport officers' mess and was allotted a camp-bed in the corner of a large empty tent. Here too, he found someone who could explain the current situation in comprehensible language.

Since the invasion of German East at Kilimanjaro in March 1916, the Germans had steadily been driven south so that they now occupied only the southern third of their colony. They had been pushed south across the Rufiji river. At their backs was another river, the Rovuma, which marked the border with Portuguese East Africa. The Rufiji, Felix's informant told him, was a huge sprawling river that divided the colony roughly in half. Von Lettow-Vorbeck, after he had been driven from the Northern Railway, had withdrawn by degrees, but with fierce rearguard actions, to the Central Railway (along which Felix had been travelling the night before). Threatened by Smuts on this front, he had again avoided a decisive battle and had withdrawn beyond his next natural defensive line, the Rufiji. Here was where matters had come to a halt, because of the imminent onset of the rains. There would be no more campaigning until March or April. Then the British Army would drive the Germans into the Rovuma.

Felix walked from the officers' mess back to his tent. Once again he smelt the musty, earthy smell and wondered what it was. Behind him the cooking fires of the vast porters' camp twinkled in the dark. He could hear strange whoopings coming from the trees beyond the perimeter fence. He wondered where Gilzean was, how the curious little man was occupying his time. Probably having a shave, Felix thought. He must need to shave about every five hours. He had wanted to ask Gilzean how far they had come, and what distance there was left to go, but couldn't face another incomprehensible reply. He hoped he hadn't appeared stand-offish.

He arrived at his tent. He felt that he had been travelling for months. First the tedious and depressing voyage to South Africa in a hospital ship full of broken South African infantry from the Western Front, with a gloomy, solitary Christmas spent at sea. Then two weeks in Durban waiting for the mountain battery to arrive from Nigeria. Afterwards the protracted voyage up the coast to Dar in the squalid *Hong Wang II*. Then the train journey through the night, Gilzean's jarring drive through the forest . . . And he still didn't know where he was.

He undressed standing on his camp-bed, as he'd been instructed to do—something about a burrowing flea one had to avoid. Then he untied his mosquito net and suspended it from hooks set in the canvas roof above the bed. He lay down and shut his eyes. This endless journeying, he thought to himself: where would it end? He made a rueful face in the dark. With Gabriel, he hoped. He allowed himself to imagine their meeting. Gabriel wouldn't believe it. "Felix!" he'd cry. "You!"

Felix grimaced. An unfortunate choice of words. With a slight change of emphasis they could be altered from incredulous delight to vengeful accusation. For a moment he felt paralysed with remorse, and the horrible subaquatic images of Charis came creeping back into his mind. He must remember—he forced himself to concentrate—to ask about P.O.W. camps the next day. Surely as they pushed deeper and deeper into German territory the advancing troops should begin to encounter some. This brought some comfort, as did the reflection that—if the conditions he had experienced today were typical—it was inconceivable that any mail for English prisoners of war would get through.

He heard something hit the roof of the tent sharply. An insect? A bat? Then he heard another and another. Rain, he realised with a smile of relief, as the drops began to patter against the canvas. Big, fat drops of rain.

It was still raining in the morning when Felix was woken up by a black servant with an enamel mug of tea. A basin of hot water had been set on a folding table and he was able to have a refreshing wash and a shave. The basin was cleared away and replaced with a plate of hot chicken, two fried eggs and a type of savoury flour cake. Gilzean stuck his head through the tent flap and said only, to Felix's relief, "Time to be off, sir." Felix pulled on his waterproof cape and went outside. Grey clouds hung low over the trees, blending with the early-morning mist and the smoke rising from hundreds of breakfast fires. Huge brown puddles had gathered in depressions in the ground and were pimpled with the constant drip, drip of water from the overhanging branches.

Gilzean was sitting on a small grey mule and holding the bridle of another which was obviously meant for Felix. Half a dozen bearers queued up behind.

Felix mounted up.

"Morning, Gilzean," he said cheerfully. "How are you feeling?"

"Oh, not so good, sir." Gilzean looked mournful. "I've got the ripples again, and—begging your pardon—an awful angry rumple fyke."

"Yes."

They joined the end of a meandering string of porters taking supplies to Felix's battalion. The road was already ankle-deep in thick mud and, from here on, passable only by men or pack animals. The jungle or forest through which they passed was monotonously familiar. Occasionally there was a ridge to ascend and descend and there were two wide, shallow rivers to ford. Transport officers rode up and down the column, checking on the uncomplaining porters with their enormous head loads. They stopped every two hours for a twenty-minute rest.

At one point the road disappeared beneath the surface of a swamp which apparently had come into being overnight. The way was marked with poles and the water came up to the middle of the bearers' thighs. It stopped raining for a couple of hours and then started again about noon. Despite the protection of his waterproof cape and the wide brim of his sun-helmet, Felix felt wet through. It was quite unlike any rain he had ever encountered in England. For a start it was warm, but there was also something thoroughgoing and uncompromising about African rain. It came down with real force, each drop weighty and loaded with full wetting potential, drumming down at speed as if falling from a prodigious height. He rode in a cocoon of constant battering sounds as it hit his cape and helmet with hefty smacks. He could see, up ahead, the drops rebounding a good six inches from Gilzean's sodden helmet.

It was the middle of the afternoon when they arrived at battalion headquarters. Felix saw what looked like small clearings of cultivated vegetable and maize plots. Then they passed a sandbagged picket and some very miserable sentries. Felix and Gilzean left the column of porters and rode into what had once been a native village. They moved through neat rows of bell tents and dismounted outside a large straw-roofed building with a bent-looking flagpole outside.

"Thank God," Felix groaned. "At last."

"We've got a wee way to go yet," Gilzean said impassively.

Felix reported to the adjutant, who welcomed him to the Rufiji front. Felix was to be attached to Twelve Company, under Captain Frearson, which was across the Rufiji on the south bank. He and Gilzean did not delay long, as it was considered advisable to cross the river before dark.

Even in the dry season the Rufiji was, at this point, over 350 yards across. Felix had never seen such an enormous river. It was a muddy brown, like milky coffee. Its lethargic flow was interrupted at many points by shiny sandbanks and the occasional small rocky island. On the north bank Indian sappers had constructed a wooden jetty that led out to a crude flat ferry—heavy planks of wood lashed across two pontoons—which was attached to wire cables that stretched across the sluggish river. It had stopped raining but thick grey flannel clouds still covered the sky. Behind the clouds the sun was setting and the scene was bathed in a jaundiced sepia light. Felix looked in awe at the Rufiji. The vegetation on either side was lush, trees and bushes growing densely right up to the banks. Felix suddenly noticed that crocodiles were basking on some of the sand bars. The dull light, the torpid river and the oppressive steaminess gave the view a pestilential, malevolent atmosphere.

Felix and Gilzean led their mules onto the ferry and tethered them to the guard-rails. When it was full of porters and their loads, a flag was waved and a large steam engine coughed into life, winding in the cables and tugging the cumbersome ferry out into the stream.

Felix leant on the guard-rail and stared in fascination at four hippopotami that were wallowing not far from the ferry's route. He turned round and looked at the crowded mob of porters, who seemed edgy and apprehensive. They wore singlets and loose py-jama-style trousers cut off below the knee. They all had canvas bags slung around their shoulders. Some carried calabash gourds, others saucepans and kettles. Felix noted that his once-smart uniform was creased and grimy. He felt oddly proud. He wondered what Holland would think of him now, in the middle of Africa, crossing this powerful brown river, surrounded by jungle and wild beasts.

By the time they reached the far bank it had started to rain again. Gilzean and Felix remounted and set off up a wide path recently cut through the undergrowth. The rain poured down, battering the leaves of the trees, turning the path into a trickling rivulet. Here, where they were hemmed in by the undergrowth, the gloom was more intense. Felix glanced upward. The setting sun had turned the clouds a sulphurous yellow-grey. His earlier feelings of awe and excitement were replaced by a mysterious depression and disgruntled impatience. When was this wretched journey going to end?

Just then he smelt a curious smell. They emerged from the trees into a clearing of sorts. Before them the pathway was flanked by an avenue of long smouldering bonfires, like huge middens or rubbish heaps that had been burning for days. Here the reek was at its most intense, a rich, choking, putrefying smell that caused Felix's stomach to heave in protest. A thick bluey smoke curled from the heaps and stung his eyes, and he could hear the hiss as the falling rain extinguished a few pale flickering flames that were visible.

Unperturbed, Gilzean entered the infernal avenue. Felix kicked his mule to follow him. Then, peering through the smoke and sheets of rain, Felix saw what they were burning. Horses, donkeys and mules, dozens and dozens of them. Great heaps of blackened rotting carcasses piled six or eight feet high, their stiff legs jutting out at all angles. As he rode between the fires he saw native soldiers sloshing paraffin over the carcasses in an attempt to get them to burn. When they succeeded, a great sheet of flame would roar up and there would be a sound of popping and cracking from the distended bellies which swelled and burst as the gases inside expanded, sending rank vile smells across the path between.

"What's happening?" Felix shouted to Gilzean.

"They're all dead," Gilzean replied.

"I can see that," Felix said impatiently. "But how?"

"Tsetse fly," Gilzean said philosophically. "Gets every horse and mule sooner or later. We burn the bodies once a week."

They moved away from the smoke. Felix could see they were approaching a village; the ground had at some time been cleared for maize and millet fields. Flimsy straw and grass shelters had been erected under the trees for the porters, and some more substantial tarpaulin-covered lean-tos had been put up to protect the piles of stores. Everywhere were empty boxes and crates and what looked like large wicker baskets of the sort used to carry laundry. Rows of tents indicated the presence of soldiers; the native carriers, it seemed, had to make the best of whatever materials came to hand.

They went through a gap in a high thorn barrier. Felix saw larger tents, some straw huts and a mud-walled rectangular building with a new corrugated-iron roof.

"Here we are," Gilzean announced despondently. "Kibongo."

CHAPTER TWO

15 APRIL 1917

Kibongo · German East Africa

Felix stared listlessly at the rain falling outside. It had been raining continuously for three months. He wouldn't have believed
it possible if he hadn't been under it himself. Twelve Company of
the 5th Battalion were still at Kibongo. Felix's platoon was on
picket duty. He had spent a damp and uncomfortable night beneath
a straw shelter. He sat now on a folding canvas chair, watching the
dawn light filter through the dripping trees in front of him. Twenty
yards away were the perimeter trenches and a machine-gun post.
The ground in front of the trenches had been cleared to a distance
of fifty yards. Gilzean was meant to be out there checking that
everyone was alert.

It had been a quiet night, as had all his nights on duty. In his
three months of active service there had been only one alarm. He

had been sitting in the mess with Captain Frearson and two of his fellow lieutenants—Loveday and Gent—when there had been a ragged volley of shots from the perimeter trenches. At once the entire camp was in pandemonium. When they got to the scene of the action they found the body of the fourth officer, Lieutenant Parrott, with a neat bullet hole in his temple. Parrott, going through a bad spell of dysentery, had wandered off in search of a convenient bush in which to relieve himself. A jumpy sentry had heard him rustling about, and without a word of warning had emptied the magazine of his rifle in the general direction of the noise. His equally nervous companions had joined in. Parrott was extremely unfortunate to have been hit.

The next day an auction of his kit was held. Felix bought half a bottle of South African brandy for £10 and also purchased Parrott's toothbrush for £1. 13s. 6d. He had an inch of the brandy left and was wondering now whether to drink it. He decided to wait until after breakfast. The extravagantly high prices were due to the fact that scarcely any supplies had got through to Kibongo since the rains had begun. The Rufiji was now six hundred yards wide, a surging, foaming mill-race that was impossible to cross. Of the entire line of supply back to the railhead, almost half the road had been washed away or else was under six feet of water. For the last month officers had been on one-eighth rations. The day before, Felix had been issued with one rasher of bacon, a tablespoonful of apricot jam, half an onion and a handful of flour. The men were living on a cupful of rice and nothing more. Everyone was frantic with a debilitating, gnawing hunger. All anyone could think of was food.

Urgent requests for more supplies merely prompted the retort that the lines of communication no longer existed and that everyone was in more or less the same state. However, the exposed position of Twelve Company at the southernmost tip of the army's advance made them suspect that if any unit was going to be hard done-by it would be theirs. The mood in the officers' mess was one of unrelieved fractious irritability. Felix thought that if the Germans ever got round to attacking, Twelve Company would surrender without demur at the prospect of a square meal.

The Nigerian soldiers, Felix had to admit, bore the deprivations with stoical good humour, setting a far better example than the English officers and NCOs. When he had arrived at Kibongo in January there had been a more or less full complement of soldiers in the company—some one hundred and twenty—plus about three hundred porters. Since then, over a hundred porters and thirty soldiers had died from various diseases, the most common being malaria and dysentery. But lately many more of the porters were dying through eating poisonous roots and fruit in a desperate search for nourishment.

A week before, one of Felix's men had shot a monkey. The animal had been divided equally among the platoon, Felix being presented with the head in token of his seniority. His cook and servant, Human, had scraped as much flesh from the skull as possible and had been seasoning Felix's meagre rations with slivers of monkey's cheek, monkey's lips and the like.

The thought of food sent Felix's gastric juices into a prolonged gurgle. Felix leant out of his grass shelter. The rain seemed to have slackened a bit. Under a tree he saw Human crouched over a small fire.

"Human," Felix called, and his servant squelched over. Human, Felix believed, was in his thirties. He had won a medal in the Cameroon campaign against the Germans in West Africa. He had proudly informed Felix that he had personally shot three "Europes," as he called them. He had been wounded himself, though, in the process and, no longer fit enough to be a front-line soldier, had been kept on by the regiment as an officer's servant. For all the fact that he was fifteen years older than Felix, Human looked remarkably young and boyish. This was partly due to his diminutive size—even smaller now due to the recent privations—and his smooth, unlined face.

"Yes, sar," Human said.

"Food, Human. I need my breakfast quickly."

Human dashed back to his fire and fiddled around with his cooking utensils. He brought Felix his breakfast. On his tin plate was something that looked like a bluey-grey fish cake spread with apricot jam. Despite the evidence, Felix's salivary glands filled his mouth in anticipation. With a fork Felix broke off a piece and tasted it. There was a strong flavour of charcoal; bland, pasty, warm flour; a hint of onion; the sweet jam, and something else he couldn't identify. Felix chewed it up slowly while Human watched.

"Not bad," Felix said. "What's in it?"

"Everything, sar," Human said. "And monkey."

"Monkey? I thought we'd finished the monkey."

"No, sar. There is more."

Felix wolfed down the rest.

"What?"

"Monkey brain, sar."

"Brain." That was the other flavour. . .

"Yes, sar. I put monkey brain inside."

At eight o'clock Felix and his men were relieved on the perimeter by Gent and his platoon. Gent was the most innocuous of Felix's fellow officers. Gent was always whistling to himself, tunelessly, and when he wasn't he seemed to breathe through his mouth all the time, his mouth hanging open like an idiot's.

Felix heard his mindless fluting coming up the path from Kibongo a good two minutes before the man actually appeared.

"Hello, Cobb," Gent said. "Quiet night?" Gent had been quite portly in January. Now he looked like a sick man, skinny, with a clammy sweat on his face.

"Have you got something, Gent?" Felix said. "If so, keep away."

"Touch of fever," Gent said, seemingly unaware of Felix's hostility. "Should shake it off before too long."

Gent's ragged platoon occupied the perimeter trenches. Felix and Gilzean marched their men away, up the gentle slope that led to the village. Once there, the men were dismissed and Felix went into the officers' mess. The mess, as they grandly called it, was the mud hut with the corrugated-iron roof. It had no amenities whatsoever and was only valued as being the driest place in the camp.

Inside were four folding canvas chairs and a trestle table. Captain Frearson was sitting in one of the chairs writing up the company diary. Felix told him it had been a quiet night. Frearson had a plump, soft face, like Philip II of Spain. He was a timid, indecisive man whose endless dithering, Felix believed, had needlessly caused them to be isolated in Kibongo. As the Rufiji had risen it became increasingly obvious that they would be cut off, yet Frearson refused to request to be withdrawn, thinking it would look like "bad show." He had seemed to be giving way under the combined pressure of Felix, Parrott, Gent and Loveday when the rising waters washed away the ferry and the matter was forcibly closed.

"Any news?" Felix asked automatically. Semaphore and—on the rare occasions when there was a break in the cloud—heliograph were the only means of communication that existed between Twelve Company and the rest of the battalion on the other side of the Rufiji.

"Battalion's pulling back to the railway at Mikesse," Frearson said.

"Good God! What about us?"

"We'll have to wait, I'm afraid. It seems the river's falling. They say they'll try to rig up a ferry again."

It was the first indication that their ordeal might soon be over. Felix felt an irrational lightening of his heart.

"That's marvellous," he said. "Absolutely marvellous."

Frearson looked at him suspiciously. At that point Loveday came in. Loveday was the biggest irritant in the camp but today Felix's benevolence could extend even to him.

"*Sacrebleu!*" Loveday said. "Three more porters dead in the night. Seems they've been digging up the mule carcasses again. Can't seem to make them understand." He shrugged. "*Pauvres idiots.*"

Loveday was a brash young man with a thin moustache who regarded himself as a sophisticate, a fact he felt was made manifest through his constant use of French exclamations. In pre-war days he would have been known as a "masher" or a "knut."

"Have you heard the news?" Felix said. "We're going back to the railway."

"Yes," Loveday said. "Not before time, I say."

The three of them remained silent for a while, taking this in.

No bond exists between us, Felix thought. This experience had only driven them apart. Frearson took out his pipe and sucked at it noisily. The pipe was empty—everyone had run out of tobacco weeks ago. This was Frearson's particular habit that tormented Felix to a near-homicidal degree, like Gent's whistling or Loveday's schoolboy French. Felix realised, with something of a shock, that during his three-month spell in the "front line" he'd never seen a single enemy soldier. His animosities were all claimed by his colleagues. He found it hard to think about home, about Charis or Gabriel. His ludicrous "quest" had fizzled out in the mud of Kibongo, his high ideals and passionate aspirations replaced by grumbles about the damp and endless speculation about what to eat.

The mess was silent, filled only with the sound of Frearson's spittly sucking. Felix felt a powerful desire to ram the pipe down Frearson's throat. His mood of elation hadn't lasted long.

"I'll be off," he said, trying to keep his voice under control.

"Cheer-ho," Frearson said.

"À bientôt," said Loveday.

Felix squelched through the mud towards his tent, suddenly feeling very tired. He smiled cynically to himself, thinking about the "great quest" again. He seldom thought of Gabriel; his musings, such as they were, seemed petty and wholly self-centred. He knew nothing of the war in Africa, had forgotten about the war in Europe. Gabriel might even have been released and repatriated by now. What kind of a war was this? he demanded angrily to himself. No enemy in sight, your men slowly being starved to death, guarding a huddle of grass huts in the middle of a sodden jungle?

He was surprised to see Gilzean standing outside his tent. Gilzean reported that Loveday had ordered him to take a burial detail and remove the bodies of the three dead porters. For a moment Felix thought of going back to the mess and making an issue out of it but decided to let it pass.

"Very well, Gilzean," he said wearily. "Let's get on with it."

Gilzean collected half a dozen men from the platoon and they set off to the carrier camp. The three dead men had been dragged from their shelters and left for the burial party. The men were naked, their scraps of clothing and few possessions already appropriated. Their eyes were screwed tightly shut and their huge swollen tongues, strangely white and chalky, protruded inches beyond their lips.

"Poisoned," Gilzean said flatly.

The dead bodies were carried down a narrow path to the Rufiji. Unceremoniously they were pitched into the turbulent brown water. Felix and Gilzean stood and watched their bodies being swirled away.

"They're for the kelpies," Gilzean said. He seemed unusually depressed, Felix thought—far more so than normal.

"What a way to go," Felix said, wondering if he should ask what kelpies were. Fish? Crocodiles?

"It could be us yet," Gilzean added, doomily. They walked back up the dripping path. "Aye, and to think I asked to come out here."

"Did you?" Felix said, keen to capitalize on a moment's lucidity. "So did I."

"Twae brothers deed in France. I thought, don't go there, Angus. Thought it would be easy out here, ye ken? Look at us noo."

Gilzean had never been so forthcoming. Felix looked at his dark, troubled face with sympathy.

"I came out here to find my brother," Felix confided. "He's a prisoner somewhere."

"We get our lawins, sure enough," Gilzean said bitterly.

Felix sensed meaning beginning to edge away. He tried one more time.

"If I find him," he said, feeling a twinge of guilt at his lack of commitment, "I'll die happy."

"This cackit place," Gilzean growled in hate, not listening. "They poor darkies. A greeshie way to go." He clenched his fists. "I'm a snool, a glaikit sumph. Nocht but rain, howdumdied all day o'boot. I've lost my noddle. Camsteerie bloody country." He gave a harsh laugh. "No strunt. Any haughmagandie? Never. Dunged into the ground . . . I could greet, I tell you." He flashed a glance of scowling malevolence at Felix. "Aye, and those primsie Suthrons— you apart, sir—I'd no tarrow to clack their fuds. . . ."

Felix let him ramble on as they plodded through the mud back to Kibongo. Gilzean's Complaint—it seemed powerful enough to warrant a capital letter—would do for all the men in Twelve Company, the dead porters too. He only understood one word in three, but this time he thought he knew how the little man felt.

CHAPTER THREE

15 JULY 1917

Nanda · German East Africa

"Look what I've got for you here," Liesl said, placing a straw basket on the dispensary table. Gabriel looked, wondering if she could hear his heart beating. He hadn't seen Liesl for three days. She had travelled the seventy miles to Lindi to meet her husband. Gabriel had missed her intolerably. She took off her sun-helmet and adjusted the pins and combs in her frizzy ginger hair, stretching the material of her blouse across her breasts. Gabriel swallowed and gripped the edge of the table. A nervous tremor had started in his left hand some weeks ago. It quivered constantly, as if possessed of some ghostly life of its own.

Liesl took out a cloth bundle, a knife and a jar of syrupy fluid. She unwrapped the cloth, revealing a dark-brown loaf the size of a brick.

"Banana bread," she told him delightedly. "Made with coconut too. No butter, but"—she held up the jar—"plenty of honey."

Gabriel smiled, his heart cart-wheeling. "How amazing. Where did you get it?"

"Erich has friends. He is an important man now. Staff officer with Von Lettow himself."

"Any news?" he said as casually as possible. He needn't have worried, he knew; Liesl told him everything.

"Bad news," she said unconcernedly. "The English have landed at Kilwa. Everywhere we are retreating." She frowned. "There has been a lot of fighting."

"So we are winning."

"Oh, yes. Some of the wounded are coming here. They've evacuated the hospital at Lukuledi. So"—she shrugged—"we shall be busy again."

Gabriel shifted uneasily in his seat. For the last six months Nanda had been almost deserted, the ward never more than half full, the town populated by the remains of its native population and about thirty German women and children. Deppe had gone—for good, they were promised—to establish a new base hospital at Chitawa some fifty miles to the south-west. Nanda hospital had belonged to Liesl again. They sat out the rainy season with little to disturb their routine. This now consisted mainly of distilling the quinine substitute that the German forces used, a vile-tasting potion made from Peruvian chinchona bark of which, surprisingly, there were considerable supplies, stockpiled before the war began. Every fortnight freshly filled bottles and containers were sent out to the *Schutztruppe* companies. Liesl handed over the administration of this to two other women, Frau Ledebur and Frau Müller. Gabriel was employed in the actual distilling process, a simple but delicate job relying on perfect timing in order for the quinine distillate to be potable. Gabriel spent most of the time supervising the process out at the back of the hospital where the two huge boiling vats were set over open fires. He filled the bottles and passed them over to Frau Ledebur, who organised their despatch to the varying *Schutztruppe* bases.

It hadn't been difficult to ascertain the positions of these bases, and he now had a good idea of the state of the fighting. Hidden in a niche in the wall of his hut he kept a tattered dossier, which he annotated and altered as fresh information came in. The news of the landings at Kilwa would have to be added tonight. By his calculations that meant the British Army was now only a hundred and fifty miles or so away from Nanda. It was true that the Portuguese had occupied Lindi some months previously, but they didn't count.

This new awareness of the proximity of the British forces brought with it a succession of conflicting emotions. His leg wound had been healed for many weeks now. Deppe's posting had made it no longer necessary for Gabriel to be regarded as injured. Liesl was quite unworried by his presence, and their friendship made it unlikely that she would ever insist on his being transferred to another P.O.W. camp. Indeed, she had saved him from being reincarcerated in the Nanda camp just three weeks previously. The stockade had been reopened for captured European NCOs. There were now ten British, four Rhodesians and two Portuguese behind the barbed wire, supervised by a grotesquely fat Dutchman called Deeg and a gang of fierce-looking native auxiliaries known as ruga-ruga. These men were armed with old rifles but wore no uniforms apart from the odd scavenged pair of trousers or forage cap. It was rumoured among the prisoners that the ruga-ruga were recruited from a tribe of cannibals. Certainly some of the men had filed teeth and this was taken to be sufficient proof of their taste for human flesh.

One of Deeg's first moves had been to imprison Gabriel, but Liesl had refused him permission, saying that not only was Gabriel an officer and couldn't be billeted with NCOs but also that he was still under medical observation and, besides, had given his parole. Deeg had been forced to accept her instructions, but he insisted that Gabriel be confined to the hospital and its grounds and not be allowed to wander freely around Nanda. This restriction had to be accepted, and Deeg also let it be known that he was lodging an official protest. Nothing further, however, was heard of this. Presumably the military authorities had more pressing matters on their hands.

Liesl sat down opposite Gabriel, her eyes bright with pleasure as she prepared to cut the banana bread. Gabriel released his grip on the table and rested his trembling hand on his knee. He looked at

Liesl's plump freckly face, her curious upper lip, the way she seemed constantly to be either on the point of speaking or biting back words. She had three distinct horizontal creases in her soft neck. All her clothes seemed several sizes too small for her and were consequently always patched by sweat stains. She tucked a wisp of her hair behind an ear. Gabriel felt the blood pulse in his head. He felt dull and thick-tongued with hopeless love. Since Deeg's arrival and the restrictions on his movement he had not dared to creep round to her bungalow at night. But somehow, feeding on his memories made the experience almost more intense. He knew every inch of that beautiful large body. The long hanging breasts, the almost invisible salmon-pink nipples, the creamy freck-led belly, the ginger-gold hair in her groin and armpits . . .

"Gabriel," she said, "is this enough for you?"

"Oh. Yes, thanks."

And yet she knew nothing of his feelings. She had left to see her husband without a word of goodbye. It had been Frau Ledebur who had told him of her departure. His clenched fist drummed gently on his knee. As Liesl grew plumper and sleeker, he seemed to be falling apart. He was thinner than ever, his leg wound was healed but it still ached, he walked with a limp and now there was this nervous tremor in his hand.

He watched her spoon some honey onto the two slices of bread she had cut and spread it thickly over the surface. She handed his piece over and, not waiting for him to begin, took a huge bite out of her own. Honey spilled off the crust and ran slowly down her chin.

"Verdammt," she swore, collecting the dribble with a forefinger and licking it clean. She shut her eyes, chewing slowly, a dreamy look crossing her face as she savoured the taste.

Unaccountably, Gabriel felt tears brim in his eyes and a sob form in his throat. He was literally helpless, he knew. The tears flowed silently down his cheeks and his features trembled in a cry-ing grimace.

Liesl opened her eyes. "Gabriel," she exclaimed in alarm. "You haven't eaten. What's wrong?"

Gabriel hung his head. "I'm sorry," he tried to explain. "It sounds stupid, I know, but it's just that—suddenly I felt very happy. I have been very happy here. It's ridiculous, I know, but I have."

Liesl tried to stop herself smiling. "Gabriel, you fool." She laughed, throwing back her head. "You can't be happy *here.*" Her breasts shook as she gave a great hooting laugh. "You stupid!" Her eyes were shut; the room was filled with the unrestrained noise of her mirth.

Gabriel didn't care. He had declared himself.

She was calming down. "Oh. Oh, that's sore. Oh, *grosser Gott.* Oh, Gabriel, don't do that to me. Did you say something?"

"Me?" Gabriel said. "No, nothing." He took a mouthful of banana bread. "Mmm," he mumbled, "this is superb."

As Liesl predicted, the hospital at Nanda soon filled up with wounded men from the fighting around Kilwa. One of the wounded was a Captain von Steinkeller who appeared to be an officer of some importance, judging from the high-ranking visitors he received. He had been very badly injured in the hip. Liesl patched it up as best she could, but it was agreed that he would have to be moved to Chitawa, where Deppe could examine it. Shortly before he was transferred he was visited by Von Lettow's adjutant himself, another captain, called Rutke.

Gabriel was standing in the dispensary when two askaris carried Von Steinkeller out to a waiting wagon.

"Don't worry," Rutke shouted. Then he spoke some phrases too quickly for Gabriel to translate. "November," Rutke then said. "Wait until November. We have *das chinesische Geschäft.*" A ragged cheer went up from the men in the ward. After Rutke left, Gabriel heard the phrase being used again as the men referred to it. *Das chinesische Geschäft.* He asked Liesl for a translation.

"What would you say? 'The Chinese Exhibition'? Perhaps. 'The China Show'? It's curious. What is it?"

"I don't know," Gabriel said. "I heard the men saying it in the ward."

Liesl shrugged. They left it at that. Gabriel wondered if it was important.

CHAPTER FOUR

19 OCTOBER 1917

Lindi · German East Africa

In October 1917 the third battle of Ypres—Passchendaele—was
well on its way to its half-million casualties. Between the four-
teenth and sixteenth of October the most savagely fought battle on
African soil took place at Mahiwa. British columns, advancing south
from the Rufiji and inland from the ports of Kilwa and Lindi, were
fiercely attacked by the supposedly retreating Germans at some innocuous hills near a bend in the Mahiwa river. Out of five thousand
African, Indian, British and South African troops, twenty-seven
hundred were killed or wounded.

Fifty percent casualties in a single battle. Three battalions of the
Nigerian Brigade were at the forefront of the fighting and suffered
heavy losses. Among those not taking part, though, was Twelve
Company of the 5th Battalion. On the days of the battle of Mahiwa,
Felix's platoon was digging latrine trenches at the brigade's head-

quarters at Redhill Camp, Lindi. Gent's and Loveday's platoons were escorting supply wagons up to the front line.

After their privations at Kibongo it was recognised that Frearson's company had endured more than most, and as a reward they received three weeks' leave in Zanzibar. Fully recovered, Twelve Company rejoined the battalion at Morogoro, where they spent the next few months training new recruits, making roads and strengthening culverts and embankments.

As the polyglot British Army marched south, the Nigerian Brigade was involved in many of the small actions that took place whenever the Germans' rearguard was encountered. It soon became clear to Felix that Frearson's company was unlikely ever to be with them. They guarded supply dumps, provided escorts for labour battalions and assisted District Commissioners to establish administrative authority in the newly conquered territory. Felix's platoon personally flattened a small hill for an extension to an aerodrome's runway; built, with mud bricks, a new wing for a field hospital; escorted without incident one hundred tons of rice from Kilwa to Mikesse—a distance of eighty miles—and, for the last three weeks, had been responsible for looking after the brigade's sizeable baggage train.

At first Felix found nothing to object to. His months at Kibongo seemed a sufficient ordeal for anyone to have gone through, and life at the rear, though agonisingly dull, was tolerably comfortable. Loveday occasionally made warlike noises (*"Aux armes, mes braves!"*) but Frearson was insistent that there was nothing he could do. The word was that morale had been laid so low at Kibongo that Twelve Company was unlikely ever to regain its full fighting capacity. Furthermore, its ranks had been depleted by sickness, and the calibre of the new recruits was suitable only for depot duties.

It wasn't until a German field-ambulance team was captured near Mahiwa that Felix sensed any alarm over his lack of activity. He stood at the gate of Redhill Camp and watched the Provost Marshal and his men escort the prisoners in. There were one surgeon, three German nurses and some native dressers. The Germans looked rugged and bush-hardened but seemed quite pleased to be captured. Amongst the wounded they had been tending when they were overrun were three British officers who had been captured a month previously; they were loudly cheered as they were stretchered into the base hospital. Since then, more and more German civilians had been interned as the advancing British columns occupied the small villages and mission stations around the Lindi area. The south-eastern corner of the country had become the supply centre for the *Schutztruppe* in the last year and was fairly heavily populated. As the hard-pressed German Army retreated towards the Rovuma and the border with Portuguese East, more and more prisoners and wounded men were abandoned by them in the interests of swifter progress.

It was the sight of these liberated English P.O.W.'s that most forcefully reminded Felix of his neglected "quest" and stirred him out of his shameful complacency. He asked and was given permission to go to Kilwa to see if the headquarters staff intelligence department could provide him with any information about his brother.

Kilwa was like any number of East African coastal towns. A palm-fringed beach, a prominent old fort, barracks, a whitewashed church and narrow dirt streets lined with single-storey, mud-walled shops and houses. On the sea front were large imposing residences once owned by the richer merchants and the colonial administrators. Felix was directed to one of these, which, he was told, housed the offices of GSO II (Intelligence). Inside the hall of this particular building—sturdy, two-storeyed and pillared on the ground floor—was a list of the offices it contained. Opposite the title GSO II (Intelligence) was the name of the incumbent: Major R. St. J. Bilderbeck. The name rang a bell. Bilderbeck: Felix suddenly remembered that it was from one Bilderbeck that they had heard the full details of Gabriel's capture. He felt a sudden excitement. This was surely some sort of omen. He walked up the wooden stairs. At the top there was a capacious landing off which were half a dozen doors. On a board were numerous typed orders. Loose telephone wires were looped haphazardly across the walls. From the rooms came a sustained rattle of typewriters. Every now and then an orderly clutching a sheaf of papers would emerge from one room and go into another. None of the doors had any notices on them.

Standing in the middle of the landing was a very fat man with a thick black walrus moustache. His uniform was shabby and faded. He wore dirty riding boots, a frayed spine pad, no tie, and his shirt-sleeves were rolled up to the elbow. Felix was only marginally tidier. The closer one got to base, the neater everyone became. Dar-es-Salaam was full of immaculate staff officers. Clearly this man had just come from the front.

"Excuse me," he said, turning to Felix. "Can you tell me which is Major Bilderbeck's office?"

It took Felix a second or two to recognise his accent as American.

"I'm afraid I can't help you," Felix said. "I'm looking for the same man."

"Oh," he said. "Well, I guess we just go on in." He chose a door at random and knocked. Felix heard someone shout "come in." The American opened the door and looked into the room.

"God, *no!*" he said vehemently, and shut the door abruptly. He turned on his heel and headed for the stairs at speed.

"I've got to go," he said to Felix as he passed.

The door he'd knocked on was flung open and an immensely tall, thin figure appeared.

"Smith," it shouted, "it's *me*. Reggie. For heaven's sake. Didn't you recognise me?"

The American—Smith—halted on the stairs, turned and climbed slowly back up, his head bowed.

"Wheech-Browning," he said tiredly. "I thought it was you."

"Come on in, old man," the Wheech-Browning person exclaimed with evident pleasure. "Haven't seen you for yonks."

"Excuse me," Felix said. "I'm looking for Major Bilderbeck."

"Oh, that's me, sort of," Wheech-Browning said. "Temporary Major Wheech-Browning. You'd better come in too."

Felix followed the American into Wheech-Browning-Bilder-beck's office. They were waved into a couple of wooden seats. Felix introduced himself.

"Dear old Smith," Wheech-Browning said fondly, paying no attention to Felix. "Fancy seeing you again." He looked up at Felix.

"Smith and I are old comrades-in-arms, aren't we, Smith?"

"What do you mean by saying you're Bilderbeck *sort of?*" the American said with a hostility Felix found surprising. "I'm looking for him too."

"You're both out of luck," Wheech-Browning apologised. "Bilderbeck's disappeared. Dead probably. Gone mad, by all accounts. You know the sort: he was one of those fearless chappies, always wanting to be in the thick of it. He used to sneak off to the front lines all the time. A few weeks ago he got caught up in a rather nasty battle at a place called Bweho-Chino. Apparently he used to stand on the parapets of the trenches at night yelling insults at the jerries. Then one night he cracked. He was last seen sprinting off in the direction of the enemy, waving his gun, screaming something about his 'girl' and how the Huns were preventing him from finding her." Wheech-Browning shrugged. "Doesn't make much sense, I'm afraid. He was never seen again." He threw his thin arms wide. "Sorry," he said. "But, ours not to reason why, and all that. I've taken over from him. Let me see what I can do. This Bilderbeck fellow kept a phenomenal number of files. Seemed to have some sort of compulsion to write things down." He frowned. "Actually, I'm not sure if I'm allowed to let you have any information. I think all the gen is classified. Still, as it's you, Smith, we'll pretend it's all been officially cleared, eh?" He gave a conspiratorial smile. "Fire away."

"I'm looking for information about a German officer called Von Bishop," Smith said. "Can you tell me if he's been captured or if you know if he's been killed?"

Wheech-Browning jumped to his feet and went to a row of filing cabinets.

"We've got records of every officer in the *Schutztruppe*," he said proudly. "Here we are. 'Bishop, von, E. (major of reserve). Owns a farm near Kilimanjaro . . . um, Maji-Maji rebellion . . . commanded a company at Tanga. Present at Kahe. Moved to Kondoa Irangi. Now believed to be on Von Lettow's staff.' That's it. If he's dead there's a 'D' beside the name. If he's a prisoner there's a 'P.' Stands to reason, I suppose. There's no 'D' and no 'P.' That answer your question?" Wheech-Browning looked disgustingly pleased with himself, Felix thought.

"So he's still out there," Smith said grimly. "Theoretically at least. Good."

"That's right," Wheech-Browning said. "Why?"

"I've got a score to settle. He was the man who commandeered my farm, remember?"

"We've all got a score to settle with the Huns," Wheech-Browning said pompously. "What did this man do?"

"All sorts of things," Smith said, non-committally. "Ruined me, for one. He stole my Decorticator for another."

"Oh, God, that bloody great thing. Stole it? How can you steal something like that?"

Felix wondered what on earth they were talking about. They sounded like schoolboys squabbling. He interrupted with his own request about released prisoners of war.

Wheech-Browning returned to his files and drew out a small dossier.

"What did you say your brother's name was?"

"Cobb. Gabriel Cobb, captain. Captured at Tanga."

"Oh. Tanga." Wheech-Browning and the American exchanged glances. "Less said about that . . ." Wheech-Browning ran his finger down the list of names. "Cobb, Cobb, Cobb. No, sorry. No Captain Cobb here. Half a mo, they've just liberated a big camp at Tabora." More rifling through files continued. "There's a Godfrey Cobb from the Universities' Mission to Central Africa. That wouldn't be him, would it? I suppose not."

He shut the drawers of the wooden filing cabinet. "Drawn a blank, I'm afraid. Mind you, there are other camps in occupied territories. Places like Chitawa, Massasi and Nanda." He pointed them out on a wall map. "He may be in one of those. Also," he added, "the German columns always tend to carry some prisoners with them. Ones they don't want freed, if you know what I mean. I shouldn't give up hope. The Germans are quite good about supplying information—deaths, that sort of thing. If we'd heard anything it would be down here somewhere."

Felix felt his face suddenly grow hot. "What about letters?" he said. "Do letters to British prisoners get through?"

Wheech-Browning sat down. "It depends. We send food parcels to the camps. Any letters usually go along with them. Bit erratic though."

"Can you tell me if a letter has been sent on to my brother in the last six months or so?"

"My dear Cobb, I haven't the faintest." Wheech-Browning spread his hands. "I've only been here a couple of weeks, since old Bilderbeck went bonkers. He'd be the man to tell you. It may have been passed on. We can never tell. We have to rely on jerry supply officers. Not exactly grade-one material, I believe."

Felix felt only slightly composed. He took out a notebook and recorded the names of the P.O.W. camps. Then he stood up and said he had to go. The American got to his feet also. Wheech-Browning invited them both to lunch at the "quite decent little officers' club" they had in Kilwa. Felix declined; the American emphatically followed suit.

Wheech-Browning saw them down the stairs. At the front door he halted them with a story.

"Listen to this," he said. "Something Bilderbeck came up with. It's called the 'China Show.'" It was a plan, he told them, formulated by the Germans to fly a Zeppelin out to East Africa to give aid and succour to Von Lettow's army.

"Extraordinary idea, isn't it? Keep your eyes peeled for an airship." He raised an imaginary shotgun to his shoulder and fired both barrels. "Can't see what it's got to do with China, though."

Felix and the American left Wheech-Browning and walked down the palm-lined coast road to the centre of the town.

"That man keeps turning up in my life," Smith said. "And somebody always seems to get killed."

"Wheech-Browning?"

"The same."

Felix said nothing. The news about letters was worrying. A silence fell and they walked on together without talking. For want of something to say, Felix brought up the Zeppelin story. They both agreed it was probably some kind of fantasy dreamed up by the deranged Bilderbeck.

They reached Felix's motor car.

"They're big, aren't they?" the American said.

"What?"

"Those Zeppelins."

"Yes. I think they are. But it will have to land in Redhill Camp if I'm to see it. My company's been in reserve since April."

"Ask for a cross-posting to the K.A.R."

"It's my brother, you see. It's extremely important that I find my brother."

"Yes." Smith nodded, but he looked as if he only half-understood. There was a pause.

"Tell you what," the American said. "We found a camp last week but it was full of Portuguese. If we come across any more I'll look out for your brother. What's he like?"

"He's fair. Gabriel Cobb, that's his name. He's tall, strong-looking. He doesn't look like me at all."

On the drive back to the camp Felix thought about the idea of a cross-posting. New K.A.R. battalions were constantly being raised; it shouldn't be too difficult.

When he arrived, he found a long-faced Gilzean standing outside his tent.

"Hello, Sergeant," Felix said. "What's wrong?"

"We're on the move, sir," Gilzean said gloomily. "Twelve Company's going up to the front. Attacking a place called Nambindinga."

CHAPTER FIVE

19 NOVEMBER 1917

Nanda · German East Africa

Gabriel eased his position slightly, trying to make as little noise as possible while he found a secure perch in the bushes outside Liesl's room. Tonight the house was full of German officers and he knew he'd have a long wait before she came to bed. The branch he was sitting on suddenly gave with a green crack, and with a loud rustle of leaves deposited him gently on his feet. He stiffened with alarm but no one seemed to have heard anything.

For the last three days Nanda had been like a garrison town. Von Lettow's retreating headquarters had set up base there temporarily. Over a thousand askaris and their camp-followers had occupied every available building. Gabriel had confined himself to the quinine distilling sheds and his own small hut, concerned not to draw undue attention to himself. Liesl had told him Deeg planned to make representations to Von Lettow in an attempt to get him incarcerated, but she told him not to worry, as she thought it extremely unlikely that Deeg would even get near Von Lettow under the circumstances. Headquarters would be moving on in a day or so, she said; the British were getting so close.

"Máybe the war is nearly over for us," she said matter-of-factly. "You can go home soon to your family."

Gabriel had never told her about Charis. "What will happen to you?" he said, changing the subject.

"Perhaps I'll go to Chitawa with Deppe."

"Deppe?"

"I hope not." She gave a brief laugh. "Or Dar-es-Salaam. All civilians are being sent to Dar."

She had continued speculating in a dreamy, offhand way. Gabriel said nothing. For the first time the reality, and proximity, of his salvation was apparent to him. British troops were fifty miles away. He'd been a prisoner for three years. In a day, two days, it would be all over. He would be free.

Why then, he asked himself, did he feel assailed with doubts and dissatisfactions? His life in Nanda had been curiously secure and uncomplicated; the future seemed to consist only of problems, realignments and responsibilities which he wasn't sure he could cope with in the same way he had before the war. Uncomfortably, he found himself thinking of Charis and of the identity which he felt he had shed when he was bayonetted. The approach of the British Army stirred hibernating instincts and forgotten values. Now that he had to face up to them, they seemed, if he was to be honest, unfamiliar and—more worrying—unwelcome.

Responding to these new pressures, he had slipped round the back of the stockade and passed on the news of the advance to the NCOs behind the wire. "Good on yer, sir," one of them said, as if he'd done something heroic. There were whispered mutters of agreement from the others. "Be careful, sir," one of them counselled.

As Gabriel had crept away, for a moment he saw himself as they did: a young officer in the midst of the enemy camp, carrying out a dangerous double game, risking his safety—his life perhaps. . . . Back in the hospital he was suffused with a sense of shame and guilt when he considered the reality of his case. He felt loyalties and emotions tug at him in conflicting directions. What should he do? He could provide no answers, so he did nothing. He felt maddeningly helpless. There was no solution in inertia, yet that seemed all he was capable of.

The feeling of mounting frustration was exacerbated by Liesl's presence. She was being unusually solicitous and kind, as if the thought of their coming separation had caused her to re-examine and revalue their curious relationship. That afternoon she had come out to the palm-roofed shelter where the chinchona bark was boiled in huge metal vats. Gabriel stood bare-chested, stirring the bubbling fluid with a bamboo pole, the clouds of steam and the heat from the fires covering his thin chest with gleaming perspiration. He broke off when she arrived. She held two "real" cigarettes—"from Erich," she said. They had stood in the shade of a large mango tree, smoking, and talking about the future.

"You'll be glad to go home?" she asked.

"Yes. Yes, I will. I suppose."

"Perhaps you will go to Leamington Spa."

"What?"

"I visited Leamington Spa once. Erich's mother lived there."

"I've never been."

"It's a pleasant town."

The bland exchange had affected him with unbearable poignancy. He was gripped by a sense of fear. He felt like a new boy on his first day at boarding school: everything ahead was strange and perplexing. In what ways would he have to prove himself? What demands would be made on his character?

A precise and cruel sense of his own inadequacies and weakness was suddenly revealed to him. He felt chastened and desperately in need of some support. He glanced at the strong and placid woman beside him. She was looking at the sun on the wasted grass beyond the pool of shade. The hand that held the cigarette was poised, a cursive rope of blue smoke rose into the heavy dark-green leaves above their heads. Gabriel was suddenly possessed of the awful feeling that nothing beyond this moment, outside Nanda, in the rest of his life, would be as sure or certain again. For as long as it lasted he immersed himself unreflectingly in the confident tranquillity. Then Liesl had left, and the self-doubts, like homing pigeons, returned to roost.

Memories of those seconds in the shade had driven him to take the risk of creeping through the plantations to Liesl's bungalow that night. Troops were billeted everywhere and he had to make his way with extreme caution. But he wanted to see her once again if he could, see her pale and unsuspecting, freeze that image in his mind for ever.

But as soon as he saw the little bungalow, he had known his luck was out. On the rickety stoop sat a group of German officers in very grubby, tattered dress whites. Liesl sat with them and two other planters' wives. Gabriel recognised Von Bishop, Liesl's husband, his head shaven nearly bald, his large nose and gaunt cheeks giving him a surprised, faintly pop-eyed look.

Gabriel crept round to his usual position, hoping nonetheless that Liesl might still come into the bedroom, but it remained dark. He decided to wait. He heard the guests leave the stoop and assemble in the main room of the little bungalow. Soon servants were ferrying steaming bowls of food from the kitchen shack behind the house and he heard the chatter of conversation around the dinner table increase as the assembled guests relaxed. Gabriel tried to find himself a secure perch in the bushes, knowing he had a wait of several hours before him, and it was then that the branch broke.

There was no pause in the conversation. From his position in the bushes he could almost catch individual words. He wondered vaguely if he should make an attempt to eavesdrop, but decided not to bother.

Then he became aware of some activity and a babble of servants' voices by the back door. He realised that suspicions had been raised by the noise he'd made. He had to leave instantly. He forced himself to remain calm. Any precipitate flight would only give him away at once. The servants were milling round the rear door. They clearly were undecided about what to do. Very slowly Gabriel dropped to his knees. Not taking his eyes off the group by the back door, he began to inch backwards through the bushes. He saw a lantern being carried from the kitchen shack, saw a white face peer from the back door.

"*Halt,*" a soft voice said behind him.

Gabriel felt his guts churn. He turned round. A white officer and two askaris stood above him. The askaris covered him with their rifles. Rifles with fixed bayonets. Gabriel felt the blood rush from his head as he heard steps running from the rear door. The bobbing light from the lantern slid up and down the dull steel blades. He fainted.

He came to on Liesl's stoop. He was sitting on a cane chair with his head between his knees. His eyes focussed on the rough wooden boards. Between his boots he saw a flying ant with only one wing walking round and round in a futile, imbalanced attempt to get from A to B. He looked up into the circle of German faces. Behind the officers he saw Liesl. A furious conversation was going on. Voices were raised. His discovery seemed to be causing an astonishing fuss.

"How long were you outside?" he was asked sharply in German.

"*Fünf Minuten,*" he lied automatically, before he realised what this gave away. He decided to speak English. "Five minutes," he repeated stupidly. He caught Liesl's worried gaze for a brief second before he looked down again. His left hand was trembling violently. He covered it with his right.

He heard more conversation, this time some of it hushed. He heard Liesl speaking, then some shouted orders. He sat on in silence. The next thing he saw was Deeg's grinning face. He was hauled roughly to his feet and marched off between a guard of four askaris. He was taken down Nanda's main street to a small wooden store shed set to one side of the prisoners' stockade. Some sacks of mealie flour were removed before he was pushed inside. There was the noise of a bolt being slid home, a mutter of voices and then silence. He couldn't tell if a man had been left on guard or not.

He felt his way round the dark interior of the shed. It was

small, about six feet by nine. The wooden planks that made up its four walls had been crudely put together and there were many thin gaps through which a faint moonlight entered. The roof was made of grass and was full of rustling insects and lizards.

Gabriel sat down in a corner. He felt, to his surprise, quite calm. He wondered what would happen to him. He peered out of a slit at the back but saw only shadowy, indistinct forms. After a while he heard voices. The door was opened and two men, one carrying an oil lantern, came in. Gabriel got unsteadily to his feet. He recognised Von Bishop, his big nose oddly illuminated by the swinging lantern held by the other man, a slim dapper figure. Gabriel remembered him: it was Rutke, Von Lettow's adjutant.

"Just one question, Captain Cobb," Von Bishop said in English. Gabriel was surprised at his high-pitched voice. He sounded tired rather than hostile.

"Are these yours?" He handed Gabriel a little tattered bundle of papers. Gabriel took them. It was his "dossier." There seemed no point in denying it. He handed them back.

"Yes."

"Herr Deeg has informed me—" Here an evilly grinning Deeg stepped into the hut but was shooed out by Rutke. Von Bishop began again. "Herr Deeg has informed me that you are under parole. These acts of espionage constitute a breach of your parole. Your word as an officer. What do you have to say to that?"

Gabriel said nothing.

Rutke stepped forward. "What do you know about *das chinesische Geschäft?*"

"Nothing," Gabriel said, and realised he'd spoken too quickly once again. "I mean, I don't know what you're talking about." He decided to be honest. Be honest where you can: it was a rule of interrogation that he'd learnt somewhere.

"I've heard the name," he said candidly, "but I've no idea what it is."

Rutke and Von Bishop looked at each other.

"Well," Von Bishop said wearily, "I'm afraid you will have to stay locked up a while longer." He paused, then stuck his forefinger in an ear and wriggled it about. "You were wounded at Tanga, weren't you?" he said in a more friendly voice. "Do you know an English officer called Bilderbeck?"

"Yes," Gabriel said. "How do you know?" He thought back to those days on the *Homayun* and on the battlefield three years ago. It seemed like a lifetime.

"He's dead," Von Bishop said, looking at the end of his finger. "He died a few weeks ago. I was at Tanga. I met him. I seem to remember he was a friend of yours."

"Yes. Well, I suppose he was. In a way."

"I thought you'd like to know."

"Thank you," Gabriel said. "Thank you for telling me." What a peculiar man this Von Bishop was. He wondered how Bilderbeck had died. He wondered if Von Bishop was making a threat of some kind.

The next day passed with unbelievable slowness. In the enclosed hut the air was hot and fetid. Hundreds of flies hummed and skittered in its darkness. Twice Deeg came and led him to a latrine trench behind the prison cage. He was escorted on each occasion by Deeg and four of his ruga-ruga. On the second journey some of the prisoners cheered him as he limped by on the way back. "Keep it up, sir," they shouted. "Don't worry, our boys'll be here soon." Gabriel managed a smile and a wave. The ruga-ruga dashed forward and prodded fiercely through the wire with their rifle butts. His food that day consisted of a bottle of water and a bowl of mealie porridge.

That night he stretched out on the beaten-earth floor and tried to find a position that would be comfortable enough to let him sleep. His leg wound was aching dully and his entire left arm seemed to be trembling now. He shut his eyes. He wondered how long it would be before the British Army arrived.

He turned over. The floor was hard; whining mosquitoes seemed to be biting every exposed inch of his body. God alone knew what kinds of ticks and vermin existed in this sort of store shed. He heard a distinct rustling sound. Oh, my God, he thought with alarm, sitting up. There's a rat in the roof, or a snake . . .

"Gabriel!" a voice whispered.

He jumped in fright. It was Liesl behind the shed. He crawled over. Through a large slit between the planks he saw a pale section of her face.

"Are you all right?" she asked.

"Yes," he said. "Is there a guard?"

"No. Listen, Gabriel. I've got news. They're going to take you with them."

Gabriel felt a thump of fear in his chest. "Who? Where?"

"Our troops. They're crossing the Rovuma into Portuguese East."

"Oh, my God. When?"

"I don't know. Tomorrow. The next day."

"Oh, God." Gabriel felt cold, fluttering sensations of panic. "But why? For God's sake, why me?"

"I'm not sure. Erich won't tell me. I think he is suspicious. A bit. They say you know some secret."

Gabriel could feel the breath from her words on his cheek. Their faces were only an inch or so apart, separated by the wooden wall.

"A secret? What?"

"I don't know. They say you know a secret, that's all."

Gabriel felt like weeping. What could he know that was so important? He thought of the information on his dossier. It was weeks out of date. Surely that wouldn't warrant their taking him into Portuguese East?

"What secret can it be?" he repeated frantically.

"I don't know, Gabriel. They won't tell me."

"You've got to help me, Liesl," he said desperately. "I've got to get away. They mustn't take me."

"I told them," she said. "I said you weren't strong, that you needed medical attention."

"That's right," Gabriel agreed, almost whimpering. "It would kill me."

"I told them."

"What did they say?"

"They said they had doctors. It didn't matter."

"You've got to help me, Liesl." Gabriel raised his voice.

"Ssh. Of course I will." It sounded like the most reasonable request in the world.

"I've got to escape." Gabriel thought quickly. "Bring me something to dig with. A knife or something. And some food and water . . . How far away are the British?"

"Near Nambindinga, I think. Forty-five kilometres, I think."

"That's north?"

"Yes, north directly."

"Bring everything tomorrow night, can you?"

"Yes. At the same time. Erich thinks I am on duty at the hospital."

They were silent for a second. Gabriel saw a gleam of light in the jelly of her eyeball.

"Gabriel?"

"Yes."

"Why were you outside my house?"

He swallowed. "I came to see you."

"Me? Why?"

"For some reason. I wanted to see you."

"Because of the end of the war?"

"Yes," he said. "That's it."

"But Erich and Rutke and Deeg say you are a spy. That you have been spying all the time."

"It's not true." Then he added, the honesty making his voice hoarse, "It was just something I did."

"Why?"

"To console myself."

"I told them you weren't a spy." She paused. "I should go now."

Gabriel had a final thought. "Liesl. Tomorrow night. Can you bring me some paper and a pencil?"

"Paper and pencil? Are you sure? All right. I will."

The next day passed as slowly as the one before. On his trips to the latrine, Gabriel became aware of more bustle in the town: columns of marching men, officers speeding up and down the street on bicycles, a general air of preparing to move. He prayed they wouldn't pull out before dark. In the afternoon he thought he heard a distant sound of gunfire but he couldn't be sure.

That night Liesl came as she had promised. She slipped a flattened iron bar through a crack between the planks. It felt like part of a heavy hinge. In ten minutes he had dug a hollow beneath the wooden walls big enough for his thin body to squirm under. Liesl helped him to his feet. She handed him an old sack.

"There's some food and a bottle of water," she whispered. "Some matches, a bit of cheese and two candles for the dark. Don't go far, Gabriel, please. Just go away and hide. They won't wait to catch you. A lot are staying behind to wait for the English. Go and hide for two days; then you can come back."

"Right," Gabriel said. He had hardly taken her words in. They were standing up against the back wall of the shed. A quarter moon provided only enough light for Gabriel to see the bold features of her face. Her shadowed eyes, her nostrils, the gash of her mouth. Their whispering meant that they stood only a foot apart. Gabriel could smell her: a faint scent of cigarette smoke, fresh smells of perspiration. He could sense the bulk of her soft body in the dark so close to his. He felt an overpowering urge to take her in his arms. Just once to feel her breasts crush against him. Just once to kiss her neck, somehow to be swallowed up and immersed in one quintessential embrace . . .

"Gabriel."

"Yes."

"I forgot the paper. I put in *Die Leiden des Jungen Werthers.* Is that all right? There is room on the pages to write."

"Yes," he said. "That's fine." He felt flooded with an inarticulate gratitude for this strong, stubborn woman. He rubbed his forehead. He felt the sense of helplessness descend on him again as he thought of what he had to do. If only they hadn't caught him outside Liesl's house, if only . . . He could have patiently waited for the arrival of the British.

"The town is very quiet," Liesl said. "They have made a line, north, about ten kilometres. Be careful. Here—" She handed him a stub of pencil.

"Thanks." Gabriel put the stub in his pocket.

"For *Jungen Werthers*," she said. "A souvenir."

Gabriel felt an intense sadness descend on him. He felt as if he were about to embark on some long, arduous voyage. His eyes were full of inappropriate tears.

He stepped back. "I'll go now," he said, trying to stop the quaver in his voice. "Down this way, then work around the town through the plantations."

"Be careful. Just for two days. Find somewhere safe. Then come back here." There was no note of pleading in her voice, just natural concern. She expects to see me again, Gabriel thought. He felt suddenly that it was only right that he should tell her something of his feelings for her. It would in some way justify what she was doing, the risks she had taken. He tried to think of safe words he could use.

She touched his elbow.

"You should go."

"Thank you, Liesl," he began. "I don't know . . . I feel. What I—"

"Don't worry. It's not important. Come back when they have gone."

"Right," he said. "Two days." He picked up the sack, gave a brief wave in the dark with his trembling left hand and set off carefully down the rutted track that led to the trees.

CHAPTER SIX

22 NOVEMBER 1917

Nanda · German East Africa

Von Bishop and Rutke looked at the hole Gabriel had made under the wooden wall of the shed. A sweating, nervous Deeg came round the side, holding the metal hinge.

"This is it," Deeg said in an outraged voice. "This is how he did it."

"But how did he get it?" Von Bishop asked. "What about the guard?"

"Ah, well. There was no guard last night. We had many duties and Cobb was a sick man. Weak. There were secure bolts on the door. I thought—"

"Someone helped him," Rutke said. "It's obvious. But who?"

A little man on a bicycle came free-wheeling down the slope from the main street and stopped beside them. He had a cigarette in his mouth. Von Bishop and Rutke saluted. Deeg went into a quivering attention, chin up, thumbs at trouser seams. He was General von Lettow-Vorbeck.

"He's gone?" Von Lettow confirmed. "The man who knows about the China Show?"

"Last night," Von Bishop said. "But he's weak; he can't be far."

"I see." Von Lettow paused. "You'd better catch him, Erich."

"Me, sir?"

"Yes. Take some of the irregulars."

It was the last thing Von Bishop wanted to do. "Are you sure, sir?"

Von Lettow frowned. He took off his sun-helmet and wiped his stubby head with a handkerchief.

"Yes," he said firmly. "We are crossing the Rovuma up by the Ludjenda confluence. In two or three days. Meet us there. But don't waste time, Erich. A Zeppelin is not going to make much difference once we're over the river."

Von Lettow and Rutke left to rejoin the main *Schutztruppe* column some five miles away at Newala. It was from there that Von Bishop had been summoned at first light by a message from Deeg. Nanda was now, to all intents and purposes, clear of troops. There remained only the large numbers of sick and wounded in the hospital, two dozen women and children from the surrounding plantations, Deeg and his squad of ruga-ruga and the sixteen NCO prisoners.

Von Bishop told Deeg to select three of his best men to form the tracking party. Deeg and the other ruga-ruga were to stay behind in Nanda and surrender to the British when they arrived.

Von Bishop walked wearily up the deserted main street towards the hospital. All the sick and wounded had been assembled here. The hospital was so crowded that many were laid out in the shade beneath trees. Others were lying in hastily erected grass shelters. Across the road from the hospital the NCO prisoners formed a curious group by the main gate of the stockade.

Von Bishop saw Liesl standing on the narrow stoop that ran along the front of the hospital. She stood like a man, her hands behind her, feet apart, gazing out over the drab view, rocking gently backwards and forwards. She was smoking a cigarette and, Von

Bishop noticed with a squirm of irritation, wearing her coloured glasses.

She saw him approach. "Erich!" she exclaimed. "What are you doing here? I thought the *Schutztruppe* were at Newala." Some wounded men lying on stretchers at one end of the stoop looked up in mild curiosity.

"They are," he said. "I came down this morning." He paused, scrutinising her face. "He's escaped, you know."

"Who? Gabriel? No, I didn't know. When?" She seemed quite unconcerned. She puffed at her cigarette, then glanced at its glowing end. Von Bishop stared in frustration at the dark, opaque lenses of her glasses. She had called him Gabriel.

"Yes, *Cobb,*" he said pointedly. "Somebody in the town must have helped him."

She shrugged. "He's been here a long time. All the boys know him."

"I'm going after him," he said. "Von Lettow's orders."

"As you wish, Erich," she said and blew a stream of smoke into the sunlight.

Von Bishop tightened the girth on his saddle. His mule munched contentedly on some dry grass. A few yards away stood three of Deeg's ruga-ruga. He felt unsettled and irritated. He had said goodbye to Liesl, and it had turned out to be both infuriatingly formal and non-committal. He had told her he would be rejoining Von Lettow's final column when he had recaptured Cobb and that she, no doubt, would be interned in Dar for as long as the war went on.

"We must continue to fight," he said without much fervour. "At all costs."

"Of course, Erich," she had replied.

He said goodbye and stepped forward to kiss her. She removed her coloured glasses, and, briefly, their lips touched. Von Bishop stepped back and held her at arm's length, his hands on her shoulders. He looked uncomprehendingly into her eyes. His wife seemed a total stranger to him. He suddenly noticed the fleshiness of her shoulders and upper arms, how the material of her dress was creased and tight across her bosom. She used to be a handsome woman, he thought sadly to himself. How this war has changed her!

With a sigh he heaved himself up onto his mule. He saw Deeg walking over from the P.O.W. cage.

"I'm sure he'll head north towards the British," Deeg said. "I've told my boys to ask local villagers. They see everything. With a bit of persuasion . . ."

"Good, good," Von Bishop said testily. Really, people like Deeg were a disgrace. "Do your men speak Swahili?"

"Ah," Deeg said apologetically. "I regret, very little. But they are obliging fellows, quick to learn. You can easily make them understand any order."

Von Bishop looked round at the ruga-ruga. Two wore brimless felt caps. The third was bare-headed, his skull shaven apart from a round tuft of hair above his brow. They were draped in coils of tattered, evil-smelling blankets and armed with old .70 rifles. Large machetes hung at their waists. They smiled winningly at him, revealing their filed, pointed teeth. Absolutely the worst sort of irregular, thought Von Bishop. Still, they would know the country. Cobb wouldn't get far.

"Let's go," Von Bishop said. He kicked his mule into action and trotted off down the main street, the ruga-ruga loping behind.

CHAPTER SEVEN

22 NOVEMBER 1917

The Makonde Plateau · German East Africa

After he left Liesl, Gabriel crept into the rubber plantations and waited for dawn. As soon as there was a faint light he set off through the comparatively open bush, keeping the rising sun on his right-hand side. It was fairly easy going. The countryside was sparsely wooded, the ground covered in thick, waist-high grass with the odd tangle of thorn thicket. He kept to paths only if they headed due north. He wanted to make as much distance as possible while he was still fresh. He bypassed native villages but made no real effort to hide himself. The main German force was south of Nanda now, he knew, based at Newala. There was a rearguard to the north-west of the town on the road that led to Nambindinga. His plan was to strike north for a day or two—depending on progress—then strike east, forming the two sides of a right-angled triangle to the Nanda–Nambindinga hypotenuse. He calculated that he should meet up with the advancing British column in three days or thereabouts.

After an hour or so the ground began to rise as he entered the gentle foothills of the wide Makonde plateau, a sizeable spur of which separated Nanda and Nambindinga. In the dips and valleys the vegetation grew thicker and for a lot of the time he passed through thin woods composed of spindly trees. At mid-morning he found a safe place to stop, a dry gully with a thick screen of bushes and scrub. He found a patch of shade and ate some of the hard unleavened bread that Liesl had supplied and drank a few mouthfuls of water.

He felt curiously exhilarated and quite pleased with himself. His limping gait had carried him along tolerably well. His leg was barely aching. He took from the sack the book Liesl had given him, *Die Leiden des Jungen Werthers: "The Sorrows of Young Werther,"* he translated. He had never read it, just used its fine pages to make cigarettes. The first eighty-seven pages were missing. He started to write on the upper and lower margins of the first available page. A little self-consciously he wrote, "Report of Capt. G.H. Cobb att. to 69th Palamcottah Light Infantry. Taken prisoner at Tanga 4/11/1914. Account of imprisonment and escape." He paused. He knew that he might fail in his endeavour and the request to Liesl for writing materials had been made with this in mind. If his body should be found, he wanted his identity to be ascertainable, and some record of the facts to be established. That was most important.

"Next of kin," he wrote. "Major——" He paused and scratched out "Major" and replaced it with "Charis Lavery Cobb, The Cottage, Stackpole Manor, Stackpole, Kent." As he added the full stop, the point of his pencil stub broke. He swore. Writing Charis's name and the familiar address brought back long-dormant memories. He found himself thinking of their days in Trouville, their walks along the promenade. He brought to mind an image of Stackpole in high summer, the field in front of the house, the river, the willow pool. He remembered the boiling afternoon he had gone swimming with Felix, the dinner when the electric light had failed, the major furiously ringing a silent bell. He felt a debilitating sense of home-sickness sweep through his body.

He looked down at his legs stretched before him as he sat. His decrepit boots, his tattered socks, his thin knees freshly scratched from the thorn. He touched his right knee, pushing at the knee-bone with a forefinger. It slid, oiled and easily, at his touch. As it moved, the sun caught the springy golden hairs that covered it. His fingers travelled higher, pulling back the frayed hem of his shorts to expose the wasted thigh, the contorted pink and white scar that stitched together the severed halves of his muscle. He pulled the trouser leg down. His wound was aching a little more; his leg seemed to be stiffening up. He rubbed his jaw, hearing the rasp of the bristles of his three-day beard. Above him the sun beat down as mid-day approached. Locusts and grasshoppers kept up their mo-notonous shrilling whine in the surrounding bushes.

He lay down and pillowed his arms beneath his head. I must rest, he told himself. I'll set out again in the afternoon, when the heat's gone from the sun. He'd look for a flint later and try to sharpen some kind of point on the pencil, so he could write down the details of his escape. At least the facts would be there, if his body were found. He tried to replace this grim thought with some-thing more agreeable. He made an effort to conjure up a picture of Charis's face, something he hadn't done for many, many months, thinking uneasily of the few days they had spent together as man and wife. He screwed up his eyes in concentration but he found he was thinking only of Liesl. Liesl in the bath, her heavy breasts drip-ping with water, the maid pouring it over her shoulders, rivulets sluicing over her belly, dampening the pale coppery triangle of hairs between her thighs . . .

He sat up. A problem suddenly became obvious to him. How could he write of Liesl's part in the escape? How would it look to anyone—Charis—reading about it? He decided to wait to think about it later.

He set off again in the middle of the afternoon. The day was still hot, but he found the slope he was moving up well-provided with shady trees. His leg had stiffened up considerably and he didn't make the good progress he had in the morning. As he skirted some fields on the edge of a native village, some children shouted at him and some stones were thrown, but he kept on going. It took him two laborious hours to break out of the trees and reach the edge of the plateau.

The sun was lower in the sky; the air was dusty and soft. Ahead stretched a vast grassy plain dotted with small stone hills—kopjes—occasional brakes of trees and bushes and delicately beautiful flat-topped acacias.

He set off across the grass plain. He would walk as far as he could before night fell. Then he would make a fire at the base of one of the kopjes. In the morning he would change course and march into the rising sun. By the end of that day, or perhaps the next, he would meet the advancing columns of the British Army.

CHAPTER EIGHT

22 NOVEMBER 1917

Near Nambindinga • German East Africa

The 5th Battalion of the Nigerian Brigade plodded along the dirt road to Nambindinga, Twelve Company in the vanguard. Felix walked beside Gilzean in the stifling late-afternoon heat. He looked back at his platoon, green fezzes bobbing in an untidy column, the slap of their bare feet on the hard earth of the road. Frearson was somewhere behind. Gent's platoon was pushed out on the right wing. Young Waller, Parrott's replacement, was slogging up and down the crumpled foothills and gullies of the plateau on the left Loveday's platoon was fanned out across the road several hundred yards ahead.

"*Sacrebleu!*" Loveday had exclaimed on being told his position. "Advance guard, my, my."

They had been making slow progress all day without meeting any opposition. This was their first occasion at the head of the column of troops pushing inland from Lindi—"Linforce," as it was known. To the north was another column, from Kilwa and imaginatively dubbed, in true army fashion, "Kilforce." It was these two columns that were driving the remains of Von Lettow's army out of German East Africa.

Felix looked at Gilzean. His khaki shirt was soaked with sweat. In the shade cast by his sun-helmet he looked pallid and drawn, his chin and jaws blue-black against his white cheeks.

"Are you all right, Sergeant?" Felix asked.

"Oh, aye. It's just unco hoat."

Frearson came puffing up from the rear at this point.

"Didn't you hear the bugle?" he demanded angrily. He seemed furious.

"No, sorry What for?"

"We're pulling back. Lines of communication too extended. Bivouac by the side of the road, then march back to camp tomorrow. Pass the word to Loveday and the others, and keep your ears open in the future."

Just then, beyond the curve in the road ahead, there was a loud explosion. A column of smoke and dust shot up high in the air, followed by the rattle of falling stones and gouts of earth. There were shouts and cries of alarm from Loveday's platoon. Everyone fell to the ground.

"My God! Artillery?" Frearson gasped, alarm tensing his putty features.

"Scairdy gowk," Felix heard Gilzean mutter behind him.

There were no more explosions. They got to their feet and ran round the corner. In the middle of the road was a crater surrounded by Loveday's excited platoon. By its side lay Loveday, or rather his top half. There was no sign of his legs or much of anything below his waist. None of his platoon seemed hurt, beyond a few cuts and bruises. They were voluble with nervous excitement over their narrow escape. Half a dozen men must have walked over the mine before Loveday's boot set it off. What would Loveday have said? Felix found himself wondering. *"Nom d'un nom"? Zut alors"?*

Felix turned away and looked at the landscape. The road sloped down slightly at this point, affording a panorama of the countryside.

The burnt grass plains, the thorn scrub, undulating hills fading out into the evening haze in the south, the lusher green of the Rovuma basin away in the distance. No sign of a German anywhere.

They spent the next morning and afternoon laboriously retracing their steps to the camp they'd left the day before. After a quiet night they buried Loveday at the foot of a baobab tree in the morning. After the burial service Felix returned to his tent for a breakfast of corned beef, mashed sweet potato and a local variety of bean which an ever efficient Human had ready for him. He was half-way through his meal when Gilzean approached with a tin can in his hand.

"What is it, Gilzean?" Felix asked.

"Could you take a keek at this, please, sir?"

Felix looked. It contained a thick, albuminous, dark liquid.

"What's this—coffee?"

"No. It's aidle from my cullage."

"Oh, yes?"

"I've been passin' this drumlie loppert water for a week. I just get a mitchkin, ye ken. A jaup."

Felix frowned. He was about to ask Gilzean to repeat himself when he saw a vaguely familiar lanky figure sauntering over.

"I say, Cobb?" it shouted. "Captain Frearson said I'd find you here. Got some interesting news. It's me, Wheech-Browning, Kilwa, GSO Two (Intelligence). Remember?"

"Oh, yes. Have a seat. I won't be a minute." He turned to Gilzean and handed him back his tin.

"Let me get this straight," he said. "Is this something to do with your health?" He wondered what Wheech-Browning wanted.

"Aye. I'm fair doited with worry. This grugous stuff . . ."

"How are you feeling?" He wanted to dismiss Gilzean, but the man was persistent.

"A bit tired. But it's oorie. It could be a clyre in my culls."

"Yes?" Wheech-Browning was staring curiously at Gilzean.

"Or my moniplies. My jag. Yes, my jag even."

Felix felt confused; by now he'd come almost to understand Gilzean, but when the man was upset, his language retreated into the obscurities of his arcane Celtic vocabulary. He knew suddenly that Wheech-Browning had news of Gabriel.

"I shouldn't worry," he told Gilzean, "if you're not feeling too bad otherwise. I'm sure it'll clear up, um, whatever it is. See the M.O. if any complications arise." That seemed to cover everything.

"Thank you *very* much indeed, sir," Gilzean said gratefully, saluted and walked off with his curious tin.

"That's remarkable," Wheech-Browning said. "What language was that man speaking?"

"English."

"Never! Quite incomprehensible."

"A Scottish version, anyway."

"Can you understand him?"

"It took a while, but I can catch the basic drift now." He paused. "You said you had some news."

"Yes," said Wheech-Browning. "About your brother. We've come across some traces of him. You remember that American chap, Smith? He telephoned yesterday from a place called Nanda."

Felix felt a sinking feeling in his body, as if all its vital fluids were being dragged towards his feet.

"Have you found him?"

"Not exactly. But we do know where he was, up to a few days ago. I've cleared it with your captain. You can come along with me."

Wheech-Browning explained what had happened as they bounced down the road towards Nanda in his Ford. "Kilforce," moving parallel to but faster than "Linforce," had captured Nambindinga the day before, found it deserted and had advanced on to the next village down the road, Nanda, where they had discovered a small P.O.W. camp. The prisoners had passed on information about Gabriel. How he had escaped just two days previously.

Felix and Wheech-Browning drove past columns of Linforce troops marching briskly down the road. Loveday's mine crater had already been filled in by the Pioneers. Felix wondered if anyone really knew what was going on in this war. Why had Kilforce been halted and Linforce advanced? *He* could have marched into

Nanda. . . . He felt a spine-snapping tension in his body. He was buoyant with a kind of nervous expectation and yet couldn't ignore the forebodings that nagged at him. What would happen when he met Gabriel again? Could he tell him his fateful news?

Wheech-Browning was in a chatty mood.

"Remember that Zeppelin I told you about? Well, it set off all right a few days ago. The nineteenth, I think. Crossed the Med and headed down over the desert in Sudan. Just as it got to Khartoum, our chaps in signals sent it a message in code, German code, saying: 'German forces in East Africa have surrendered.' We've got the jerry codes, you see. We captured them in 1915. Bilderbeck's work again. Great loss, that man." His face looked solemn for an instant. "What do you think happened?"

Felix wasn't really listening. "What? Oh, um, no idea."

"Turned right round and went straight back home, that's what. Bloody marvellous, don't you think?"

Nanda was full of King's African Rifles. Felix looked about him as he drove into the little town. He saw the row of cramped mud-walled, tin-roofed buildings lining the main street; the shade trees planted here and there; the tin and wood bungalows of the planters' families; the long stone buildings of the former agricultural research station; the wire enclosure of the small P.O.W. stockade.

Wheech-Browning reported to battalion headquarters, which had taken over one of the larger bungalows. They were told where they might find Walter Smith and walked down the main street in search of him.

Behind the hospital, sitting in the shade of a large mango tree, were a disconsolate group of German women and children. Some little way off, Walter was talking to one of them. Felix and Wheech-Browning approached. Walter broke off his interrogation and greeted Felix with some enthusiasm and Wheech-Browning with less.

"What are *you* doing here?" he demanded of Wheech-Browning suspiciously.

"I'm GSO Two (Intelligence), for heaven's sake," Wheech-Browning protested. "This is a matter for my department."

Walter inclined his head in the direction of the German woman.

"That woman is the wife of the bastard I'm chasing," he said. "But wait for this. He's chasing your brother. Isn't that extraordinary?"

Felix wasn't interested in the American's observations. What was coincidence to him was merely irrelevant to Felix.

"But why? Why is he chasing him?"

"Your brother escaped two days ago. It seems they think he was a spy."

"A *spy?*" It didn't make any sense. "Gabriel?"

"Yes. But Frau von Bishop says he wasn't a spy." Walter frowned, as if he, too, was having trouble comprehending everything. "Anyway," he went on, "the Germans believe your brother is in possession of vital information, which is why they're after him."

"I wonder what it is?" Wheech-Browning said.

"Doesn't she know?" Felix asked.

"No. Or at least she isn't saying. She says she has no interest in the war at all."

"But where's he gone?" Felix said. It seemed the most malevolent cruelty to have allowed him to get so close.

"North," Walter said. "That's all she knows. She keeps saying not to worry. She says your brother will come back here any day. She says he's just hiding out in the bush somewhere."

"How does she know all this?"

"Your brother was in the hospital here for a long time as her patient. It seems she got to know him then."

Felix felt lost. He couldn't really grasp what was going on.

"Look," Walter said. "I'm going after this Von Bishop. They won't be long off. If I catch him, your brother might not be far away."

"I'm coming too," Felix said. "But I must ask this woman a question first."

"Let's get out of the damned sun first," Wheech-Browning said, pushing open the door of an outhouse. "Cooler in here. I'll just have a look." He ducked inside. Ten seconds later he came out, red-faced, scrupulously wiping his hand with a handkerchief.

"Good God!" He seemed genuinely shocked. "Barbarians! The place is covered in . . . human ordure!"

"That's right," Walter said calmly. "I should have warned you."

Felix walked over to the German woman, Walter and Wheech-Browning following. The woman was plump and strong-looking, with a pale freckly face. She had a mango leaf in her hands and was tearing it methodically into tiny pieces.

"Guten Tag, gnädige Frau," Felix said, striving to remember his German.

"She speaks English," Walter said.

"Oh, good." Felix started again. "I believe you know my brother, Gabriel Cobb. He escaped from here two days ago."

The woman's placid expression suddenly became curious. She stared at Felix's face.

"You are Gabriel's brother?" she said.

"Yes. I just want to ask you one question," Felix said slowly "Can you tell me if, during the time he was here, he ever received a letter? A letter from England."

"A *letter?*"

"Yes."

"No. No, I'm sure."

"Sure he didn't?"

"He never had any letter."

Felix felt a delicious sensation momentarily envelop him. A feeling of supernatural release, a floating, an ecstatic removal of terrible worries and tormenting fears. Gabriel knew nothing. Now all he had to do was find him.

"Thank you," he said with heartfelt sincerity to the woman, and rejoined Walter and Wheech-Browning.

"Were you speaking German then?" Wheech-Browning asked.

"What? Yes, just a word or two."

"You don't happen to number Portuguese among your many tongues, do you?"

Felix was still overcome with the information he'd just received. He couldn't be bothered with the idiotic, insane questions of this ludicrous beanpole of a man.

"Portuguese? Yes, I speak it fluently."

"You wouldn't care for a job with GSO Two (Intelligence), would you?" They were walking round the hospital back to the main street. "It seems my next task will be to liaise with our Portuguese allies, if and when Von Lettow crosses the Rovuma, and I don't speak a word."

"No, thank you," Felix said firmly. "I'm fully committed to the Nigerian Brigade."

"Are you coming?" the American asked casually, as if he were offering to drive him to the local railway station. "I've got orders to scout north anyway. They think there's another column heading south from Tabora trying to rejoin Lettow."

Felix paused. He experienced a sense of mounting desperation; he felt the imponderable obstacles of army custom and regulations hemming him in.

"I've *got* to come," he said finally. "But my captain has only cleared me for today. What can I do?" he asked Walter.

"Easy," Walter said. "Get Wheech-Browning here to say his motor car has broken down. We shouldn't be more than two or three days."

Wheech-Browning held up his hands. "Sorry, old chap. Not on, I'm afraid."

"Come *on,*" Walter persuaded. "It's his brother, for God's sake."

"It could be his great-grandfather for all I care," Wheech-Browning said cheerily. "No can do."

Felix felt like killing the man. Wheech-Browning was a major. Frearson wouldn't suspect anything.

"Jesus Christ," Walter swore incredulously. "Can't you say it's a matter of vital security?"

"Oh, yes," Wheech-Browning agreed. "I can say that. But then I'd have to come along, too, do you see. I couldn't say that, then send Cobb along in my place, could I now?"

Walter's face set. He looked at Felix. "Is that all right with you?"

"Yes," Felix said desperately, "anything."

"Jolly good," Wheech-Browning said. "Let's pop back to battalion HQ. I'll give your company commander a call."

CHAPTER NINE

24 NOVEMBER 1917

The Makonde Plateau · German East Africa

Von Bishop had hoped to catch up with his quarry long before, but it had proved harder than he thought to pick up his trail and necessitated a tedious to-ing and fro-ing between native villages, and the issuing of bribes and threats before reports started to come in. Once they had reached the plateau he thought it would be only a matter of hours, but Cobb's course was so erratic that the ruga-ruga kept losing his trail. Cobb had been on the move now for two full days: by all accounts he should be collapsing from exhaustion. It was remarkable that he'd got so far.

As dusk fell, the ruga-ruga made their unwillingness to continue evident. They hadn't expected to be away from Nanda this long either, but Von Bishop pressed them on regardless. Each night when he camped, Cobb lit a fire—judging from the remains they found. Von Bishop hoped that tonight they would be close enough to him to spot it glimmering in the darkness. He had been on the point of calling a halt—the sun had disappeared and only the shred of an orange-pink sunset lightened the sky—when one of the ruga-ruga up ahead gave a whistle. A kilometre or so away, at the base of the darker mass of a rock kopje, was a tiny twinkle of flame.

They stopped where they were and waited until it became fully dark. The ruga-ruga stood together whispering excitedly, clearly glad the chase was finally over. Von Bishop, too, felt a vague relief. He began to plot their next moves. They would have to head west for a while before wheeling south to the Ludjenda confluence. He wished suddenly that he had had the foresight to bring another mule. If Cobb was sick and weak, their progress would be considerably impeded. Perhaps he could get the ruga-ruga to procure him one from a village; they couldn't afford to waste any more time.

He wandered a little way from the group, staring at the twinkling point of light. There was a moon rising but it was too thin to make detection likely. He frowned with concentration, staring at Cobb's fire—a tiny flicker in the vast encroaching darkness of the plateau—until his eyes watered.

What had made Cobb come to his house on that particular night? Sheer chance? Or was he really gathering intelligence? He'd known about Cobb for a long time, known that the wounded Englishman was one of Deppe's long-term projects. He'd even seen him once or twice: a manifestly sick, limping officer on parole who sometimes helped out in the ward. . . .

He walked back to his mule. He waved one ruga-ruga twenty metres out to the left. He positioned another similarly on the right. To the third he gave the reins of his mule. He himself took the middle position. He could just see the ruga-ruga on either side. He unholstered his revolver. They would creep silently up to the fire. He was looking forward to seeing Cobb's face when they stepped out of the gloom and into the firelight.

He waved the men forward and they moved silently across the dark grass plain towards the glimmering fire. They were about a hundred metres away when Von Bishop caught a glimpse of Cobb moving about in front of the flames. He seemed to be collecting twigs and wood for fuel. Von Bishop hissed at the ruga-ruga on either side to stop. He would wait until Cobb had settled once more.

Just then his mule whinnied. Not very loud—perhaps the ruga-ruga leading it had drawn it up too fiercely—but to Von Bishop it sounded deafening. Swearing under his breath, he dropped to one knee, peering ahead at the fire. It still burned on. Cobb evidently felt there was no need to extinguish it. Von Bishop allowed himself a small sigh of relief. The African night was full of sounds, especially those made by animals.

For safety's sake, though, he and the ruga-ruga remained where they were, crouched in the knee-high grass for another ten minutes before moving slowly forward once again. As they drew closer, Von Bishop felt a tightening in his chest. Cobb had made his camp between two spurs of rock at the foot of the kopje. Slowly more details emerged. A stunted thorn tree grew out of a large fissure. The flames caused shifting knife-edged shadows to be cast by the jagged rocks on each side. They inched closer. Then Von Bishop suddenly stood up. Cobb had gone.

He strode angrily into the deserted campsite, followed by the chattering ruga-ruga. Cobb had obviously left at once, and in haste, abandoning everything as soon as he heard the mule snicker in the dark. Von Bishop looked at the dry tufts of grass around the fire. One had been flattened from the pressure of a body. A sack hung from the thorn tree. A heel of unleavened bread lay on the ground beside a small bundle of sticks. A box of matches had been placed neatly on a round stone. . . .

Von Bishop looked around him vainly. The light from the fire made the surrounding night impenetrably black. One of the ruga-ruga unhooked the sack from the thorn tree and brought it over. Von Bishop reached inside and drew out two candles. He reached in again and his hand closed on a book. He frowned with surprise. A book? He took it out. The worn black and gold leather binding was immediately familiar. He held the spine to the fire, attempting to read the faint lettering of the title: *Die Leiden des Jungen Werthers.*

He recognised the book as his own. How curious, he thought; how on earth did Cobb come to have it? And where were all the missing pages? He tugged at his bottom lip in puzzlement. For what possible reason would Cobb want to read Goethe while on the run? Did he tear out each page after he had read it?

His eye caught some faint writing on the top margin. "Report of Captain G.H. Cobb," he read. "Account of imprisonment and escape." He turned the pages with new interest, thinking that here would be some significant clues, but there was no more writing. Another frustration. He felt mildly disappointed.

There was a rattle of falling stones from somewhere high on the kopje. They all looked up at once.

"Get him!" Von Bishop shouted excitedly at the startled ruga-ruga. They had seized their rifles. "Go on, you idiots!" Von Bishop shouted again. He tried Swahili. "Get him, I tell you!" What was Kikuyu for "catch"?

One of the ruga-ruga yelled something in their gibberish language. He brandished his rifle in the air like a spear. Von Bishop mimed grabbing movements in desperation. Why couldn't they understand? How did Deeg speak to them? Dutch? Afrikaans? "Yes," he yelled exasperatedly, baffled by their reticence. Every second counted in this darkness. "Go on, yes?" He gestured at the black mass of the hill. "Catch?" He tried Swahili again. No effect. "Quickly, for God's sake, catch him." This was ridiculous. Cobb was getting a head start while Von Bishop floundered around with languages.

Then one ruga-ruga suddenly turned and shouted something to the other two. The three of them scrambled off into the dark, up the rocky slope of the hill. For several minutes he could hear them calling out to each other, and heard the slither and fall of the stones dislodged by their feet. Then their cries became fainter. It sounded to him as if they were now on the other side of the hill. Soon he could hear nothing above the endless noise of the crickets.

He threw some more wood on the fire and sat down. He stared glumly at the flames. He felt tired. He still held the book, he realised. He reached forward and dropped it on the fire. It burnt away to ashes very quickly. It was a kind of evidence, he supposed. Theoretically, he shouldn't have destroyed it. He pursed his lips and rubbed his nose.

He poked at the ash brick that was all that remained of the book, letting the flakes crumble and fall into the embers of the fire. He thought suddenly of Cobb, out there alone on the dark plain, running. Running frantically from the ruga-ruga. He shivered with sympathy. The man would be terrified out of his wits; any man would. You could die from that sort of terror. Racing blindly through the night, heart pounding, lungs bursting, tripping and falling down, the shouts of your pursuers in your ears.

Von Bishop woke up just before dawn. He felt stiff and hungry. There was a lemon-grey lightening in the east. He relit the fire, took some mealie-flour cakes from his saddle-bag, spread them with the last of his raspberry jam and ate a lonely breakfast.

The ruga-ruga didn't return for another hour or so. Von Bishop saw them first in the distance, coming round the side of the hill, just the three of them in single file. So Cobb got away, he thought, briefly elated for some reason. But then the prospect of another day's chase made him miserable again. Still, Cobb knew about the China Show. He had his duty to do.

He built up the fire and then took his rifle from his saddle holster. He would try to shoot a bird or a small antelope for the ruga-ruga. It was a safe bet that they wouldn't move off again until they had eaten.

The ruga-ruga marched into the hollow between the two spurs of rock ten minutes later. Von Bishop sat on a boulder, his rifle between his knees. The leading man, he noticed, had unslung his blanket and carried it over his shoulder like a sack. Perhaps they've got their own food, he thought, bending down to remove a speck of dust from his rifle bolt.

There was a soft heavy thud and Von Bishop looked up. A yard from the toe of his left boot lay the severed head of Gabriel Cobb, his nose pressed uncomfortably into the dusty earth, his staring eyes and gaping mouth swarming with tiny insects.

CHAPTER TEN

The Makonde Plateau · *German East Africa*

Walter rode between Wheech-Browning and Felix. A hundred yards up ahead his two askari trackers paced easily along, leading their mules, following the conspicuous trail left by Von Bishop and his men. They had been up early that day and had made good progress. Walter calculated that they were only two or three hours behind Von Bishop now. He stood up in the saddle and stared ahead over the grass plain. Up here on the plateau the morning mists lingered. There was still something of a haze on the horizon, softening the details of the landscape.

He looked round at the faces of his two companions: Wheech-Browning sleepy and stupid, Felix tense and expectant. They made a strange group, he thought.

"You said this Von Bishop man was the same one who commandeered your farm, didn't you?" Wheech-Browning asked.

"That's right."

"I thought he was your neighbour. Did you have some kind of feud going, or something?"

"No," Walter said. "Not until he destroyed my farm." Walter looked grim. "What kind of man is it, I ask you, who one day can talk to you about sisal farming—in a perfectly interested and friendly way—and then, the next moment, steal away your livelihood?" Walter looked to Felix for a reassuring reply, but he clearly wasn't listening.

"Sounds like a shrewd businessman to me," Wheech-Browning said with a squawk of laughter.

"Just what do you mean by that?" Walter said in a steely voice. "You don't know what you're talking about."

"Sorry, I'm sure," Wheech-Browning said huffily. "But you did ask."

Their argument was interrupted by a shout from one of the askari scouts. The man stood at the base of a stone kopje a little way to the right. They wheeled their mules and rode over. In a hollow between two spurs of rock were the remains of a camp-fire. Walter dismounted and ran his fingers through the ashes.

"Ouch," he said. "Still hot. They can't be more than an hour away." He picked something out of the ashes. "Looks like a piece of leather binding from a book. What do you make of that?"

Felix held up a sack. "Empty. Is this Von Bishop's camp? Or Gabriel's?"

Walter looked around. There was a pile of droppings from a mule. "Von Bishop's," he said. There was also a small rough mound of freshly dug earth. "I don't think your brother would bother to bury his rubbish."

"Who left the sack then?"

There was a shout from Wheech-Browning, who hadn't dismounted.

"About half a mile away," he called. "Masses of birds wheeling around."

Walter and Felix remounted and trotted after Wheech-Browning. True enough, a dozen kites and vultures circled and flapped above something in the grass. They saw Wheech-Browning get off his horse and run forward, windmilling his arms and shouting. Five or six birds shrugged themselves awkwardly into the air. Walter and Felix dismounted a few yards off and walked through the grass towards Wheech-Browning. A subdued droning noise filled the air from thousands of flies. The grass stems all around them were blackened and weighed down with a fruit of shiny bluebottles and duller blowflies. Each step raised a temporary cloud, like a thick animated dust.

Wheech-Browning stumbled towards them, his face white.

"Good Lord," he said. "Christ. It's a body." He put his hand on his throat. "No head."

"No head?" Felix said with alarm.

"Bloody flies!" Wheech-Browning said. "Where do they all come from? A huge empty plain. That's what I want to know."

Walter walked forward with Felix. He looked across at him. Felix's face was slightly screwed up, as if he were walking through a cloud of smoke or gas.

The body lay on its belly in a wide clearing of violently torn and trampled grass. The birds had already pecked away both calves, and the porcelain gleam of exposed ribs shone beneath the tattered shirt.

"Army boots," Walter said, not wanting to speculate further.

"Looks too small for Gabriel," Felix said bravely. "He was a big chap, Gabriel."

Wheech-Browning re-joined them. By now they were all covered with flies, flies crawling all over their faces, oblivious to their waving hands. Walter took some paces to one side.

"It's been chopped off," he said. "That wasn't an animal."

"My Christ," said Wheech-Browning. He suddenly leant forward from the waist and vomited. He straightened up unsteadily, wiping his mouth. "Phew," he said. "There goes breakfast."

As if on some unspoken order they withdrew to the mules.

"What the hell is going on?" Walter said. "Who chops off a man's head in the middle of the veld?"

"I'm pretty sure it's not Gabriel," Felix said. He swallowed heavily. "I think. I mean you can't tell. Without . "

"Who is it, then?" Walter said. "Von Bishop?"

"Where's the head, though?" Wheech-Browning asked. "Why carry off the head? I don't understand."

Walter suddenly recalled the mound of earth at the camp. "You stay here," he said to Wheech-Browning. "Keep the birds off. We're going back to the campsite."

"Scarecrow," Wheech-Browning said, holding his hands out from his sides. "That's what the chaps called me at school."

Walter and Felix rode back to the campsite.

"What is it?" Felix asked.

"I think they've buried the head there." Walter indicated the mound.

"Oh, God."

"Shall I do it or will you?"

"I think you should."

Walter got down on his knees and began digging away the loosely tamped earth with his hands. Six inches down his fingers struck something soft. He felt his mouth swim with saliva. He dug some more. The head was wrapped in a square of blanket.

He turned away. "It's here," he called to Felix, who was standing some yards away. Felix came over. Walter could see his jaw muscles were clenched with effort. His top lip and growth of beard were dewed with sweat. He looked down at the blanket-wrapped head. He took a long quivering breath.

"Could you . . . please."

Walter reached down into the hole and carefully unwrapped the head. He saw a squarish handsome face, very white and thin, with open eyes and mouth. He wiped away some of the larger ants. The hair was pale-brown and tousled. Something about it made it look artificial.

He looked round and saw Felix crying silently, his hands over his face, his shoulders shaking.

"Poor Gabe," he heard him say.

Walter wrapped the head again. Then he stood up and walked over to Felix. He put his hand on his shoulder for a second. He didn't know what to say. He felt an inexpressible sorrow for the young man. Walter walked away from him, past the two scouts who tended their mules, kicking savagely at the grass as he went.

He took some deep breaths, looked up at the sky, beat some dust from his trousers. Off in the distance he could see Wheech-Browning capering madly around the corpse, waving his long arms at the wheeling birds as if he were putting on a performance for them. His yells and whoops carried faintly across the grass.

Walter walked back to Felix.

"What made him do that?" Felix asked hoarsely. "Why did he need to do that?"

"I don't know," Walter said. "I don't have any idea."

"What's his name?"

"Von Bishop."

"I just don't understand," Felix said softly, a tremor distorting his voice. "What would make anyone do a thing like that?"

"I don't know," Walter said with some vehemence. "It just doesn't make any kind of sense at all."

PART FOUR

After the War

CHAPTER ONE

15 MAY 1918

Boma Durio · Portuguese East Africa

"Snap!"

"Eh?"

"Snap. I win," Felix said. *"Ganhador.* Me."

"Oh. Oh, *sim."*

"Terminar?"

"Sim. Sim."

Felix noted down his victory. It took his score to 1,743 games of snap. His opponent, Capitão Pinto, had won 34. Felix put the cards away. The capitão turned for consolation to his erotic books.

Capitão Aristedes Pinto was dying of tertiary syphilis. Or so he said. This fact didn't bother Felix so much as the histrionic way the captain flicked through his small but well-handled collection of pornography. As he turned the pages of dim photographs and extravagant etchings he would sigh wistfully and shake his head as if to say,

"Look at the trouble you naughty girls have got me into." Occasionally he would give a fond chuckle and pass one of the books over to Felix for his perusal. Initially, Felix had indeed been intrigued to look at the pictures—mainly of plump girls in bordellos, with their breasts hanging out of satin slips, or skirts routinely raised to reveal huge creamy buttocks or luxuriant pudenda—but now it was just another irritation. The girls all smiled and posed with little coquettishness, almost as if they were drugged. Felix thought of his own solitary encounter with a prostitute in Bloomsbury Square. It seemed like decades ago, in another world.

Pinto was a small fat man with a pencil moustache, a festering sore in one nostril, and one smoked blind eye. His uniform was constantly smeared and dirty, but for all that he was an amiable sort of fellow, Felix thought, and he seemed to find it not in the slightest bit out of the ordinary that he—a non-English speaker—should have to liaise with an English officer who in turn spoke no Portuguese. Felix had been sharing quarters with him at Boma Durio for getting on for three months, and thanks to the absence of a common vocabulary, they had never had a cross word.

Pinto pushed the book across the table and Felix obligingly scrutinised the picture.

"Francêsa," Pinto moaned. He parted his lips in a grimace of ecstatic pain, exposing his four silver and two gold teeth. "Diabólica!" He blew on his fingertips and launched into a lengthy reminiscence in Portuguese. It was an impossible language, Felix thought, full of thudding consonants and slushing noises. He'd been trying to learn it for three months with the aid of a crude dictionary he'd bought in Porto Amelia but he couldn't even pronounce it. Pinto had been making better progress with his English and spoke a little French, and through a combination of all three languages they just about managed to communicate. It was almost as difficult as talking to Gilzean.

Felix shifted in his seat uncomfortably. He worried that he'd let Gilzean down rather, given him false hopes. His gloomy sergeant had died of black-water fever three days before Christmas 1917. Poor Gilzean.

Pinto went back to his book and Felix took the opportunity to stroll outside.

Boma Durio was a huge earthwork fort, roughly two hundred yards square, set on a hill a mile away from Durio village somewhere in the middle of Portuguese East Africa. In one corner of the square was a redbrick tin-roofed building which was Felix's and Pinto's quarters. Nearby were half a dozen large but flimsy grass huts which housed Pinto's servants, his three young Negro concubines and the half-company of Portuguese native troops and their camp-followers. The rest of the square was empty. That morning it had been filled with six hundred porters and their loads of yams, manioc, rice, sugar-cane and sweet potatoes—provisions for some of the twelve thousand British and Empire troops still chasing Von Lettow and his small army up and down Portuguese East Africa.

It was late afternoon. The light was soft and damp. Noting Felix emerge from his quarters, Human came over to see if there was anything he wanted. Human was Felix's sole remaining contact with the Nigerian Brigade, all of whom had been shipped home some months previously. Human had volunteered to follow Felix in his cross-posting, and Felix had been touched and surprised by his loyalty.

Back in November 1917, after Von Lettow had successfully crossed the Rovuma at the Ludjenda confluence, the Nigerian Brigade had been recalled to Lindi. There, after a few weeks, they had learnt they were to be sent back to Nigeria. Felix had immediately applied for a cross-posting to the King's African Rifles—now some twenty battalions strong—on whom the future brunt of the war in East Africa was to rest. For some mystifying reason it had been turned down. In desperation he recalled Wheech-Browning's offer of a job with GSO II (Intelligence). He got in touch with Wheech-Browning, applied and was immediately accepted. He became a Special Services officer seconded to the Portuguese Army. No one ever thought to check up on his qualifications. "Believe me, Cobb," Wheech-Browning had said with great enthusiasm, "your Portuguese is going to be the most tremendous asset."

Felix imagined he would be in the front line liaising between the K.A.R. and the Portuguese units who were being led a merry dance by Von Lettow. In a confident mood he sailed from Lindi to Porto Amelia in northern Portuguese East Africa. It was from Porto Amelia that the main thrust inland by the British columns—designated "Pamforce" by the ever-imaginative army staff—was issuing. But, instead of fighting, Felix discovered that he was to be a requisitions officer organising food supplies for the K.A.R. troops. He had been sent to Boma Durio, some hundred and fifty miles from Porto Amelia in Nyana Province, which was in the midst of a fertile area of farmland. Here he received his instructions for supplies for Pamforce. Pinto and his men collected the food from surrounding farms and native settlements, and carriers transported it to whichever area the British Army happened to be fighting in.

Anguished complaints and protests to Wheech-Browning at headquarters in Porto Amelia had achieved nothing. "You're doing a vital job, man," Wheech-Browning said. "You can't treat the war as a personal vendetta."

So Felix lingered at Boma Durio, unable to pursue Von Lettow, feeling frustrated and hard done-by. Pinto did all the real work with surprising efficiency. Felix signed requisition orders, paid for the food and kept accounts. Every fortnight or so he received a visit from Wheech-Browning, who kept him in touch with the course of the war and brought him a few home comforts from Porto Amelia.

But for all the deadening monotony of the work and the steamy lethargic atmosphere of Boma Durio, Felix found his hatred of Von Bishop never left him. He thought about Gabriel's death constantly, trying to puzzle out what had happened on the plateau, what dreadful struggle had torn up the grass, why his brother's body had been mutilated. His desire for revenge never left him. It was like the nagging pain of an ulcer. Some sort of normal life was possible, but the pain never went away.

Felix walked across the compound and climbed the steps onto the earthwork ramparts. Below the walls ran a deep ditch, and beyond that the ground sloped down to a small river. The road from the Boma crossed it on a small wooden bridge and meandered downhill for a mile or so to Durio village. The countryside around was lush. Lining the river were huge stands of bamboo, some of the central trunks as thick as a man. On either side of the track to the village, where the ground wasn't cultivated, elephant grass grew to a height of nine feet. Anything stuck in the ground here took root at once, Felix had observed. Human had cut some poles to act as supports for a washing line. Within two weeks new shoots and leaves were sprouting from them. Now they resembled miniature trees.

Felix lit a cigarette and blew smoke at the flies buzzing round his head. Two days ago it had been Gabriel's birthday. He would have been thirty-one. He thought back to that terrible day on the Makonde plateau. They had buried Gabriel at the side of his final camp, in the hollow between the two spurs of rock. Wheech-Browning and Walter had carried the body over and the askaris had dug the grave. Felix had done nothing, overwhelmed by the enormous grief and the surging emotions in his body. They covered the grave with rocks, and Wheech-Browning said the few words he could remember from the burial service. Walter had marked the kopje accurately on his map so that they would know where to find it again. By then there was no point in continuing after Von Bishop, and they had returned to Nanda. Felix had wanted to speak to the Von Bishop woman but she and the other civilians had already been moved to Dar. Shortly after this, Walter learnt that he was being recalled to Nairobi. He said he was glad to be leaving. He left Felix to continue the chase.

Felix threw his cigarette over the ramparts and turned to look at the cluster of huts in the Boma. He saw Pinto emerge from their brick building and watched him stretch and stamp his tubby frame into activity.

"*Feliz!*" Pinto shouted, looking around for him.

"Aristedes," Felix replied. "Up here."

Pinto puffed up the steps to the ramparts.

"*Telefonada,*" he panted, showing his array of gold and silver teeth. "Wheesh-Brownim. Stokesh gonz." He prattled on. Felix registered Stokes guns. Wheech-Browning was coming with Stokes guns. But when?

"Um. Ah . . . *presentemente?*" Felix asked.

"*Não.* Eh . . . *Demain. Sim. Demain.*"

"Tomorrow."

"*Não. Demain. Demain.*"

"*Sim.*"

They nodded and smiled at each other. Then they turned and surveyed the view. It was extremely familiar. Nonetheless, Pinto started pointing out features in the landscape, but Felix didn't understand him. All the same he nodded, and said *sim* from time to time.

The sun began to sink and the light thickened. In the ditch, frogs croaked and the first crickets began to trill. The mosquitoes came out from the shadows they had been resting in all day and began to whine around Felix's ears. He felt a great weight of melancholy descend easily on him; an acute sense of how futile all his efforts had been, of all the human cost of the last two years. Charis, Gabriel . . . The list went on. Gilzean, Cyril, Bilderbeck, Parrott, Lovejoy. Then there were the wounded: Nigel Bathe, Cave-Bruce-Cave, his father. Then there were the unremembered casualties: the men in his platoon and company, the poisoned porters at Kibongo. And that was just one person's list. Think of all the people with their own lists: Walter, Wheech-Browning, Gabriel, Aristedes. . . . Then everybody in East Africa and Europe. He could only mourn in the vaguest sense for the others, but when he thought of his personal roster of names he felt his anger return. How could he just *accept* these casualties? He couldn't be fatalistic about them any more. That was why he had joined up after Charis's death, why he felt he had at least to try to find Gabriel. . . . He ruefully acknowledged his own dishonesty here. There had been other motives too: fear, self-preservation, worry, guilt. But it didn't matter. The important thing was that efforts had to be made, responsibilities shouldered, blame apportioned. He couldn't simply let it go. But he had his guilty man now. Von Bishop carried the heavy freight of all his grievances.

He accepted another cigarette from Pinto, who was still talking away. Felix thought about Stackpole. He had written a long letter home about Gabriel, telling them that Gabriel had died while escaping from prison camp with vital military secrets of an unspecified sort. But then he'd torn it up. It was better, he felt, to let them live on as long as possible in ignorance. He realised he'd been away from Stackpole for nearly two years. To his surprise he found himself feeling homesick for the ugly house. He set his face, feeling an unfamiliar twitching below his eyes.

To distract himself he looked back at Pinto. But the melancholy mood of the African dusk seemed to have affected the captain too. His plump features were slack; a hand worried at the sore at his nostril. He had abandoned his disquisition on the landscape and returned to his favourite theme: his illness. His voice was doleful and slurred with self-pity. He cupped his fat groin in both hands. Felix saw his eyes glistening with tears as his pathological litany softly continued with the evening gathering kindly about them.

Wheech-Browning leapt awkwardly from the Packard lorry. He sneezed and reached into his pocket, extracted a large checked handkerchief and blew his nose into it.

"Ah, Cobb. Good morning. Stinking cold. Somehow you never expect to get a cold in Africa. Touch of the flu as well if I'm not mistaken."

Pinto wandered up.

"Ah, morning, *Capitão* Pinto!" Wheech-Browning dropped his voice and turned to Felix. "How do you say 'Good morning,' Cobb? I can never remember."

"Bom-dia."

"Bom. Dia. Senhor. Capitão." He enunciated each syllable very clearly.

Pinto bowed. He was still very depressed. *"Dia,"* he muttered.

"Marvellous gift you have, Cobb. I say, is old Aristedes all right? He looks a bit white around the gills."

"It's his syphilis. It's getting him down."

"I see. Extraordinary man. Rather hard luck, though." He turned to the askaris jumping from the back of the lorry. "Come on, you men, let's get those guns out."

While the guns were being unloaded, Wheech-Browning explained his mission. Apparently a column had broken off from Von Lettow's main force, had wheeled north and was heading in the general direction of Boma Durio in search, it was assumed, of stores and supplies. Two companies of K.A.R. askaris were being marched down from Medo as reinforcements, but in the meantime it had been decided to strengthen the Boma's defences with two Stokes guns.

"I said you knew how to fire them, Cobb. That's right, isn't it?"

Felix said yes. He had spent many days at Morogoro after Twelve Company had returned from the Rufiji, learning how to fire the simple mortars.

The guns were taken up onto the earthworks and aimed at a stand of bamboo that stood at the edge of the cleared ground around the fort. Pinto had cheered up at the prospect of a private firing and stood by the Stokes guns expectantly, waiting for instructions.

"Right, Cobb," Wheech-Browning said. "Over to you."

Felix thought fast. "I'll tell you what," he said. "I'll explain everything to the *capitão* and then he can drill his men. I'm a bit rusty on the technical terms."

Some dummy rounds were brought up. Felix dropped in a charge, set the sights on the bamboo stand approximately one hundred yards away, then fitted the round dummy bomb—rather like a large wooden toffee-apple—into the top of the muzzle.

"Normally this is done by three men," he explained.

"Que?" said Pinto.

"Three. *Três*, um, *homem. Três homem.*"

"Eh?"

"Sim."

"Good, Cobb. Excellent."

"Stand by." Felix jerked the lanyard at the base of the barrel. There was a loud report, causing everyone to leap back in alarm. Smoke coiled from the barrel and every fissure in the gun. The bomb remained fixed at the end of the muzzle.

"Good Lord," said Wheech-Browning.

"Let's try the other gun," Felix suggested.

The sighting and loading procedures were repeated, the lanyard jerked, and this time with a dull thump the bomb went sailing high into the blue morning air and dropped into the jungle a good fifty yards beyond the bamboo stand. Pinto clapped.

"Bit off target," said Wheech-Browning.

Felix adjusted the elevation of the barrel. Another round was fired. This one went almost straight up and when it came down bounced off the hard ground some thirty yards short. Pinto's men had by now gathered at a safe distance farther along the earthworks, and were looking on with a mixture of apprehension and sceptical curiosity. Pinto himself seemed enormously pleased.

"What's going wrong?" Wheech-Browning said.

"I can't seem to get the range."

"I was told these things were infallible. Child's play to operate. Not much of a show you're putting on, Cobb."

Felix looked darkly at Wheech-Browning. "The dummy rounds. They're too light." He told himself to stay calm. He took out his spectacles and slipped them on to check the small calibrations on the sighting mechanism. Everything seemed to be in order. He suspected it must be something to do with the imbalance between the charge and the dummy round. He explained as much to Wheech-Browning.

"Try a real one then," Wheech-Browning said, taking out his handkerchief and snorting into its folds. "Only for God's sake get it on target. We're looking a right pair of fools." He smiled and waved at Pinto. "At this rate, a bunch of schoolgirls could capture the place."

A live round was loaded. Felix adjusted the elevation and jerked the lanyard. The round bomb sailed high in the air and again landed beyond the bamboo, throwing up a puff of white smoke as it exploded with a very loud bang.

"They make a lot of noise," Wheech-Browning said slowly to Pinto, as if he were addressing a three-year-old. "Noise. BANG!"

"*Sim,*" Pinto agreed. "BOOM!"

"Come on, Cobb," Wheech-Browning said in a low voice. "Hit the wretched target."

Felix loaded another live bomb. He couldn't understand the gun's erratic performance. Then he had a thought. If one gun had malfunctioned, maybe the other gun was doing the same.

"Just a moment," he said. "I think there's something wrong with the sight. I'm going to pace out the range."

"You won't exactly be able to do that if the Germans are storming the place, you know," Wheech-Browning said scathingly.

But Felix had leapt over the rampart and slithered down the side of the earthworks, leaping across the ditch as he went. He strode quickly across the open ground counting out the paces through gritted teeth. He was determined to land the next bomb right in the middle of the bamboo stand, and shut Wheech-Browning up for good.

At the count of ninety-two he reached the bamboo and turned round. He was surprised to see Pinto energetically pacing out the distance behind him. The stupid idiot evidently thought this was something to do with the training exercise.

"Não, Aristedes," Felix called with forced geniality, going back to meet him and waving his hands. "Não importante."

He saw the puff of smoke from the earthworks before his incredulous ears registered the report from the Stokes gun. He even saw the speedy climb of the bomb, a black streak against the blue sky.

"Run!" he screamed into the startled face of Pinto. "Run!"

Felix turned and began to run.

There was an immense roaring noise. He felt as if he'd been caught by several huge ocean breakers in quick succession, buffeted, lifted, tossed. He felt a searing pain in the back of his head, as if a nail had been driven into his skull. Then he hit the ground.

He lost consciousness for a matter of seconds. He opened his eyes to find himself surrounded by swirling smoke. His mind seemed to be functioning with hypersensitive lucidity; he remembered everything, understood what had happened.

He got groggily to his feet, staggered a bit, then looked down at his body. He was shocked to see he was totally naked apart from his boots, which remained. Such bits of his body as he could see between the strands of swirling smoke were either bloodlessly pale or mottled with grotesque livid bruises. Blood dripped from his chin onto his chest. He touched his face and head and looked at his fingertips. Blood seemed to be pouring from his nose, ears and *eyes* The back of his head felt numb and wet. He lurched a bit. He seemed to be getting more dizzy, not less. He looked around for

Aristedes, squinting through the gaps in the smoke for him, but there was no sign. He tripped over the lip of the fresh crater. The torn earth was warm, like bread that has just been pulled from an oven. As if in some kind of a dream he saw what he took to be precious stones or jewels glittering amongst the steaming clods. With difficulty he groped in the earth and picked one up. He held it close to his baffled eyes. It was a golden tooth. Aristedes had disappeared.

He fell back on the ground. He sensed his faculties leaving him as if being tugged away by invisible hands. Through the one remaining gap in the enveloping smoke he saw Wheech-Browning's agonised looming face, heard his shocked voice, clear as a child's.

"The lanyard, Cobb. I sneezed. I was holding it in my hand. It just went off. I'm sorry, Cobb. I'm sorry.   "

CHAPTER TWO

13 NOVEMBER 1918

Kasama · Rhodesia

Von Bishop looked at Rutke, whose teeth were chattering with cold even though the morning sun was bearing down with its usual strength.

"If you ask me, you've got influenza," Von Bishop said bluntly. "But go and see Deppe; he'll tell you."

"Oh, God, please no," Rutke said heavily. Three officers had already died from Spanish influenza. He walked off, shoulders slumped, in search of the doctor. Not that Deppe would do much, Von Bishop thought. A useless doctor, worse than useless. Von Bishop was still suffering from the high-pitched ringing in his ears that he'd contracted in Tanga. Four years ago now, and still no release. Angrily he wriggled his little finger in his left ear. If anything, it seemed to be worse.

He walked out from beneath the awning he'd been standing

under and looked up and down the deserted main street of Kasama.
A dust road, a straggling avenue of flame-trees, mud and wooden
houses, tin and straw roofs. Up ahead he could see the men of his
company standing guard behind some hastily erected barricades. It
was a pleasant morning.

He returned to his patch of shade and told his servant to bring
him a cup of coffee. He sat down in a cane chair and leant forward,
resting his elbows on his knees, supporting his head in his hands.
He wondered if Von Lettow felt as tired as he did. In the last year
they had marched south, deep into Portuguese East Africa, innumerable Portuguese strongholds surrendering at the first shot, fighting a constant rearguard battle against the plodding English columns
in pursuit. Then in July they had turned north again. Winding back
up through Portuguese East, back across the Rovuma into German
East once more. In August their progress had been retarded by a
curious epidemic. At first Deppe said it was "bronchial catarrh."
Then he changed his diagnosis to "croupous pneumonia." Now,
after three Europeans and seventeen natives had died, he was telling
everyone it was "Spanish influenza." Von Bishop furiously wiggled
both little fingers in his ears. And the man called himself a doctor.

In October, still pursued by the relentless British columns, the
tattered *Schutztruppe* turned west and invaded Rhodesia. Little resistance was encountered and many stores were captured. Von Lettow
halted his small army for a few days near the border town of Fife.
Here, English newspapers provided the first information about the
war in Europe that they had had for months. The news was not
good. An offensive had been launched by the Allies in September.
The Americans were advancing in the Argonne, the French and the
British at Cambrai and St. Quentin. Von Bishop and many of the
other officers wondered if Von Lettow would consider surrendering. But at a meeting the general announced that captured medical
supplies had brought their quinine reserves up to fourteen kilos, and
that they had four hundred head of cattle, sufficient to last until
June 1919. He planned to advance across Africa, westward into the
Congo, perhaps as far as the Atlantic coast.

And so mobile detachments were sent down the road from Fife
towards Kasama. A week earlier, Von Bishop had marched into the

town after the garrison had fled southwards. Shortly after, the main body of the *Schutztruppe* had gathered in Kasama and was preparing to march off again in pursuit. Some patrols had gone ahead. Von Bishop was to remain behind for a few days as part of the rearguard.

Von Bishop looked up. His coffee was ready. His boy had also brought him a tin plate filled with strawberries, which grew in plentiful supply in Kasama's kitchen gardens. He took one of the plump berries and popped it into his mouth, crushing it against his palate with his tongue. His mouth was filled with the sweet juice and pulp. How Liesl would love this! he thought suddenly. His smile drooped. He wondered where and how she was. He wondered if she knew that Cobb was dead.

He stirred his coffee slowly, thinking about that night on the plateau. A terrible mistake. A lack of communication, that was all. That morning he had hastily buried the head and then had made off straightaway to the Ludjenda confluence and the meeting with Von Lettow. He intended to have the ruga-ruga arrested and executed for murder but they disappeared the next night. There was nothing he could do. He couldn't ask them why they had done it; they couldn't tell him. He had some suspicions that they may have been acting under instructions from Deeg, but that was something else he couldn't confirm. He told Von Lettow that they had found Cobb's dead body and had buried him. He assumed that Cobb had died from starvation and exposure out on the plateau.

He drank his coffee down and got to his feet. It was over now. He didn't like to think too much about that particular episode. It had been a tragic error. By rights Cobb should have been with them now in Kasama, along with the other British prisoners in the *Schutztruppe* column. He checked himself; there was nothing to be gained by that sort of reflection.

He walked up the street towards his men, his mind still dwelling on the events of that night. If Deeg hadn't given his men secret instructions, could the responsibility be laid at his—Von Bishop's—door? Had he done anything or said anything that the ruga-ruga could have construed as an order to kill Cobb? No, he was sure. He questioned himself with punctilious honesty. But he had not ordered the ruga-ruga to kill the man. "Get him," was all he had said—in a language, moreover, that they could not understand. No, his conscience was clear.

He joined his men. Like him they wore a mixture of ragged German uniforms and captured Portuguese clothing. All their weapons were by now of Portuguese or British origin. Some askaris sat behind a stone wall; others lay in shallow firing pits. Von Bishop's sergeant, a European, came up and saluted. Everything was quiet.

The sun beat down. The road they were guarding led back towards Fife and the border of German East some two hundred kilometres away. Fife was now occupied by the pursuing King's African Rifles. Von Bishop stayed for half an hour and then set off back down the main street towards his billet.

Then, from a side road, he heard the put-put of a motor bike. Curious, he waited. Presently the bike emerged into the main street. The driver stopped and removed the goggles he was wearing. Von Bishop walked closer. He was an English soldier.

"Where is everybody, mate?" the man said cheerfully. " 'Fraid I'm lost. Can you tell me where the Kasama garrison is?"

Von Bishop realised that in his tattered faded uniform he looked more like a farmer than a German officer. It was awkward but he didn't have a gun with him either.

"This town has been occupied by the German Army," he said apologetically.

"Oh," said the despatch rider. "Am I captured then?"

"Yes, you are," said Von Bishop, feeling rather foolish.

"Haven't you heard?" the despatch rider said. "The war ended the day before yesterday." He took a stiff canvas folder from the bag slung round his body and handed it over.

Von Bishop read the message it contained.

Send following to Colonel von Lettow-Vorbeck under white flag. The Prime Minister of England has announced that an armistice was signed at 5 hours on Nov. 11th and that hostilities on all fronts cease at 11 hours on Nov. 11th.

Von Bishop looked up. He felt suddenly weak with relief, a tingling in his knee joints, a slackening of his bowels. Finally it was all over. Two days late, but at last it was finished. The despatch rider was holding his hands above his head in an attitude of surrender.

"Oh, it's all right," Von Bishop said, smiling broadly. "You don't need to bother with that now."

CHAPTER THREE

2 DECEMBER 1918

Nairobi · British East Africa

Sir Nigel MacMillan's house in Nairobi looked rather like a larger version of the grey granite bungalows that can be found in the more genteel streets of any Scottish country town. It too was stone; the roof was slate, the guttering ornamental and cast-iron, the windows leaded. The only concession to the African climate was a wide, pillared verandah on which were arrayed pots of plants and wooden chairs and settees, and which overlooked neatly mown lawns and weed-free gravel paths. In 1917 Sir Nigel had lent it to the British and Empire forces in East Africa for use as a sanatorium For officers only.

Felix Cobb sat bolt upright in one of the armchairs, his spectacles held in both hands, staring blankly at the trio of African gardeners hoeing a flower-bed. In his lap was a letter and a copy of the local newspaper, *The Leader of East Africa,* which he'd just been reading. He looked like a man who had just received a nasty shock.

To compose himself he picked up the letter, put his spectacles on and read it again. It was brief and from his mother.

> *Stackpole Manor*
> *30 August 1918*

Darling Felix,

> *We were most distressed to hear of your accident with the bomb-gun, but relieved to know that you are steadily recovering from your injuries.*

> *I am writing in haste to tell you of your father. I am sorry to say that he has become progressively more unwell since your departure for the war. After much heart-searching and lengthy consultation with Dr. Venables, Cressida and I have decided that it would be best for everyone if he went away for a while. Dr. Venables has found a quiet and pleasant nursing home near Bournemouth, called St. Jude's. He says it comes highly recommended. Dr. Venables hopes that when this war is finally over and you and Gabriel come home, life may eventually return to normal.*

> *Nigel Bathe has a splendid new pair of hands and is much more his old self. Your friend Holland has gone to Russia to join a revolution there. He telephoned the other day to ask news of you.*

> *With fondest love from us all,*
> *Mother*

Felix put the letter down, momentarily overcome with sadness for his old mad father. He wished he had written home with the news about Gabriel at the time. It was going to be impossibly hard to relate the facts of his death now. He smiled ruefully. He was full of retrospective wisdom, twenty-twenty vision as far as his hind-sight was concerned.

He stood up, his right hand going automatically to the back of his head to feel the bumps and ridges of scar tissue there. As he got to his feet, the newspaper slid off his lap onto the floor. He bent down to retrieve it and felt the giddiness come on as the blood rushed into his brain.

He tucked the newspaper under his arm. He needed to wait a

while longer before he could bring himself to read it again. He walked down the steps into the garden.

He had made an almost complete recovery since the day Wheech-Browning had blown him and Captain Pinto up with the Stokes-gun bomb. A chunk of shrapnel had fractured his skull at the back of his head and caused lesions to the occipital area of the brain. The swirling ropes of smoke he had seen at the time of the explosion had in fact been a symptom of the partial blindness caused by his injury. What happened subsequently was that only parts of either eye could see. It was like looking through a shattered pane of frosted glass. The remaining shards were the blind areas, demarcated by a swirling effervescent grey smoke, like a cloud of glittering mica dust. The partial blindness had lasted for nearly four months; then it slowly began to clear as his wound healed. The only lingering effect was, he discovered, that it returned for a day or so if he was ever close to a loud noise: a viciously slammed door, a high-pitched shout, gunshots.

He was to be invalided out of the army and was due to sail back to England from Mombasa in three weeks' time. Those intervening weeks were to be spent convalescing on Walter Smith's farm near Kilimanjaro. That, at least, had been the plan. Everything had changed since he'd read today's newspaper. For a year now he'd been waiting in hope for the news it contained.

As he drew near a group of patients, a curiously shaped man detached himself from it and came sidling up. It was the Reverend Norman Espie, Walter's father-in-law and an annoyingly regular visitor to the "gallant injured boys" in the sanatorium. It was through Espie, though, that Felix had renewed his acquaintance with Walter, and he was grateful to him for that.

The Reverend Norman Espie ducked a non-existent shoulder and held up three fingers in front of Felix's eyes.

"How many fingers, Lieutenant Cobb?"

"Three, Reverend," Felix said impatiently. Espie always did this. "I'm not blind."

"Praise the good Lord," Espie said. "Walter has asked me to relay the message that he will meet you at the Norfolk Hotel at ten of the clock, the morn's morn."

"Ah. I'm afraid there's been a change in plan. I won't be coming now. At least, not for a while."

"Goodness me. Not any sign of a relapse, I trust."

"No. I have to go to Dar-es-Salaam."

"Dar! What on earth for, my dear young man?"

"Official business. To do with the death of my brother. Walter will understand."

Felix repeated his apologies and left the Reverend Norman Espie to his visiting. He walked back to his seat on the verandah. What he had told Espie wasn't strictly true. It was a plan he'd concocted only minutes before. He still had arrangements to make, official permissions to secure, but he had every intention of going to Dar.

He sat down and opened *The Leader* again. It contained a long article about the surrender of the German forces at Abercorn in Northern Rhodesia on the twenty-fifth of November.

> . . . *von Lettow made his formal statement of surrender in German and then repeated it in English. General Edwards accepted the surrender on behalf of His Majesty King George V. Von Lettow was then presented to the officers present, and in return introduced his own officers. The German forces numbered 155 Europeans, 30 of whom were officers, medical officers and higher officials, and 1,168 askaris.*

Then followed a list of those German officers who had surrendered. Felix's heart began to beat faster as he searched again for the one name he was looking for. He felt a slight sensation of nausea when he found it. "Von Bishop, Erich, Maj. of Reserve." Von Bishop was still alive. Fate had allowed him to survive the war. Felix shut his eyes and conjured up an image of Gabriel's severed head. The waxy skin, the staring eyes, the dull, tousled hair. He thought of his half-eaten body in the trampled grass. The questions that had nagged relentlessly at him for a year rose again in his head. What had happened to Gabriel out there on the plateau? What hellish torments had he endured?

He opened his eyes again and looked out at the quiet garden, with its civilised lawns and groups of strolling invalids. Since this war had begun, not one thing in his life had turned out the way he had planned. Oxford, Charis, the search for Gabriel, the hunt for Von Bishop. He realised that he'd been a soldier now for nearly two and a half years—since July 1916—and he had never fired a shot in anger. What kind of a war was it where this sort of absurdity could occur? And yet he'd been sick, half-starved, insanely bored, had seen his brother hideously murdered, shared a house with a syphilitic Portuguese who spoke no English, and been almost killed by a bomb fired by his own side. He knew that he was not responsible for the way events had turned out, that it was futile to expect that life could in some way be controlled. But surely everyone had some vestigial power to influence things at his disposal? He had sworn to himself that before he left Africa, before he was done with this mad, absurd war, he was going to exercise that power and fire at least one shot in anger. He was going to put a bullet in Von Bishop's brain. As far as he was concerned his war would not be over until then.

CHAPTER FOUR

5 DECEMBER 1918

Dar-es-Salaam · German East Africa

After the surrender, the German Army remained at Abercorn for two weeks before being marched to Bismarckburg on Lake Tanganyika. From there a steamer took them to Kigoma, the terminus of the Central Railway from Dar. The journey back to the capital took several days. First they stopped in Tabora, where the askaris were to be interned. The officers and European officials were being taken directly to Dar, where they, along with the rest of the German civilian population, were to be repatriated as soon as possible.

As the train approached Dar, Von Bishop began to feel distinctly nervous at the prospect of meeting Liesl. He hadn't seen her for over a year. Their last unsatisfactory goodbye had taken place under very strained circumstances on the steps of the hospital at Nanda. He wondered if she would be at the station to meet him At

Morogoro, when the train had stopped, the remaining German population of the town had turned out in force to provide a lavish
welcome. Tables had been set out on the platform. Fresh bread,
fruit, beer and wine had been in plentiful supply.

The sight of the coconut groves behind the city made Von
Bishop's nervousness increase. It crossed his mind that somehow
Liesl might have found out about Cobb's death. If not, she would
surely ask him what had happened. He shut his eyes for a moment,
a flutter of panic beating at his throat. What could he say? What
answer could he give?

"Don't look so worried," Rutke said. "We'll be home soon."

Concealing his annoyance, Von Bishop looked at Rutke, who
was sitting opposite him. Rutke was pale and thin. But he had been
lucky. Five more Europeans had died of Spanish influenza since the
surrender. Rutke had pulled through after forty-eight hours in a
high fever.

"It's all right for you," Rutke went on heedlessly. "Married
men with homes to go to. Us bachelors have to live in a camp."

A big crowd was waiting at the station. As the train pulled in, a
hearty cheer of welcome rose up. The officers got out and were
marched up Unter den Akazien to a tented camp set up in the
botanical gardens. Von Bishop hadn't seen Liesl among the faces at
the station, but someone told him that the wives of prisoners would
be waiting at the camp. Slowly they filed through a large, airy tent.
Their names, ranks and particulars were noted and they were presented with a new cotton-drill suit, three shirts, collars, underclothes and a shaving kit.

His arms full, Von Bishop stepped outside into the sun

"Erich," he heard a voice call.

"This way," the English sergeant said and led him off to where
the group of wives was waiting.

Liesl was wearing a white high-necked blouse and a long grey
skirt. On her head she had a man's sun-helmet. The first thing Von
Bishop noticed was that she was much thinner. For the first time in
years she bore some resemblance to the woman he had seen off on
the boat to Germany in 1913. For some reason the change seemed
to him an indication of new hope.

She took the clothes from him. "You were meant to be here yesterday," she said. "What happened?"

"A delay at Morogoro," he said. He bent his head and touched his lips to hers.

"Liesl," he said. "You look wonderful. Very well."

"I've been sick," she said, her voice sharp with irritation. "A month of fever."

Von Bishop felt his heart brim with love at her retort. Now everything, he was sure, would be fine.

They took a rickshaw back to the quarter of the town that was reserved for German civilians. Formerly a temporary development for junior officials on the railways, it lay behind the marshalling yards and was composed of small corrugated-iron bungalows raised two or three feet off the ground on brick piles. German civilians were permitted to move freely around the town during the day, but after dark a curfew was imposed and they were obliged to stay indoors.

It was a curious sensation to be riding through Dar again. Von Bishop looked about him. English soldiers were everywhere, Union Jacks flying from the highest buildings, English street signs at road junctions. German East Africa didn't exist any more.

Their bungalow was mean and unprepossessing, smaller even than their house in Nanda. The streets in the neighbourhood were rutted and narrow. Pie dogs and skinny hens sniffed and picked at piles of rubbish which mouldered at the side of the road; shade trees were few and far between.

Liesl's house boasted a ravaged hibiscus hedge and a cinder path to the front door marked by freshly whitewashed stones. Inside there was a sitting room, separated from the single bedroom by a narrow hallway. A kitchen shack and privy stood a few yards from the back door. The Germans were allowed only one servant per household. Kimi, Liesl's maid from Nanda, welcomed them at the front door

Inside it was fetid and warm. Von Bishop sat down on a wooden upright chair.

Liesl stood by the window, fanning herself with a piece of card.

"It gets cooler at night," she said non-committally.

"I suppose it's better than being herded in a camp."

"Oh, the English are very fair."

The maid brought Von Bishop a glass of beer.

"My God, beer!" he exclaimed. "I haven't had it for years." In fact, he'd drunk bottles at Morogoro.

Liesl looked pleased. "I saved it for you."

Von Bishop got to his feet, went over to her and kissed her on the cheek. Then he stood awkwardly at her side staring through the open shutters at the spindly hibiscus hedge and the cinder path with its whitewashed stones.

"Erich," Liesl said, still looking outside. "I have to ask you. What happened to Gabriel Cobb?"

"You don't know?"

"I heard nothing. They moved us here almost immediately. After those men set off after you."

Von Bishop almost dropped his glass of beer. He forced himself to relax.

"We found him," he said gravely. "On the Makonde plateau. He was dead, from starvation, weakness. . . ."

Liesl looked at her left hand, which rested on the window sill. She prised up a splinter from the dried and cracking wood.

"I knew it," she said sadly. "When I heard nothing I knew he was dead." She paused. "Erich, I——"

"We found him quite alone," Von Bishop went on quickly. "His clothes were rags. He had nothing with him. No food, no water. 'Unaccommodated man,' as Shakespeare says. A brave but foolish attempt."

Liesl looked round at him sharply. Von Bishop shrugged his shoulders. "We buried him there. I went on to the Ludjenda confluence, rejoined Von Lettow. You never heard anything from, ah, the men following me?"

Liesl opened her mouth as if she were going to say something, then closed it. Her shoulders relaxed.

"No," she said, exhaling. "Nothing. But I saw one of them yesterday. He reminded me of it all."

"Here? In Dar?" Common sense stilled his alarm. He'd been in captivity a month. If he had been accused of anything he would have learnt of it by now.

"Yes," Liesl said, looking round with mild curiosity.

"Did he see you?"

"I think so. He must have."

"But he didn't say anything?"

"No, nothing. I don't think he recognised me."

Von Bishop cleared his throat to hide the relief. "They couldn't have found the grave, then."

"No." Liesl took her bottom lip between her teeth. "I suppose not."

Von Bishop set his beer glass down and put his arms around his wife and pulled her to him. She was thinner but her body was still soft. He felt a sense of happiness wash through him. He squeezed her shoulders.

"Soon we'll be in Germany," he said. "But perhaps one day they'll let us come back."

CHAPTER FIVE

9 DECEMBER 1918

Dar-es-Salaam · German East Africa

Felix stood in the dappled moon-shadow beneath a cotton tree looking at the Von Bishops' house. He cursed his luck. How typical of the way everything had gone that within two days of arriving in Dar he should practically fall over Von Bishop's wife outside the Kaiserhof. He had looked right through her, pretending not to recognise her face, and had turned and walked off quickly. He couldn't tell if she recognised him, however, and to allay any possible suspicions he had not stirred from the hotel for the next few days.

Now he pulled the collar of his linen jacket up above his ears. He was wearing civilian clothes. A cool breeze was coming off the sea. He seemed to have been standing under this tree for hours. He shifted his weight from foot to foot, feeling as he did so the barrel of his service revolver scrape across his pelvis. The gun was too large to go inconspicuously into his jacket pocket, so he had thrust it into the waist of his trousers. He took the gun out now and opened it, catching the moon's gleam on the six brass cartridges. He wondered if the time was right for him to make his move but decided to wait a few more minutes. One of the rooms of the tin bungalow was lit; the other was completely dark. He looked up and down the dusty streets. They were deserted. The moonlight had turned the dust an ash colour and despite the balminess of the night the scene looked cold. Felix decided to wait a few more minutes. Just in case.

Getting official permission to come to Dar-es-Salaam had presented few problems. He had telegraphed to the Provost Marshal in Dar, saying he had information about the death of his brother, Captain Gabriel Cobb, that might constitute it a war crime. Permission was promptly granted and he went by train to Mombasa, and from there by coastal steamer to Dar. At the Provost Marshal's office they had been most helpful. He told them the story of Gabriel's death, leaving nothing out except Von Bishop's name. The harassed and overworked young lieutenant appointed to investigate the case had provided all manner of information about the surviving German officers. Securing Von Bishop's address had not been difficult.

He had set wheels in motion, but he knew they would move very slowly, such was the clutter and chronic disorganisation of Dar-es-Salaam. Other cases of alleged German brutality were also pending, let alone the myriad of usual disciplinary matters attending a large and idle occupying army. Felix's accusations would just have to wait their turn.

Then he had seen the Von Bishop woman and, in the interests of safety, had lain low in his tiny room at the top of the Kaiserhof for three days. During this period of inactivity he concentrated on sustaining the mood of hatred and desire for retribution which he'd felt so fiercely all these months. But somehow, now he was almost in sight of his quarry, he felt his resolve wavering. He decided to let Von Bishop speak for himself, to see if he had any defence to offer.

Those few moments when a voice in his head asked him if it was worth persevering were easily overcome. He simply had to conjure up the images of that dreadful day on the plateau. The only trouble was that they brought a train of associated but unwanted memories. Memories of Gabriel and Charis on their wedding day, of Charis's appallingly misleading reassurances on the train between Aylesbury and London, of her own frightful death. Soon he would be shaky with guilt and unhappiness again, fully aware of his own problematic motives, and yet above all conscious of the overwhelming imbalance, the dreadful unfairness of everything. He was lucky, he reminded himself. He had it in his power to do some squaring up, knot a few of the dangling loose ends. At these times when he was most low, he would try to imagine Von Bishop's face, try to visualise the features of the man who had killed his brother. Walter had said it was thin, shaven-headed with a large, sharp nose. It was not much to go on but in his imagination it readily acquired the lineaments of despicable cruelty. He felt instinctively that he would recognise Von Bishop anywhere.

He weighed the gun in his hand. It was time to go. Keeping as much as he could to the shadows, Felix moved towards the Von Bishop house. Not far off a dog began to bark, but it soon fell silent. As he crept towards the bungalow, the gun held in readiness by his side, he felt suddenly possessed of an avenging strength and confidence. There was, he decided, an irrefutable rightness in the doctrine of an eye for an eye. It had a logic that brooked no back-sliding; it allowed man some say in his fate, some little control of the order events took upon his planet.

He saw the shadow of a figure against the lighted square of window. He wondered if it was Von Bishop. He crept up to the house. He could hear no conversation. He thought suddenly of Von Bishop's wife, and the fact that she might be a witness. He paused. It would be necessary to mask himself somehow. Felix felt through his pockets. He had no handkerchief with him. It was paramount that he disguise his face.

Cursing under his breath, he took off his linen jacket and wrapped and knotted it awkwardly under his chin. Simply by pulling up one fold, he could effectively mask his face. But somehow this *ad hoc* pragmatic operation had deprived him of his mood of vengeful omnipotence as swiftly as it had arisen. He felt foolish and vulnerable, and try as he might, he couldn't help wondering what he must look like with his jacket wrapped round his head. Already he was bathed in perspiration, sweat running uncomfortably down his muffled neck.

He looked again at the gun, hoping that the sight of the agent of destruction would inspire him once again, but it only brought another unwelcome thought to mind. When he fired, when he pulled the trigger, the noise in an enclosed space would be deafening. Without doubt it would bring back his partial blindness again, his fractured vision. What would he do then? How would he get away? He threw back his head in desperation and looked at the vague stars in the sky. Why now, at the eleventh hour, were all these obstacles massing in his path? Don't think, he told himself angrily, just *do*.

He eased round to the dark end of the house. Here the shutters, to what he assumed was the bedroom, were flung wide to cool the room as much as possible prior to the occupants' retiring. Reaching up, he grabbed the sill. The gun in his hand clanged noisily against the corrugated iron. He dropped immediately into a crouch. But there was no reaction from inside. Ordering his leaping heart to still itself, Felix stuffed the gun back in the waistband of his trousers, stood up and, with some effort, clambered into the empty bedroom. He stood by the window listening for any suspicious noises from the sitting room. All was quiet.

Slowly his eyes grew accustomed to the darkness of the bedroom. A wooden chest against one wall. The tall shape of a cupboard. A stand with a basin on it by a bed. The two beds themselves with tall, crude cast-iron bedsteads, rumpled sheets on one of them—

He felt a silent scream of shock echo through his head. *One of the beds was occupied.* He tried to swallow but his Adam's apple seemed to have swelled to block his throat. As silently as he knew how, he drew the gun from his waistband and took a tentative step nearer the bed. The person lay on its back, sound asleep, its large sharp nose silhouetted against the pale wall.

Felix felt his stomach churn with nausea as he realised that the sleeper was Von Bishop. He took another small step nearer the bed.

Miraculously there was no squeak from the wooden floor-boards. He had him now. He aimed the gun. It trembled wildly in his grasp. but he was so close he couldn't miss.

"Von Bishop," he hissed. "Wake up."

There was no movement from the bed.

"Wake up," he croaked. "Wake up."

Von Bishop slept on peacefully.

Felix lowered the gun. What now? He took a step closer. He stood almost above him. Felix could hardly hear the sound of his breathing. Hand wobbling, he levelled the gun at Von Bishop's shadowed face.

"Wake. Up." He reached forward to shake him by the shoulder. This was absurd, he thought; it was going to be impossible to shoot the man now.

Behind him the door swung open.

"He's dead," Liesl von Bishop said in a calm voice. "Leave him alone."

Felix reeled round in horror and aghast surprise, frantically hauling the folds of his jacket up over his face. He lost his balance and staggered, a hand slamming down on the bed for support, thwacking Von Bishop's immobile leg.

The light from the oil lamp she carried illuminated Von Bishop's face. His eyes were shut, his mouth slightly open, his skin looked stretched tight.

"Oh, my *God*," Felix exclaimed tremulously, bending over, gasping for air. "Oh, God, Jesus!" He felt as if he were about to fall apart, so critical was the shock he'd received.

"He died this evening," Liesl said dully. "About three hours ago. Influenza. Spanish influenza, the doctor said."

Felix felt his rioting body come under minimal control.

"What's wrong with your face?" she said.

"What?" Felix touched the masking folds of his jacket.

"Your face, why is it covered? And a gun," she said with more alarm. "Why have you got a gun?"

"In case," Felix improvised, tearing away his jacket, hoping he wouldn't have to try to explain that. "Self-protection," he concluded lamely.

"I saw you oustide," she said, "standing under the tree. I was waiting for you to come to the door." She gave him a weary, tolerant smile, as if he were an idiotic child who kept getting into trouble. She moved to one side to let him pass, and Felix walked out of the bedroom into the narrow hall. He put on his jacket and tucked his gun away with some embarrassment.

"You wanted to ask Erich about Gabriel?" she said.

"Yes." It was odd hearing the sound of his brother's name on her lips, she used it so familiarly.

Her face went serious. "I must tell you. You know that he's dead?"

Felix nodded. "I know. I found him." He looked again at this perplexing woman. He remembered that she had known Gabriel for what amounted to the last two years of his life.

"Did your husband . . . did he tell you what happened? About Gabriel?"

"Oh, yes," Liesl said.

"But *why?*" Felix said imploringly, suddenly aching for some sort of explanation. "That's *all* I want to know. Why? Why? Why?"

"Why what?" Liesl frowned.

With an intuition of dreamlike clarity, Felix realised that she knew nothing of the truth of Gabriel's death. She had no idea of what happened that night on the plateau, had no conception of her husband's part. He decided at once not to tell her. He knew, again with a surprising sense of conviction, that it was better to leave it as it was. After all, he thought sadly, we all have our secrets to keep. The heavens wouldn't fall for such a trifle.

EPILOGUE

Mombasa · British East Africa

"It's ironic," Felix said. "After four years of war, to die of influenza."

"To say the least," Walter agreed.

"Over half of them have died, you know," Felix went on. "Of the surviving German officers."

"I heard," Walter said. He seemed preoccupied. "Anyway, what happened after that?" he asked. He, his wife and Felix were standing on the quayside on Mombasa Island. Felix was going back to England. The Smiths had come to say goodbye.

"We talked on for a short while," Felix said. "I asked about Gabriel. She said she knew him very well. She liked him a lot. 'A very nice man,' she said. 'Very quiet, very kind.'" Felix paused. "I didn't say anything about the plateau. I thought nothing would be served."

Walter stroked his moustache.

"What's she doing now?"

"Still waiting to be repatriated. She said she was looking forward to that."

"She didn't talk about Von Bishop at all? In any way?"

"No. Not at all. I thought—you know, given that he was lying next door . . ."

"Yes, of course, I see." Walter seemed agitated. "She didn't by any chance mention the word 'Decorticator,' did she?"

"What?"

"Decorticator. She didn't give any hint as to what Von Bishop may have done with it?"

"No," Felix said. "What's a Decorticator?"

"So the secret dies with him." Walter put his hands on his hips and looked at the ground. "It's a mystery," he said. "I've searched every German farm on Kilimanjaro and the Pare hills. No sign. Nobody knows what happened to it. It seems to have disappeared into thin air. But how could it?" He looked genuinely distressed. "Did they melt it down, or what? Break it up? But it was too big." He looked to his wife for support. "Wasn't it, dear?"

"Of course," Mrs. Smith said, gazing dreamily out to sea. "Extremely big."

She reminded Felix of his mother. And this thought brought Stackpole to mind. What would life be like when he got home? No Gabriel, no Charis, his father shut away. He was filled with gloomy foreboding.

Farther down the quayside a military band struck up a jaunty tune, dispelling his morose reflections. Drawn up in neat ranks was a battalion of Indian troops preparing to embark. A dazzlingly white-suited official inspected the guard of honour. Four light artillery pieces attended by spruce K.A.R. gunners stood with their barrels pointed out to sea in preparation for the official salute.

"When those guns go off they aren't going to do your eyes much good," Walter said.

"Oh, I think I'm better now," Felix said without much confidence. "Finally got rid of Wheech-Browning's legacy. I'd hate to be reminded of him every time there's a loud noise."

"I warned you," Walter laughed. "Do you remember? The first time we met."

"What happened to Wheech-Browning?" Mrs. Smith asked.

"God knows," Felix said. "I never saw him after the explosion."

"I wonder where he is?" Walter said.

They were all quiet for a while

"It's another mystery," Felix said.

"You can't know the answers to everything," said Walter. "Life doesn't run on railway tracks. It doesn't always go the way you expect."

"That's a very profound remark, dear," Mrs. Smith said.

Walter looked at her. "Are you making fun of me, Matilda?" he said, a little annoyed.

"Of course not." Mrs. Smith touched her husband's arm reassuringly.

"Well, it was good of you to come and see me off," Felix said to them both. "It's a long way, for a goodbye."

"No trouble," Walter said. "I wanted to come to Mombasa anyway. I'm going out to a rubber plantation this afternoon." Walter made an expansive gesture with his arm, and for a moment looked transported with his vision. "I see the shores of Lake Jipe as one great green rubber forest."

There was another pause. They didn't know each other very well.

"At least it's over, anyway," Walter said. "We should all be thankful for that."

"What?"

"The war."

"Oh, the war. Yes, that's true." Felix thought about the news he was carrying back to England.

A boy came and picked up Felix's case. The launch was ready to take the few passengers to the liner, the *Conway Star,* which rode at anchor some sixty yards away from the quay.

Felix said goodbye.

"Come back soon," Walter said. "Don't wait for another war."

"I might," Felix said. "You never know."

*   *   *

Felix leant on the wooden guard-rail around the sun-deck, looking around the beautiful bay. Mombasa Island seemed very green and pretty from this side. Beyond the harbour buildings, scattered among the trees, were splendid white houses with arches and long verandahs. In the distance was a line of hills. A small promontory showed a silvery stretch of beach. A cluster of palm trees leant out towards the sea. Around the *Conway Star* were other ships. A liner for the Indian troops, an old steamer, some dhows and two small, tidy destroyers.

Felix looked back at the wharf. Walter and his wife had promised to stay until the boat sailed, and true to their word, they had remained. Felix saw them at the edge of the small group of well-wishers who had assembled to say goodbye. He waved, and Mrs. Smith waved back. Walter had moved a few paces away and was looking at the crowd that had gathered to see off the Indian battalion. Felix squinted up into the sun. Above him stretched an immense deep-blue sky occupied by a few small clouds. The sky seemed higher in Africa, he thought vaguely. On shore, the military band broke into "God Save the King" as the colonel of the battalion embarked. Felix returned to his musing. How can the sky be higher? He rebuked himself: the sky has no height. He looked again. Then he realised, with an absurd sense of achievement, that it was the clouds which were higher in Africa. They sailed higher than the clouds in Europe, and that was what made the encompassing blue seem so toweringly out of reach.

BOOM! went the first of the guns in the farewell salute. The other three followed in quick succession. Felix felt the shock and crash of the cannonade echo in his head. The view before him trembled, misted and then fragmented, as he had known it would. The quay, the ships, the sea, the leaning palms, glimmered fitfully between the swirling chasms of mica dust. Never mind, Felix told himself in resigned compensation. It would be quiet on the voyage. He waved at the place where he thought Walter was standing, just to show him that he was all right and, in case he was concerned, to put his mind at rest. The guns boomed again. Quiet on the voyage, he repeated, dazzled and distracted, looking up at the small unfailing clouds dancing quite contentedly in the repercussing air.

ALSO BY WILLIAM BOYD

THE BLUE AFTERNOON

Sprawling between three continents and two historical eras, William Boyd's lushly atmospheric novel opens in Los Angeles in 1936, when architect Kay Fischer is approached by an elderly man named Salvador Carriscant, who claims to be her father—and who insists she accompany him to Lisbon in a search for the great lost love of his life. Suspenseful, stylishly written, and teeming with historical detail, *The Blue Afternoon* is a triumph.

Winner of the Los Angeles Times *Book Prize in Fiction*
Fiction/0-679-77260-X

THE DESTINY OF NATHALIE X

In these eleven startling, exotic, and deliciously inventive stories, William Boyd charts the euphoria of love, the anguish of loss, and the gnawings of ambition. A tourist stranded in the Dordogne valley in the 1920s returns to his hotel to find a beautiful French countess waiting amorously in his room. And in the story "Cork" a widowed Englishwoman and a Portuguese poet meet every Christmas in 1930s Lisbon to enter a shared erotic delirium before parting for another year.

Fiction/Literature/0-679-76784-3

VINTAGE INTERNATIONAL
Available at your local bookstore, or call toll-free to order:
1-800-793-2665 (credit cards only).

"*Any Human Heart*...stands up as one of his most enjoyable novels to date: generous, witty and sneakily profound."
—*Evening Standard*

Any Human Heart

A novel

BY WILLIAM BOYD

From the acclaimed author of *Armadillo* and *The Blue Afternoon* ("pitch-perfect"—*New York Times*), a new novel that invokes the tumult, events, and iconic faces of our time as it tells the story of Logan Mountstuart—writer, spy, and man of the world—through his intimate journal.

Available in February 2003 in hardcover from Knopf.
$26.00 • 0-375-41493-2

Please visit www.aaknopf.com

Also by William Boyd
available in paperback from Vintage:

Armadillo • 0-375-70216-4
The Blue Afternoon • 0-679-77260-X
The Destiny of Nathalie X • 0-679-76784-3
A Good Man in Africa • 1-4000-3002-1
An Ice Cream War • 0-375-70502-3
The New Confessions • 0-375-70503-1
On the Yankee Station • 0-375-70511-2
Stars and Bars • 0-375-70501-5